MAITLAND PUBLIC LIBRARY
3 4200 00096 6883
WITHDRAWN
P9-DDG-160

Falling Stars

V.C. Andrews® Books

The Dollanganger Family Series
Flowers in the Attic
Petals on the Wind
If There Be Thorns
Seeds of Yesterday
Garden of Shadows

The Casteel Family Series
Heaven
Dark Angel
Fallen Hearts
Gates of Paradise
Web of Dreams

The Cutler Family Series
Dawn
Secrets of the Morning
Twilight's Child
Midnight Whispers
Darkest Hour

The Landry Family Series
Ruby
Pearl in the Mist
All That Glitters
Hidden Jewel
Tarnished Gold

The Logan Family Series
Melody
Heart Song
Unfinished Symphony
Music in the Night
Olivia

The Orphans Miniseries
Butterfly
Crystal
Brooke
Raven
Runaways (full-length novel)

The Wildflowers Miniseries
Misty
Star
Jade
Cat
Into the Garden (full-length novel)

The Hudson Family Series
Rain
Lightning Strikes
Eye of the Storm
The End of the Rainbow

The Shooting Stars Series
Cinnamon
Ice
Rose
Honey
Falling Stars

My Sweet Audrina
(does not belong to a series)

Published by POCKET BOOKS

Falling Stars

POCKET BOOKS
New York London Toronto Sydney Singapore

Following the death of Virginia Andrews, the Andrews family worked with a carefully selected writer to organize and complete Virginia Andrews' stories and to create additional novels, of which this is one, inspired by her storytelling genius.

POCKET BOOKS, a division of Simon & Schuster, Inc.
1230 Avenue of the Americas, New York, NY 10020

ISBN: 0-671-03986-5

First Pocket Books hardcover printing December 2001

10 9 8 7 6 5 4 3 2 1

For information regarding special discounts for bulk purchases, please contact Simon & Schuster Special Sales at 1-800-456-6798 or business@simonandschuster.com

Printed in the U.S.A.

The truly insane perform on many public stages. The sane stage their performances in the privacy of their own minds. Everyone is an actor. In the end, everyone wants applause.

Madame Senetsky

Falling Stars

Prologue

Now that I was definitely going to the Senetsky School of Performing Arts in New York City, I asked Mommy to tell me once again what it was like for her to come to America from Russia when she was just a little older than I was now. I was hoping she would give me some secret, some special new power with which I could overcome my fears and anxieties and stop the spasms of trembling that made my spine rattle like the infamous snake—warning, warning, warning.

I'm sure it wouldn't be difficult for anyone to understand why I was afraid. I had spent all my life on this corn farm in Ohio. The moonlight always looked warm and soft and protecting to me. I was able to see the sky blazing with stars, not a single constellation washed out by streetlights and the lights of tall buildings. On a mattress of freshly cut grass, I could sprawl out on my back, look up, and feel like I was drifting into space, drifting toward the bedazzling beauty of other galaxies and solar systems. I could feel like I was part of something far greater than myself. In a city as big and overwhelming as New York, I knew you could feel insignificant.

The noises I heard outside my window every night were sounds made by owls and frogs, peepers, and occasionally a coyote or two who had wandered close by in search of prey. The symphony being played was familiar music of the night to me. It soothed me. I drew it over me like an additional blanket, and fell asleep to the lullaby I trusted. I was never afraid to close my eyes. I was never afraid of the darkness.

However, I knew that, very soon, whenever I put my head down on my pillow to sleep, I would hear the hubbub of city traffic—horns and car wheels, sirens from ambulances and fire engines or police cars, announcing someone's trouble and pain. There would be the continuous murmur of strange voices, an undercurrent of indistinguishable words caught in the ebb and flow of human drama. In New York City, I would see more people in an hour than I had seen in a month back on the farm. I would be a small fish in a big ocean full of dark waters, searching for the light. I was so afraid my dreams would rot into nightmares.

How had Mama managed to come from a world so similar to the world I lived in now without getting herself lost? Where had she found the courage? She and her aunt had traveled across the ocean. She was coming to marry my father, a man she had never met. The lights of the great city that greeted her surely had to have filled her with terrible uncertainty. She was so far from the voices and the smiles that had given her comfort, embraced her warmly when she was frightened, and promised her that she would be all right, promised her she would always be safe.

Mama paused before answering. I could see she wanted to tell me something important, something that would help me. Her own memories flowed in a continuous stream behind her eyes, some bringing smiles, some making her nod thoughtfully.

"It's like being born again, Honey. Not in a religious sense, but in a more everyday sense," she began. "Everything is so new and different: the odors, the sounds, the sights, colors, everything. You don't know where to look first. You hesitate to take a step, but you do, and then you take another and another. Soon you're walking, just like everyone around you. Suddenly, one day, you feel like you belong. No one can tell you have come from a place vastly different.

"You'll see," she said confidently. "It will happen to you, too."

She was right, of course. But I often wished she wasn't.

1

Curtain Up

How numb and panicky I felt the day Daddy, Mommy, and I set out for New York City in Daddy's new black Lincoln Town Car. It had luxurious black leather seats that still smelled as fresh as the day they were made. The dashboard resembled an airplane console with its sound system, its climate controls and GPS locator screen, and its ground positioning system.

Daddy had bought the car soon after my Grandad Forman had died. There was a great deal more money than any of us had imagined in the legacy, money buried away in interest-bearing accounts Daddy was unaware existed until the will was read. My grandad was a frugal man who believed it was a sin to spend money on anything other than what he deemed absolutely necessary.

A big, beautiful, luxurious car was certainly not absolutely necessary, but Daddy had always wanted one, and Grandad had always discouraged it. I should really say, forbidden it. Grandad Forman had been more than just the head of our household. He had ruled our lives with a stern, fundamentalist religious eye, seeing potential evil everywhere—even, I was to learn, in his own face every time he looked in the mirror. As terrible as it was to think it, when he died, it was truly as if a heavy weight had been lifted from our shoulders. We could breathe, enjoy the fruits of our hard labor and not be afraid to laugh, listen to music, and appreciate beautiful things for themselves and not only their practical uses.

Nowhere was this more evident than in Daddy's face every time he gazed appreciatively at his new automobile. He had an expression similar to the one on his face whenever he gazed out at a field of fresh, healthy corn and knew we were going to enjoy another successful year. His heart was full. He was proud of himself. I could see it in his eyes. He was fulfilling promises I was sure he had made to himself, and maybe even to Mommy, years ago.

Daddy had also fulfilled a promise to my Uncle Simon, and built him his greenhouse right behind the cow barn. Uncle Simon, Daddy's older half-brother, was a giant of a man who, despite his size and strength, was the gentlest man I knew. Grandad had treated Uncle Simon poorly all his life, forcing him to leave school at a young age and do hard labor on the farm. He even moved him out of the main house and into a makeshift apartment above the cow barn.

Despite his great strength and size, Uncle Simon accepted his lot in life, but put all his best efforts and love into his flowers. He nurtured them as parents nurtured children, fingered the petals as someone would handle very valuable jewels, and even talked to them. They were almost always vibrant, healthy, and very beautiful. Soon his flowers became very famous. People stopped by to see them often, and then started to offer him money for them. Eventually, with Mommy's help, he had turned his hobby into a successful little business.

Later, when I learned he was really Grandad's son, the result of an affair Grandad had had with one of his farm worker's wives, whom he later married after the worker's death, I understood better why Uncle Simon conjured up guilt in Grandad's mind, stinging his overblown conscience, and thus why he had tried to separate him from the rest of us.

Thankfully, that had never worked.

Now, with the farmhouse itself being refurbished, Mommy's new kitchen appliances installed, new rugs, new furniture, and bright new colors in our home all having been acquired, Daddy turned his full attention to me and my attending the well-known Senetsky School for the Performing Arts in New York City, where I had been accepted to develop my talent as a classical violinist.

The school was owned and managed by an internationally famous former stage actress, singer, and dancer, Madame Edith Senetsky. Her son, Edmond, was a theatrical agent, and often sent prospective candidates he had discovered during his various travels around the country to audition for her performing arts institution. It had a worldwide reputation for developing talent and creating stars of the stage and screen. Its list of celebrated graduates was impressive.

I had no idea yet just how small the school's population was and how personal the attention to each student would be. In my mind, when I thought of a school, I conjured up images of students in classrooms, bells ringing, schedules to follow, rules to obey and homework to do.

However, Madame Senetsky was very critical and selective. Candidates who would be well sought after and accepted at other, more traditional schools of performing arts were quickly rejected. Mr. Wengrow, my violin instructor, constantly impressed upon me how significant it was that I had been chosen. To him, it was explicit proof that I would become a major success. It was almost as if my career would be guaranteed as long as I followed Madame Senetsky's orders and guidance.

Even my boyfriend, Chandler Maxwell, a talented pianist who had taken duet lessons with me, was convinced of this, of my success beyond his own. It all made me very nervous. The level of expectations was high. To fail after being given such an opportunity was almost, to use Grandad Forman's terms, a cardinal sin.

And then there was my great desire to fulfill all the promises I had made to my Uncle Peter, my daddy's younger brother, before he had died tragically in a plane crash. He was a wonderful, handsome man, whose joy and happiness and carefree ways flew in the face of Grandad's stern warnings. Uncle Peter was the one who had bought me my wonderful violin and started to pay for my lessons. He had great faith in me, more than anyone.

"You've got to do this for him then," Chandler once said, when I told him more about Uncle Peter, my first pretend boyfriend. "Almost as much as you have to do it for yourself. I wish I had someone like that to please," he added with some bitterness. His family, especially his father, wasn't very excited about his interest in music. Chandler had been accepted to Boston University, and I would be in New York, but we promised each other we would remain in close contact, and he vowed he would visit me as soon as there was an opportunity to do so.

"I'll come to New York as often as I can," he pledged.

Now I was actually leaving. The day had come. Daddy had put my suitcases in the trunk. He and Mommy sat up front and I sat in the rear, clutching the bouquet of red, white, and pink roses Uncle Simon had just cut from his bushes and given to me as a bon voyage gift.

"They'll keep all the way to New York," he promised. "Put the stems in water at the motel you stay at tonight."

I thanked him, and he promised to send me fresh flowers now and then.

"I don't imagine you'll see much greenery, living in New York," he muttered. "Cities are full of concrete and steel," he added distastefully.

I kept the door open and he lingered there, kicking a small stone with his big foot. Sometimes, when I thought of him, I thought of Paul Bunyan.

"It's not that bad there. They've got parks, Simon, with ponds and ducks and everything," Mommy told him.

He nodded, but he didn't think much of that. I could see it in his eyes, and I could see the loneliness he was anticipating the moment we drove off.

"I'll write you and I'll call you often, Uncle Simon," I promised.

"I'm not much with letters," he replied.

"You don't have to write me back. Just send your flowers when you want."

He smiled, nodded, lifted his big hand to say good-bye, and walked toward the greenhouse.

A fugitive tear charged out of the corner of my eye and fled down my cheek to my chin. I closed my eyes to stop the flood that threatened to follow. Uncle Simon had always been there, watching over me, doing my chores for me so I would have more time to spend on my violin, calling me one of his precious flowers, taking pleasure in my blossoming. Although my leaving was inevitable, he, even more than my parents, hated to see me go. It made me think of how hard it was for him to give up his flowers to buyers. Mommy convinced him he was sharing his love of their beauty with other people, and that was only right and good.

She told him my talent was so rare and beautiful, I had an obligation to share it, too, with others. I know that was meant to help me feel better about going, as much as it was meant to help Uncle Simon.

Still, it was hard for him to say good-bye.

It was so hard for me, too.

"Here we go. Fasten your seatbelts," Daddy declared with a dramatic flare and started the car.

Moments later we were on the highway, cruising toward the interstate and on our way to New York City. The scenery flew by, all of it quickly becoming a blur through my tear-fogged eyes.

Wasn't all this a terrible mistake? Even with the great vote of confidence I had received by being chosen, was I seeking to do something I could never do? Could I live so far away from home and be on my own, I wondered. As we drove on, I realized that I had never spent a single night out of my home. I had never slept in a bed other than my own—no pajama parties with girlfriends, no family trips to stay at hotels, no relatives for me to visit. And yet, here I was, going off to live in a strange place and go to school with strangers.

A part of me wanted to shout, "Stop driving, Daddy. Turn back. I can't do this. I won't do this."

My tongue actually tried to form the words. Why? Where were my feelings of joy and excitement? I had great reasons to feel that way. The faces of all those envious of me flashed across my eyes. Their covetous words echoed in my ears.

"You're going to school in New York City! Wow!"

"A school where you learn how to be a professional entertainer? I'm just going back into English, history, and math to get myself a liberal arts degree. You know how many freshmen flunk out of college? You don't have to worry about failing exams."

"You're so lucky you've got a talent, Honey."

Was I?

How often had I asked myself, is this a blessing or a curse?

How often had I wondered, where would all of it really take me?

Soon, I would know.

* * *

Fortunately, we had great weather all the way to New York. We had to spend one night on the road. Daddy had planned the trip like a battle, figuring out how many hours it would take to get to our first rest stop, our lunch, our motel and dinner. Some road work and traffic backups spoiled his plan and slowed us up, but Mommy wouldn't permit him to go too fast.

Occasionally, at Mommy's request, I took out my violin and played for them while we rode, and especially when we were stuck in traffic. Daddy thought it was amusing to open all our windows and let the people in cars around us hear me play, too. Some people actually applauded.

"It's better than this CD and radio!" Daddy cried. "We have our own built-in musical artist, performing live!"

Daddy was never as talkative as he was on this journey. Mommy was the same, and when they were quiet, I rattled on and on, talking about things my school friends had said, asking questions about places we passed. For a while, it was as if we were all afraid of any long silences, afraid of permitting our dark thoughts to get control. Our little family was splitting up and it was very traumatic, even if it would be good for my future.

The reality of what was happening and what I was doing didn't set in until we confronted the great New York skyline. Traversing the George Washington Bridge, we rode in awe. I kept thinking, *I truly am crossing from one world over to another.* The bright day made the skyscrapers sparkle, their windows like precious jewels catching the sunlight. *Wasn't this a good omen?* I thought. *Please, dear God, let it be.*

As soon as we turned into the traffic, the tension was palpable in our car. Horns blared around us. Drivers, especially taxicab drivers, stuck their heads out of their windows and screamed, waved fists, and cursed. Mommy sat forward, cramped with nerves. Daddy began to mutter aloud, wondering how human beings could put themselves into such a horrid situation day in and day out. It seemed to take forever to reach the exit we were told to take off the East River Drive. Once we were in the city proper, however, the wonder returned. Mommy laughed at the way people hurried along.

"It looks like the sidewalks are moving!" she cried. "I forgot how exciting it is here."

She marveled at the shops, the restaurants with their patio seating, the fashionable women in high heeled shoes and designer outfits.

"What fashionable women?" Daddy asked, his eyes suddenly going like windshield wipers.

"Just keep your eyes on the road, Isaac Forman. I'll watch the people," she admonished.

Her feigned concern brought a smile to my frozen face. Now that we were actually here and I was really going to do this, my blood seemed to congeal and my heart go on pause. I kept holding my breath, and finally realized I was embracing myself so tightly, I nearly suffocated.

We followed the detailed directions and soon turned onto streets that seemed magically removed from the hustle and bustle. The buildings looked immaculate, all with security guards in crisp, bright gray and burgundy uniforms, either in front of or just inside their lobbies. There were black and gray iron gates and parking restrictions everywhere I looked, emphasizing how special and restricted these places were. We turned down one more street, and then all of us, almost simultaneously, released a sigh of amazement.

It was truly as if we had left the city and entered a magical kingdom. A high, black wrought iron gate fenced in the property, upon which there were sprawling maple trees, fountains, stone benches, walkways, and gardens. There, at the center of it, was this enormous mansion with a very busy roof line consisting of spires, pinnacle turrets, gables, and shapely chimneys, confronting us with its majesty, its formidable size. To me, it was larger than most hotels. The grounds were certainly larger than my own school grounds!

It's impressive, I thought, but it was strangely dark with its black shutters like heavy lids over stony dark eyes, almost an illustration in a book of fantasy, a castle rising from the bog, spreading over several acres in magnificent but intimidating grandeur. When the sun took a fugitive position behind a passing cloud, it became even darker, more foreboding. Would I cross a moat and be made a prisoner, or kept secure, safe, far from the demons that lurked in what Grandad Forman always called Satan's city?

"This is a school?" Mommy asked, astounded. "How can it be?"

"It's the right address, isn't it?" Daddy said, slowing down, somewhat skeptical himself.

"Yes," Mommy said, gazing at the directions. "This is the Senetsky School address."

There were no signs announcing it as so. We paused at the gate. It was closed.

"What do we do now?" Daddy asked.

"I don't know."

"That looks like some sort of a call box to let people know you're at the gate," I said, pointing to it.

Daddy inched closer, and then lowered the window and pressed a button.

"Yes?" we heard a female voice ask.

"We're the Formans. We're bringing Honey Forman to school. This is the Senetsky School of Performing Arts, isn't it?" Daddy asked.

"Of course it is. Drive up when the gate is opened," she snapped back. A moment later we heard the buzz, and the grand wrought iron gates opened slowly, reluctantly, the metal groaning with displeasure about being disturbed. We saw a video camera on the stone column turn toward us, its lens aimed like the barrel of a gun at our moving vehicle.

Daddy raised his eyebrows and gazed at Mommy and me.

"I guess you need to live like this in New York City," he said.

Mommy nodded, but she was too interested in everything to speak. Daddy paused after driving through the gate, took a deep breath as if we were about to go under water, and then he started slowly ahead.

A long driveway wound up to the grand house. Along the way, we gazed more closely at the elaborate

Grecian fountains, the stone benches embossed with angelic figures, the beautiful gardens and pruned bushes. A grounds worker was busy trimming a tree off to our right. Squirrels leapt about nervously, pausing to glance at us, tweak their noses, and then demonstrate their ability to make a quick, successful retreat up trees whenever they needed to do so.

"Simon would appreciate the grounds," Mommy remarked.

"He'd probably show them where they are doing things wrong, planting the wrong flowers, foliage," Daddy replied.

Mommy nodded, but there was no way to diminish the look of appreciation in her eyes. Seeing how much she was dazzled made me feel better about being here.

Close up, the mansion was even more impressive. It was a three-story structure fronted by a rather long gray stone staircase, with stone railings on both sides. The grand double wood doors were in an arch, as were the large multi-pane windows on either side. The building went back so far, Daddy said it looked as long as the east corn field back home.

All of the cornices with elaborate moldings, the shallow relief carvings, and ornamental metal cresting made the house look Gothic and bespoke its age, although it was far from worn-looking anywhere.

"Well," Daddy said, turning off the car engine, "it certainly beats any school I ever saw."

"I am sure the Czar would have lived in such a house," Mommy remarked, her eyes small with her memories of her own Russian history.

For a long moment, none of us attempted to get out. The opening of the front doors put us into action. Daddy hurried around to get my suitcases, and Mommy and I took my smaller bags. We started up the steps and quickly recognized Madame Senetsky's personal assistant, Laura Fairchild, the woman who had greeted us at my audition.

Her dark brown hair looked shorter, trimmed about mid-ear. She wore a navy blue suit and a white blouse with blue trim around its collar. Her eyeglasses hung around her neck on a thin gold chain, the frames decorated with tiny jewels. I hadn't taken much note of her when we had gone to the audition. I had been too nervous to look at anything long or remember anything. Afterward, I was convinced I had failed, and buried the whole experience in the pool of forgets.

Now, when I looked at her, I thought Laura Fairchild's eyes were too small for her long, rather thin and bony face. She had a small mouth as well, but when she smiled—or really, more like grimaced—those lips suddenly became very elastic, slicing into her sunken cheeks and opening themselves just enough to reveal her diminutive teeth. She wore a beautiful cameo on her suit jacket, just above her nearly nonexistent bosom.

"Hello," she said, jerking out her right hand almost as if she was going to stab Daddy with her long, thin fingers and sharp nails. "I'm Laura Fairchild, Madame Senetsky's personal assistant."

"Yes, I remember you," Daddy said. He put one of my suitcases down so he could shake her hand.

She extended her hand to Mommy.

"Hello," Mommy said. "What a beautiful place this is, and what an unusual house."

She greeted me quickly, so quickly one would think I might be contaminated, but I wasn't upset about that. Her thin fingers in mine were corpse-cold.

"The house is of Chateauesque style, of course, popularized in this country by Richard Morris Hunt, the first American architect to study at France's prestigious École des Beaux-Arts," she replied pedantically with a perfect French accent. "Many of his wealthy clients built homes in this style, including the Vanderbilts. This particular residence was built in 1896, and has been in the Senetsky family ever since."

"It's quite a farmhouse," Daddy said, nodding and smiling.

Laura Fairchild looked at him as if he had just gotten off a boat, and then turned back to Mommy and me.

"I'll show you to your room, give you your class schedule and your orientation packet. Please follow me. Do you need any more help with your luggage?"

"No, we've got a handle on it," Daddy said.

She smirked, nodded, then turned and led us into the house.

The entryway itself was circular. On both sides were enormous Greek theater masks in what looked to be archaic stone. One was the face of tragedy and the other of comedy.

"These look real!" Daddy said.

Laura paused and turned to them.

"Of course they're real. They come from ancient Greece, the theater of Dionysius in Athens."

"Old as Grampa's whiskey," Daddy remarked.

"I think quite a bit older than that, Mr. Forman," she said sarcastically, not realizing Daddy was not being literal. He looked at Mommy, who smiled to herself. She was staring down at the beautiful marble tile floor, admiring how it glittered and wondering how often it was washed, I'm sure.

The hallway leading in was of similar marble, its walls decorated by paintings depicting famous scenes from Greek, Elizabethan, and nineteenth-century theater, all in rich, thick, wooden frames. There was more statuary, and here and there a vase with imitation flowers. I clung more tightly to Uncle Simon's real roses. Adorning the walls as well were oval mirrors, framed in thick, rich mahogany. Above us ran a line of chandeliers with tear-drop bulbs raining light down the long corridor. On the left, about midway, was a dramatic grand spiral staircase with a dark cherry wood balustrade. The steps were carpeted in a tight, light beige stitch and looked never stepped upon.

"I will conduct a more elaborate tour of the building for Honey and the others once she is settled in and meets our other students. All," she added pointedly, "who have long since arrived, when they were scheduled to do so."

"We got caught in some nasty traffic," Daddy started to explain. "There was road work and—"

"Unfortunate," she muttered.

She glanced at her watch.

"We're actually a bit behind schedule, I'm afraid, so we'll have to make this quick. Please continue to follow me," she said, starting for the stairway.

Mommy threw a disappointed look in the direction of the great rooms ahead of us on the right and the left. Laura was at least charitable enough to throw a gesture that way and add, "Our studios, lecture halls, dining room, and parlor are all downstairs, of course. We do have a costume storage room on the third floor, however."

Daddy, struggling a bit with my two large suitcases, started up after her, Mommy and I trailing behind and gaping at as much as we could, from the paintings to the wainscoting. Everything looked sparkling, immaculate. Every bulb in every chandelier worked, and there must have been a few hundred.

"What about the medical facilities?" Mommy asked even before we reached the second landing.

Laura Fairchild turned so abruptly, Daddy nearly tripped over the next step and had to fight to keep from falling forward. She looked down at us, her right eyebrow hoisted a little higher than her left.

"Some of New York City's most respected hospitals, with international reputations, are just minutes away, and Madame Senetsky's personal physician is always available to make a house call, if need be, but we have never had such a need."

"I was just wondering," Mommy said softly. She practically added, "I didn't mean to sound critical." I could see it in her expression, but she bit down on her lower lip to shut in the actual words and continued to follow Daddy, who struggled along behind Laura.

The upstairs floor was thickly carpeted in the same light beige. The walls up here were filled with paintings similar to the ones below, but also included portraits of actors and actresses, singers and dancers, some of whom I recognized, but many I didn't. There were marble-top stands, upon which rested busts of famous theater people, including Greek playwrights like Sophocles and Euripides, their names embossed at the base. Some pedestals held small figurines: ballet dancers, pewter couples doing a dance routine, people cast in brass performing dramatic poses out of some opera or drama, I was sure. And more vases with imitation flowers.

Without real flowers, the air was filled with the scent of cleaning agents, polishes, window cleaners. Uncle Simon's roses still had their sweet aroma. I was more grateful than I thought I'd be for that.

Laura paused at the first door on the left.

"This will be your room," she declared, and reached for the doorknob. We gathered behind her as she opened it to a surprisingly large room with a four-poster canopy bed and matching night stands, all in a milk-white wood. The floor was covered with a rich, thick, pinkish-white carpet. There was a large window on the west side that faced a metal balcony and some metal stairs going upward.

"I'm afraid your view of the city is disturbed somewhat by this mandatory fire escape the city made the Senetskys build years ago."

"It comes in handy if there's a fire," Daddy remarked cheerfully.

"Yes," Laura said dryly. "But I wish they could have built it more off to the side. This landing is for two rooms, and then there's another for the next two, and so on and so on," she said with a deep, deprecating tone of voice.

She walked to the closet door and opened it to show me how big it was. Then she pointed out the dresser and the smaller one across from it. There was a pretty desk in the left corner with a lamp and a chair.

"I'll set your computer on that, okay, Honey?" Daddy said, nodding at it. We had brought along my notebook. Chandler and I had promised to e-mail each other as often as possible.

"There is only one phone line in each room," Laura quickly said. "It's a direct line, so you can take down the number before you leave. Our students hardly have time to dawdle on computers, anyway. Most of what they need to know they will find here at the school. Theory is put to practice very quickly. We don't assign homework in the traditional sense. There is no research except for the research you do on your own skills and talents."

"I'll just use it for E-mail," I said.

"Yes, you and Miss Rose Wallace, it seems. Madame Senetsky finds it a very impersonal way of communicating and refuses to have a computer. We still communicate the old fashioned way, via letters and actual phone conversations," she added.

Mommy, who was about as versed in modern technology as an Eskimo might be, squeezed her eyebrows toward each other and smiled with confusion.

"Well, now, here is your daily schedule," Laura Fairchild said, pulling a small packet of papers out of the leather folder she had under her left arm, "and here is our orientation booklet," she added, handing them all to me. "We'll be going over all this in great detail when you're all together." She checked her watch again.

"Please have your clothing unpacked and be ready to meet with me for a tour of the school in forty minutes," she said, and turned to Mommy and Daddy. "You should say your good-byes quickly, Mr. and Mrs. Forman. Honey has a great deal to do in a very short time because of the hour you have arrived."

"But don't we get to meet Madame Senetsky, too?" Mommy blurted.

"Madame Senetsky is interested only in her pupils, not their families," Laura Fairchild replied firmly.

"But that seems so unusual," Mommy said.

"Of course it's unusual. This is not a public school or in any way like a common college. Everyone who comes under her guidance and instruction does so completely, without any reservation, and with the realization he or she has been given a rare opportunity."

She paused, darkened her eyes with new intensity, and lifted her head stiffly.

"The world of entertainment is often a world of loneliness," she continued to explain. "Madame believes it is very important—in fact, essential—that her wards immediately develop a sense of independence."

"I don't see what harm it does to say hello to people," Daddy muttered.

"It's been nice meeting you," Laura Fairchild said in return. She flashed a plastic smile at Mommy, and then turned to me. "If you have any questions, save them for our general meeting, in what is now thirty-five minutes," she threw off, nodded at Mommy and Daddy, and strutted out of the room, closing the door behind her.

We all stood there, gaping after her.

"Nothing wrong with that woman that a good dose of old man McCarthy's rot-gut gin wouldn't solve," Daddy remarked.

"Stop it, Isaac," Mommy chastised. "She'll hear you."

"I wish she would."

Mommy started to help me unpack. Daddy walked about the room, studying it like some prospective buyer or building inspector. Mommy worked with a sense of frenzy to keep herself from bursting into tears. I could see the small look of terror in her eyes as the time for them to leave was closing in on us. After I replaced the fake flowers in the vase on my desk with Uncle Simon's roses, I put my hand softly on her shoulder, and she turned to me, her eyes glazed.

"I'll be all right, Mommy," I said. "Really, I will."

"Of course she'll be all right," Daddy nearly roared.

Mommy gave him a quick look of rebuke. He shifted his eyes and studied the closet door hinge rather than look at me.

"I don't like bringing you here and dropping you off like some sort of package," Mommy muttered. "Parents should be shown about and given a sense of relief, too. They need to know their children are secure."

"Look at this place," Daddy said, his arms wide. "Video security, gates, bars. It's built like a fortress."

"All right, Isaac."

She looked at me.

"You can call us if you need us. We can fly here quickly if we have to."

"You're making it worse," Daddy muttered, almost in a whisper.

She gave him a look full of fire and then she calmed down, looked at me, smiled, and hugged me.

"I was hoping we would take you to a nice dinner, maybe meet some of your new friends," she moaned. "Just dropping you off and turning right around to go home..."

"Sophia."

"Okay, okay." She dropped her arms in defeat, gazed around the room, and then walked to the doorway. "Oh, make sure she has money, Isaac," Mommy reminded him.

He reached into his jacket and produced an envelope stuffed with bills.

"Use this to set up your account," he said. I saw there was quite a bit of money.

"How much is here, Daddy? It's too much," I concluded, flipping through the big bills.

"Never mind that," Mommy said. "New York is expensive."

Daddy smiled at me, hugged and kissed me, and wished me good luck.

They paused at the door, looked back at me as if they were watching me leave on a boat or a plane, and then turned and walked out and down the stairs. I stood for a moment, gazing at the open doorway, tears now unabashedly pouring down my cheeks. My heart felt like a clump of mud. Just as I started to flick the tears off my cheeks, a thin boy with long, ripe-corn-yellow hair down to his shoulders stepped in the doorway.

"You're not crying real tears, are you?" he asked with a crooked smile. He had a long, narrow nose, prominent cheekbones, and a round jaw with a slight cleft in his chin. His lips had a somewhat orange tint. He wore a light brown athletic shirt with the words *Go Beethoven* written in bold red letters and a piano keyboard in coal-black and milk-white beneath them. The shirt hung loosely over the waist of his very battered jeans, which had rips at the knees. His rather large feet were in dark brown Air Jordans with his sweat socks bundled loosely around his ankles. When he brushed back the strands of hair from his left ear, I saw a diamond stud in his lobe.

He stepped into my room without an invitation, his light turquoise eyes practically circling like a wheel of fortune as he looked at everything.

"These rooms are all about the same. I'm just across the hall," he said, smelling my real flowers, "but don't worry about noise."

I nearly jumped out of my own shoes when he stepped closer to the wall and slammed his fist against it to demonstrate. There was a dull thud.

"Whoever built this, built it to last a thousand years. You won't hear a thing and I won't hear a thing, so you can sob all night if you like."

"I'm not sobbing all night," I said. "I just said good-bye to my parents for the first time ever."

"Really?" He flopped into the chair at my desk so hard, I thought he would crack it in two. "I think I've said good-bye to my parents more than I've said good morning or good night. From the day I could walk and talk, they found places for me to go. Sometimes, I think they bribed my relatives to take me in for a week-end or so.

"My mother says I give her nerves," he continued, taking barely a split second to breathe. "How can you give anyone nerves? 'We're all born with nerves,' I told her," he continued, rubbing the arm of the chair with his fingers as if he was trying to sand it down as he spoke. " 'I mean you make my nerves nervous,' she replied. Ever hear anything so stupid? Making her nerves nervous? What's your name?" he asked before I could respond.

"Honey Forman."

"We hardly know each other," he said. "Really. I've been with aggressive girls before, but for you to call me honey as soon as we meet..."

"That's my name!" I exclaimed. Now he was giving me nerves. I wanted to tell him I understood what his mother had meant.

He sat forward, folded his fingers between each other, clasped his hands behind his head, and then sat back.

"Great. Every time I call you or talk to you, everyone will think we're lovers."

"Not if I can help it," I shot back at him, and he laughed. "Do you have a name or should I just call you Nervy?" I demanded, my hands on my hips.

"Very funny, Honey. I have a rather ordinary name, I'm afraid: Steven. I'm named after my great-grandfather, Steven Jesse, credited with inventing, patenting, and producing a better candy-vending machine. It was the better mousetrap of its day, and as a result, my family became filthy rich.

"What's your specialty?" he asked before I could say a word or ask him another question.

"Specialty?"

"We're all specialists here, Honey. I'm into piano. Back home, I'm known as the boy with the Mozart ear."

He ran his fingers over an imaginary keyboard and then hummed the notes to what I thought sounded like Mozart and said so. He held his hands in midair and smiled.

"What number?"

"I'm not sure... 22?"

"23, but that's very good. Are you here as an instrumentalist?"

"Violin," I said, nodding at my violin case on the floor beside him.

"Oh, right. I thought it might be a small machine gun," he joked and jumped up so fast, I stepped back.

He performed a stage bow.

"Proper introductions, then. I am, as I have said, Steven Randolph Jesse, child prodigy, musical genius—in short, a mystery to my parents, who demonstrate no musical abilities. My mother is literally tone-deaf. My father's favorite song is *Row, Row, Row Your Boat.* I have a younger brother, who is currently the star halfback at our high school and listens to Ricky Martin, N Sync, hip-hop, whatever, and thinks piano keys unlock the piano.

"However, he's Mr. Popularity, class president, and consistently voted most likely to become state senator, which I imagine he will, if my father has any say in it.

"How many brothers or sisters do you have?"

"None," I said.

"Lucky you. All Mommy and Daddy's attention comes your way. Were they happy you were chosen by the queen to be here?"

"Yes, they were. Of course, they were. I wouldn't be here if they weren't."

He ignored me, knelt to open my violin case, peered at it and whistled.

"Stradivari, impressive."

"My uncle bought it for me."

He rose like a jack-in-the-box. Watching him move about was like watching someone flip channels on a television set.

"Ironically, my mother bought a piano to dress up the grand living room and never expected her toddler would wander up to it one day and actually begin tapping out sensible sounds. At first, everyone thought it was a novelty, and then my daycare teacher decided I might be a genius, because all I had to do was hear a melody to reproduce it. At the age of five!" he emphasized, throwing his hands in the air. "Thus, the boy with the Mozart ear! Get it?

"Where are you from?" he asked. New thoughts just popped out of his mind and mouth at random, it seemed.

"Ohio. We just drove into the city."

"I'm from Syracuse." He marched toward the door, paused, and walked back.

"You meet any of the others yet?"

"No, I was literally just brought up here by Miss Fairchild."

"*Ms.* Fairchild," he corrected. "Please, get that right. She corrected me with an electric cattle prod when I made the mistake. Your parents drove you all the way here?"

"Yes."

"Mine just put me on a hopper flight. My mother wanted to come, but my father said, 'The boy's a genius, isn't he? He can take care of himself.'"

A sudden burst of loud laughter flowed down the hallway to my door.

Steven spun around abruptly.

"That's this weird girl Cinnamon Carlson and Howard Rockwell the Third or Fourth. I can't remember what he said. Howard's from Boston, one of those families that goes back to the Boston Tea Party or something. Don't worry, he'll make sure you know. Cinnamon is from just north of the city, some small out-of-the-way town close to Yonkers."

"Why is she weird?"

"She looks like a relative of the Munsters or the Addams Family—remember them?"

Who was he to make fun of the way someone else looked? I thought.

"She's an actress," he said, as if actress meant someone strange anyway. "And Howard is an actor, or should I say thespian. That's what he calls himself. There are two other girls here, but I haven't met them yet."

Again we heard laughter.

"Let's see what they're up to. Ms. Fairchild made the mistake of telling them where the costumes are stored, and the next thing I knew, they went up to the third floor and carried on like a couple of kids in a candy store. C'mon."

"I've got to unpack still."

"You've got time. This isn't exactly a military camp, you know. No one's coming around to inspect your room, despite what Ms. Fairchild says. C'mon," he insisted. "You've got to meet them sometime."

He reached for my hand and practically tugged me out the door.

We crossed the hall to the doorway of another room and looked in. Cinnamon Carlson, her coal-black hair down to her shoulders, where it lay over the metal breastplate she had fastened on, stood with a sword in her right hand. Kneeling at her feet was Howard Rockwell, who was also wearing a breastplate and holding a helmet in his hands. He had his back to us, so I couldn't see what he looked like, but Cinnamon was wearing a translucent white lipstick and had her nails painted black. She had a very light complexion, almost pale, which made her heavy eyeshadow and eyebrow makeup look that much more stark in contrast.

She glanced at us, but didn't stop her speech, which pronounced Howard a knight as she touched the sword to his shoulder. She called herself Jeanne d'Arc, Joan of Arc.

" 'I shall place my very life at your disposal,' " Howard declared and rose slowly. He put on the helmet, and then turned to look at us.

"And who be this strange new woman you dare to bring to our court?" he cried at Steven.

I thought Howard was the handsomest boy I had ever seen. He had eyelashes I knew some girlfriends of mine would sell their souls to have, and Paul-Newmanblue eyes, eyes that you just knew would make him as cinematic as could be. He had a perfect Roman nose and a strong, firm mouth, with high male-model cheekbones, all his features perfectly symmetrical. I judged him to be at least six feet one or two inches tall, with a trim figure. The helmet didn't quite hide his rich apricot-brown hair.

"She happens to be my honey," Steven said.

"Already? Swift work, knave. Enter," he cried at me, "and pay homage to our blessed Joan."

"Approach, dear maiden," Cinnamon declared.

"Actors," Steven said disdainfully.

"Why don't you two go up and choose some costumes? You won't believe how much there is," Howard suggested. "Go ahead, Steven, show her."

"I've got to get back to unpacking," I said. "I just arrived."

"She's worried about Lady Fairchild inspecting and then being locked up in the tower for failure to fold socks or something."

"Ridiculous," Howard declared. "Don't you realize who we are, sweet child? We," he cried, his arms out, "are the crème de la crème."

"*The Prime of Miss Jean Brodie!*" Cinnamon cried. "I love that play."

"I had the lead role in our high school production," Howard told her.

He turned back to me.

"What's your name really?"

"My name really is," I began looking at the smirking Steven Jesse, "Honey Forman."

"Well, Miss Forman, are you a thespian, too?"

"I'm a violinist," I said.

"Pity. I thought we could do a scene from *Jean Brodie.* I would direct, of course."

"Of course," Cinnamon sneered. "He's already telling me the things I do wrong."

"I keep telling her, first you establish a sense of place. Where you are. You must know, before you say a single line. Would you say the same words the same way on a boat as you would in the middle of a city street?"

He looked at me.

"Understand?"

"I guess. It makes sense," I said, and he broadened his smile.

"You sure you've never done any acting?"

"No," I said. "I better finish my unpacking," I added.

Cinnamon unbuckled her metal plate and brushed her hair back. I thought she was unusual-looking, but not weird, as Steven had suggested. In fact, she was very pretty, with a very nice figure. She looked at me for a moment and then turned to Howard.

"Would you be so gallant as to put all this back for me?" she asked him.

He looked shocked.

"Me?"

"A minute ago you were pledging your life to her," Steven remarked.

"That was on stage. Now we're mere mortals, Mozart."

"You, Howard Rockwell the Third or Fourth, a mere mortal? Hard to believe," Steven said.

Howard grimaced.

"Usually, I have some stage assistant do that sort of thing. But," he added, reaching for her sword and breastplate as if it took an enormous effort, "under the circumstances," he told Cinnamon, "I will do you this favor this one time. Naturally, I'll expect something in return."

"*Naturally* you can expect whatever you want. What you'll get is another thing."

Steven laughed, but Howard just continued to smirk.

"Come on, Honey," she said to me. "I'll help you finish up."

"The owl has cried," Howard screamed so loudly I thought he would surely bring everyone in the grand house to the door. "Minutes to go before we face Madame Senetsky and the possibility of being beheaded on the spot. Come on, Mozart. Help me with this stuff while the womenfolk do what womenfolk do."

Humming Beethoven's Fifth, Steven helped gather up the costuming.

Cinnamon laughed.

"He's good," she said, "but he's obnoxious."

My heart was pounding. Who were these other students? Was this how geniuses behaved?

Was I crazy to come here, or was this going to be more fun than I could have ever imagined?

Something told me it wouldn't be much longer before I knew the answer.

2

Madame Senetsky

"I didn't start out thinking I was going to become an actress," Cinnamon said as we walked across the hallway to my room. "Acting was just something that came naturally to me, I guess. My mother and I did a lot of pretending in the attic of our house, where we found things that went back to the original owner and his family. He was a famous Civil War general, and we used to do a great deal of role-playing, imagining ourselves back then. It was fun, but I never thought of it as training for a career. My drama teacher at school kept after me, and finally, I took a part in the school production, a big part.

"What about you and the violin?"

"My uncle Peter, my father's younger brother, told me I was drawn to the violin like a fish to water. He used to say it plays me rather than I play it."

"What do you mean, used to say?" she asked as we entered my room.

"He was killed in a plane crash. He was a crop duster back in Ohio, where my family has a corn farm."

"Oh," she said. She looked like gloomy, dreadful news was not shocking or upsetting to her. It was almost as if she had expected to hear something like that.

"Anyway, he bought me my violin and paid for my early lessons."

I started to finish my unpacking. She looked at the picture of Chandler I had brought.

"Who's this?"

"My boyfriend," I said, holding the picture and smiling. "He goes to Boston University. Just starting. I miss him already. He plays piano and we took duet lessons together. That's how we met. I mean, I knew him in school, but before that we didn't so much as say hello."

"He looks...smart," she said, "and he's good-looking, too," she added. "I don't have anyone special," she continued before I could ask her. "I don't think I want to get involved with anyone until I'm forty. Not seriously, that is."

"Then you don't want a husband and a family?"

"No," she said quickly. "I won't torture them. You know how hard it is for someone to be in the theater and have any sort of normal life. Once we start this, really start it, we've got to become dedicated, like nuns married to the Church or something. That's what Howard says. I suppose he's very good. He doesn't lack for ego, that's for sure. He'll be the first to tell you how good he is. He claims you have to have that sort of confidence to do what we do. He won some sort of national drama award, like the Academy Award of high school theater or something."

"I want a family," I said. "Maybe even more than I want a career."

She shrugged and started hanging up my blouses for me.

"I don't think I can give anyone as much love as he needs right now and be true to myself.

"But that's just me," she said quickly. "Maybe it will be different for you."

"Do you have any brothers or sisters?" I asked.

For a moment she looked like she wasn't going to answer. She kept hanging up my clothes. My words seemed to linger in the air, frozen.

"I almost had a sister. My mother miscarried."

"I'm sorry."

"It was very bad. I mean, she took it very badly. She actually had a sort of mental breakdown.

"She's all right now," she added quickly.

"That's good."

"Hi," we heard someone say, and turned to see a very attractive girl with strawberry blonde hair and very bright green eyes. She had the demeanor of a fashion model, with a natural air of confidence. "I'm Rose Wallace," she said, entering.

"Cinnamon Carlson. This is Honey Forman," Cinnamon replied.

The three of us stood there a moment, contemplating each other like three gunfighters unsure of what one or all of us would do next. Were we going to be great friends or ruthless competitors?

Rose glanced around my room.

"Aren't these rooms nice?" she asked. "The whole place is so incredible. For New York City, that is." She gazed out my windows. "I'm right next door. See, we both look out over the gardens. I thought you were next to me on the other side," she told Cinnamon, "but someone else is in there. She's had her door closed since she arrived. Ms. Fairchild told me her name is Ice. Either of y'all know her or meet her?"

"I just arrived," I said.

"No, I haven't met her either," Cinnamon said. "Why is she locking herself up in her room?"

"I didn't say she was locking herself up. She just hasn't come out yet."

"If she's shy, she's in the wrong place. That's for sure," Cinnamon said.

"I don't know what's the right place for shy people anymore, except maybe on the Internet. You can talk to people without facing them," Rose said. When I raised my eyebrows, she added, "Not that I do that. My half-brother Evan does, but he's disabled, in a wheelchair, and stays at home. Lately, I've gotten him to go out more.

"Actually, he and I never met until this year."

She stopped and looked from Cinnamon to me.

"Why do I feel like I'm babbling at y'all?"

"Maybe you're as nervous as we are. Where are you from?" Cinnamon asked her. "Somewhere in the South, I can hear."

"Georgia; and you?"

"Yonkers."

"I'm from Ohio," I said.

"What about Ice?" Cinnamon asked. Rose shrugged.

"I don't know any more about her than her name."

"Maybe she's frozen in there," Cinnamon told her, and we all laughed. "Are you an actress, too?"

"I'm a dancer, but you know here we're supposed to work on the *whole* creative person," Rose said, repeating what we were told about the schooling.

"I play the violin," I said. "I don't think I could act and I'm not much of a dancer. I like hiding behind my music."

Cinnamon stared at me a moment. She had a way of making her eyes so small, her gaze so intense, that you couldn't look away or ignore her. The rest of her face seemed to freeze and become a mask.

"We're all hiding behind something," she said. "When you act, you're someone else. You're escaping yourself."

"Maybe that's what really brought us all here," Rose blurted. "I mean, not that we're criminals or anything. We're just not comfortable without our dramatic personas."

The air was heavy with that thought for a moment.

"I don't know what I'm even saying to y'all," Rose declared, and Cinnamon laughed.

"I haven't met her yet, aside from seeing her briefly at my audition, but I'm sure Madame Senetsky certainly wouldn't like that idea to be our prime motive for dramatic and artistic training."

"Hardly," Rose agreed. "Although sometimes I've thought actors are lucky. They can spend a good part of their lives being someone they'd like to be."

"What if they have to play evil people?" I asked.

Cinnamon turned to me sharply.

"Who says we don't want to be evil sometimes?" she fired, almost in anger. "Haven't you fantasized yourself doing something forbidden?"

I blushed and started to shake my head.

"And what's going on in here, pray tell?" Howard Rockwell asked, leaning against the doorjamb. He turned his collar up and put an unlit cigarette into the corner of his lips. "You dolls are up to something, see? I can tell, see? Don't try to put anything over on Rocco, see?"

"Edward G. Robinson," Cinnamon declared.

He smiled and took the cigarette out of his mouth.

"Correct. And who have we here?" he asked, stepping up to Rose. "What's your name, sweetheart?"

"I'm Rose Wallace, Edward."

"I'm not Edward," Howard said, laughing. "I was just doing an imitation of Edward G. Robinson."

"A mediocre one, I might add," Cinnamon said.

He gave her a sharp, angry look and then smiled again when he turned back to Rose.

"My name is Howard Rockwell. Howard Rockwell, Jr., actually, but I'm dropping the Jr. for now. You sound like you're from... Georgia," he declared.

"How did you know that?" Cinnamon asked suspiciously. I'm sure she thought he had been standing just outside my door, listening in on our conversation.

"Accents are my forte. You have to be able to master that skill if you want a wide range of performances," he declared, as if it was so obvious even an uneducated person would know.

"You're pretty good at it," Rose said.

"I know," Howard replied.

"Howard here doesn't suffer from a low self-image," we heard as Steven Jesse came in behind him.

"If you lack confidence in yourself, you don't belong on the stage. It's a breeding ground for egos, and rightly so. I'm not ashamed of my self-confidence," Howard lectured.

I had never seen anyone who could leap onto a soap box and preach as quickly. His eyes fell on me.

"You're all going to be out there, naked."

"Pardon me?" I asked.

"Not literally, although," he added, shifting his eyes toward Rose, "you might consider posing for Playboy or something to help spike your careers. False modesty has no place in our world."

"What if it isn't false?" Rose countered.

"Lulu Belle, darlin', all modesty is false when it comes to being in the spotlight."

"My name's not Lulu Belle," Rose shot back sharply.

"Just funnin' with ya, darlin'," Howard continued.

"Give it a rest, will you, Romeo," Steven said, stepping forward. "And let her meet a real Romeo. I'm Steven Jesse, pianist extraordinaire."

He reached out to shake Rose's hand, but when she extended hers, he pulled his back.

"Sorry, but I have to protect my fingers. They're insured by Lloyd's of London for ten million dollars."

"Really?" I asked.

"Of course... *not!*" he cried, laughing.

Rose looked at me with an expression asking if Steven and Howard were for real. I shrugged.

"Let's go help Ice defrost," Cinnamon said.

"Who's Ice?" Howard inquired.

"The girl who's behind the closed door. No one has met her yet and, if you look at the time, we all have to be downstairs to meet Dracula's daughter," Cinnamon told him.

"Dracula's daughter?" I asked.

"Ms. Fairchild," she replied.

Steven thought that was very funny.

"Go on and laugh," Howard said, stepping closer to him. "Until you find her at your neck."

"Something tells me he'd enjoy it," Cinnamon muttered.

Even I laughed at Steven's shocked look.

"Hey, just a minute here," he cried as we all started out to knock on the door of the last one to be introduced.

Cinnamon knocked, and we waited. When Ice did not come to her door, Cinnamon looked at us, and Howard suggested she might have gone ahead.

"I doubt that," Cinnamon said.

"What are you, psychic?" Steven asked. He was still smarting from the way she had made fun of him a moment ago. She turned those beady eyes on him.

"Yes, so watch yourself. I'll know exactly what you're thinking," she said. She glared into his face and he stepped back.

Just then the door opened and the most striking African-American girl I had ever seen stood there gazing out at us. She was about my height, with a rich light-chocolate complexion and jeweled ebony eyes.

Her hair was styled and cut just below her earlobes. She wore a belted white dress and a pair of sandals.

"Your name is Ice?" Howard asked in a skeptical tone.

I saw the heat quickly build in her face, her eyes becoming brighter, like the flash of two candles flaming in his direction.

"That's right," she said. "That a problem for you?"

"No, no. It's great. I'm Howard Rockwell. This is Cinnamon, Rose, Honey, and Mozart," he added, nodding at Steven.

"My name is Steven Jesse," Steven corrected. "He's an idiot."

Ice nodded as if she had known for years.

"Hi," I said, extending my hand. She looked at it, at me, and then shook it quickly.

"We're just stopping by to get you," Cinnamon said. "We've got to get downstairs quickly. Are you all right?"

Ice nodded, her eyes washing over all of us, skeptical of our motives and full of distrust. She stepped out and closed her door behind her.

"The rooms are very nice, aren't they?" Rose asked her.

"Yes," she said.

"Where are you from?" Cinnamon asked.

"Philadelphia," she said.

"What do you do?" Howard practically demanded as we all headed for the stairs.

"He's worried about the competition for top billing," Steven explained.

"Hardly," Howard said.

"I sing," Ice said.

Despite his confident facade, Howard looked relieved.

As we descended the stairs, we all grew quiet. Getting here, unpacking and settling in our rooms, meeting each other briefly had occupied us and kept us from worrying, temporarily corralling our nerves. It was apparent to me that none of us really knew what to expect next, even the overly confident Howard Rockwell, Jr. Instinctively, we all remained pretty close to each other as we turned and started down the corridor.

Ms. Fairchild stepped out of the parlor. She had a clipboard in her hand and was reading it as we approached.

"All right, ladies and gentlemen," she began, looking up, "please follow me. As you can see," she said, nodding at the parlor door, "this is the parlor. We greet our guests here, and it is everyone's responsibility to keep it as neat and as clean as you see it is now. We do not, and I repeat, do *not* permit smoking in this house or on these grounds, by yourselves or your guests.

"Unlike traditional schools, there is no system of demerits. If you violate one of Madame Senetsky's rules, you will be summarily dismissed—any rule, no matter how small it might seem to you. I hope that is very clear from the start."

"Quite," Howard muttered.

She looked up from the clipboard and then nodded at the hallway.

"Follow me and pay attention," she said.

She took us first to the room designated as the dance studio. There were practice bars, what looked like a brand-new shiny wooden floor, and mirrors on all the walls. After that, came a small theater with seats for about fifty people.

"When Madame Senetsky decides you are ready, you will conduct performance nights here," Ms. Fairchild explained. "The guests include managers, producers, booking agents, and from time to time well-known performers, any of whom might take an interest in you and might help you with your professional careers. Most of them will be former students," she added. "Madame Senetsky has instilled a sense of responsibility in her graduates. They all want to give something back, help fledglings such as yourself."

"Fledge what?" Steven asked Howard, who poked him.

All of us contemplated the empty stage for a moment. This was where we would be judged, where we would either soar or sink. I imagined Rose saw herself dancing up there and Ice saw herself singing.

"Not too shabby," Howard remarked. "How are the acoustics?"

Ms. Fairchild looked annoyed by the question.

"I don't think you should have any concerns about that," she replied. "The best theater architect in the world designed this little theater as a special favor for Madame Senetsky."

"I know that," Howard said defensively. "I just wondered."

"Sure," Steven said.

"I did. What do you think, it's some top-secret information? If you bothered reading about the school..."

"Let's continue," Ms. Fairchild snapped.

She took us to a room about half the size of the dance studio. There was a grand piano in it. She said this was where the instrumental lessons would be held and where the vocal lessons would be conducted. Steven went to the piano and tapped out some notes.

"Please," Ms. Fairchild said. "Not now."

"I can't help myself. I'm obsessed," Steven cried.

"Distressed is more like it," Howard muttered.

Ms. Fairchild showed us the large dining room, and then led us toward the kitchen.

Along the way we saw a wall full of framed photographs. She explained that they were all various shots of Madame Senetsky in her prime, each capturing another famous moment on a European stage. Costuming indicated productions from the Greeks through Shakespeare and into more modern plays, but there were also news clippings and reviews explaining the productions as well. When she was younger, she was quite striking, I thought. I was sure I might have seen her in an old movie.

After the display of photographs were a number of trophies, plaques, and citations Madame Senetsky had won. They were encased in glass. Some had been awarded by royalty. We clumped around them, reading as much as we could.

"You can look at all that some other time," Ms. Fairchild said, rushing us along.

We stopped at the kitchen, where a short, elderly woman with her hair under a net was preparing what looked like roast duck. She glanced at us, but kept her attention solidly on her work.

"Mrs. Churchwell is responsible for all the cooking

and food preparation here at the Senetsky school," Ms Fairchild explained. Even while she talked about her, Mrs. Churchwell kept her concentration on her work. "She runs the kitchen and has it organized as she needs it to be. No one is to move a cup out of place. All of you, on a rotation basis, will help with kitchen chores, cleanup, and the like. Tonight, your first night here, is the one exception.

"For tonight," she continued, "Madame Senetsky has hired help to conduct the dinner. That is because you will meet all of your teachers at dinner tonight, and Madame Senetsky wants you to give all your attention to them. I will show you where I will be posting messages, the roster, scheduling, and anything else you all need to know. It will be your responsibility to check the board daily," she emphasized.

"Chores?" Howard moaned. "What is this, summer camp or something?"

"Clothing," she announced instead of responding, and continued down the hallway to the laundry room. "You all are responsible for your own bedding, clothing, towels, et cetera. Anyone who needs instruction about working the washer and dryer will speak to Mrs. Ivers," she said.

On cue, a tall, thin, dark brunette entered behind us. She wore a short-sleeved white uniform and white, thick-heeled shoes. Her arms, although very slim, looked muscular, veins and arteries well embossed against her skin. Her lower lip looked smaller than her upper and seemed to lie unhinged, showing her bottom teeth.

"The soap powders and softeners are kept in this

closet," she instructed, opening a closet door to demonstrate. She stepped back to pull a handle and lower the ironing board. "The iron is right here. Anyone who wants clothing sent to the dry cleaners should leave it in of these bags before nine A.M.," she said, showing us a drawer full of plastic bags. "The bill will be given to you and needs to be promptly paid," she said and looked to Ms. Fairchild.

"Thank you, Mrs. Ivers. Any questions about this, ladies and gentleman?"

"What if I want to send out my laundry?" Howard inquired. "Entirely."

Mrs. Ivers looked to Ms. Fairchild.

"Madame Senetsky frowns upon any ostentatious show of wealth," she replied. "You will hear many times how important self-reliance is for people pursuing careers in the theater."

"I just don't want to waste my time," Howard moaned.

"Your time and how it is used and not used will be organized efficiently, believe me," she told him sharply. "Learning how to be independent is not a waste of time."

"But..."

"Let's continue," she said.

Howard turned crimson with frustration and anger.

Ms. Fairchild marched us down the hallway until we reached a pair of dark brown, thick double doors embossed with flowers and birds. Then she stopped, turned, and addressed us.

"This is where the school boundaries are drawn. Beyond these doors lies Madame Senetsky's private residence. Under no circumstances, ever, for any reason whatsoever, are any of you permitted through these doors. If there is a reason for you to speak with Madame Senetsky, you will contact me and I will so inform her. I will now show you my quarters, so you will know where to go if you have any special requests.

"You enter the building only through the front door. You are permitted to walk on the grounds, of course, but do not, I repeat, do not enter the building through any side or rear doors, especially at the rear of the building. Any questions about this?"

We all stared at her and then looked at each other.

"I repeat, if anyone violates this important rule, he or she will be summarily dismissed."

"How else can you be dismissed but summarily?" Howard muttered.

"You could be court-martialed first," Steven quipped.

Ms. Fairchild did not smile. She glared at Steven, who quickly shifted his eyes toward a painting.

"Please follow me," she continued and took us to a door she said was the door to her quarters. "I repeat, come directly here if you have a problem that needs my attention. Do not discuss it with anyone else, not even your teachers and certainly not with anyone outside our school."

She checked her clipboard, looked at her watch, and told us to follow her back to the parlor.

"Wait here," she ordered. "Madame Senetsky will be addressing you all in a few minutes."

She turned and left us.

"A work roster?" Howard immediately cried. "How

come no one told me about that at the audition? Anyone else here ever told we'd be washing clothes, clearing dishes, taking out garbage?"

"You would if you went to an ordinary college, wouldn't you?" Rose asked him.

"No. I wouldn't go to just *any* college."

"Why don't you just think of it as another role or something," Cinnamon told him. "The butler in a big mansion or the owner's deranged, illegitimate son."

I saw how Ice's eyes filled with amusement.

"I never washed my own clothes before," Howard moaned.

Ice raised her eyes toward the ceiling, smiled, and shook her head.

"It's not rocket science," Rose said.

"You know how much we're all paying for tuition," Howard complained. He looked at Ice. "Anyone here want to take my turn at kitchen duties and take care of my clothes for me? I'll pay," he said.

She turned to me and Cinnamon, the small muscles in her jaw tightening. Her name might be Ice, I thought, but she looks like she could explode in a ball of fire.

"Why are you looking at me?" she asked Howard. "You think I've been working as someone's maid?"

"No. I'm looking at everyone. What about you, Honey?"

"You're not showing a good attitude, Howard," Cinnamon said. "You won't build character if you buy off your responsibilities."

"I've got character!" he exclaimed.

"Yes, but *which* character? Doctor Jekyll or Mr. Hyde?" Steven quipped.

Everyone laughed. Howard shook his head and plopped on the sofa.

"The instrumental studio looks pretty good, doesn't it?" Steven asked me.

"Yes," I said.

"Piano is in tune. Actually, I've got the same one at home."

We all found seats and kept our attention on the doorway.

"What was all that about not entering Madame Senetsky's private area?" I asked.

"The reason is pretty obvious," Howard said in a condescending tone.

"Really? Enlighten us, oh great guru of the theater," Cinnamon said.

"Madame Senetsky simply needs to separate her private life from her public one. We'll all have that problem some day. At least, I expect to," he concluded.

"He's probably right," Rose said.

"Of course I'm right. I'm sure all of you have things you'd rather the rest of us didn't know."

He smiled at Ice, who gazed back at him with such a cold, hard expression, she wiped the smug smile off his face and he sat back.

"I wonder how long we'll be kept waiting," he muttered.

"Waiting is something with which you had better make acquaintance," we heard, and all turned to the doorway to see Madame Senetsky enter.

If any of us have ever wondered what it would be like to be in the presence of royalty, we surely were finding out at this moment, I thought. With a regal air that seemed to precede her and wash over us to make commoners of us all, Madame Senetsky appeared. Ms. Fairchild remained a few feet behind, as if it was forbidden to stand too close to her imperial self.

In her left hand Madame Senetsky held a jeweled cane with a meerschaum handle. She wore a dark suit with an ankle-length hem, the jacket open to reveal her pearl silk blouse and prominent bosom. There were strings of pearls around her neck and her blue-gray hair was pinned tightly in a chignon and fastened with jeweled combs. She wore a large faced antique watch on a gold band on her left wrist and on her right were coils of gold bracelets. Almost all of her fingers had rings, ranging from simple gold bands to large rubies and diamonds.

The news clippings I had barely scanned in the hallway had told me she had to be at least in her mid-sixties, yet she had the complexion of a woman far younger. Her skin had almost a silvery tint, with only tiny wrinkles around her eyes but a remarkably smooth forehead. Her cheeks were a bit sunken, which served to emphasize her high cheekbones and the sharpness in her perfectly straight nose.

Elegance and sophistication were defined by such a woman, I thought. She truly had perfect bone structure, with a very strong, firm mouth, the lips of which were just barely tinted a light crimson. When she drew closer, I saw that her surprisingly youthful appearance owed a great deal to the smart use of makeup. Even so, her blue eyes were girlishly bright and intelligent, gathering information about us in seconds. In the face of her perfect posture and slow, confident air, we could barely shift our eyes an inch away from her. This was a woman who not only demanded attention, but easily commanded it as well.

She considered each of us, lingering on our faces as if she wanted to be absolutely sure that no imposter had come into this school under false pretenses.

"Perhaps in the theater more than anywhere else, Mr. Rockwell, patience is a virtue."

Howard started to respond, but she pulled her head back as if she held invisible reins on his lips, and he kept them firmly sewn shut.

"I am here not only to welcome you today," she began. She didn't have an English accent as such, but her pronunciation was so careful, so precise, I couldn't help but be impressed and self-conscious about my own. "But to welcome you to hard work, dedication, and sacrifice. There is no pretending that isn't required. Here at the Senetsky school, the only illusions we permit are the illusions we create on the stage."

She paused, took a step closer, and once again perused each and every one of our faces as if she was looking for some sign of weakness and defeat already. Ice looked more annoyed and angry than frightened. Cinnamon stared up at her with two unmoving and unflinching eyes, revealing little emotion. Rose looked calm, a soft smile on her lips. Steven shifted his eyes but looked quite unimpressed, even a bit bored, and Howard nodded as if he was hearing exactly what he had expected to hear.

Was I the only one whose heart was pounding? I gazed back at her, holding my breath.

"You have all indicated a desire to succeed in the most difficult of vocations. Doctors, lawyers, teachers, almost any tradesman or tradeswoman can hide, bury, or find some excuse for failure, but when you people fail, you all fail right in front of the public. There is no question that you've failed, no equivocating, and very few other people with whom to share your blame. A series of bad notes," she said, directing herself toward me and then toward Steven and Ice, "is as obvious as beautiful notes. A terrible stage performance, a lack of concentration, sticks out under the lights," she added, looking at Howard and Cinnamon and Rose.

"In short, you will all be judged severely. You will all be competing with people as talented or more talented, even those less talented who have compensated with more effort and dedication, and your reputation will be only as good as your last performance. In the arts, it is most difficult to coast on your past successes and be tolerated long.

"I have often been asked what is the secret of success in the arts. Let me tell you all now and forever. It is easily a proportion of sixty percent talent to at least forty percent perseverance and attitude.

"You are all here because you have proven you possess the raw talent. I will have your talents developed and nurtured by the finest teachers in New York City, indeed in all the entertainment world, but I, myself, will be in charge of developing the proper attitudes in you all.

"To do this, I will literally, from this day forward,

take charge of your life. You will dress, eat, walk, talk as I instruct. You will learn how to hold yourself properly, how to converse properly, how to present yourself properly, for appearance is an essential ingredient in our lives, far more than it is in the lives of ordinary people. Therefore, I will be in judgment of you constantly, even when you are merely crossing from one room to another, spooning soup or sipping tea, talking to each other, or sitting and reading a book.

"We are, in short, always performing, always on one stage or another.

"You will be unhappy a great deal of the time, as anyone under a microscope of criticism would be, but if you have the grit and determination, if you are sufficiently ambitious, you will survive and grow into the successful performer a Senetsky graduate becomes."

She pulled her shoulders back even more and gazed down at us all, searching for some sign of defiance, I thought. No one so much as breathed hard.

"Why all this effort? Why this opportunity? I will give you my philosophy, simple and sweet. Along with all the fame, the accolades, the money, and prestige comes an enormous amount of responsibility. We are the truly chosen few, given talents for a purpose.

"We fill the lives of ordinary people, brighten their dreary world with meaningful distraction. We show them beauty where they would see none without us. We help them appreciate their own powers of perception, their own senses and emotions. We are truly the prophets and the clergy showing them what God means for them to worship, to love, and to cherish the most in this world.

"If you are unable to meet the tests I give you, you were not meant to be one of us and to bear this great responsibility. I will surely send you on your way.

"Any questions or comments so far?" she asked.

Only Howard dared lean forward to speak.

"That's really my philosophy, too," he said. "I believe in it."

"Believing in it is one thing. Performing it is quite a different thing," she replied firmly.

She looked at the rest of us to see if anyone else would dare utter a word. No one did.

"When I say you must meet my tests, I do not mean only my instructions and requirements for your education in this school of drama. I especially mean not indulging in the degenerative practices so common to people your age these days.

"Consequently," she began, stiffening her posture again and seeming to rise above us even higher, "anyone caught smoking, drinking hard liquor, or using drugs will be immediately discharged—and that means indulging in these bad habits off the premises as well as on. From this day forward, you represent this school. You are a Senetsky student," she declared, her voice plush with pride, "and that means you bear my name and you live under the shield of my reputation. I will not tolerate the smallest stain on that reputation.

"In short, you are to live like the old-time studio contract players once lived in Hollywood. Everything you do, you do with my permission first. Even your love affairs and your marriages should be planned to help further your careers."

Steven started to laugh.

"You must have more dedication and commitment than nuns and monks," she insisted, her eyes on him, instantly freezing that laugh into a weak smile.

I glanced at Cinnamon, who looked at Howard. He was beaming with a light of self-satisfaction that would outdo the gleam of most arrogant people in comparison. All over his face were the words, *I told you so.* However, I had the sense that he had read her words somewhere and was simply mouthing them to us.

"Ms. Fairchild has your behavior contracts," Madame Senetsky continued.

"Behavior contracts?" Steven whispered loudly.

"After I leave," she continued, ignoring him, "you are all to read them and then sign them. If you do not want to sign them, please pack your bags and arrange for your departure. I have a number of students on standby.

"Tonight, you are all invited to dinner with your teachers. I will expect the gentlemen to wear jackets and ties and the ladies to dress appropriately. I would prefer to see a minimum of makeup," she added, focusing entirely on Cinnamon.

"Makeup is an art form. I will be bringing in professionals to evaluate each and every one of you and instruct each of you on how to dress your face to an advantage. Why, you wonder, is that so important now?" she continued, as if she could read our very thoughts.

"I repeat, a Senetsky student is always performing, always on one stage or another, always being judged, evaluated, considered. Do not step out of this house without taking that attitude along.

"I never do," she concluded, softly tapped her cane on the floor, and turned to nod at Ms. Fairchild, who shot forward instantly to hand a behavior contract to each of us.

We watched Madame Senetsky leave and then began to read the contract.

There was a curfew for weekday nights and another for weekends.

Any guests had to first be approved before they could visit us.

We were never to have any guests in our rooms.

We were solely responsible for the upkeep of our rooms and we were to care for the house as if it was our very own.

Repeated in bold print were the prohibitions against smoking, drinking, and drugs, with the codicil that all the rules applied to our behavior off the property as well as on. In essence, we were simply never off the property. The world had become the Senetsky School of Performing Arts.

"How come we weren't shown all this before we auditioned?" Steven Jesse mumbled. "This is worse than living at home."

"You do have a choice," Ms. Fairchild told him. She appeared to enjoy telling him. "Don't sign and leave."

"Thanks," he replied dryly.

"I don't see any problems," Howard said, signing the contract with a flourish. "I know what I want, and it's not wasting my talent."

Ms. Fairchild didn't nod or smile at him. She took his contract and waited for the rest of us to finish reading the fine print.

Each of us signed the contract and handed it to her.

"Dinner will be served at seven o'clock. Madame Senetsky insists on everyone being on time for any class assignment, any event, any meeting whatsoever. In the theater, promptness and responsibility are essential. She views lateness the same as missing a cue.

"You're all dismissed for now," she concluded, pivoted almost in military style, and walked out.

For a moment it was as if all the air around us had stagnated and become too heavy to breathe.

"I wonder what she does for fun," Steven queried, nodding after Ms. Fairchild.

"Probably pulls wings off of flies," Cinnamon said, rising.

"I'm sure it won't be as bad as it sounds," Rose said hopefully. She looked at me, and I smiled.

Ice was still staring at the floor.

"Are you all right?" I asked her.

She shook her head.

"I came here to develop my singing ability. I don't know what she's talking about: being the prophets and clergy and showing people what to worship? I thought I was here just to learn how to sing. Now she makes it sound like we're becoming someone's idea of a saint."

"Right," Steven cried.

"Wrong," Howard corrected. "You don't just sing, Ice," he continued, standing up. "If that was all you were here to do, you could do it in the shower. You're a performer. You heard what Madame Senetsky said. We're all performers, very special people with special gifts."

"I never felt like someone special," Ice said as she stood to face him.

"Well, you should," Howard insisted but backed away.

We all started out and headed for the stairway.

"I hope I can invite my boyfriend to visit," Rose said. "He's attending NYU, so he's here in New York."

"If not, you'll just go visit him," Cinnamon said.

"Unless Madame Senetsky disapproves," Howard inserted.

"Why would she do that?" I asked.

"Maybe her boyfriend is a detriment to her career," he replied. "A poor influence."

"She has no right to say that," Rose cried, pausing on the stairway.

Howard shrugged.

"You just signed an agreement giving her that right."

"I did not!"

"I'm afraid you did," he insisted.

She looked to me and Cinnamon.

"Did I?"

"Technically, I suppose, we all did," Cinnamon said.

Everyone grew quiet as we continued to walk up the stairway.

"I was wondering why my father agreed to this so quickly," Steven said. "Now I know. He wanted me to be tortured."

We paused at my room. I opened the door and, to my surprise, they all followed me in.

"He must have known what it was going to be like," Steven added, throwing himself down in my desk chair. The girls stood inside the doorway with Howard across from them, staring at Steven. He was twisting his fingers around each other as if he was trying to get something sticky off them. "No wonder he wrote that tuition check so fast."

"Wasn't he proud of the fact that you had been chosen?" Rose asked.

"He was proud of the fact that I was out of the house," Steven said. "He's put me in the hands of a monster."

"She's far from that," Howard said. "You don't know how lucky you are. None of you do," he emphasized. "But you'll realize it soon enough."

"How did someone so young get so much wisdom so quickly?" Cinnamon asked. Ice smiled, but kept her eyes down.

"I've just done my research on all this. I know how important her opinion is, in the theater world especially. We're talking worldwide reputation here. You saw the awards. You don't have to be a genius to figure that out."

"What about Mr. Senetsky?" I asked. "I didn't see any reference to her husband in the articles I skimmed. Did anyone else?"

"He was never part of her career," Howard said. "Besides, he's dead now."

"Oh."

"How did he die?" Rose asked.

"All I know is what is rumored," Howard replied.

"Really?" Cinnamon asked, her eyes narrow with skepticism and a small twist in her lips. "And what exactly is rumored, Howard Rockwell? Tell us. What else do you just happen to know?"

Howard shrugged, strutted across to my dresser, looked at Chandler's picture, and then turned to the rest of us.

"Supposedly, he committed suicide in this very house years ago. That might be another reason why Madame Senetsky has shut up a portion of the mansion, the parts that remind her of him, his office, whatever."

"Why would he commit suicide?" Rose asked. She looked close to tears, worried about the answer.

"I don't know. Business failures, maybe. As I said, it's just a rumor."

"How can suicide be just a rumor?" Rose practically demanded.

"The story was it was a gun accident."

Rose looked like she was about to faint, her face drained so quickly. We all stared at her. She suddenly looked like she couldn't move, couldn't speak. Tears made her eyes glisten like glass after a rain.

"Rose?" I said. "Are you all right?"

"What? Oh, I just... wondered."

"Well, you're right to be concerned," Howard said, moving toward her. "We should all be concerned."

"Why?" Ice asked. She had been so quiet, her eyes down, listening.

"Well, I hesitate to tell you this."

"Howard, you are so full of—" Cinnamon began.

"No," he interrupted. "It might be bad for some of you."

"What?" I demanded, impatient.

"There's a story that his ghost wanders the house, back there in the locked-up places."

"Howard!" Rose cried.

Howard started to smile.

"I wouldn't laugh at it," Cinnamon suddenly said. The skepticism and anger left her face as she sat on the edge of my bed. Her reaction took Howard by surprise.

"Oh?" he said.

"We have a very old house and often I have felt the presence of spirits."

"Oooh," Steven said jumping up, "maybe we should call Ghostbusters."

"Maybe we should call Idiotbusters instead," Ice piped up and stepped beside Cinnamon. Rose and I did the same.

The two boys looked at all of us.

"I've still got some unpacking to do," Howard said. "See you all at dinner."

Steven widened his smile and then pumped the air with his fingers and hummed the theme from *The Twilight Zone.*

He laughed and followed Howard out.

"Do you think any of that was true?" Rose asked us.

"I don't know. What difference does it make how or why Mr. Senetsky died?" Cinnamon replied. "I'm here to learn my craft and you're here to become a professional dancer. Ice will make hit records, and Honey here will be playing in Carnegie Hall very soon. Howard's right. We're lucky."

She started away.

"My father committed suicide," Rose blurted. "The

same way. It looked like a gun accident, but I was never fooled by any of that."

Cinnamon stopped and turned back to her.

"Why?" she asked.

"He was having an affair with someone and..."

"What?" Cinnamon asked.

"There was another child, Evan."

"That's why you called him your half-brother?" Cinnamon asked. Rose nodded. "What happened?"

"It got very complicated, and one day he didn't come home from a duck-hunting trip. My mother and I ended up living with Evan."

"That *does* sound complicated," I said, just to make her feel better.

"Didn't you say Evan was in a wheelchair?" Cinnamon asked.

"Yes, but he's quite a unique person. He's the one mostly responsible for my getting here. Money-wise, that is. He's a genius on the computer, too. I'll tell y'all more about him sometime. We've developed a good brother-sister relationship."

"That's nice," I said.

"I can't let him down."

"Seems like a lot of people are depending on us being a success," Cinnamon said.

"That's true enough," Ice added.

"Not the least of whom is Madame Senetsky," I said.

"She made it seem like, if we fail, we'll go straight to hell," Cinnamon said.

"Steven thinks he's already there," Rose reminded us.

We all looked at each other, and then, maybe out of

a desperate need for relief, we all started to laugh, hugged each other, and laughed some more.

"Let's promise each other right now," Cinnamon said, "never to permit those two gifted geniuses, those wonderful prophets of beauty, to get under our skins."

"Or our covers," Rose added.

Ice laughed the hardest at that.

We clasped hands in the middle like a team about to go out on the basketball court.

And suddenly I felt we were all going to be all right.

We were all going to be just fine.

Was that the first illusion I'd experience in this house, or a bit of the truth?

3

Girl Talk

When we met to go down to dinner, Cinnamon looked naked and withdrawn without her makeup—not that she was in any way unattractive, though. Even in the little time I had spent with her, I realized that her makeup was truly a mask from behind which she could feel safe gazing out at the world. Perhaps for her, more than for any of us, what Madame Senetsky had said about us performing constantly on one stage or another rang with truth. Ice and Rose joined us when they heard us in the hall.

"Where are the boys?" Rose asked.

"I'm here!"

Steven came flying out of his room. His tie knot was loose and his shirt wasn't quite fully tucked into his pants. Dressed up in formal clothing, he looked pretty much like a fish out of water. His sleeves didn't seem long enough and his jacket could use a good pressing, I thought.

"How do I look?" he asked.

"You want the truth?" Cinnamon asked.

"Of course. Don't forget what Madame Senetsky said: No illusions are permitted except the ones we create on stage," he replied.

"Okay. You look like a slob," she replied.

"Huh?"

"Fix your tie at least," Rose said and stepped up to tighten it for him.

"And get your shirt tail in," I said, coming around behind him to help him do it.

"Straighten out your jacket," Ice suggested. She tugged on his right sleeve and buttoned the shirt cuff.

We all stepped back and looked at him.

"Well?" he asked, looking from one face to another.

"I hope you play the piano really well," Cinnamon said. "Otherwise..."

"What otherwise?"

"Otherwise, there isn't much hope," she muttered.

Rose and I laughed.

"Very funny. Geniuses don't need to look good. Ever see a picture of Einstein?"

"He didn't perform in public," Cinnamon replied.

We started for the stairs.

"Where's Howard?" Steven asked, following.

"Probably stuck on his face in the mirror," Cinnamon said.

Rose and Ice laughed louder than I did.

We started down the steps.

"He's going to be late," Steven warned, looking

back toward Howard's room. He lagged a bit behind us. "Maybe I should wait for him."

"Then you'll be late, too," Rose pointed out.

I felt better with the girls around me. Rose and Ice led, both of them looking so beautiful. Maybe we really were an impressive group. Maybe Madame Senetsky wasn't wrong about our being special. I wished I could feel it as strongly about myself as some of the others did about themselves. When would I gain the confidence Howard Rockwell seemed to have at birth? Was it just around the corner, waiting for me, along with my wonderful future? Or was that one of the fantasies Madame Senetsky would eventually end?

The sound of Howard's laughter coming from below surprised all of us. We paused when we turned the corner of the stairway and saw him emerge from the parlor beside a tall man with dark, wavy brown hair and a smart mustache that curled gently toward the corners of his mouth. He wore an earthy brown corduroy jacket and a red ascot. I thought he was a very handsome man, with a dark complexion and soft blue eyes. He smiled at the sight of us.

"These are the others," Howard told him, making 'others' sound a bit inferior, I thought.

"Oh, how do you all do? I'm Brock Marlowe, your drama coach," the man said, nodding toward us. No one spoke. Finally, Cinnamon stepped forward.

"Since you've already managed to meet Mr. Marlowe, Howard, why don't you introduce everyone? Properly," she added, sending an impish glance back at me.

"Right. This is Cinnamon...Carlson, is it?"

"So short a memory, Howard? How do you manage to memorize your lines?" she shot back.

Howard sucked in his breath and forced a small smile, turning to the rest of us.

"Honey Forman. Rose Wallace. And Ice—I'm sorry. I really didn't get your last name," Howard said.

"Goodman," she said quickly.

"Ice Goodman. And that's Steven Jesse trying to hide behind them."

"Ah yes, the man with the Mozart ear. Howard's been telling me. Pleased to meet all of you," Brock Marlowe said.

"What else has our Howard been telling you, Mr. Marlowe?" Cinnamon asked with feigned sweetness.

"I don't know that much about any of you to tell any stories," Howard said quickly.

"So, he talked mostly about himself. How surprising," Cinnamon said.

Ice actually laughed aloud. I could see she liked Cinnamon, and looked forward to everything she did or said.

"No, I did not talk about myself. We talked about the theater," Howard said out of the side of his mouth. "Mr. Marlowe happens to be a hero of mine. He directed the revival of Ibsen's *A Doll's House* in the West End in London last season, a smash hit. He also single-handedly created the Player's Theater in Chicago."

"Howard has done his research," Brock Marlowe said, "but I'm not quite the only one responsible for the Player's Theater. Many good minds went into that."

He smiled at us.

"So, who are the prospective actors here?"

"I guess I am," Cinnamon said. "I am surprised Howard didn't mention it, yet mentioned Steven's piano talents," she added, sending Howard a hard, cold look that made him shift his eyes guiltily away.

"We're all supposed to develop dramatic talents," Rose remarked.

"And so you will, Rose. I am looking forward to working with you all," Mr. Marlowe said.

"So are we," Howard quickly followed.

Laura Fairchild came walking quickly down the corridor from the rear of the house, her tall, thin heels pinging like steel raindrops over the floor.

"Oh, Mr. Marlowe," she said, "Madame Senetsky was asking after you. The rest of the staff has been meeting with her in her office. She sent me for you. Girls, boys," she continued turning toward us, "follow me into the dining room for your seating."

"See you in a while then," Mr. Marlowe said, and hurried down the corridor toward Madame Senetsky's office.

"She won't spank him for being late, will she?" Steven quipped. Ms. Fairchild ignored him and led us into the dining room.

"You'll sit across from your teachers," she began. "Ice here," she said, holding the back of the chair at the near end of the long table, "Steven, Rose, Honey, Howard, and Cinnamon," she continued down the table.

She nodded at the empty chairs.

"These will be your permanent seats at this table."

"Permanent seats? What is this, grade school?" Steven asked.

"Maybe that is how our teachers will recognize us," Cinnamon wondered aloud.

"No," Ms. Fairchild said. "You'll be properly introduced when they arrive. Please be seated. Do any of you have any questions about dinner table etiquette? Which fork to use when, anything?" She looked pointedly at Steven. "Madame Senetsky prefers no one be embarrassed *or* embarrass the school."

"Does that mean we can't eat with our hands?" Steven asked.

"Not yours. They're insured for millions, remember?" Cinnamon said.

"Oh, right."

"If there are no intelligent questions, then please be seated. When your teachers enter, please stand and wait for them to take their seats before sitting again. When Madame Senetsky arrives, we all stand."

"And wait for her to take her seat before sitting again?" Steven queried with a sly smile.

"Of course," Ms. Fairchild replied. "Dinner will begin in a moment."

She left the dining room. Everyone gazed at the elaborate table with its heavy silverware, its crystal goblets, and beautiful china. There were three candles in gold candleholders, waiting to be lit. Platters of bread were already on the table, but covered with what looked like silk.

"What if she never sits down?" Steven asked. "Would we all eat standing?"

"Your wisecracks are going to get you in trouble quickly here," Howard warned him.

"That can't happen, Howard. I would just switch from piano to stand-up comic and continue."

We all sat and for a long moment just contemplated the room. One of the maids came in and put dishes of butter out. She didn't really look at any of us.

"I'm as nervous as I was at my audition," I admitted.

"Me, too," Ice said.

"I didn't have an audition," Rose revealed. Everyone turned to her.

"What?"

"Well, not a formal one like y'all had, I mean."

"How did you get into this school then?" Howard demanded, as if it was an affront to him and his talent.

"My dance teacher at school was friendly with Madame Senetsky's son, Edmond."

"So?" Howard pursued.

"He attended my performance and she brought him backstage. He told me his mother permitted him to select one student a year, and he decided to select me," Rose explained.

"That's not fair. I had to prepare and travel here and wait to find out if I had been accepted or not. I turned down the University of Southern California before knowing," Howard moaned. "He must have had a thing for you," he quickly decided.

"What?"

"How can you say that? You don't know how talented she might be," Ice piped up with such vehemence, it not only took Howard by surprise, it made us all widen our eyes.

"Maybe he's right," Rose thought aloud. "I never considered that."

Howard looked smug.

"Don't pay attention to him, Rose," I said. "Howard, you're making her feel bad."

"I'm just suggesting a possibility," he insisted.

"It's not even a possibility," Cinnamon snapped at him.

"Oh? Why not, pray tell?"

"First, if Edmond sent someone here who didn't meet his mother's standards, she would know instantly, wouldn't she?" Cinnamon asked. "And what do you think she would say or do to Edmond? Remember what Madame Senetsky told us? We, of all people, can't hide our imperfections, our failures. There's no way to fake it. You either belong here or don't," she told Rose.

"Howard," she said, sending daggers his way with her small eyes, "should know that better than any of us, and *does* know that. He's just a little jealous.

"Beware the green-eyed monster, Howard, it mocks the meat it feeds upon."

"Ha! I guess she told you, Howard Rockwell the Sixth," Steven cried and reached for a piece of bread.

"Don't!" Cinnamon barked.

He pulled his hand back as if he had burned his fingers.

"What?"

"You can't do that until everyone is here. It's not good etiquette."

"She's right," Howard muttered. "I'm surprised you didn't know *that!*"

Steven grimaced and folded his hands under his arms.

"I don't know why all this is so important. It has nothing to do with the way I play piano," he complained.

"If that's all you want, get a job in some smoke-filled dive," Howard told him.

Steven glared at him. *What a time to begin bickering amongst ourselves,* I thought, *with our teachers about to meet us.* Why was it my expectations rose and fell with roller coaster emotions? One moment I was feeling optimistic about us all enjoying this experience, and the next I was dreading another moment in this house. I gazed about the table, searching everyone's face to see if anyone else seemed to have similar feelings. They all looked lost in their own thoughts.

A grandfather clock ticked the hour.

And, on cue, our teachers began to enter the room. With Howard practically leaping to his feet first, we all stood.

A short, bald man with dull brown watery eyes and a complexion as pale as tissue paper took the seat directly across from me. He didn't smile so much as he turned his lips into each other and pulled back the corners of his mouth. He was plump, a little barrel-chested, with a necklace of fat hanging at the sides of his throat. His ears were far too large for his head. They looked tacked on at the last minute, mistakenly taken from someone else's assigned features.

Right behind him came a far younger-looking, tall, slender man with hair as black as Ice's, styled with a soft wave from his forehead back. He had bright hazel eyes with specks of green and a thin, straight nose above very soft-looking lips. Unlike the bald man, he wore a pleasant smile. He nodded at us and gave Rose, in particular, an additional and wider smile.

A very fat, robust man with thinning dark gray hair but heavy sideburns and a bulbous nose with a patch of redness over each nostril marched in firmly, nearly knocking into his chair with his stomach. He had very thick lips and large, dark brown eyes. Brock Marlowe came in after him, moving far more gracefully, and he was followed by a rather stern-looking man, about six feet tall with long, thick pecan-brown hair. He kept his lips tight, drawing a slash across his angular face.

Our teachers gazed at us and we gazed back at them. For a moment I wondered what would happen next. Then Ms. Fairchild appeared at the foot of the table.

"Ladies and gentlemen," she began, "let me introduce you to your instructors.

"Mr. Angus Masters, your speech instructor," she began, and the bald man across from me nodded at us. "Mr. Cameron Demetrius, your dance instructor," she continued. The trim-figured, gentle-faced man smiled wider and turned his shoulders as if he was scratching his back against a wall. "Mr. Alfred Littleton, your vocal instructor," she said. The heavy man opened and closed his thick lips without speaking. "You already know Mr. Marlowe, your drama coach, and this is Mr. Leonard Bergman, our instrumental and piano teacher." Mr. Bergman's eyes brightened a bit, but he didn't change expression and barely nodded.

She then recited our names and, after our instructors sat, we sat.

"Everyone settle in okay?" Cameron Demetrius asked immediately, to break the silence.

We all answered at once, and that lightened the heavy air with some laughter.

Howard then started a long story about his trip, speaking as if he was doing a scene on the stage, his hands moving like two birds circling each other.

A moment later, Edmond Senetsky entered with Madame Senetsky on his arm and everyone rose. She took her seat at the head of the table. Edmond sat at the far end, and our first formal dinner at the Senetsky School began.

We learned that Alfred Littleton, our vocal teacher, was a former light opera star, and the instrumental teacher, Leonard Bergman, was an internationally famous conductor. The more we learned about each and every one of them and their accomplishments, the more nervous and insecure I felt. Surely, they would take one good look at me and see what an imposter I was. How could a farm girl from Ohio be considered someone so talented she could compete for a place in the world's greatest orchestras?

Mr. Masters would find my speaking ability and speech patterns so flawed, he would throw up his hands in frustration. I knew I didn't have the kind of grace or muscle coordination to please a professional dance instructor, and I couldn't carry a vocal note. There would be no point to any singing instructions for me. Once all this was learned, I was sure I would be called to Madame Senetsky's office, where she would quickly inform me a great error had been made and there was someone far more qualified waiting in the wings. I would almost be relieved, I thought.

I was so frightened, I competed with Ice for the position of the most silent person at dinner. I could see how Mr. Masters was keenly listening to everyone's speech patterns. It made me very self-conscious. As I expected, Howard Rockwell led us with his questions, his eagerness to show just how much he knew about each of our teachers. When Brock Marlowe asked him about parts he had played, Howard rattled off a very impressive range of roles. I was terrified Mr. Bergman would follow by asking me how many times I had performed in public, what orchestra I had been a member of, or what my training had been up until now. I would surely look like a musical pauper.

I continually glanced at Madame Senetsky to see her reaction to everything said and asked. She maintained a stoic expression, her eyes barely confessing an emotion or a thought. I had the distinct feeling that she wanted her staff to make its own judgments about us and would do nothing to influence that evaluation.

As the evening wore on, most of us did relax. Despite the formal, stiff beginning to the dinner, each of our teachers spoke about himself and his professional experiences, and before long we were all witnessing a fascinating conversation about international theatrical events with names of famous people woven in so casually and so quickly, we didn't have a chance to react. Every so often, I looked at Cinnamon and Rose, who wore soft smiles of appreciation on their faces. Steven looked bored and from time to time fidgeted with his silverware. Ice looked like someone visiting another country, her eyes small but full of curiosity. Only Howard sat with a demeanor of confidence, as though he was a regular participant at such dinners.

Edmond Senetsky apparently knew something about everyone anyone mentioned and had stories of his own, name-dropping his clients at every opportunity. Since Howard had made his accusation earlier, I couldn't help but watch the way Edmond glanced at Rose from time to time. It was probably my imagination, but I did think he was trying to catch her eye more than he was trying to catch anyone else's attention. Howard looked directly at me when Edmond described Rose's dance performance for Mr. Demetrius, using superlative after superlative. Then Howard looked at Cinnamon, who was glaring not daggers but spikes back at him. He quickly turned away.

The dinner itself was as elegant and rich as any I had ever seen or read about, much less experienced. We did have the roast duck we saw Mrs. Churchwell preparing earlier, but it was nothing like any duck Mommy had made back on the farm; it had an orange flavor. We were served wine, which started a discussion about the quality of California wines compared with French and Italian. From the comments Mr. Littleton made, it appeared he had tasted wine all over the world. I had no idea if what I was drinking was good, great, or otherwise. Wine was still just wine to me. I was familiar only with Mommy's elderberry.

In fact, I was eating things I had never seen before, but I was afraid to ask what they were. The vegetables looked and tasted different from any I had eaten, and between courses, we were served sherbet! I thought it was odd to have dessert before the meal ended, but soon learned it was served as a device to clear the palate, so we could fully enjoy what was yet to come. There was so much to learn above and beyond my music, I really wondered if it was possible to do so in so short a time.

Was Steven right? Would any of these things matter if I could play exceedingly well? How were people judged in the world after all?

Madame Senetsky's dining room help were efficient to perfection, moving in and out, between us and over us without so much as creating enough of a breeze to move a single strand of anyone's hair. And they were so quiet, too. It was as though they were ghosts and not real people. I saw how Madame Senetsky's eyes moved from one to the other when they served, cleared away a dish, or replenished something. It was almost as if she was waiting for something to drip, something to bump so she could pounce.

Finally, just before dessert was served, she turned her attention to us.

"Well, gentlemen, what do you think of my new stable of horses?" she asked.

All of our teachers looked at us as if they were actually going to make life-changing decisions that very moment and tell one or more of us to leave the table, go upstairs, pack, and be gone. I found I was actually holding my breath.

"I think you have a charming group, Madame Senetsky," Brock Marlowe began. "Frankly, I can't wait to begin working with them."

There was a silence we all expected to be filled by one of the other instructors, but all we saw were some nods and then eyes turned to Madame Senetsky.

"Charm is something to be nurtured," she began, "but it is in no way a substitute for hard, dedicated work. These gentlemen will quickly determine if you are all making such an effort, and they will report to me on a regular basis. I have placed great faith in your natural abilities. Don't disappoint me."

"Or me," Edmond piped up, looking toward Rose in particular.

"It will be a while before you get your greedy hands on these prodigies and gobble up your ten percent, Edmond," Madame Senetsky said.

Our teachers laughed, Howard joining them as if he was an old, experienced thespian already.

"I can see my son is already counting his commissions," she continued.

"Mother," Edmond said, "you know I'm in this for the love of it and not the profit."

"Spoken like a true agent," Alfred Littleton declared. When he laughed, he laughed in silence, his heavy body bouncing, his jowls trembling.

There was more laughter, and then the discussion took a remarkable turn away from us and centered on the current New York theater and music scene. Except for Howard, who really did keep up with it, the rest of us could only be fascinated listeners.

"I'd like them to attend the new production of *Madama Butterfly* at City Opera," Mr. Littleton said.

"Puccini is not real opera," Mr. Bergman remarked. "Why don't you take them to Wagner at the Met?"

"Why not do both?" Mr. Marlowe interjected.

"Of course we will," Madame Senetsky said. She turned to us again. "Ms. Fairchild will discuss your first weekend with you tomorrow," she told us. "We have arranged for you to visit MOMA."

"Visit who?" I blurted. I think it was the wine going to my head that gave me the courage or unfastened my tongue from the roof of my mouth.

"The Museum of Modern Art," Howard quickly explained in a stage whisper.

"Oh." I felt the heat in my face. Did they all think I was a country bumpkin? "Sorry."

"Yes, and that night you will all attend an off-Broadway production of modern dance," Madame Senetsky continued, not pausing for a beat. "Sunday afternoon, there is a lecture on Renaissance theater at the New York Public Library. All of your transportation will be arranged."

"You're pretty lucky kids," Cameron Demetrius said.

"Let's hope they appreciate it," Mr. Bergman added.

"Oh, they will," Madame Senetsky said. She seemed to be looking more at me than the others. "If not tomorrow, then the day after."

She then announced that we were excused. Howard rose first and thanked her and our teachers. They stood to say good night. I couldn't help but notice how Edmond Senetsky held Rose's hand a little longer than he held Cinnamon's, Ice's, or mine, and how his eyes fixed on her face as well. Howard smiled slyly at me, and then we all left the room and headed for the stairway.

"That was fantastic," Howard began before we were too far. "It was like being on public television or something. Can you realize and appreciate who our teachers have met, worked with, known?"

"You think Mr. Bergman might have known Mozart?" Steven joked.

"Don't be an idiot. You better not fool around with Bergman or you'll be out on your Mozart ear," Howard warned him.

Steven shrugged.

"Daddy will find me somewhere else before I'm in the taxi cab," he replied.

I could see how his nonchalance infuriated Howard Rockwell. He pounded up the stairway ahead of us. At the top he turned, a wry smile on his face.

"Anyone notice how much flirting Edmond Senetsky did with Rose here?"

"Stuff it, Howard," Cinnamon snapped.

He laughed.

"Good night, girls. I'm getting some rest for the big first day."

He walked off.

Steven looked after him and then shrugged.

"I've got some calls to make. See you in the morning," he said. "Remember, don't disappoint!" he warned with a silly smile and followed Howard.

Rose looked upset.

"Don't let Howard get to you," Cinnamon told her.

"Was he right?"

"No," I said quickly.

Once again, they followed me into my room.

"Close the door," Cinnamon told Ice, and she did so.

Cinnamon then sat on the floor in front of my bed and leaned against it.

"I thought Mr. Marlowe was very good-looking, but Mr. Bergman looked like he was suffering from hemorrhoids," she added, and everyone laughed. "Sorry for you and Steven, Honey. He looks tough."

I sat beside her and sprawled. Rose followed, and then Ice sat in front of us.

"Honey's not the only one who should worry. Mr. Littleton is not going to like my singing voice. I don't sing opera," she moaned. "My daddy brought me up on jazz."

"That won't matter, Ice," Rose said. "It's like training with a long-distance runner even though you're going to specialize in the sprint."

"That's a very clever way to put it," Cinnamon said, nodding. "Were you a good student?"

"I was on the honor roll a few times, but my family moved often and I attended too many schools."

"Why?" I asked.

She looked like she wasn't going to answer, and then said, "My father was trying to avoid responsibilities."

"You mean with his other child and the other woman?" Cinnamon asked.

"Yes, and he was just a man who got bored easily. The longest we were anywhere I can remember was nearly two years."

"That didn't give you much of a chance to make really good friends or boyfriends, did it?" Cinnamon asked.

"No, but as I told you, I have a boyfriend attending NYU. When my mother and I moved after my father's death, my boyfriend Barry visited me every weekend."

"How serious are you two?" Cinnamon asked. Their eyes met.

"Serious," Rose said. "More than I've been with anyone else."

"How much more?" Cinnamon pursued.

"More," Rose said.

They eyed each other for a moment, and then Cinnamon folded her lips into a knowing smile and nodded, after which she turned to me.

"I know Honey's got someone," Cinnamon said. "She put his picture out pretty quickly. What about you, Ice?"

She shook her head.

"Looks like you and I will be on the prowl then," she told her, and Ice smiled. "Not that we need any commitments," she added. "I don't mind being compared to a nun in terms of my dedication to my efforts to develop my talents, but chastity is asking a little too much."

Rose laughed.

"It's a bit late for it anyway," Cinnamon revealed.

I felt myself blush. Ice's eyes seemed to illuminate.

Cinnamon gazed at all of us.

"I'm not the only one here, am I, girls?"

Rose didn't hold her gaze.

"That's what I thought, Rose." She looked at me. I shook my head and Ice did the same.

"Well, we're evenly matched, virgins against fallen women," Cinnamon said. "Although," she continued, her eyes distant, "when I made love with my boyfriend, we were in one of those illusions Madame Senetsky would permit. We were playing the roles of the spirits in my house."

"Spirits?" Ice asked, her eyes narrowing with a look of fear.

"Yes. I told you, the spirits of the people who first lived in it. They made me do it," she said, and then laughed.

Ice, relieved, laughed, too, and we all relaxed even more. Rose leaned her shoulder against me, and Cinnamon suddenly dropped herself lower, her head practically on Ice's lap.

We spent the rest of the time talking about our various love experiences, and what we each searched for in a boyfriend. Ice told us about a time her mother had arranged a blind date for her.

"You own mother arranged a date for you?" Rose asked her. "How come?"

"She thought I was being stuck-up because I wasn't going out much."

"How was the date?" Cinnamon asked.

"A disaster. Even though I was smart to end it quickly, my mother was upset about it."

"Why did you have to end it quickly?" I asked.

"He was a soldier on leave and he was moving too fast for me. A friend of mine at school who played piano was there and knew the band. He ended up taking me home. When my mother found out, she was upset."

"Why did that bother her? Wasn't she proud you made the right choices?" Rose asked quickly.

"No. I told you. She thought I was being stuck-up, but I'm not going to be anyone's good-time trophy," she declared with hot pride. "If that makes me stuck-up, good."

"I don't blame you for that," I said.

"Stop worrying about it," Cinnamon declared. "Madame Senetsky wouldn't permit it, anyway."

"I don't need Madame Senetsky to watch over that!" Ice said with her eyes wide.

Cinnamon stared at her a moment and then smiled.

"You know, there's no reason why you can't make them *your* trophies. Men think that sex is designed for their pleasure only.

"But that's far from true," she added. She looked at Rose. "Am I right, Rose?"

"I don't think of either of us as a trophy," she said softly. "As long as you both respect each other."

Cinnamon seemed disappointed in her response. She looked like she was searching for an ally in her war with the world.

"I'm tired," she said, rising. "This conversation is to be continued."

Rose and Ice got up as well.

"What's first tomorrow?" Rose asked.

"After breakfast, we all meet with our specialist in the morning, and then in the afternoon, we're all meeting with Mr. Masters to perfect our consonants and vowels," I said.

"There is absolutely nothing wrong with my vowels a good laxative wouldn't fix," Cinnamon said.

For a split second, all of us looked at her as if she had gone mad and then, we all laughed so hard I was sure, thick walls or not, we would bring the boys back out to see what was happening.

No one came.

We said good night and I began to prepare for my first night in a strange house, sleeping in a strange bed.

After I washed and put on my nightgown, a brand-new one Mommy had bought me, I sat at my vanity table and brushed my hair, just as I always did. For most of my life, my Uncle Simon lived across from my room at home, above the barn in a makeshift apartment. Sometimes, he would sit at his window and watch and listen to me practice my violin before I went to bed. For him, I suppose my window resembled a television screen. When I was older, I realized I had to pull down my shades when I was dressing and undressing, of course, although I never saw or felt him looking at me in any lustful way. He was always so protective of me, doing my chores for me, especially if he thought Grandad had given me something to do that was too hard. It was almost as if I had a second father, or maybe an older brother watching over me, giving me a sense of security.

I surely could use him here, I thought, and then suddenly realized that my thoughts had gone to him because I had the strangest feeling I was being watched right now. I gazed in the mirror and shifted to the left a bit. My heart stopped and started. There was a shadow in the window behind me. I was sure of it, because a moment later, it was gone.

For a long moment, my heart was pounding so hard, I didn't think my legs would support me. I rose slowly and, after taking a deep breath, walked to the window. My hands were clenched into small fists at my side. My stomach felt as tight as a drum. Inching myself to the glass, I looked out at the fire escape. There was no one there.

Breathing with relief, I stepped back. Had it been a shadow cast by the moonlight and the clouds sliding across the inky night sky? I waited to see if there was any sign of anyone and then, satisfied, returned to my table, finished my hair, and went to bed.

After I turned out the lights, I listened keenly for the sounds in the house. Back home, I had long ago become acquainted with every moan in our pipes, every whistle of the wind through loose shingles or over a shutter. I had expected we would hear the city traffic, but we were so isolated on these grounds, there were no sounds of cars and trucks. How would I have known without having been here before, of course? Occasionally, the scream of police, ambulance, or fire sirens did find its way over the iron gates, up the grounds, and into my room, but it was so muffled, it sounded like something coming from someone's television set.

No, I thought, it was far quieter than I had anticipated. The house was so firm, so solid, almost as if it had to obey the rules of etiquette, too. Every groan or burp in the pipes had to be subdued. Respect for the inhabitants required silence, or at least keeping noises to little more than a rustle and a swish.

I concentrated. Was that someone whispering, or was that part of my ever-growing imagination?

My eyes shifted toward the window again. The shadow had returned, resembling someone in a hood and a cape. I stared at it and waited. *It's only the moon and the clouds,* I told myself. I didn't move. I didn't breathe. After a while the shadow was gone again. The whispering ended, too. Darkness fell even thicker around the fire escape. Clouds had joined above like a curtain closing. The moon was shut away. Night had taken full control of the stage.

I closed my eyes.

For a while, despite my deep fatigue, sleep seemed impossible. I was simply overtired, nervous. I had underestimated how tiring and how much of an emotional strain the day had been for me. When sleep finally came, it was like a welcomed surprise, drifting in and washing over me, resembling another blanket.

But soon I tossed and turned, fretting in and out of shadows and tunnels, hearing voices, footsteps, and strange childlike singing. I woke once or twice but immediately fell back to sleep, and finally slept so well that when the sunlight opened my eyes again, it was early in the morning.

I quickly turned to my window. The sunshine glittered on the metal fire escape that had been the platform for the dance of those strange, dark shadows.

Surely what I had seen the night before, thought I had heard outside my door and windows, and my parade of distorted dreams were products of my overworked imagination, I thought. *Be happy,* I told myself. *Be hopeful. Be as proud as Mommy and Daddy were for me.*

Today is truly the beginning of the rest of your life.

4

A Shadow at the Window

"She did it deliberately!" Howard exclaimed as soon as he came through the dining room door to have breakfast. "Just because I expressed some unhappiness about it."

"Who did what?" I asked. The rest of us were long since there.

"Dracula's daughter gave yours truly the first work detail. And it's a week at a time!" he added.

"What do you actually have to do?" I asked.

Steven was sipping his coffee, his eyes barely open. Ice and Rose had bowls of cereal and Cinnamon had toast and jam. I was the only one eating eggs and a bagel.

"For one thing, clean off this table, so don't make any more mess than necessary, and then I have to set the table for dinner. Lunch is more or less staggered, depending on our personal schedules, so we're all individually responsible for that, and I'm to look after the parlor and be the last one up at night to be sure none of us has left it untidy. Next thing you know, I'll be running a vacuum cleaner."

"What of it? I have," Ice said.

"So have I," I said.

"Guilty," Cinnamon added, raising her hand.

"You're all used to that sort of menial labor. I'm not!"

"Why don't you put an ad in the newspaper and see if you can hire a part-time worker?" Steven asked facetiously.

Howard considered the suggestion.

"You think they would let me do that?"

"Of course not," Cinnamon said. "You heard Lady Fairchild expound on Madame Senetsky's opinions of ostentatious wealth yesterday, didn't you?"

Howard stared quietly a moment and then nodded.

"Don't take any more dishes than you absolutely need," he advised Steven. Then he went to get himself breakfast, pausing at the door. "How did you all get down here before me anyway?" he asked, suddenly realizing.

"We spent less time in front of our vanity mirrors," Cinnamon said.

Howard smirked and went into the kitchen. He returned with a cup of coffee and a bagel with cream cheese. Grumbling to himself, he sat.

"How did y'all sleep?" Rose asked. The way she asked caught my attention. She was asking as if she was fishing for something.

"I was out before my head hit the pillow," Steven said.

"Okay," Ice said. Cinnamon said the same. Howard only grunted, so Rose waited for me.

"I suppose it was only my imagination," I began, "but I kept seeing a shadow on the fire escape, and for a while that kept me awake."

"A shadow?" Howard asked. "So? What are you, afraid of a shadow?"

"It seemed to be a shadow cast by someone there," I added. His sarcasm brought tears to my eyes.

Steven buttered a piece of toast vigorously, ignoring me, but the girls all stared, Rose the most intensely. After a beat she said, "Me, too."

"Me, too? What me, too?" Howard cross-examined.

"A shadow, something, on my fire escape."

"Your room is on the same side as Honey's," Howard said. "Whatever cast her shadow might have cast yours. Big deal. Moonlight, clouds. What's the mystery?"

Neither Rose nor I replied. Then Cinnamon, who had continued staring my way, said, "There was no moonlight last night."

"Yes, there was," I said quickly.

Cinnamon shook her head.

"If you don't believe me, check the newspaper."

"But I saw light, a glow..."

"So you saw starlight," Howard said. "Or the light from other rooms or the lights from the grounds below. I repeat, what's the big deal here?"

"Starlight, casting shadows?" Rose asked.

"It happens. What else is it, the ghost of Mr. Senetsky? I was just kidding about that. Save your imaginations for the stage," he advised. "Listen, it's getting late." He looked at Rose. "Can't y'all clean up after yourselves, please?"

"All right," Rose said, "here's a proposal. Forget Ms. Fairchild's work roster. One for all and all for one. We all do the work duty all the time."

"Great," Howard said quickly.

"But that means *all* of us, Howard," Cinnamon emphasized. "When your duty is over, you don't disappear or leave it for anyone else. All!" she emphasized.

"Okay, okay. It's a good idea. Teamwork."

She gazed at him skeptically.

"The moment one of us fails to do his or her share, we go back to the roster," Cinnamon threatened. "Agreed?"

"Fine with me," Steven said. "However, I've got to protect my fingers, remember? I can't develop any calluses."

"Then stop licking the cream cheese off them," Ice snapped at him sharply.

All of us laughed.

We finished our breakfast and cleaned up. Then we left, breaking into our specialty classes. On the way out, Rose stepped up beside me.

"I didn't want to say anything about last night" she whispered, "but when you did..."

"What did you actually see?" I asked.

"Nothing more than you said," she replied. "I feel silly now. I'm not afraid of any shadows and I certainly don't believe in ghosts."

She continued walking quickly to catch up with Cinnamon and Howard, heading to their first drama session with Brock Marlowe. I stood there watching. Ice, who had overheard, looked at me, her eyes full of confusion. Steven poked me.

"I don't think we can be a second late for Mr. Bergman. He doesn't look like the tolerant type."

I caught up with him quickly, glancing back at Ice, who turned and headed for her vocal lesson. Rose was already at the dance studio door.

I wasn't afraid of any shadow and I didn't believe in ghosts or spirits either, but there was something else here, something that was not described in our orientation booklets, something in the heart of this old house, like a secret of the heart long forgotten, trying to be remembered, calling to anyone who would listen.

Maybe I was the first who would.

Mr. Bergman began with a thorough evaluation of our musical abilities and knowledge. He had Steven play some pieces and then he had me play my violin. He listened and watched us and then gave us other pieces to try. Before our session ended, he had us play a duet.

When I first had my duet lessons with Chandler Maxwell at Mr. Wengrow's, I thought Chandler was the most brilliant pianist I had ever heard, but I had to admit, Steven was truly exceptionally gifted. His fingers floated over the keys as if they each had a mind of their own, and when he played, all the impishness in his face, all of his lackadaisical expression disappeared. It was truly a wonder to watch his body metamorphose into someone so different from the carefree boy I was getting to know away from the piano. The instrument, the notes he played invaded his body and even his soul. When my Uncle Peter had said the violin played me and not vice versa, he was really talking about someone like Steven, I thought.

Since he went ahead of me, I was sure Mr. Bergman would see how special he was and how ordinary I was, but he didn't react that way. He didn't change expression or make any negative comments, nor did his voice take on any displeasure when I played.

He kept us at it for nearly three hours, and when our session ended, he sat silently for a long moment. I glanced at Steven, who raised his eyebrows in a question mark. Was Mr. Bergman about to tell us we weren't good enough?

"There is a great deal you both have to learn about technique," he began. "There's a tendency to rush, which is usual for people your age with your limited experiences. In my estimation, I would say neither of you have reached even fifty percent of your capabilities. In short, we have a great deal of work to do here. Much of that will seem elementary to you at first, but I want you to trust me.

"I'll want to work with you separately for a while. Who likes getting up earlier?"

"Not me," Steven replied quickly.

"I spent most of my life getting up very early to do my farm chores before I went off to school, Mr. Bergman. I don't mind it."

He smiled. Finally there was a friendly, warm expression on that critical face.

"Good," he said. "You and I will meet from eight to ten the first few weeks and Steven, I'll see you promptly at ten every morning.

"Very good," he concluded, then without further comment rose and left the room.

"Does that mean we're excellent candidates or not?" Steven wondered aloud.

"It does to me."

I was happy. In my mind I had met the first test. My instructor wanted to continue with me.

"Elementary," Steven muttered. "He's just making work for himself, if you ask me."

As if to prove his point, he sat at the piano again and began to play an entire concerto from memory, which I recognized as Beethoven's Piano Concerto 14 in C Sharp Minor. It was one of Chandler's favorites, but I never saw him do it without sheet music. Steven's eyes were closed as he played. I stood there listening and watching him and then, when I turned to leave, I saw Madame Senetsky standing in the doorway.

"How was your first lesson?" she asked me.

"Fine, I think. It was mostly evaluation."

She nodded.

Steven continued playing, oblivious to her presence. She and I looked back at him, listening.

"Extraordinary," she said.

"He's wonderful," I agreed.

"In a pure sense of raw talent, yes, but so many who have that fail because they don't realize it's only a part of who and what they are. It's very draining to give so much of yourself all the time. It's why the training is so important. You understand?"

"Yes, Madame."

She nodded.

"You have a certain je ne sais quoi," she said with her softest smile yet, "what in French is a certain quality not easily described, perhaps. In your case, I believe it comes from your innocence, Honey. You remind me a great deal of my daughter, whom I unfortunately lost at a very young age. However, just in observing you a short time, practically no time, I sense it, sense the way you have such trust in the music you play, your instrument, the mystery of all that. If you don't lose that quality, become jaded or cynical, you will be just as extraordinary a talent as Steven. I would like to see that same trust given to me, to my school," she said.

No one had mentioned her losing a daughter, I thought. I felt honored she had compared me with her.

She continued to smile.

"You look like you don't really understand, but you will, some day, I'm sure. Is everything else all right? Your room, the facilities..."

"Oh, yes," I said quickly.

"Good." Her smile lifted and was quickly replaced with that schoolmarm look. "When someone speaks to you, try not to look down so much. You need to look into the eyes of people to see how sincere they really are, what they're really up to. Most people can't hide their true thoughts, prevent them from peeking out at you through their eyes. When you avoid them, you give up an important defensive tool."

"Defensive?"

"You must always be on the defensive," she said sharply. "There are people who will lie to you to get you to do what they want, people who will lie to you to make you trust them. People like us are easily exploited, Honey. We yearn so much for applause, appreciation, opportunity. There are those, parasites, who sense it and take advantage of us. That is why our lives must be driven by a constant search for truth," she said. "And also why we must exude confidence. Pull your shoulders back. Stand firmly, otherwise you telegraph your insecurity and encourage the vultures."

When she spoke, she did seem to be on a stage delivering an important soliloquy, posturing, delivering her words with such authority.

She stared into my face so hard, I had great difficulty doing what she wanted: keeping my eyes on her.

"You're a virgin," she suddenly said. It was so unexpected I couldn't help but blush. "I'm right about that, am I not?"

I barely nodded.

"I'm glad. Don't lose your virginity for a long while yet. You're not aware of it, but it gives you a certain edge, a way of looking at everything that will change radically once you do lose it.

"I'm speaking from experience," she added. She smiled again. "Don't look so worried, my dear. You will succeed. I insist upon that."

She said it as if she could command the sky to clear, the rain to fall or not fall, the night to wait longer before pushing out the day.

"I must go look in on the others. Have a good first day, my dear," she said, patted my arm, and walked off.

Steven, who had stopped playing once he had realized Madame Senetsky was right there in the doorway speaking with me, jumped up from his piano bench and hurried over before I could release the hot breath in my lungs.

"What did she say to you? Did she say anything about me?"

"She thought you were extraordinary."

"She did?"

"But nowhere near what you can be."

"Why does everyone say that?"

"Maybe because it's true," I said, starting away.

"Wait a minute. She said something else. Something that made you turn red in the face. I saw that."

I didn't answer and he kept after me.

"Don't deny it. You were speaking with her quite a while. I pretended not to notice, but I did. Well? What did she say? C'mon. It's not right to keep secrets that involve all of us. One for all and all for one, remember?"

"It doesn't involve all of us. It was something very private," I finally turned and blurted at him.

"Oh." He thought a moment and then seemed to quickly lose interest. He shrugged. "I'm hungry. Let's see what's for lunch."

He marched ahead of me, but I was still trembling from the intimacy of my conversation with Madame Senetsky. How could anyone look at me and know if I was a virgin or not? Was it because of how I reminded her of her daughter? Was her daughter my age when she passed away?

I couldn't look at Rose and know positively that she wasn't a virgin, or even be that sure about Cinnamon, despite her sharp, knowing ways.

Was Madame Senetsky right? Virgins had a different way of looking at things, feeling things, knowing things? She was certainly true to her promise, I thought. She was involving herself in our lives far more than other teachers would. Even my own mother hadn't had such a conversation with me, warning me that once I gave up my virginity, my way of viewing the world would change and that would change how I approached my music. For now there was something important in me that Madame Senetsky did not want me to lose along with my innocence—not that I had plans to do so in the immediate future.

But was that something you actually planned? Everything I had read or seen in movies made it seem like something that had to be spontaneous. If it wasn't, it lost its essence, its loving purpose. It became something almost scientific, an experiment. I had overheard many girls at school talk about it that way. Some made love specifically to see what it was all about and couldn't care less with whom they had experienced it. What sort of a memory was that to carry into adulthood? Was I old-fashioned to think like this? Would the others eventually ridicule me? Where did I belong? Maybe I should have been the one to live in Cinnamon's home and be pretending I was a young girl during the Civil War, and not her.

Then a little voice inside me asked, "What makes you think girls were really all that different then?"

All these questions buzzed about my head like a maddened hive of bees, and just when I had so much more upon which my concentration had to be fully directed. I felt like I was standing on a top, spinning and desperately trying not to fall off.

We had an hour or so after lunch before our next session began. This one was with Mr. Masters, our speech instructor. After that we were all to report to Mr. Littleton to get vocal instruction. Ms. Fairchild continued to emphasize that it was Madame Senetsky's philosophy that, even though we all weren't talented in these various areas, exposure to them would make us far more rounded and help us in our own fields.

After lunch, Rose, Cinnamon, Ice, and I went for a walk to see the grounds. Steven had gone up to his room and Howard was looking over the little theater like an athlete checking out the playing field. All of us agreed he was the most obsessive and intense about his career.

It was a nearly perfect day, with just a dab of a cloud here and there against the light turquoise sky. Although it was in the low eighties, a breeze stirred the air around us. The lawns had just been cut that morning, so the redolent scent of fresh grass was all about us. That, along with the distinct aroma of freshly turned earth, made me somewhat homesick. I planned on writing a letter to Uncle Simon this evening, and thought I would describe the grounds with the sprawling old maples and hickory trees, the rock gardens, and fountains. I'd catalogue all the flowers that had been planted here. He would be so surprised to read that I was living and going to school in such a beautiful place.

"Did Madame Senetsky stop by to see all of you?" I asked the others.

Cinnamon said she had paused to listen to Howard and her read some lines from Shakespeare's *Julius Caesar,* but didn't stay around to speak to them afterward. Ice said she had come by and listened to her doing scales with Mr. Littleton.

"The way she was looking at me, I thought she was handing me a bus ticket home, but she nodded and spoke to Mr. Littleton, telling him she thought he had a rich field to mine. He agreed. I don't like it when people talk about you right in front of you as if you're not there," she added with a touch of fury in her beautiful ebony eyes.

"She did the same to me, talking to Mr. Demeterius, praising my graceful moves aloud," Rose said.

"Why did you ask?" Cinnamon asked me with those narrow suspicious eyes of hers fixing on my face. "Did she say something to you directly?"

"Yes."

"So? What? You look like you swallowed a mouse or something."

I didn't want to tell Cinnamon what Madame Senetsky had said about virginity. I wasn't sure how she would take it in light of what she had openly confessed the night before.

We paused at one of the stone benches and I sat. The others gathered around me, waiting.

"This must be something good or bad!" Rose declared. "She didn't tell you to leave, did she?"

I shook my head.

"What do we have to do to get it out of you?" Cinnamon asked. "Sacrifice a virgin?"

I looked up so sharply, she stepped back, her eyes full of confusion.

"What made you say that?"

"It's just an expression. You know, primitive tribes...sacrifices and virgins...why?"

"She said she knew I was a virgin. She could look at me and tell."

"What?"

"That's amazing," Ice said. "Most boys look at me and think otherwise."

"What made her say such a thing?" Cinnamon followed.

I shook my head.

"She must have had some reason."

"She said I reminded her of her daughter."

"Daughter?" Rose asked.

"Yes, a daughter who died very young."

"Before she could lose her virginity, then," Cinnamon concluded.

"I don't know. She just said I should..."

"What?" Rose blurted, impatient.

"Stay a virgin for as long as I could."

I shot a quick glance at Rose and Cinnamon. They were both quiet, both looking at me with wonder and confusion.

"Why?" Cinnamon finally asked.

I shrugged.

"She said it gave me a certain...she spoke French..."

"Savoir faire?" Rose asked.

"No," Cinnamon said for me. "I'd think it would be

just the opposite." She thought a moment. "Je ne sais quoi?"

"Yes, that's it."

"A certain something, indescribable, but there," Cinnamon said. She became very thoughtful a moment. She looked at Rose. "I guess you and I are damaged goods, and in her eyes don't have that special something."

"She didn't say that," I quickly reported. "Whatever it is might not be important for what you do. In her way of thinking, at least. I still don't understand it."

"What's she going to do, check you out every week to see if you're still pure?" Cinnamon asked bitterly.

"That woman scares me," Ice said. "How could she look at her and say that?"

Cinnamon smirked.

"Our Honey here doesn't exactly radiate sexual sophistication."

She stared at me a moment and then asked, "What are you going to do if your boyfriend wants to make love—tell him it's bad for your career?"

"I don't know. I'm confused."

"Talk about invading someone's space. Maybe she's just weird. Maybe she's lost it since her daughter's death or something. Maybe we're coming to this school too late," Cinnamon rattled off.

Everyone was lost in her own thoughts for a while.

Then Ice turned her head to the side and said, "Well, look at that."

"What?" Cinnamon said, her voice testy. I really regretted revealing what Madame Senetsky had said to me now.

Ice nodded at the rear of the mansion. From where we sat, we could see it well.

"What?" Rose asked, squinting. The sunlight was reflecting off windows and the walls.

"That door. It's all barred up. It looks like a prison door or something," Ice said.

"Yes, it does," Cinnamon agreed. "Let's take a closer look."

She started across the grass, Rose and Ice following. I got up and joined them. As we drew closer, it was clear it was a heavily barred door. The windows in the rear looked barred as well.

"Some security," Rose said.

"Why?" Cinnamon turned around. "Look at this place, with its high gate, its video security and alarms. It's not exactly a burglar's dream."

"This would take us through the rear of the building," Ice remarked.

"I guess Ms. Fairchild wasn't exaggerating when she emphasized how we should keep from entering this portion of the mansion," Rose said.

"What did she think we would do, take a saw to these iron bars?" Cinnamon asked.

"Can I help you?" we heard, and turned to see a short, stout groundsman with heavily curled dark brown hair. His shirt sleeves were rolled up over his bulging forearms and he held a pair of clipping shears pointed at us. His face was dark, and made darker by his unshaven cheeks and chin. Instinctively, I crossed my arms over my chest and stepped back. Ice and Rose did the same, but Cinnamon held her ground, even taking a step toward him.

"We were just admiring the beautiful bars on this door," Cinnamon replied. "We're students here."

"You can't go in that way," he said.

"We know," Rose said. "We weren't going to do that."

"You couldn't if you wanted," he continued, coming closer. "Those bars aren't the only thing. That there door is welded shut."

"Why would anyone do that?" Rose asked him. "Isn't that against some fire code or something?"

He shook his head.

"I don't ask questions. I do what I'm asked to do."

"How long has it been this way?" Cinnamon asked him in the tone of a detective.

"A little more than two years, I think," he replied. He looked like he didn't enjoy being cross-examined, but Cinnamon had a firm, demanding way about her.

"It was done to keep anyone from going into the private residence," I said, stating what I thought was the obvious and hoping to end this.

"Hey!" we heard, and saw Steven walking across the lawn. "Ms. Fairchild is looking for you all. She has information about this weekend's events. She sent me out to find you."

"Be careful," Cinnamon said, turning from the door to me. "She's liable to want to put a chastity belt on you. From the looks of this," she added, nodding at the barred door, "it seems like something she might do."

The groundsman squinted with confusion and then shook his head and walked off.

Rose and Ice gazed at me, and then we all went to join Steven.

Only I looked back at the door, wondering what it was that made this part of the house so inviolate.

Our lesson with Mr. Masters wasn't as unpleasant as I had anticipated. He was a very jolly man, actually, and had fun pointing out our little speech idiosyncracies. He did it in a friendly, light manner so that no one felt singled out or mocked. What he emphasized, more than anything, was how much more effective we all could be if we spoke more slowly and didn't slur our words. There were plans to record each of us individually and work with each of us on a one-to-one basis by next week.

Our vocal lesson followed a similar procedure. Mr. Littleton's main objective was to get us to understand how the voice was an instrument in and of itself. Projection, breathing combined with enunciation, and some dramatic awareness would all blend together and make us more effective in so many ways. It made sense and was truly an effort to give us a well-rounded artistic education.

Dance class served as our physical exercise class as well as an effort to help each of us develop poise, grace, and coordination. Since this first class was simply an orientation, we didn't do very much, but for the next class, we were to all dress in appropriate clothing. It was Ms. Fairchild's job to provide us with it, including dance shoes. All of us, including Steven, laughed at the image of him in a pair of tights, especially with his toothpick legs.

We all thought we would have some time to ourselves after our dance class, but Ms. Fairchild informed us that our culinary education would begin with the evening's meal. Accordingly, she wanted us to dinner a half hour earlier. It seemed Madame Senetsky, from time to time, brought in a culinary critic or a well-known New York City chef to lecture to us about different cuisines, from Cordon Bleu to Szechuan to Greek. It was here that I would taste entrees like chicken Kiev, paella, beef Wellington, and so many other things that I had only read about, and many more I had never even heard of.

This first evening we were treated to a lecture on Spanish food. Madame Senetsky began by explaining that our food lectures would be like travel guides. The speakers wouldn't just talk about food, but the cultures as well.

She introduced Senor de Marco, a teacher from a New York City culinary institute. We sat with glasses of sangria and listened to him describe how the Spanish people gathered in bars, which he described as being closer to meeting halls than a gin mill.

"In small towns in Spain, the only place to have coffee is at a bar. In others, the only place that sells ice cream cones is the bar in the central square."

He then went on to describe tapas and the variety of dishes we were about to enjoy, including paella with fish, Russian salad, chicken wings, gizzards, or hearts in sauce, and tortilla Espanola, all with sangria.

The more Steven drank, the funnier he became.

Before the evening ended, he cried out, almost in desperation, "Is everything we do here part of our education? Maybe we'll even get instruction on how to take a shower!"

"Maybe you'll get instruction on how to hold your liquor, Steven," Cinnamon countered, and everyone laughed.

Later that evening, I sat and wrote my first letter to Uncle Simon. I thought he would appreciate my description of the flora and the grounds, but I made it clear how much it all reminded me of him and how I missed him, as well as Mommy and Daddy.

Mommy called that night as well.

"I wanted to call before this," she explained, "but your father thought I shouldn't. Is everything all right?"

"Yes," I said and described all that I had done, our meals, and the other students. We spoke for nearly a half hour. "This phone call is costing so much," I realized.

"I don't care," Mommy said. "You don't hesitate to call me and reverse the charges, Honey. Promise you will whenever you feel you need to or need to tell me something, okay?"

"Okay, Mommy," I said.

Finally, she put Daddy on.

"How's life in the big farmhouse?" he joked.

I almost told him about the strangely barred rear doors and windows, but didn't. I wanted to be sure I didn't sound any sort of negative note and plant the seed of worry in him or Mommy. Besides, what was there to worry about? I was sure there was some logical explanation.

Instead, I asked him questions about the farm. He was comfortable talking about the corn crops, the market, and his new machinery.

"Finally replaced that old grain combine of Grandad's," he told me. "I did a trade on a new one. His bones are probably rattling."

I laughed at the thought.

"You just have a good time, Honey, and make us proud. I love you," he said.

It brought tears to my eyes. I told him I loved him, too, and then we ended the conversation. Maybe he was right keeping Mommy from calling me, I thought. Hearing their voices stirred up the anthill of homesickness inside me. I had been doing all I could to keep from thinking about home, and Chandler, too. He hadn't called me yet, nor had he written.

When I turned on my computer, however, I was pleasantly surprised by a "you have mail" greeting, and there was an E-mail from him, describing his arrival at Boston University, his roommate, his classes, his piano teacher and the band instructor, and then, finally, in the last paragraph, how much he missed me and looked forward to his first opportunity to visit me in New York.

I wrote back, doing some of what he had done, describing the school and the other students, but my letter talked more about how much I missed him and our times together, especially at the lake on my farm.

My heart felt like a Ping-Pong table upon which all my emotions had been bantered back and forth. I had cried, laughed, sulked, and smiled within an hour's time. Exhausted, I prepared for bed. When I came out of the bathroom after I had changed into my nightgown, however, I was shocked to see Cinnamon just inside the doorway. She was wearing a robe and slippers and looked troubled.

"What is it?" I asked after a short gasp of surprise. "You frightened me."

"Sorry, but I came to get you and had to do it as quietly as I could."

"Why?"

"We've got to go to Rose's room. Now," she emphasized. "Put on your robe quickly."

I hurried to my closet, took it off the hook, and slipped into it.

"What's wrong?"

"There was another shadow at her window," she replied.

"Oh."

"Only this time, it left something behind on the fire escape."

"What?"

"C'mon. Ice is already there," she said, and opened my door.

It was very still in the house. The lights had been dimmed. Steven and Howard's doors were shut and no one else but us was about.

When we entered Rose's room, Cinnamon shut the door behind us quickly. Rose was on her bed, Ice beside her, embracing her. It was obvious Rose had been crying.

"What's wrong?" I asked. We drew closer to the bed.

"Where is it?" Cinnamon demanded.

Ice nodded at a chair on the right, near the window opening to the fire escape. I looked and saw what appeared to be a scarf.

Cinnamon held it up and nodded.

"Recognize it?" she asked me.

Rose and Ice fixed their gazes on me to see my reaction and hear my reply. It *was* familiar.

"It's someone's scarf, isn't it?"

"It's an ascot," Cinnamon explained.

"Ascot?"

"What Edmond Senetsky wears instead of a tie," she said. "After Rose sensed someone at her window, she got up enough nerve to go to it and spotted this out there. She came for me, and I went out and brought it back inside."

A small ball of ice rolled down my spine. I jerked my head toward Rose, who started to cry again.

"What does that mean?"

"It means," Ice said slowly, "that Mr. Senetsky was on that fire escape, peeping in Rose's window tonight while she was getting undressed and everything."

I shook my head.

"Can't be," I said. "He would really do that?"

"I feel so violated," Rose cried. "About a year ago," she said, after sucking back a sob, "I was in a beauty contest. My father got his boss to sponsor me. I was brought to the dealership to meet Mr. Kruegar, a balding forty-year-old man who had inherited the business from his father. It was the first time I was paraded in front of someone who looked at me like a product—maybe in his case like a brand-new car. He even said I had nice bumpers," she said, a bit of fury replacing the fear in her face.

"After that, I could feel his eyes on me all the time I was in the contest. He even tried to get me to come work for him and wear a bathing suit. Men who do that to you make you feel...molested with their eyes," she said. "That's how I feel right now. I want to go under a hot shower for hours."

"She's right about that," Ice agreed.

I was glad I had never told them how my Uncle Simon used to sit and watch me through my bedroom window, especially when I practiced the violin. They would surely make something nasty out of it when there wasn't.

But I understood what Rose was feeling. No one liked to be spied upon, especially like this and by someone we thought was so sophisticated and important.

"Howard must be right," Rose said. "He has some other sort of sick and perverted interest in me."

"Maybe we're jumping to conclusions too quickly," I said. "It could have blown out of another window or something."

Rose looked up quickly, her eyes filling with some hope. She turned to Cinnamon, who held the scarf and then brought it to her nose.

"I recognize the scent of the nauseatingly sweet cologne he wears," she said. "It's his for sure."

She offered it to me and I smelled it. It did have the same aroma.

"I'm not saying it's not his. It might be, of course. I'm saying there might be another explanation as to why it was out there. He doesn't live here. It seems so weird that he would come back to the house to do this."

"That's true," Cinnamon said cautiously.

"Well, what should we do about it?" Ice asked. "Should we go tell Madame Senetsky?"

No one replied for a long moment.

"If we're wrong about this or if there is another explanation, she's not going to like us making such accusations," I suggested. "And Edmond Senetsky will certainly not like it."

"Honey's right," Cinnamon said. "We should be absolutely sure about it first."

"Should we tell the boys?" Rose asked.

"No," Cinnamon said quickly. "First, they would probably think we made all this up somehow. Howard would be against telling Madame Senetsky no matter what, and I don't think they'd be too sympathetic about it."

"Maybe one of them is doing it," I thought aloud.

"That doesn't explain the scarf," Rose said sadly. "I almost wish it *was* Steven or Howard."

Again we were all quiet, thinking.

"All right," Cinnamon declared, moving closer with the scarf in hand. We gathered about the bed. "If we don't mention it or in any way act different because of it, he might very well come back."

"I don't want him to come back!" Rose wailed.

"Just a minute, will you? I have an idea. Tomorrow night, about the time we all retire to our rooms, the three of us will sneak into yours and camp out under this window. If someone appears on that fire escape, we'll be ready for him, and then there'll be no doubts about it."

"What if he doesn't show up until after she goes to sleep?" Ice asked.

"Chances are he is more interested in seeing her undress than under the covers, Ice," Cinnamon replied dryly.

"Just asking," she said.

"Let's just try it and see what happens," Cinnamon said. "Okay?"

No one spoke.

"Okay?" she asked forcefully.

"All right," Ice said.

I nodded.

"It's not just you, remember," Cinnamon told Rose. "He was at Honey's window."

"Is that what you think?" I asked.

"Boy, you *are* innocent," Cinnamon replied. "If you saw something on your landing and it's the same as Rose's landing, why not?"

"How come you didn't suggest such a possibility when I mentioned it at dinner?" I asked, a bit stung by her words concerning my naivete.

"I thought…it might be spirits," she admitted.

"So did I," Ice said.

They stared at each other a moment, and then simultaneously broke into a laugh.

"Some spirit," Cinnamon said. "Wearing a scented ascot."

"What are we going to do with it?" Rose asked.

"Keep it as evidence, what do you think?"

"I don't want it in my room," Rose said, leaning away from it as if it was contaminated.

Cinnamon gazed at it and shrugged.

"No problem. I'll keep it in mine. Unless one of you insists on keeping it," she said to me and Ice. Neither of us offered any opposition. "Thought not," she said and folded it. "Let's go back to sleep."

"What if he returns tonight, looking for the scarf?" Rose asked, the thought searing across her forehead, forming one deep line of worry and anxiety.

"If you hear anyone out there, Rose, come and get me," Cinnamon said.

"Come get us all," Ice added.

I looked toward the window. Something from above dropped a sheet of dim light over the darkness, enough light to silhouette someone standing on the fire escape if someone was actually there, I thought.

"No one will be out there anymore tonight," I said in nearly a whisper. It was really more of a prayer.

Ice walked to the window and stood there a moment.

"What makes it glow out here?" she asked. Cinnamon stepped up beside her.

"Light from a window above, I imagine."

And then, almost as if every word we spoke could be heard, the light went off.

And the world outside the window was dark.

As dark as it would be if a curtain had closed.

I heard an audible gasp from Rose's lips.

Or was it coming from my own?

5

The Room Upstairs

I remember a line I once read in a famous short story, calling truth "a hard deer to hunt." If ever sleep was a "hard deer to hunt," it was so this night. I closed my eyes and turned on my side with my back to my bedroom door, but I couldn't help anticipating the sound of it opening, and then seeing either Cinnamon or Ice or Rose herself there to tell me he had returned. At times my eyes popped open and I stared at my own window. The darkness played tricks, metamorphosing into someone's silhouette and then turning back to nothing.

Steven had been right about the house itself. It was so well built, sounds familiar to me from my own home back in Ohio were not audible here. Pipes didn't groan, boards didn't creak, shutters didn't tap a beat to the marching wind. At night this house tightened like a fist, not to open again until the first light of morning.

The silence was not welcome, however. It caused me to feel shut up, entombed with my own childhood fears. I heard my own little groans, heard myself breathing. For hours I tossed and turned and fought with my pillows. Every once in a while, I glanced at the illuminated face of my clock and panicked a bit at the hour. I would get no sleep whatsoever, I thought, and tomorrow, I would be a mess and make one mistake after another during my violin lesson.

Once, before I actually did fall asleep—or, rather, pass out—I heard what sounded like approaching footsteps in the hallway and lifted my head from the pillow, expecting the door to open. Whoever it was paused, but then turned and descended the stairs. Stillness overtook the echo of those steps, and once again, I was drowning in silence. I let out a breath, closed my eyes, and tried desperately to think only good thoughts, to visualize my beautiful little lake back on the farm, remember Chandler's laughter and smile and all the wonderful things we whispered to each other so I could drift into sleep.

Sleep finally came, but like it would if I had been anesthetized. When sunlight streaked in, it stood at my bedside and waited impatiently for me to acknowledge morning. I knew that was true because when I finally did wake up, it was more than a half hour later than I needed to make my new schedule. After all, I had promised Mr. Bergman I could manage the earlier session. I had even bragged about how easy it was for me to be an early riser. Now what would he think of me?

I literally threw off my covers and leaped off the

bed, rushing around to get myself showered and dressed, and did it all in less than half the usual time. I practically flew down the stairs.

There was still no one else at breakfast yet. Except for Mrs. Churchwell, there were no servants around either. Before I was finished eating, however, the girls and Howard began to stream into the dining room. I could see from the sleepy eyes on all the girls that I was not the only one who had been in a desperate battle for some rest.

Steven, who looked like a somnambulist himself and who was the last to come to breakfast, was oblivious to how the rest of us looked, but I could see Howard had suspicious eyes. He continually glanced from one of us to another and asked delving questions like, "Anyone hear a lot of moving about in the hallway last night?"

Rose was the most obvious, turning constantly to Cinnamon for the answers. Finally, Howard came right out and asked what we were all up to.

"Who says we're up to anything, Howard?" Cinnamon returned.

"You look like a pack of conniving conspirators, Roman senators planning the assassination of Julius Caesar or someone of similar importance."

"Maybe you?" Ice said, smiling coolly.

"Very funny. What's up, girls? What am I missing here? The silence speaks volumes."

"We stayed up late comparing notes about old boyfriends," Cinnamon replied. "And decided that none of them compared to you."

Steven laughed and Howard smirked and nodded.

"Okay," he said. "Have your little girlie secrets. See if I care."

"Thanks for giving us permission," Ice said. She didn't say much, but when she did, it carried the chill that her name suggested.

Howard glanced at her and then quickly returned to his breakfast. There was no question she intimidated him far more than Cinnamon did.

"I've got to get to an early lesson," I said. "I'll take care of my own dishes."

"Butter him up for me, will you?" Steven cried after me.

Actually, my morning went relatively better than I had expected it would. Somehow, when I put my fingers to my bow and held my violin, my fatigue took a back seat to my enthusiasm, and I was able to play well enough for Mr. Bergman to give me a real compliment. However, it was couched in one of those between-the-lines type of remarks.

"Madame Senetsky certainly has a gift for recognizing exceptionally talented young people," he said. He had taken me through what he called the basics, moving me along quickly because of his satisfaction with my performance at almost every level.

"Thank you," I said. He looked at his planning book and kept his eyes glued to the pages, ignoring me, as if thank yous were unnecessary and even embarrassing for him.

"We'll continue the same time tomorrow," he said as a way of dismissing me.

I met Steven on my way out.

"How is he?" he whispered.

"Like a hungry raccoon," I said. "He'll tear through anything."

"Huh?"

I laughed as I hurried away.

With the time I had in between my violin lesson and my next session, I mailed out the letter to Uncle Simon and then finished cleaning and organizing my room. While I was doing so, I heard footsteps above and paused to listen. It was the first time I had heard anything above me. There was a shuffling and even the squeaking sound of something metallic being opened and closed. Both Howard and Cinnamon should be in their drama class with Mr. Marlowe, I thought. Ice was in her vocal lesson. Rose was at dance class, and I knew where Steven was. Mrs. Ivers was in the laundry room and Mrs. Churchwell was in the kitchen. I had seen Madame Senetsky and Laura Fairchild conversing in Madame Senetsky's office below when I had hurried to the stairway. Who was that up there?

Daddy used to say curiosity could often be like a worm to a fish, dangling on a hook, drawing you closer, drawing you into trouble, but it was hard to resist.

I checked my watch, saw that I still had some time, and went to the stairway leading up to the third floor. All I had been told was there was a costume room up there. I had yet to see it. I listened for a while at the foot of the short stairway, but heard nothing. Then I slowly ascended.

The third floor was quite unlike the rest of the house in which we lived and worked. There was only a single light fixture in the center of the ceiling, halfway down the corridor. It was a weak light at that, casting thin, soft shadows that caused the gray walls to look like stone.

Apparently there was only one room up here. I paused at the door, listened again, and then opened it. The slight illumination from the hallway spilled in before me to reveal rows and rows of costumes. They began just inside and ran the length of the room. I found a light switch on the right side and flipped it on. A series of bigger and brighter fixtures in brass lamp shades lit up the room well enough for me to see everything. On shelves above the costumes to my left were all sorts of hats and helmets. Against the right wall was another set of shelves, upon which were props—the swords Cinnamon and Howard were playing with the day I arrived, the armor, canes and magic wands, as well as crowns with imitation jewels. Below that were pairs and pairs of shoes and boots, slippers, and Indian moccasins.

The room felt dusty. Stepping into it, I sensed that once I moved something, a parade of particles would begin to float through the air, swimming from one set of costumes to another. The smell was musty, stale, as if the door to the room hadn't been opened in years. Of course, I knew otherwise.

If this was the only room up here and there were no other doors, who had been moving around? To do what? No one had come down the stairs.

"Hello?" I called, wondering if someone was deeper in the room, perhaps behind some costuming. There was no response. I walked in further and then followed the aisle on my right, past the rows of costumes organized by century and style, from the Middle Ages to the Roaring Twenties, with lots more from other eras and styles on the opposite side of the room.

I reached the rear of the room and started to go around the other side in order to return to the doorway when I saw what I realized was another door, behind a pair of gowns that looked like they could have been worn by Scarlett O'Hara in *Gone With the Wind.*

Where did this door go? It had a key in the lock. Why was it practically hidden from sight, I wondered, and I lifted the gowns away to turn the lock and then try the knob. It turned, but the door opened to another door. Still curious, I put my ear to that door and listened. I thought I could hear someone singing to the music of what sounded like a mandolin. I knew the sound well. It was a form of lute.

"Who's in here?" I heard, and spun around to see Laura Fairchild in the doorway. She seemed to swell in the doorway, her neck stretching, her eyes beaming with rage.

As quietly as I could, I closed the door, locked it again and stepped out into the aisle.

"Honey? What are you doing here?" she demanded.

"I was just curious," I said. "I heard about the costumes and wanted to see them."

"I've already instructed Howard and Cinnamon not

to touch anything in here again until they are told to do so. You had no permission to be up here."

"I'm sorry," I said. "I didn't really touch anything."

She pursed her lips and gazed at me skeptically, after which she looked into the room as if she would be able to tell in an instant if I had moved a single dress or boot.

"There's no reason for you to be on this floor," she emphasized.

"I thought I heard someone above my room, and thought it might be one of the others," I explained. I knew it couldn't possibly be one of my fellow students, but she made me feel so guilty, her eyes narrowing with cold suspicion, that I thought I had better come up with some other sensible explanation, even though all I was guilty of was curiosity.

"Isn't it time for your next session?" she asked, or more like commanded.

"Yes."

"Then you had better get going."

I started out and she went further in. I hesitated in the doorway. What was she doing? Was she really checking to see if I had taken anything? How could anyone keep track of all that was in here anyway? And why would I take anything from the room?

I lingered in the doorway and watched her trace my steps toward the rear. Then she surprised me by lifting away the old gowns as I had done and then testing to see if the door was still locked. Suddenly she spun around, as if she could feel my eyes on the back of her neck.

"What are you doing?" she demanded.

"Nothing," I said quickly and hurried away and down the stairs.

Where did that door go? Was someone singing behind it? Who? Curiosity was certainly a worm on a hook for me, I thought. And like the perennial fish, it would get me in trouble, too. I felt sure of that.

After our speech lesson, during which we were each recorded reading a selection from James Joyce's *Ulysses* for Mr. Masters, I pulled Cinnamon aside and told her what I had heard and what I had done.

"I didn't see any door in the rear of the wardrobe room when Howard and I went up there," she said. "But maybe that was because I didn't go all the way back and didn't look behind those costumes you said were hanging in front of it. Howard and I got excited over the armor, which was close to the front, and got into that. Our Ms. Fairchild did tell Howard to tell me to stay out of the room until we were instructed to go there for a specific thing, but I didn't think much of that. You said you distinctly heard footsteps and then you heard someone singing?"

"Yes, I'm sure that's what it was," I said. "Of course, it could have been someone listening to music."

"You're sure of what?" Ice asked, catching up with us.

I told her all of it briefly. She didn't look surprised.

"I've heard someone above at night," she revealed,

"or what I thought was someone above, but I haven't heard anyone singing or any music playing."

"I never did before," I said.

"Ice's room is directly under the costume room," Cinnamon remarked.

"I'm sure I heard footsteps, but there was no one there in the costume room," I said.

"Did you try to open the second door?" Cinnamon asked.

"I didn't have a chance. Ms. Fairchild appeared as suddenly as a ghost. I closed the first door and locked it again as quickly and as quietly as I could."

Ice groaned.

"Let's not think it's Howard's ghost of Mr. Senetsky again," she pleaded.

Cinnamon thought a moment. Rose was coming along with Steven.

"Don't say anything to Rose just yet. She's spooked enough by what we found last night."

We agreed and went on to our vocal class. Mr. Littleton had decided to turn us into a little chorus, with Ice, of course, singing lead. We had an opportunity to really hear her vocalize, and all of us, even Howard, were very impressed.

Later, when we confronted each other in dance class in our dance costumes, Steven took a lot of ribbing from Howard, who baptized him Mr. Toothpick Legs. Mr. Demetrius employed Rose as his assistant to help us develop fundamental moves and exercises. She truly had a striking figure, and moved with such grace and ease, she was inspiring to watch and to try to emulate.

She seemed made of rubber, able to turn, twist and move in defiance of gravity itself.

While we were working in the studio, Cinnamon nudged me and nodded toward the doorway.

There, apparently observing us for some time, was Edmond Senetsky. Rose saw that we were looking behind her and turned and saw him there as well. She suddenly became very nervous. A moment later, he was gone. She looked back at us and then caught Howard gazing at her, a big fat Cheshire cat smile spread over his face.

"Did y'all see him?" Rose asked immediately at the end of the dance session. "Maybe he returned to the school to get his scarf."

"Not in the daytime," Cinnamon insisted. "He couldn't risk being seen up there. He'd have no explanation for it."

"One of us has a real fan," Howard Rockwell sang as he walked by us. He rolled his eyes and laughed.

"Stuff it, Howard," Cinnamon called after him.

"There's no doubt in my mind that if Howard found out what we've discovered and planned to do, he would make more trouble for us," Ice remarked, glaring after him with eyes that looked capable of drilling a hole through a steel wall.

"Forget about him," Cinnamon said. "We'll follow our plan tonight."

After we completed the school day, we all went up to shower and rest before dinner. Tonight, we were told, we would be enjoying a French meal, and we would be given a lecture about wines as well. Madame

Senetsky would be at this dinner to observe us, Laura Fairchild said.

"French food happens to be her favorite," she added. "Everyone is to be on his or her best behavior and look presentable."

After I took my shower and lay down to get some rest, I fell into a deep sleep. I was that exhausted from tossing and turning, fretting in and out of nightmares the night before, and now, equally tired from a day of tension as well. Unfortunately, I slept so deeply, I didn't wake even when the others were talking and making noise outside my room. I didn't even hear Cinnamon knocking on my door. I woke only when I felt her shaking me vigorously.

"Whaaa... ?"

I gazed at all three of them, dressed and ready for dinner, standing beside my bed.

"Oh, no!" I screamed and sat up. "What time is it?"

"You've got only ten minutes," Cinnamon sadly pointed out, nodding at the clock.

"What will I do?"

"Just throw something on quickly," Rose advised.

I flew out of the bed and threw open my closet. Everyone did something to help...Rose finding my shoes, Ice going for the hair brush and brushing mine into some semblance of order, while I slipped into my dress and tried to adjust it. Cinnamon dampened a washcloth and told me to just scrub the sleep out of my face. I did that and then put on the little lipstick we were permitted, only I didn't realize some of it had smeared at the side of my mouth. The others were so worried about being late that they rushed out the door ahead of me.

Less than ten minutes later, still groggy, I followed them to the dining room, where Madame Senetsky was speaking to the French chef who would be lecturing us. She turned when we entered. The boys were already seated. As if she had some sort of built-in radar, she focused on me alone, her eyes growing small with displeasure. I knew my hair, despite Ice's attempts, was nowhere near as neat as it could be or should be. And I suddenly noticed that one of the buttons on my dress was unbuttoned. I made a quick attempt to fix it, but I didn't want to attract too much attention.

"I'd like to introduce Christian Rambaud, the chef at Champs-Elysees, a world-famous restaurant in New York. Tonight he will discuss wine as well as food. Please pay attention to everything. My graduates attend worldwide functions, galas, charity events, and award ceremonies in the most sophisticated cities. Actors especially, of course," she continued, centering on Cinnamon and Howard, "should do everything possible to expand their educations.

"Monsieur Rambaud," she said with a slight nod at the tall, dark, and what I thought was a rather lean man, for a chef. He smiled and stepped to the head of the table.

"Good evening," he sang, and began his lecture. "Let me begin with my favorite topic...wine."

He smiled and held up a glass of white wine.

"Give me a bowl of wine. In this I'll bury all unkindness," he quoted. "Shakespeare's..."

"Richard the Third," Howard finished.

"Très bien," Monsieur Rambaud said, impressed. "You are, of course, correct."

Madame Senetsky looked pleased and Howard beamed, shot a quick glance at the rest of us, and sat back.

"Winemaking in France dates back to pre-Roman times, but it was the Romans who disseminated the culture of wine and the practice of winemaking throughout the country," Monsieur Rambaud lectured.

"Wine is the product of the juice of freshly picked grapes, after natural or cultured yeasts have converted the grape sugars into alcohol during the fermentation process. The yeasts are normally filtered out before bottling. The range, quality, and reputation of the fine wines of Bordeaux, Burgundy, the Rhône, and Champagne in particular have made them role models the world over."

I could see Steven was getting bored. Howard continued to look like an attentive student, and the girls were all looking at each other, me, and sneaking a glance or two at Madame Senetsky, who sat and stared at us with a grouchy face. I couldn't look directly at her. Whenever I did so, her eyes seemed to burn into my heart. Cinnamon brushed the side of her mouth with her hand and made faces at me, but I didn't understand what she was trying to convey, and with a glance at Madame Senetsky, she gave up.

"France's everyday wines can be highly enjoyable, too, with plenty of good value wines now emerging from the southern regions. Each of ten principal wine-producing regions has its own identity, based on grape varieties and *terroir.* Appellation control laws guarantee a wine's origins and style," Monsieur Rambaud continued, and then captured our attention, especially Steven's, by pouring from different bottles and passing the glasses along for us to taste.

"Wine-tasting is an art in itself," he instructed. "There are three things to consider: Color, nose, and taste."

"Nose?" Steven asked, grimacing.

"Smell," Monsieur Rambaud replied.

"Real hard to figure that out," Howard muttered under his breath.

"I'm not as sophisticated as you, sue me," Steven retorted.

"I wish I could."

Madame Senetsky tapped her cane and they both came to stiff attention.

"The appearance of the wine gives you an idea of the type of grape, the age, and whether it is good or bad. Hold the first glass up to the light," he instructed, and we all did so. "This is a buttery-yellow white wine. Obviously either a Chardonnay or a French Burgundy. The intensity of the wine, whether it is opaque or closer to transparent, tells us about its age. Older wines tend to be brownish at the edge. If it's cloudy, it's probably spoiled.

"Now let us nose...smell it," he said. "Swirl it in your glass as so, and then take a whiff."

"It smells like apples," I said.

"Ah, yes. It is a Chardonnay. Finally, let us taste

the wine. Take a small sip and suck the air between your teeth. Hold the wine at the center of your tongue for a few seconds longer to allow the character of the wine to be apparent. Let's try this Merlot," he said, switching to another glass he had poured for us all. Everyone took his or hers. "We are checking for acidity, tannin—which will tell us if it's bitter or easy to drink—body or weight, oakiness and finish, the aftertaste.

"Now," he said, "let us continue. First, we'll finish with the whites..."

There were no less than ten bottles of white and ten of red. We were supposed to only take a sip from each and not swallow, but Steven took some good gulps. By the time he reached the fifteenth glass, his face was tomato red and his eyes were glassy. He was making one silly remark after another, and Howard was countering. I could see Madame Senetsky losing her patience with them.

Finally it ended and we went on to the food. By the end of the evening, I felt stuffed. I saw Steven had grown sleepy. His eyelids were practically shut. We finished the meal with a dessert called Chocolate Mousse Le Pain Perdu, which was a bread pudding topped with a caramel sauce. It was all delicious and I ate far too much. I was actually somewhat nauseous at the end of the meal. I wanted to get up to my room as soon as possible, but when we were excused, Madame Senetsky asked me to stay.

Because of the tone of Madame Senetsky's voice, the girls looked at me with pity as they filed out.

Madame Senetsky thanked Monsieur Rambaud and then, after he left, she turned to me.

"How dare you come down to one of my formal dinners looking so unkempt? Did I not impress upon you how important presentation is in our world?"

"I—"

"Did I not stress that when you are a Senetsky student, you are my representative, and what you do reflects directly back on me?"

"I'm sorry," I began. "I was tired and I—"

"Wipe off that lipstick," she ordered, but before I could, she stepped forward and did it herself with a silk napkin. Roughly, too.

"There are no excuses for failure in our world," she snapped before I could offer any explanation. "One either is successful or not. Excuses, mitigating circumstances, accidents, fate, whatever you reach for to save you will not change one moment of a poor performance. Audiences are unforgiving and the critics couldn't care one iota about our personal issues. Once we're on stage, our lives, our real lives, are forgotten. We can't use them to help us or protect us or excuse us. The curtain rises, and when it does, we must be ready to give the public what it has paid for and what it has a right to expect. After the curtain falls, it is over, ended, a fait accompli.

"I told you, all of you, every moment you're in this house, studying with these fine teachers, you are on stage. Is there any part of this you still don't understand? Well?" she asked, pounding her cane.

"No, Madame Senetsky." I looked down at the table.

"I'm disappointed. If I had to choose one of you who would fail me first, I would never have chosen you. I thought I had made the reason clear to you the other day," she added, referring, I'm sure, to her telling me about her daughter.

I looked up at her, my eyes so glazed with tears, I felt as if I was looking at her through a veil.

I started to say I was sorry again, but quickly choked back the words.

"I do not permit many mistakes, Honey. Be warned," she concluded, smacking her cane to the floor again and standing. I stood quickly, too, my eyes down again.

"You're excused," she said, and I hurried out of the dining room.

I felt the tears break over the dam of my lids as I pounded up the stairway. How disappointed Mommy and Daddy would be if I were sent home in disgrace. How would I ever face Uncle Peter's gravestone again?

The girls and Howard were standing in the hallway, waiting for me. From the sounds I heard coming out of Steven's room, I knew he was vomiting.

"The idiot is paying the price for drinking instead of tasting the wines," Howard commented after a particularly loud, ugly noise. "What did she want from you?"

I looked at the girls and then just hurried into my room before I burst into hysterical sobs. I felt like I was going to vomit any moment, too, and had to get some cold water on my face. All the girls followed me.

"Are you all right?" Rose asked, coming to my side.

I shook my head.

"She was so angry I thought she was going to ask me to leave right then and there. I had this buttoned wrong," I said, turning to show them. "And my lipstick was smeared. She wiped it off herself, practically taking some of my skin and part of my lip with it."

"I tried to warn you," Cinnamon said.

"She called me disheveled, a great disappointment. She said I was the last one she expected to disappoint her."

I looked in the mirror. My hair was every which way.

"I'm sorry. I tried to get it neat for you," Ice said.

"It's no one's fault but my own," I wailed. "I feel sick to my stomach."

"That dinner was too rich," Cinnamon said. "We had too much to taste."

I nodded and went to my bed, where I just flopped on my back.

"At least none of us are as bad as Steven," Rose said.

"He is going to feel it more in the morning," Ice said. "I remember how my mother was sometimes, many times. She would go drinking with her girlfriends and suffer the next day, but it didn't stop her," she pointed out.

"Your father let her?" Rose asked.

"He worked as a security guard, often at night, and she just was frustrated. She's a beautiful woman, and thinks she messed up her life by marrying and having me."

"My mother went through something like that, too," Rose said. "She wanted to regain her youth, but she was being influenced, poisoned by someone else."

She looked at us when we gave her expressions of confusion.

"Who poisoned her?" Cinnamon asked.

"The sister of the woman with whom my father had his affair and other child. Her name is Charlotte Alden Curtis. She's rich and has a house nearly as big as this."

"Why did she do that to your mother?" Ice asked.

"Her sister died in a terrible car accident on the way to meet with my father, and Charlotte blamed him and wanted to unload his sins on us. She trapped us by inviting us to come live with her and help her care for my half-brother Evan because he was disabled and in a wheelchair. My mother was an easy target—gullible, trusting. We didn't have any money. My father barely left us enough to eat. We had no home. My mother didn't have good job skills." Rose turned to Ice. "She, too, was full of frustrations. That made her an easy target, I suppose. She finally realized what was happening, but it was almost too late."

Everyone was quiet.

"I wonder if that will be my destiny, too," she added. "I'll end up one day so frustrated and disappointed in my life, I mean."

"It won't happen to any of us. Not if we stick with our career goals and be what we need and want to be," Cinnamon insisted. "Whether we like it or not, Madame Senetsky can help us get there. We'll have to put up with everything."

"Even a sick Peeping Tom?" Ice asked.

No one spoke for a moment, and then Cinnamon

firmly said, "No. We'll put an end to that if it happens again. Everyone still up for the plan?"

"I might get sick," I warned.

"So? Better you do it with one or more of us around to help you. Let's all get into our nightgowns and robes and meet in Rose's room in ten minutes. It's about that time."

"What do I do?" Rose asked.

"Nothing different. This is a trap we're setting. We don't want to give him any warnings. Okay? Everyone agreed? Well?" she pounded.

"Okay," I said.

Ice nodded.

I took a deep breath, fought back my nausea, and prepared to join them in Rose's room, half hoping it would be a waste of time.

It wasn't.

I had never had or participated in a pajama party. Ice and Cinnamon said they had never, either, but Rose told us she had when she was fourteen.

"I had made some friends and thought I was finally going to have a life. Shortly afterward, my father came home and told my mother and me we were moving again. I remember I cried a lot this time, just rained a storm of tears down my cheeks until the well of sorrow inside me dried up and left my heart aching."

"I bet you were afraid to make friends after that," Cinnamon said.

"Exactly. I was terrified of becoming too close to anyone or too involved in any activity. Good-byes were like tiny pins jabbed into my heart."

She stared at the sad memories flashing over her eyes.

We were all sitting on the floor, each of us wrapped in the blanket we had brought along. We were situated so that we were just below the window. Rose, at Cinnamon's suggestion, left the bathroom lights on, making it look as if she was still in there, perhaps taking a shower or a bath.

"It doesn't seem like all that much of a big deal now when I think back," she continued, "but I do remember how much fun it was sharing secrets with your girlfriends. Everyone just seemed to be more honest, frank, and unafraid of revealing what a girlfriend of mine called *heart thoughts.*"

"Heart thoughts?" I asked. I looked at Cinnamon and Ice, who both shook their heads.

"She had this theory that some thoughts don't come from our brains. They come directly from our hearts, traveling up to our brains, and finally, when we're being honest or care to be revealing, out through our lips."

"That's silly," Cinnamon said. "Your heart doesn't have the neurological cells to form thoughts."

Rose shrugged.

"She just meant that some feelings originated there and got translated into thoughts, I guess. Of course, she was mainly referring to our crushes on boys and our..."

"What?" Ice asked.

"Our sexual fantasies, I guess."

"Like what?" Cinnamon asked. Just asking brought a crimson glow into Rose's cheeks.

"One girl described closing her eyes while she was

taking a bath and imagining a boy she liked a lot kneeling beside the tub and washing her body with a soft sponge."

We were all suddenly very quiet. Rose traced her finger along the carpet.

"When I was twelve," she continued, "I was at a friend's house. She had a swimming pool and some boys were there. We were all flirting and splashing each other. One boy, Neil Rosen, kept going under water and grabbing at our legs. He popped up in front of me and I fell backwards. As I fell, he reached out and grabbed the top of my bathing suit, allegedly to stop me from falling. It came off, and I screamed. I was so embarrassed I wished my head would sink into my neck. I felt like drowning myself afterward.

"Anyway, I told the girls the story, but I made it seem like a fantasy and not a true story. I felt guilty about it because I was letting them tell their true life secrets and I was hiding mine."

She looked ashamed.

"You shouldn't have worried about it. Half the things people write as fiction come from real events in their lives," Cinnamon said. "I was an expert liar, creative liar, I called it, but I based my tall tales on some thread of truth. We all do it."

I was going to disagree, but didn't. Maybe she was right. Maybe there were things I had said and done that I didn't want to expose.

"Whatever," Rose said. She took a deep breath and smiled. "We had a good time nevertheless, and with everyone around everyone else giving support, we called boys we dared not call on our own. I remember I was sorry the night came to an end. We all fought sleep until we were too exhausted to keep our eyelids open. Everyone was dragging around so dreadfully the next day, our parents thought we had participated in one wild party. I remember my mother saying, "Darlin', you look like you chased Mr. Sandman out of your bedroom forever."

All three of us were smiling at her, actually feeling quite envious, as if keeping yourself up all night talking and flirting with boys over a telephone was a rich, wonderful experience. Maybe it was. Maybe we had somehow missed out on so much.

I lowered myself to the floor and laid my head on a pillow.

Cinnamon was talking, describing what it had been like for her when her mother had been committed to a mental clinic after she had miscarried. It was a sad story, and interesting, too, but I was having trouble keeping myself awake. The food, the wine, the emotional tension made me very sleepy.

And then, suddenly, the feel of Ice's hand squeezing my ankle popped my eyes open.

"What?"

"Shh," Cinnamon warned. Everyone was quiet.

A dark shadow moved over the window.

"He's back," Cinnamon whispered.

My heart began to pound like a parade drum. Cinnamon edged closer to the wall and slowly, ever so slowly, began to lift herself toward the window.

We scrunched down and crawled up beside her. She held her hand out to be sure we were still.

"Someone is out there," she whispered. "That's definitely no shadow or spirit."

"Oh, no," Rose moaned.

Then Cinnamon leaped up, throwing the window open at the same time.

We all stood.

Someone rushed off the ledge and up the ladder.

"Who's out here?" Cinnamon yelled. "What are you doing here?"

She started to climb out.

"Wait," Ice said. "Maybe you shouldn't."

"We've got to," Cinnamon insisted. She went onto the fire escape ledge. Ice followed, and then I did the same. Rose hung back in the window.

"Look," Cinnamon said, pointing above.

We saw a figure climb the flight and step up on the ledge above. Whoever it was disappeared into the open window.

"That's on the side of the house off limits to us," Ice commented.

"Not anymore," Cinnamon said and started toward the ladder.

"No," Ice said, holding her back. "You'll make a big scene."

"We should."

"Maybe not yet," Ice said.

"This is disgusting. A grown man doing something like this, and a well-known theatrical agent, too," I said.

"Let's deal with it tomorrow. We'll just approach Madame Senetsky and hand her the ascot," Ice said. "Let her handle it. It's her problem, too."

Cinnamon stood there, deciding, and not making an effort to come back inside.

"What would you do anyway? Climb up the ladder and go through that window? Please," Ice begged. "Come on back inside."

She and I crawled back into the room. Cinnamon still lingered, looking up.

"Cinnamon?" Ice said.

She remained a moment more and then followed us in. Ice closed the window behind us.

"I don't think he'll be back after this," I said.

"I should have gone up," Cinnamon insisted, her eyes on the fire escape.

"Madame Senetsky will still believe us," Rose said. "Won't she? We'll all be able to tell her what we've seen. She's got to believe it if all of us tell her, right? Cinnamon? Right?"

"Yes. Okay," Cinnamon said, frustrated and angry. She turned to the door. "Let's go back to our own rooms now and get some sleep." She paused. "You all right, Rose?"

"I think so," Rose said.

"Keep the curtain closed tight and forget about him," I said.

"Okay. Thanks, everyone," she replied in a small voice.

We started out, closing the door softly behind us.

"He won't be back. That's for sure, isn't it?" I asked Cinnamon.

She stood there, her eyes darkening with thought.

"I don't know. There is something very odd about

all this. Look at the hour," she said, holding up her watch. It was close to midnight. "He doesn't live here, right? Why would he be here so late and how would he explain all this to Madame Senetsky?"

"What are you saying?" Ice asked. "That's his ascot you have hidden in your room, isn't it?"

"Yes, but..."

"But what?" I asked her.

She put her finger to her lips so I would speak more softly.

"Whoever that was wasn't wearing any shoes," she said.

"What?" Ice asked.

"He was barefoot," Cinnamon insisted. "I saw bare feet flash against the metal steps."

We were all quiet.

"Why would he be barefoot?" Ice finally voiced.

"And the feet," Cinnamon said.

"What about them?"

She turned to me.

"They looked...small."

"You mean it was a child?" Ice asked.

"I don't know what it was, who it was, I mean."

"What the hell is going on out here?" we heard, and saw Howard in his doorway. "You're keeping me up." He was standing in his pajamas. "What are you doing? Planning your assassinations again?"

"We're not doing anything exciting, Howard," Cinnamon said. "Rose had a nightmare."

"Really? Must have been the wine."

"Right," Cinnamon said.

"Howard," I said.

"What?"

"Your barn door is open," I said, remembering Uncle Peter's sense of humor.

"What?" He grimaced.

"And the cow is about to leave."

"Huh?"

He looked down at his pajama pants and quickly closed the door.

How good it felt to laugh.

Even if it was only for a few seconds.

6

Looking for Answers

"I think it was Laura Fairchild," Cinnamon whispered to me at breakfast the next morning.

"What was? Who?"

Cinnamon drew closer to me before answering, even though we were alone. Howard was in the kitchen getting his breakfast. Ice, Rose, and Steven were not yet down.

"On Rose's fire escape last night," she said. "I thought about it for quite a while before I fell asleep last night. I went over and over what I saw and I'm convinced that the bare feet I saw were the feet of a woman," she concluded.

"The feet of a woman? I don't understand. And anyway, why Laura Fairchild?"

"Who else could it have been? It wasn't Mrs. Churchwell or Mrs. Ivers, and it certainly wasn't Madame Senetsky. The other servants don't sleep here."

"But Laura Fairchild? Why would she do such a

thing? And what about the ascot that belongs to Edmond Senetsky, that had his cologne on it?"

She shook her head.

"I can't answer any of that yet, but I don't want to do anything or say anything until I can, especially to Madame Senetsky."

We both looked up as Rose entered. She looked tired, but somewhat excited.

"My brother Evan contacted me early this morning," she whispered as Howard returned to the table. "I asked him to use his computer to do some research on Madame Senetsky and her husband after Howard told us that fantastic story."

"So?" Cinnamon asked.

Rose revealed some pages she had printed off her computer.

"What's that?" Howard asked.

"Notes on yesterday's food and wine lecture, Howard. Don't you remember? We're having a test this afternoon about it?" Cinnamon said.

He froze for a moment and looked from Rose to me and then to Cinnamon.

"You're kidding, right?"

"Of course not, Howard. We don't fool around when it comes to our careers," she replied.

He stared and then he shook his head and sat.

"You're all wacky," he muttered and started to eat.

After a moment we returned to the pages. I looked over Cinnamon's shoulder and began to read.

It was a reprint of some news stories about Madame Senetsky's husband Marshall and his apparently very unexpected suicide. Friends and business associates were quoted as being taken by complete surprise, one associate claiming he had just been talking to him on the phone a short while earlier and had no indication of unhappiness. Madame Senetsky had no comment and avoided the press.

According to the news stories, Marshall Senetsky's body was found slumped over his desk in this very house. He had shot himself and had not, according to the articles, left any note explaining his action. However, because of the forensic evidence, the police investigation had concluded it was suicide.

Some people conjectured about the Senetsky fortune, but evidence indicated there were no serious financial difficulties. All of the articles mentioned that surviving him were his wife and son Edmond, who at the time was only nineteen years old. There was no mention of the daughter who had died.

"Evan is going to continue to dig for us," Rose whispered. She glanced toward Howard, who was pretending not to try to hear what we said.

"Wait until later," Cinnamon told Rose, her eyes on Howard. She folded the pages and handed them back to Rose, who went for her breakfast.

Before Ice and Steven arrived, I left for my early session with Mr. Bergman. My lesson went well, and he gave me the music he wanted me to prepare for our next session. Essentially, we had completed what he had called the basics and were now going to begin a study of more involved compositions.

On my way back upstairs, I ran into Rose, who

looked very distraught. She was rushing to get to her dance session, but she looked frantic, her face already as flushed as it would be at the end of her exercises.

"What's wrong?" I asked.

"Oh, I'm so stupid, Honey. I don't know how I could have forgotten it, but I did and when I went back, it was gone."

"What?"

"Those pages on Madame Senetsky's husband's suicide," she said. "I put them beside my chair on the floor and ate my breakfast. Then Steven and Ice arrived and Ms. Fairchild burst in to give us the weekend's schedule. Yours is up in your room. I got so involved listening to it because there's not a moment in there for me to meet up with my boyfriend Barry. We're all going to a play on Friday night and then a matinee on Saturday. That night we go to a dinner with Madame Senetsky at Monsieur Rambaud's restaurant so we can show off our new knowledge of wine and food, and then we're off to the ballet. On Sunday, we're going to lunch and then immediately to the Museum of Modern Art for most of the afternoon. We return here for another special dinner and start of another week. I thought I'd have Sunday afternoon off at least!" she cried, her arms up in frustration.

She shook her head.

"I guess it got me so upset, I forgot what I had brought down and went upstairs to get ready for my dance class. I was up there twenty minutes before I realized what I had left in the dining room, but when I rushed down to get it, it was gone! I asked Mrs.

Churchwell if she had seen the pages, but she said she hadn't."

"You mean when you and the others cleared off the table, you didn't realize it was there? No one did? I can't believe that. One of the boys must have it. Did you ask Howard?"

"Actually, he and Cinnamon left before Ice, Steven, and I did. I know Steven didn't have it. I must have kicked them under the table or something, but they're gone. Where could they be? Could someone have just thrown it all in the garbage?"

I shook my head.

"I don't know. What does Cinnamon think?"

"She worries that Ms. Fairchild might have found it or someone else did and gave it to her. She thinks she would give them to Madame Senetsky," she moaned.

I didn't want to say it, but I thought that was very likely. I tried to ease her concern.

"Why would she do that?"

"Why? We're living in a prison," she wailed. "Spied upon in every which way and I don't mean just Peeping Toms. I can't even get an hour to see my boyfriend. I'm terrified about asking Madame Senetsky to let me have any time off."

She shook her head, sucked in her breath, and hurried on to her class.

I looked after her, thinking about what she had said. Cinnamon suspected the silhouetted person on the fire escape was Ms. Fairchild. Could Rose be right? Could it be we were all being watched? How bizarre, I thought.

The remainder of the day was uneventful. I still half suspected Howard had swiped the pages, but if he knew anything, he didn't reveal it. Rose remained depressed and anxious. We tried to cheer her up, but her boyfriend had called and expressed how disappointed he was, too.

"Y'all know what happens when you can't see them, don't you?" Rose asked. No one wanted to answer, even though everyone knew what she meant. "They find someone else who is able to see them. I can't blame them, either."

"I'm sure you'll have free time next weekend," I said. Neither Cinnamon nor Ice looked optimistic about it. "He'll wait. He'll wait if he really cares for you.

"I described the same situation to Chandler and he understands," I went on. "It's a bigger trip for him coming in from Boston, and he wants to be sure he can spend a lot of time with me before he comes."

"Well, good for you," Rose said, her eyes welling up with tears.

"I didn't mean..."

She turned and walked quickly out of my room with her arms folded, her head down.

"Rose..."

"Leave her go," Cinnamon said.

"But I didn't mean to make it sound like my boyfriend is better than hers."

"The way she is right now, she's going to jump down anyone's throat."

I told her what Rose had said concerning our being in a prison, being under glass.

"Maybe you're not so wrong suspecting Ms. Fairchild," I said.

"Suspecting her of what?" Ice asked, and Cinnamon told her.

She grimaced and shook her head.

"It all seems so spooky," I said.

"That's not spooky. That's downright sick. And what about the ascot?" Ice asked. "How does it figure into this?"

Cinnamon shook her head.

"As I told Honey, I can't explain it." She thought a moment and then nodded. "There's only one thing to do."

"What's that?" I asked.

"One night we've got to climb the ladder and look into those windows above us."

"It's not where Ms. Fairchild stays," Ice reminded her. "That window is in the private residence. If Madame Senetsky finds us up there peering into her apartments, we're all going to get the boot."

"Right now, I'm not so sure I would mind," Cinnamon retorted and walked off.

She almost got her wish. An hour later, Laura Fairchild came upstairs to tell us we were all to report immediately to the parlor.

"What's this about, I wonder?" Howard asked as all of us headed down the stairs.

"Maybe some of the silverware is missing," Steven quipped.

Ms. Fairchild told us to take seats and wait for Madame Senetsky. Rose looked from me to Cinnamon and Ice. She looked absolutely terrified.

Howard rose quickly when Madame Senetsky entered. Steven jumped up a moment after he had.

"Sit," she barked as if they were both dogs. They did so quickly.

Everyone was very quiet. She stood straight, firm, her cane in front of her, both hands on it.

"From time to time, I have someone under my wing who doesn't belong. When you all first arrived, I told you success in the arts consisted of sixty percent raw talent. The other forty percent really comes from character, charm, inner strength. Your teachers all agree that every one of you has the gift of talent, but alas, I am afraid that not every one of you has one or more of the other ingredients."

She paused and turned to Laura Fairchild, who practically leaped forward and handed her Rose's computer pages.

"Who left this in the dining room for my servants to find?" she demanded, holding up the familiar pages.

"What is it?" Howard asked.

"It's that aspect of this business I despise: gossip, invasion of privacy, everything that dehumanizes us. Well?" she asked again. "Who put this in the dining room?"

Rose began to stand, confession written on her face.

"I found it in my closet," Cinnamon said quickly.

"What?" Madame Senetsky replied. "Your closet?"

"Yes. I didn't know what to make of it. Someone must have left it there. I brought it down to give to Ms. Fairchild, but I forgot and left it on the floor."

"It was found next to Rose's chair," Laura Fairchild said skeptically, glaring at Rose.

"What is it?" Howard asked again.

"I passed it over to Rose, who looked at it and then put it away when the others came to the dining room," Cinnamon said, making up her lies as fast as questions could be asked. "That's why Howard keeps asking what it is," she said, looking at him. "He didn't see it. Neither did Steven, right, Steven?"

"I didn't see anything," he declared. "I don't know what this is all about."

"Well, what is it?" Howard cried.

"I'm sorry, we left it there. Who was in my room before me?" Cinnamon then asked. "Whoever that was must have forgotten it when he or she left the school."

"That's ridiculous. Those rooms are cleaned until they are spotless after each group of students leaves us," Laura said.

"Well, someone missed a spot. It was at the back of the closet. I wouldn't have found it myself if I didn't have a dress fall off the hanger."

Madame Senetsky stared at her and then panned all of us. Steven looked absolutely confused. Howard looked annoyed. Rose shifted her eyes guiltily away, and Ice and I looked down.

"The least I would expect from all of you is loyalty," Madame Senetsky said. "Loyalty that comes from sincere appreciation. I would hate to learn that one or even more of you were not grateful for this opportunity," she said. "Leaving something like this about my home is not a way to show it," she added, shaking the papers.

"Are those old news stories true?" Cinnamon bravely asked.

Madame Senetsky straightened her back into a pole of steel and glared down at her.

"That is not your concern here. Your concern is development of your talents, nothing more, nothing less, and certainly not to take dips into the pool of nasty gossip. Is that understood?"

"Yes, Madame, and I do apologize for being so careless. If I find anything else..."

"You will not find anything else!" Madame Senetsky practically screamed. She pounded the floor with her cane.

"Yes, Madame," Cinnamon said. She sat back.

The stillness in the room was so thick, I thought I could hear Madame Senetsky sucking air into her nostrils like a bull. After another moment, she said, "You're all dismissed," then turned and left the parlor, with Laura Fairchild glaring back at us furiously before following on Madame Senetsky's heels.

For a moment it was as if she had taken all the air in the room out with her.

"Man, oh, man," Steven muttered.

"What the hell was that all about?" Howard asked. "I got in trouble with all of you. I demand to know and know now," he said.

"Relax, Howard. It was just copies of old news stories about her husband's suicide," Cinnamon told him.

"Her husband's suicide?" He thought a moment. "Where did you really get them?"

"You heard me. I found them in my closet. Go look

in yours. Who knows what you'll find?" she said and winked at me.

She stood up and we did the same.

"Why are you poking about her private life and her family history? What's that got to do with why we're here? You're going to get us all into big trouble. I won't stand for it," Howard cried.

"So sit," Cinnamon said.

We all started out.

"Why did you do that?" Rose asked Cinnamon. "Why did you take all the blame for what I did? You could have been thrown out."

"I didn't think so, but if you had told her the truth, I don't doubt she would have considered excusing you, and you're too good a dancer, Rose. You're going to be a real star," Cinnamon predicted confidently.

Rose smiled.

"Thank you, Cinnamon." She looked at Ice and me. "Thanks, all of you."

"Remember, one for all and all for one," Cinnamon said.

The boys passed us on the stairway, Howard continuing to mumble to himself.

"I feel a little ashamed," Rose said when they were far enough ahead.

"Why?" I asked.

"I'm missing a skirt and a blouse outfit."

"Missing?" Cinnamon asked. "Are you sure you just didn't bring it?"

"Yes. I'm positive because I remember hanging it up."

"Why did you say you were ashamed?" Ice asked. "You thought one of us took it?"

"I didn't know what to think."

We were all quiet for a moment.

"Okay," Ice said. "I'm missing something, too, a sweater. I wasn't sure if I had brought it or not, though, so I didn't mention it."

"Well, we have no maids cleaning our rooms. Who are we going to accuse? Laura Fairchild?" Cinnamon asked.

"Maybe one of them," Ice said, nodding toward Steven and Howard. "Steven's too weird for me."

"I can't believe that," I said. "Why would he want our things?"

"It's called fetishism," Cinnamon said. "We mentals know that lingo. Someone puts lust or love into an inanimate object related to someone he wants. I hate to tell you what he might do with your sweater, Ice, or your skirt and blouse, Rose."

We all stared at the empty hallway before us.

"But we shouldn't accuse anyone or think anything like that until or unless we know it's true," I said.

"You're right, of course," Cinnamon quickly agreed. "Who wants it to be true anyway?"

She started away.

"Boy, I hope I can get some rest tonight," Rose declared when we paused by our rooms.

"You will," Cinnamon said.

We hugged each other and went to our respective bedrooms.

Thankfully, there were no more incidents at Rose's window that night, or for the remainder of the week for that matter. And no one lost any other articles of clothing. We all became too involved with our classes and teachers to think about anything else anyway.

On Wednesday, I received a delivery of flowers from Uncle Simon, a beautiful mix of his favorites. The girls were all jealous. I immediately sat at my desk and wrote him a long thank-you letter, feeling guilty for being so busy I had written only one letter up until now. I told him how much the girls loved his flowers and told him I would call home to speak with him soon, too.

Meanwhile, Rose's brother Evan sent her another E-mail, claiming he was running into what he called "an unusual number of dead ends" regarding information about the Senetskys' tragedy.

"My brother believes there is something very strange here," she told us Thursday afternoon.

"Why?" I asked.

"He's very good at what he does on the computer. He's able to break into highly sensitive areas. He told me he once even broke into the Pentagon!"

"What does he suspect, that it wasn't a suicide?" Cinnamon asked.

"I don't know, but he promised me he would keep trying. Should I tell him to stop?"

Cinnamon thought a moment and then shook her head.

"No. Just don't print anything out and leave it anywhere. I'd like to know more. Everyone okay with that?" she asked.

I was nervous, but I didn't say anything. Ice just shrugged and looked as stoic as usual.

"Whatever pushes your buttons," she muttered.

"It's not much different from what pushes yours," Cinnamon said. "Only yours have to be pushed a lot harder, I guess."

Ice stared at her a moment. I held my breath. It was like waiting for a second shoe to drop.

And then Ice laughed, and we all did the same.

The weekend was as full and exhausting as it had promised to be. Laura Fairchild was our chaperone and guide. We were driven about in a van, which made us feel like younger, high school students, but it was a very convenient way to get around the city. It was nice having our van outside the theater waiting for us while the mobs of people fought for taxicabs. We were able to keep to the ambitious schedule.

I did enjoy all the performances, the lunches, and even the Saturday night dinner at the Champs-Elysees. I had to admit to myself that it made me feel important to be at a big table with all the waiters, the maitre d', and Monsieur Rambaud himself fawning over us. I could see from the way people were staring at us that they thought we were some very important group, and of course, a number of people came over to say hello to Madame Senetsky, some to get her autograph. A well-known Broadway star and his wife stopped by as well, and we were all introduced to him as prospective stars ourselves. Howard beamed and looked most determined.

At the end of the evening, Madame Senetsky complimented us all on our behavior and what she called our social performances. Exhausted, we all looked forward to our comfortable beds. When we visited the museum the next day, we were all quite subdued. Steven looked like he was sleepwalking, in fact. A professional guide had been assigned to lecture us about the exhibition.

After we had passed through about half of the museum, Rose stepped up between Cinnamon and myself and said, "Cover for me. I'm going to tell Ms. Fairchild that I'm going to the bathroom, and then I'm going to get lost for a while."

"What?" I cried. "Don't, Rose. You'll get in terrible trouble."

"Your boyfriend's here, isn't he?" Cinnamon asked her.

She smiled.

"In the lobby," she whispered. "I told him where we would be and he and I planned a secret rendezvous. Cover for me."

"Rose, please don't take the chance," I urged.

She stepped back, muttered something to Ms. Fairchild, who looked displeased, and then hurried away before Ms. Fairchild could prevent it.

The guide concluded his comments on the artwork before us and we moved to another room. I kept looking back at the doorway. I was very nervous for Rose.

"Don't worry about her," Cinnamon said. "She'll get away with it. She's just as good an actress as she is a dancer. You've seen her in Mr. Marlowe's improvisation classes. If you keep looking after her, you raise the temperature of suspicion in Ms. Fairchild's thermometer."

"Where's Rose?" Ice whispered, coming closer. "Ms. Fairchild is growing very upset. She muttered, 'That girl,' twice under her breath."

"Bathroom," Cinnamon said. "Terrible cramps."

Ice smiled.

"Terrible cramps. Suddenly, huh?" She tilted her head. "Her boyfriend's here, right?"

"Boys don't usually give me terrible cramps," Cinnamon replied, and we laughed.

"If you're not interested, you can at least be courteous and quiet," Laura Fairchild admonished.

We straightened up quickly. Howard and Steven glanced back at us, Steven smiling wryly.

"Hey," he said, realizing Rose was not there, "where's Ginger Rogers?"

"Bathroom," I replied, but Laura Fairchild was staring at the door behind us, her increasing anger making her neck turn redder and redder.

"Excuse me, Mr. Longo," she said to our guide, and then turned to us. "You all continue—and pay attention. I'll go look for our little lost lamb."

"I can go," Steven volunteered.

"You can go back to where you came from, too," she replied sternly.

Howard laughed at Steven's look of shock.

We watched Laura Fairchild march off, the fury stiffening her neck and turning her hands into small fists. Her heels clicked off down the corridor like an old clock ticking down to the launching of a rocket.

"I wouldn't want to be our beautiful Rose right now," Steven declared.

"Don't worry. You'll always be a weed," Cinnamon told him, and we all laughed.

"Ha, ha. You're a riot."

"Can we continue with the tour, ladies and gentlemen? I have another in about twenty minutes," Mr. Longo said, twisting his lips with obvious disgust.

"Oh, please do," Steven told him.

We subdued our giggles and followed along. His voice droned on, but our eyes went from the works of art to the door. Some other visitors came up behind us and listened to his lecture, but neither Rose nor Ms. Fairchild appeared until we were almost finished.

Just as Mr. Longo began his summary, there was Rose again, a great look of satisfaction on her face, her eyes full of glee.

"Did you see Laura Fairchild? She's looking for you," Cinnamon whispered.

"No."

A few moments later, Ms. Fairchild appeared, her face now as red as her neck, her eyes blazing as brightly as sunlight off a tin roof. Some of her perfectly obedient strands of hair were loose and curled like broken piano wires. She glared at Rose, but held back her rage so she could thank Mr. Longo for his tour on behalf of Madame Senetsky and the school. He bowed, looked a bit disgusted at Steven, and then walked off to begin his next tour.

Laura whipped around on her heels and practically lunged at Rose.

"Where were you?" she clamored. "I checked every women's lounge in the museum."

"I went to the bathroom, just as I told you I would,

Ms. Fairchild. When I came out, I got lost and wandered through the wrong rooms," she added. "I was getting so desperate, I swear I could hardly breathe. Finally, some kind stranger put me on the right path. I'm so sorry for any inconvenience I might have caused y'all, ma'am."

Laura glared at her, but Rose held her innocent gaze. It served like water dousing a fire finally, and Ms. Fairchild relaxed her shoulders.

"You should have paid attention to where we were and how to get back. It's not very bright to get lost in a museum. You people are supposed to be special."

"The crème de la crème," Cinnamon declared.

"The icing on the cake," Steven added.

"No," Cinnamon said. "We *are* the cake."

"All right. That's enough. Follow me out to the van and let's not have anyone else get lost," Ms. Fairchild warned, her eyes still shooting darts at Rose, who continued to look as innocent as a kitten.

We marched obediently behind her. Ice, holding that soft, smart smile on her lips, Cinnamon's eyes full of mischief, and me alternating between holding my breath and keeping up with my pounding heart. Howard looked annoyed, of course, but Steven was suddenly very awake.

It was still quite a beautiful, warm day, with some dabs of white moving between the skyscrapers. On the way home, Ice led us in song. Someone would shout out a line from a show tune and she would pick it up and do the verses while we all sang the chorus. It was fun. Even Ms. Fairchild seemed to melt some of her cold facade. I know our driver loved it because he joined in from time to time. We sang right up to the steps of the mansion.

"Be sure you are all down to set the table in time," Laura Fairchild called as we hurried up the steps and into the building.

"I'm exhausted," I admitted.

"It was easier in public school," Steven cried.

"Can't wait to hit that shower," Cinnamon said.

However, when we got upstairs, we waited until the boys disappeared into their rooms and then grabbed Rose and pulled her into her room.

"Tell us what you did," Cinnamon ordered.

"I couldn't believe how long you dared stay away," I said.

Rose smiled and sat on the edge of her bed.

"It was wonderful," she said, embracing herself and closing her eyes. Then she opened them and looked excitedly at us, her attentive small audience, far more attentive than we were in the museum.

"What was?" Cinnamon asked, impatient.

"Even after just this short time, Barry somehow looked older, more mature. And much more handsome!

"He was happy to see me. We didn't care. We kissed right in front of a crowd of people and then we snuck outside to the side entrance. We were both talking so fast, trying to get so much in, that we finally both stopped and laughed and just kissed again and again.

"He's enjoying college, has a great roommate and some great new friends. He wants to bring them around to meet y'all. I told him you were taken, Honey, so he'd only bring two. Unless you want me to tell him otherwise," she added, looking at me.

Cinnamon and Ice waited to hear my response.

"You should have agreed to see other people while you're apart, maybe," Cinnamon said when I hesitated.

"I guess that's all right, but I'm not going to fall in love with anyone else," I insisted.

"Famous last words," Cinnamon said.

"Those aren't last words," I asserted. I looked at each of them. "They're not!"

"Okay, okay. Don't get your strings in an uproar. Besides, we're being a bit optimistic here. We can't all ask to go to the bathroom and sneak away, and you can't do it again, Rose," Cinnamon warned. "I'm sure she's reporting you to Madame Senetsky as it is.

"Although," Cinnamon added with a small smile, "I think you pulled it off. I must admit, I was quite impressed with the performance."

"All the world's a stage for us now," Ice declared with exaggerated emphasis. "Remember?"

Everyone laughed.

Then we heard a ding. I think our collective hearts went on pause.

"What was that?" Ice asked in a deep whisper.

We were all quiet for a moment, listening keenly.

"Did the noise come from the fire escape?" I asked, my heart pounding so hard I could barely hear myself speak.

Cinnamon started to turn to the window to see when Rose jumped up.

"Oh," she cried. "It's my computer! I forgot I left it on. It means Evan has sent me something."

She sat at her desk and we all gathered around her as she brought up the E-mail.

Dear Rose,

I have retrieved what you wanted to know, I think. It's too weird to send over a computer or talk about on the phone. It would take a long explanation, also.

I've decided to leave the house and make the trip we talked about me eventually making. I'll just make it sooner than I had expected. It's too quiet around here to suit me these days, anyway. You can blame yourself for that. You know, how you gonna keep them down on the farm…

In other words, I'm coming to New York. Aunt Charlotte is not happy about it, of course, but I'm working on the arrangements. I'll let you know when. And don't worry about me. I can do it. Actually, this is the most exciting thing I've ever done, and don't forget, you were always lecturing me on my not getting out enough.

Of course, going to New York City is a bit like jumping from a bathtub into a pool or even ocean, but what's the good of it if it's not a challenge? Right?

As to your inquiries and some of the things happening at your school that you've described to

me…for now, I'll just use our favorite line: "Something's rotten in the state of Denmark."
I'm sure you know what I mean.

Love,
Evan

"What does that mean?" I asked.

"It's from *Hamlet,*" Cinnamon said. "It just means that there's something very wrong, something deeply troubling, some stream of horror running under the surface."

Rose nodded.

"Exactly."

"Well, why didn't he just tell you?" I asked, frustrated.

"You can see he wants to come here to see Rose very much. He's using it as a reason," Cinnamon said. "I don't think any of us can blame him, from what you told me about his life with his aunt, Rose."

"No. I hope he'll be all right though. It's not like taking a trip down to the market or mall."

"It sounds to me like he's very smart and knows what he's doing," Cinnamon said. "It also sounds like he has something that will knock our socks off."

We all stared at the screen and then looked at each other, thinking the same thing.

None of us would get a good night's sleep tonight.

Maybe not tomorrow night either.

And once Evan came and we learned what he had discovered through his computer searches, maybe not ever again, if we continued to sleep here.

7

Stepping Out

As if there was a concerted plan to challenge us or drive us to the very limits of our stamina and determination, our teachers bore down on us in the days that followed, keeping us in sessions longer, demanding we practice our various talents more, criticizing us continually. The warm, encouraging beginnings were turned into distant memories by the long hours, the constant repetition, and practical disappearance of compliments. Everyone but Howard began to wonder if we were now seen as potential failures, and this was Madame Senetsky's way of ending the struggle. Perhaps she hoped to drive us out or cause one or more of us to quit.

Cinnamon especially began to have those suspicions. She and Howard were practically hoarse every morning. They were working with Mr. Marlowe on stage now, and he was after them to project, project, project. He no sooner had them memorize one scene from one play when he handed them another and told them they were to do it without scripts the following morning. Their evenings were absorbed by their rehearsals. That and the regular voice and diction classes kept their vocal cords very busy.

Madame Senetsky began sitting in on all our sessions, pounding her cane after each criticism and complaint as if to put a dramatic period or exclamation mark at the end. She rarely smiled. All of us felt her eyes on us. They were like two pinpointed lights searching for weaknesses, mistakes, and signs of discouragement.

She lived up to her promise about the makeup artist, too. Each of us was analyzed and then redesigned, so to speak. Ice was infuriated about the cutting of her hair. Cinnamon hated her makeup, the new lipstick and nail polish that were brighter than her usual colors. Ironically, Rose thought she was being neglected because the consensus was that she should be left "natural," except for a little lipstick. Her hair was tied in either a pony tail or a bun when she danced in rehearsal. I was given some highlights, but my hair was only trimmed at the bangs. I was directed to use a different shampoo and conditioner and made to feel like an absolute country bumpkin when it came to taking care of myself.

"Stop this griping and whining! Experts are necessary to handle you when you are in the theater or on the stage," Ms. Fairchild lectured when she overheard Ice mumble a complaint. It was as if she was lingering just around corners or behind a door. She pounced on us.

"You need people not only to advise you on how you should look and dress, but publicists to handle your public appearances and relationships. It is the price you pay to be famous. The trade-off is you become a public commodity. In other words, your life isn't your own, not the same way it is for so-called everyday people."

"You mean, like you?" Cinnamon fired back at her, her eyes taking on that small, dark, darting look she often had.

"No," Ms. Fairchild said, barely skipping a beat. "I'm one of the experts Madame Senetsky depends upon when it comes to her students.

"And as one of those experts, I would advise all of you to contain your negative comments and show more appreciation. There is literally a line of candidates just chafing at the bit outside this very door. Why, the wind stirred up by your exit won't even die down before one of them takes your place."

She glared at us and left.

Despite her comments, Steven was vocal about his displeasure concerning what they asked him to do with his long hair. He could keep it long, but they wanted him to have it more styled, neater.

"I'm a pianist, not a male model. Can you imagine someone telling Beethoven how to wear his hair?"

Howard, on the other hand, acted as if he was comfortable with every suggestion, soaking up the criticism and comments like some medical patient who had turned his whole life over to a specialist.

He infuriated us all by saying, "Ms. Fairchild is right. She's not my favorite person, but what she's telling you is correct."

"Like we need to be reminded every day by her and now by you," Cinnamon retorted. "And if I hear one more time about the line of candidates just outside this door..."

"Do you doubt it?" Howard asked her.

"I'm beginning to," she said, which took him by surprise.

Soon after our makeovers, Madame Senetsky began to pop up everywhere, and not only in our classes and sessions. Just like Laura Fairchild, she seemed to lie in wait, ready to swoop down on each of us, criticizing the way we walked, held our shoulders and heads, dressed, ate, and, I began to think, even slept. It wasn't long before we were all turning somewhat paranoid.

"Every once in a while, I have this tingling at the back of my neck and turn around looking for someone," Ice revealed. "It's like someone's there, someone's always watching."

"I could swear the shadows in this house move when I move," Rose added.

I had to admit having the same feelings often.

"Maybe we really are being observed every single moment of the day," Cinnamon conjectured. "Maybe spying on us through windows is just the tip of the iceberg. Who knows? Our phones might be tapped. There might even be cameras secretly placed in our rooms."

"Then I'm glad Evan didn't tell me anything over the phone," Rose said.

He had informed her that he was coming in ten days, which would be in time for what we learned was to be our first Performance Night. For this, Madame Senetsky relented and, through Laura Fairchild, informed us we could each invite two guests. Naturally, it was expected we would invite our own parents, if possible, but friends were permitted.

My mother and father wanted to come, but Daddy was pressured with the fall harvest. I called Chandler, and he said he would try to be there. He had a friend at Columbia University who could arrange for him to stay at his place. Cinnamon was trying to get her parents to come, but her father had to have some adjustments made on his pacemaker and would be in the hospital and under observation that weekend. Her mother wasn't sure she would come without him.

Rose revealed that her mother was coming into New York this week specifically to have lunch with her. She worked up the courage to go to Madame Senetsky to ask for the day off, and Madame Senetsky approved of the schedule changes so Rose could meet and spend time with her mother.

Ice was quiet about her parents. Whenever we asked her, she said, "I'm not sure yet."

Then, on Wednesday, she joined Cinnamon and me in Rose's room and told us her parents were getting a divorce.

"I told you how my daddy had been shot on his security job and how long his recuperation has been. Mama's lost patience with him and, I just found out, she has moved out of the house."

"Is he all right by himself?" I asked.

"He's fine, but still not a hundred percent, he says.

He wanted to come himself, but I told him to wait until the next Performance Night."

"What about your mother?"

"She's busy with her new social life. She said she would try, but I'm not holding my breath, and I'm not exactly sure how I would treat her if she did come."

Everyone was quiet, the depression as heavy as bad humidity, and then Rose looked up and said, "Maybe the theater will become our new life, and everyone in it our new family. Maybe Madame Senetsky isn't wrong about any of it."

No one disagreed, but it was apparent from the looks on all our faces that no one was completely happy about what that meant. Sure, we could get close to other members of casts, directors, other musicians and even producers, but after the performances ended, they were all gone and we were alone again. The stage would become an empty place and our voices would just echo inside us. All of us were well aware that too many people in our line of work ended up on psychiatrists' couches, looking for answers. Who wanted to spend a lifetime having no one to confide in but psychotherapists?

Rehearsals were now stepped up in preparation for the Performance Night. Ms. Fairchild began dropping the names of people who had been invited and would attend. Most were, as we were promised, people from the theater, producers and actors, as well as some critics. Every dinner began with the announcement of another acceptance. I think it was designed to build the pressure on us.

Madame Senetsky was not subtle about that. One night at dinner she lectured us about how important it was for a performer to learn to deal with anticipation and with the pressure that came from an impending appearance.

"Even the most seasoned actors and musicians experience stage fright, butterflies, shattered nerves before stepping on stage. One never gets blasé about the fact that hundreds of people, even thousands, and with television, millions are looking at you and only you at times, watching, listening, noticing mistakes. People are just naturally critical. It takes so much to please them, and even when you have a major success, there are those who detract from it, who find fault, who can never be satisfied. You know that, and yet you go and expose your talents and your efforts under the spotlight.

"It takes courage, fortitude, and a great deal of self-confidence. There is quite a difference between self-confidence and arrogance, however. Arrogance will always get you into trouble. Self-confidence will insulate you against the slings and arrows."

"Hamlet," Howard whispered to us, in case we didn't get the "slings and arrows" reference.

Contrary to its purpose, Madame Senetsky's lectures served to make me, at least, more nervous than I had been before she pointed all these things out. She was so eager to do it, I thought it was exactly the result she was looking to achieve. As our big night drew closer and closer, I found myself developing a trembling in my hands. Mr. Bergman noticed it as well and had been making me pause, take breaths, and start again in our rehearsals.

Finally, one day, with Madame Senetsky sitting and

watching me work, he slammed his palm down on the piano and cried, "Stop!"

I held my breath as he paced.

"Sit," he ordered, and I did, holding my violin in my lap and glancing furtively at Madame Senetsky, who herself sat like some alabaster statue, her eyes frozen on the space between me and Mr. Bergman.

"You're thinking too much," he began. "You are not separating yourself from the performance. You're worrying over every note and making it all sound mechanical. You are no longer submerged in the music, which was the well from which your talent has drawn its strength, its life's blood."

I glanced at Madame Senetsky, who nodded slightly, but continued to stare.

Mr. Bergman looked at me hard, too.

"Follow me," he suddenly decided and marched to the door, where he turned and waited. I was so confused that for a moment I just sat there. "Well, get up and bring your violin and your violin case along," he commanded.

I looked at Madame Senetsky and then rose and followed Mr. Bergman out the door. He led me down the corridor to the front door and held it open.

"What are we doing?" I asked.

"Getting rid of pretension," he declared. "Go on. Walk out."

I did and he followed, closing the door behind us. He walked down the steps and started down the driveway. Now, more confused than ever, I walked behind him, carrying my violin in its case and looking back occasionally at the house. He had me go all the way to the gate and then stopped and opened it. He stepped out onto the sidewalk and folded his arms over his chest.

"Come along," he directed. "Out here!."

I did as he asked. Pedestrians along the sidewalk and across the way gazed at us.

"Take out your violin," he said.

"What?"

"Take it out of its case. Now."

I did so.

He placed the case open at my feet and stepped back.

"Begin your piece," he commanded.

"Here?"

"Exactly," he said. "Play."

I lifted the violin and began. The music carried over the street. People who had paused gathered in a small crowd, and others began to join them. The air was cool, crisp, with just a slight breeze that seemed to lift my melody higher and higher. Before long, there was a sizeable crowd collected. I closed my eyes and I let the music carry me off as well. When I finished the piece, the people in the street all applauded, most throwing coins and dollars into my open case.

I looked at Mr. Bergman.

"There," he said. "You've played for an audience in New York. It's out of your system. Now think only of the music, and if you develop that trembling again, come down here and play again on the sidewalk, if you like, but get yourself out of that box that is suffocating you. Understand?"

"Yes," I said. "Thank you."

"Very well. We'll return to our studio," he said, and

we headed back to the house. I saw a curtain move in a window on the third floor and imagined Madame Senetsky had been watching the whole time, but when we returned to the studio, I saw her in her posh office making phone calls.

Later, I told everyone what Mr. Bergman had done.

"I actually made seven dollars!"

Steven said he would have a hard time wheeling the piano down and then up the driveway, otherwise he would do it, too.

"You don't have her problem," Howard told him. "You have the opposite problem."

"Oh, yeah, and what's my problem, oh mighty master of the stage?"

"You could care less about the audience."

Howard meant it as a criticism, but Steven thought a moment and then nodded.

"You're right," he admitted. "It's me and my piano and everyone else can go to hell."

"Whatever works for you, works for you. It doesn't necessarily work for the rest of us," Rose told him in a very angry tone of voice, which was so out of character for her it raised everyone's eyebrows.

Actually, Rose had been unusually quiet since she had met her mother for lunch. She didn't tell us much about it until early Friday evening. Ms. Fairchild, as usual, dictated our weekend schedule to us at dinner. At eight o'clock we were going to attend a lecture on the theater that was being given at the New York Public Library. On Saturday we would go to a matinee of a play that had just been brought over from London, and Saturday night we would attend a performance of *Madama Butterfly* at the Metropolitan Opera. Sunday was finally free.

Rose had made arrangements to meet her boyfriend Barry. Since Chandler was coming the following weekend, I couldn't ask him to come Sunday. Rose proposed that Barry bring along three of his new college buddies. Cinnamon thought it might be a good idea. She suggested we all go to the zoo in Central Park.

"It's supposed to be a very nice late fall day. What do you think, Rose?" she asked.

"Why not?" Rose replied. "We're all in our little cages. We might as well look at some fellow sufferers."

Her bitterness and depression was finally too much.

"What's wrong with you, girl?" Ice snapped. "You been saying ugly things ever since you met your mama."

Rose just stared at the floor.

"Well?" Ice pursued.

We were all in my room, relaxing before we dressed for the lecture.

"My mother is getting remarried," Rose revealed. "She's fallen head over heels in love with a man five years younger than she is. He's a salesman working for a company out of California. He sells air time on radio and independent television stations."

"Did you meet him, too?" Cinnamon asked.

"No and yes."

"Huh?" Ice said. "How can it be no and yes? Either you did or didn't, right?"

"He wasn't actually there with us at lunch, but I felt like I met him. That's all my mother talked about. She hardly asked a question about me and what we're doing here. She's like some teenager, I'm telling you."

"When is she getting married?" I asked.

"She wants to get married next week, but his travel schedule makes it difficult, so they're getting married as soon as he has the time. She said it would just be one of those justice of the peace ceremonies. They might even do it in Las Vegas," she said. "Maybe they'll get an Elvis impersonator as a witness," she added bitterly.

"And then what? She moves to California?" Cinnamon asked.

Rose nodded.

"Is she coming to the Performance Night?" I asked.

"Maybe. It depends on his schedule, but I kind of got the idea she wouldn't."

"What's his name?" Ice asked.

"Warner Langley. He was married once before, but it lasted only a month."

"That's more like a long date, not a marriage," Cinnamon said.

"This might be as well," Rose muttered. "Sorry I've been such a drag around y'all."

"What's it been like in dance class?" I asked, thinking about my own session with Mr. Bergman.

"Not bad," Rose said, perking up. "When I'm into a routine, doing exercises, moving to the music, I forget everything else. Mr. Demetrius said that even when I'm dancing to the same melody, I have a natural tendency to vary it just a little, almost making it more beautiful, more touching. He really cheered me up."

"He's right, of course. That's why you're so good,

Rose," Cinnamon said. "That's why you're going to make it, despite all the rest."

"Then maybe she is right," Ice said. We all turned to her.

"Who?" I asked.

"Madame Senetsky. Maybe she's right. We should become like nuns and marry ourselves to the stage."

Cinnamon nodded slowly.

"It's a way to escape," she said.

"From what?" I asked.

"Who we really are," she replied.

"I don't want to escape from that," I said.

"There's nothing about your family, your past, yourself that deep inside you hate?" Rose asked, her eyes forbidding.

I thought about Grandad Forman and his ruthless religious fervor that made me feel guilty about all my loving feelings, tying me as tight as a drum inside, making me feel as if a simple kiss, a trembling in my breast was all leading to some enormous sin. It nearly kept me from winning Chandler's affections. Even now, even after all the promises and wonderful things we had said to each other, there was still some of that inside me, and I always feared it would keep me from giving myself truly and wholly to anyone who loved and gave himself to me. I used to think it was like a stain on my heart, corrupting my emotions.

"Maybe," I confessed.

"We all want to escape from something," Cinnamon insisted. "One day you'll realize exactly what it is and you'll be happy you've been given a way to do it. You can't change your mother or stop her from making another mistake, Rose, and neither can you, Ice. Let's all stop trying to change our pasts. Let's just change our futures."

Rose nodded and then smiled.

"What about Sunday? What should I tell Barry?"

Cinnamon looked to me.

"Honey?"

"I don't care. I'm not getting married Sunday," I said. I put on a brave face, but my heart was pounding. If Chandler found out, he might not come the following weekend.

"Good," Cinnamon said. "Let's have a good time. Forever and ever," she added, "let's have good times. A vow, come on," she said, holding out her hand. Then she closed her eyes and recited, "Be gone, all unhappiness. Come, sweet lips of pleasure, Kiss us all, every one."

Ice smiled and put her other hand over Cinnamon's. So did Rose, and then so did I. We held onto each other and for a long, wonderful moment, it seemed very possible, very much within our grasp, to do what she prayed for: to enjoy life.

The lecture that night at the library was very interesting. We were surprised by the special guest, who turned out to be one of Broadway's most famous producers. He had wonderful stories about productions, stars, critics, and people like ourselves on the verge of attempting to break into the world of entertainment. On the way home in the van, Howard picked up where the producer's talk had ended as if he had already known it all and had the experiences to confirm the lessons we were given.

"I'm surprised you even bother to come to this school, Howard," Cinnamon said with feigned softness, dressing her face in a small, gentle smile.

"Why?"

"Why? Because you know everything there is to know about the theater. It must be terribly boring for you being around people like us."

There was a heavy silence for a moment.

"Well," Howard said, incredibly or deliberately missing her sarcasm, "you must be willing to be generous on the stage, especially when you're performing with others and your rhythm is so dependent on someone else being on cue, in sync, so to speak.

"The truth is, Cinnamon, the better you are, the better I'm going to look, especially next weekend," he replied, so satisfied in his response, he looked absolutely invulnerable, like some prince sitting on a throne miles above his peasant followers.

"Oh, I'm so happy I will be able to help you win the Academy Award, Howard."

"Go on, laugh, but in your heart of hearts, you want that Oscar in your hands almost as much as I do. You can pretend to be unaffected and uncaring about the glory, but in your heart, you're just as ruthless."

"Don't tell me what's in my heart, who I am and what I want, Howard Rockwell the Third, Fourth, and Fifth. You don't know anything about me. Anything. Understand? Well?"

"Very well," he finally replied.

Cinnamon had looked ready to leap over her seat and claw out his eyes if he didn't respond. How were these two able to get on stage and perform their dialogues from *Romeo and Juliet?* I wondered. They must be great actors if they can convince an audience they are in love.

Later, I asked Cinnamon about it. She said she used the advice her high school drama coach, Miss Hamilton, gave her.

"Pretend the other person is someone you really like, if you have to like his character on the stage, or someone you really hate, if that's the character. You fill your mind with those people and not the actual actor."

"That seems like good advice."

"It works. I can tell you I wouldn't be here if it wasn't for Miss Hamilton," she added. "Getting me on stage practically saved my life.

"And," she added, "nearly ruined hers."

"Why?"

She told me how she and Miss Hamilton spent some time alone together rehearsing, and how a jealous student spread ugly rumors about them that almost cost Miss Hamilton her job.

"Someone took a picture of us through a window while we were rehearsing and she was pretending to be the male lead."

"How mean!"

"Don't believe all the glorious things we're told about the stage and performing. Howard makes it sound like a new version of heaven, but just like the real world, it has its sharks swimming at your feet," she advised.

Listening to Cinnamon, and to Ice, especially, I often wondered if my isolated life on the corn farm in Ohio was really a blessing after all. It was all right to be like I am if I would never leave the farm, I thought, but if I was going to be in The World, as Steven liked to refer to what was going on just outside our gates here, I needed to be more cautious, more distrusting, more aware of the demons.

"Innocence," Cinnamon once quipped, "was only an asset in the Garden of Eden, and there's no chance we're getting back into that."

The play we saw Saturday afternoon was wonderful and later that evening *Madama Butterfly* tore my heartstrings. I never thought I would cry at an opera, of all things. The aria "Un Bel Di," "One Fine Day," was planted forever and ever in my mind. I heard it in my sleep and couldn't wait to play it on my violin.

We girls were in a good mood Sunday at breakfast. Howard and Steven realized we were going off to meet some boys. They threatened to follow until Cinnamon made it a point of pride for Howard.

"You can't find yourselves girls? You've got to depend on us?"

"I was just joking," Howard quickly replied. "I happen to have a friend who's already fixed me up with someone for dinner and a movie."

"I thought *we* were going to dinner and a movie," Steven complained.

"That was before I received this phone call," Howard said. He was a good actor, but not so good a liar. At least, that was what I thought.

When it was time to go, Cinnamon—living the closest to New York—became our titular travel guide. She hailed our cab at the corner and rattled off some of the places we passed.

"I haven't even walked on Fifth Avenue yet," Ice complained.

"We'll do it after we go to the zoo," Cinnamon promised her. "Window shopping is fun."

The taxi driver, at Rose's request, stopped in front of the world-famous Plaza Hotel. It was there we were supposed to meet Barry and his three college buddies. Less than a minute went by before another cab pulled up to the curb and they got out. Rose ran to Barry and they hugged. The three of us watched, all of us smiling softly as they kissed.

"Let's all get introduced," Barry declared, realizing everyone was standing around watching him and Rose. He was a tall, dark-haired boy, easily six foot one and very good-looking, with a real mature air about him. I could see why Rose was so fond of him. He was someone upon whom she could lean, someone she really needed. But equally obvious to me was his devotion to her. He seemed unable to turn his eyes from her, to stop holding her hand, to move another inch away. Chandler and I were like that, I thought.

With Barry were Larry Martin, Reuben Kotein, and Tony Gibson. Larry was taller than Barry and very lean. We quickly learned he was a star on the basketball team and had been nicknamed Hoop when he was only twelve. He lumbered along when he walked, and seemed incapable of passing a garbage basket without rolling up something and tossing it in. He came from Jersey City, where he had been a basketball star in his high school. He seemed awkward and shy around girls, and maybe for that reason gravitated toward Ice, who still had a very quiet way about her. It was easy to see how he was trying to impress her from time to time with a leap or a turn to throw something into a basket.

Reuben Kotein wasn't much taller than Cinnamon. He was a dark complected boy with very deep hazel eyes, a wide forehead, short brown hair, and a firm, athletic build. Of the three, he was the most introspective, and because of the way his forehead went into small folds, looked like he was thinking something profound all the time. His slightly sarcastic tone immediately attracted Cinnamon, and before long they were sharing comments and reviews about people they saw on the street. Reuben created a game for them: guessing about people, their pasts, their personalities, from the way they walked and were dressed. Then they turned it into deciding what animal each person would be if they were changed into one.

Tony Gibson was by far the handsomest of the group. He was as good-looking as Howard, but without Howard's arrogant eyes and demeanor, which to me made his attractiveness a waste. The girl Howard eventually chose had to be willing not only to love him, but worship him.

Tony's personality was light, carefree, and so unassuming, it was as though he had no idea how good-looking he was or cared. It was easy to be relaxed with him, even for someone like me who kept thinking about her boyfriend and how this simple little walk in the park was somehow a betrayal.

He came from Rhode Island, where he said he did a lot of sailing, which explained his deep tan, a shade that emphasized his cerulean eyes and sparkling white teeth. He told me the sea was in his blood, even to the point where he wanted a career in maritime law.

"Girls I've kissed," he said, "tell me I have the saltiest lips."

He smiled coyly, and I heard a small alarm go off inside me. First, it was warning me how attracted I was to him, but then it was also suggesting his carefree, almost aloof approach was possibly a good act or technique. There were surprises, not only in what he said and how his soft eyes often turned deeper and more intense when he looked into mine, but by the way he suddenly managed to find my hand or touch my shoulder to take me away from the others, ostensibly to see something he had just discovered.

"I understand you play the violin," he said. "Really well, too."

"I hope I'm good. I'm working hard at it."

"I bet you are good. I hope to hear you play someday."

"I hope so, too," I said, but I meant in a place like Carnegie Hall.

He smiled as if I had agreed to go to bed with him.

"Have you ever been on a sail boat?" he asked.

"No."

"I can take you sailing sometime. A friend of my father's has a boat docked at the seaport. What about next weekend?" he followed so quickly, he nearly took away my breath.

"I can't," I said. "That's our big weekend at the school. We have family and friends coming to the Performance Night."

"Oh. Well, we'll try for another date," he said. "I'll call you, if that's okay."

"Let's catch up with the others," I told him instead of committing and walked quickly toward them.

We had a lot of fun with the monkeys, fed the ducks, and then found a restaurant near Lincoln Center and had pizza. The truth was I had never been out with a group like this, everyone so carefree and exuberant. The magnificent fall day with a nearly cloudless blue sky kept our faces bright with smiles. Here I was, sitting just across the street from the world-famous theater in what everyone agreed was the most exciting city in the world. All of our dreams and ambitions did seem within our grasp. Depression and defeat were things of the past.

The energy that came from our laughter and conversation made me feel drunk on life itself. We would all become stars. Maybe someday we'd all share an apartment in New York and have elegant clothes and go to sophisticated restaurants. Our pictures would be taken frequently. People would hover about us, clamoring for our autographs. The day was going so well, I no longer felt nervous and constantly on guard.

Then Barry and Rose revealed they were heading back to his fraternity house. Ice, who wanted to walk Fifth Avenue, was going there with Larry, and Cinnamon and Reuben had decided to go to the YMCA to hear a poet they both were familiar with who was doing a reading.

"What do you want to do, Honey?" Rose asked me.

"I think I'll head back to the school," I said.

"That sounds so boring. You can come along with us if you like," she suggested, obviously hoping I would refuse.

"No, I'm fine," I said.

"We can walk," Tony suggested. "It's a great day for it, and it's not really all that far."

"Oh, I thought I would just take a cab."

"That wouldn't be nice of me, letting you do that. At least let me be a nice guy," he prodded.

The others looked at me. They knew what made me hesitant, but they also looked like they thought I was being foolish.

"You're not getting married," Cinnamon reminded me in a whisper.

I took a deep breath and nodded.

"Okay. It is too nice to take another cab."

"You'd only go right to practicing, anyway," Rose said. "We know you, Honey."

"We know ourselves," Ice said. "That's what we would all be doing."

There was confession and then laughter. The boys paid our bill and everyone went his and her separate way, no one apparently as nervous about it as was I.

"Is this the fastest way?" I asked Tony almost immediately.

"Sure, but do you really want to get back so

quickly? It's such a nice day and New York is a great city for walking. From what I understand, you girls work pretty hard all week and even have obligations on the weekends. You don't get much free time, right?"

"No, but we're not here for that."

"Everyone's here for some of that," Tony insisted, grinning at me with teasing devilry. Then he grew serious and added, "It's hard enough being at a big college with lots of girls in the same situation as you are, but to go to such a small school and have so few friends, especially in New York City, must be difficult, huh?"

"No," I said. "I'm too busy to worry about any of that," I insisted, half to convince myself as well as him.

"You sound so dedicated."

"I am. You have to be if you want to do what we're setting out to do."

"That really applies to everything, Honey. I'm going to have to work hard, too," he said.

"I didn't mean to make what you're doing sound inferior. I meant..."

"I know," he said, laughing. "I thought if I made you feel guilty, you'd be nicer to me."

"I'm being nice to you."

"Sure. Rushing to get away from me is being nice to me," he said. "Am I that distasteful to be with?"

"I didn't say you were. I..."

Should I tell him about Chandler now? I wondered. Would he think I was making it up? Why did I agree to this afternoon date if I was going so hot and heavy with someone else, he would surely wonder.

"I'm sorry," I said. "I'm just very nervous."

"Me, too," he said, laughing.

I looked at him skeptically.

"I am!" he insisted. "I don't know why girls assume every boy in the world is a Don Juan full of experience. The truth is, I've been serious with a girl only once in my life, and if you have to know, she dumped me! She cheated on me and then she rubbed it in my face.

"She dumped the guy she had dumped me for shortly afterward," he said with disgust. "I've been extra careful about the girls I date ever since. Sorry for the speech," he ended and walked along, his head down.

I felt terrible and caught up to him.

"I'm not really in any hurry to get back," I said. "You're right. We should all learn how to relax, too."

He looked at me and then he smiled.

"Good. I've got an apartment that overlooks the East River," he said. "Actually, it's not my apartment. It's my uncle's, but he's in Europe until February, so I've got it to myself for a while. Hey," he said, suddenly stopping, his face full of excitement, "you're into music, right? You've got to hear this stereo system. It's built into the walls with Surround Sound and everything. When you're sitting there listening, you can close your eyes and feel like you're at a live performance in Carnegie Hall or the Met or someplace like that.

"Who's your favorite composer?" he demanded before I could comment one way or another on his invitation. "Come on. Who?"

"Well, I enjoy playing Mozart."

"Great, perfect," he said, slapping his hands together. "He has all the Mozart albums. Come on. Now I do want to walk faster."

"But..."

He pulled my hand and we crossed a street against traffic. The horns blared.

"Don't worry," he said, "it's New York. Everyone jaywalks!"

I ran along with him, caught up in some whirlwind, my conscience trailing far behind like some loyal but exhausted puppy, losing me.

Maybe forever.

8

A Shocking Discovery

"Are we close to my school?" I asked when we rounded a corner and headed toward an apartment building. Despite our pace, we had been walking for quite a while.

"Oh, sure. It's only about a dozen blocks south of here. No problem," Tony assured me.

We stopped before a tall building just at the corner. It had a gray brick front and a faded burgundy awning over the entrance.

"This is it," Tony said. "Wait until you see the view. It's on the fifteenth floor," he said, and we entered the small lobby.

There was nothing much to it, some mail boxes on the right and a bench just under them with packages that were delivered for the tenants. I thought the elevator was very small, too, and it looked old and worn, so much so that I became anxious when the doors closed and he pushed the button for fifteen. I didn't want to say, but I had never been higher than the third floor in any building. I heard the metal cables grinding and groaning above us as if we were close to the maximum load or something.

"From one of the windows you can see the cable car that takes people to Roosevelt Island," he said.

I smiled and nodded as if I knew what he was talking about, but by now I was so nervous, I wished I had simply gone straight back to the school.

The elevator opened on a narrow hallway with pale yellow walls. I noticed scuff marks along the sides near the chipped and broken molding. The hallway floor was covered in a grayish brown rug that was very worn and dull. From some apartment came the heavy aroma of a pot roast cooking. Was that the way it was in New York apartments? Everyone knew what you were having for dinner? Why was he so excited about living here? I wondered.

We stopped at a door and he dug his hand into his pocket to produce the keys that opened three door locks. I laughed to myself, thinking how we never locked our door back in Ohio.

"Voilà," he said, stepping aside after he had opened the door.

I walked in slowly. There was no real entryway. The doorway opened on the small kitchen. Mama would laugh at it, I thought. Our pantry was bigger. The appliances looked old and the walls were almost as faded as the hallway walls.

"In here," he guided, taking my elbow and turning me into the living room.

It, too, was rather small, with one oversized dark brown sofa, two matching chairs, and a glass coffee table. There was a scratched and dull hardwood floor with one oval area rug that looked like it needed a good shaking out. On the far side of the room was a sliding glass door that opened to a balcony just big enough for two people if they stood side by side, and close to each other at that. A curved black iron grating was set in the balcony walls. It curved inward with arrow heads as if to discourage anyone from leaning over too far.

The walls of the living room were papered in a vanilla ice cream shade. There were two large framed prints on opposite walls, both rather uninteresting pictures of city scenes, put up for their color coordination more than for their artistic merit, I thought. Even the frames were drab. The room itself was quite messy: some dirty dishes with remnants of sandwiches, dirty glasses with the soda now flat and oily-looking like some stagnant pool, dirty silverware, a few empty cans of beer lying on their sides, another on the floor by a table holding a pizza box. Magazines and books were strewn over the sofa and one of the chairs and on the floor beside a pile of notebooks.

"Looks like a boys' dorm, I know," Tony said, and started to clean up. "I had a few of the guys over two nights ago for a study session."

"Two nights ago?"

"Well..." He smiled. "I was never one for housework. Take a look at the view," he urged, and I went to the sliding doors. He rushed ahead to open them for me. "Go on, step out. It's safe," he promised.

I was grateful for the fresh air. While I stood on the

balcony, he scooped up the dishes and cans. I heard him knocking about in the kitchen, throwing things into a garbage can and putting dishes into the sink. The view was impressive, although not enough to get me to want to live here, I thought. Some cargo boats were moving up the river, and I could see the line of traffic on what I knew was the East River Drive. It seemed so long ago when Mommy and Daddy and I drove on it.

"From the window in the bedroom, you can see that cable car I described," he said, coming up behind me. "This is why people pay the high rents."

"High rents? This is expensive?"

He laughed.

"An apartment in this neighborhood with these views? Thousands and thousands."

I shook my head in disbelief. If Uncle Simon stood out here, he would grimace with such distaste and disgust, the owner of the apartment would think about moving out that day. You had to look hard to see any real greenery. Even up on this floor the traffic noise was considerable—horns sounding, brakes squealing. Suddenly, my heart had such a longing to be back on the farm, to look out over our seemingly endless fields, to feel the warm, fresh breeze and smell the flowers, to simply dig my hand into the soft, warm and moist earth.

"Pretty nice, huh?" he asked.

I smiled at him.

"I guess I'm too much of a country girl, Tony. It's nice, but not what I would like."

He held his smile, but I saw the warm excitement go

out of his eyes like a snuffed candle. Did he really think I'd be so impressed?

"Sure, I understand. Frankly, I like being on the open sea the most. There's nothing like sailing, like feeling the wind in your hair, the sea spray on your face and looking out at the never-ending horizon. You feel…free," he said.

That did bring a deeper smile to my face. That I could understand.

"It sounds wonderful."

"I gotta get you out there, Honey. You'd hear music you've never heard before, and all of it composed by Mother Nature herself, with terns as the chorus."

I guess my eyes brightened, and that encouraged him enough for him to take the liberty of bringing his lips to mine before I could even prepare for a kiss. It wasn't a long kiss, just a smack on my mouth, more like a firecracker.

"Sorry, but I had to do that," he said. "You look so fresh. Hope you're not mad."

He turned before I could reply and headed for a cabinet. When he opened it, I saw the audio equipment. It looked elaborate, sophisticated, and technical. He pushed some buttons and lights began blinking. Then he opened a drawer and began sifting through a thick pile of CDs.

"I know I've seen a whole section on classical music…"

I walked in and stood behind him, waiting, wondering why I didn't get upset with his impulsive kiss. Was I giving him the wrong idea by not being angry? Should I just say I was leaving? How can someone kiss you and behave as though it was nothing more than a handshake? What would Cinnamon do? Ice? Even Rose? Was I suffering through this moment of confusion because I had such little experience with boys?

"Here they are," he declared and held one up. "A collection of Mozart. I knew it."

He held up what I recognized as the sound track of *Amadeus,* the movie about Mozart.

He slipped it into the CD player and pressed some buttons.

"Sit right here," he said steering me to the center of the sofa. "The speakers are all around you. Just close your eyes and listen while I get us something to drink."

It did sound very good, but it was nothing like being at a live performance. Perhaps he really had never been to one, I thought. I tried to be polite about it. He seemed so excited and wanted so much to please me, how could I be otherwise?

"Great, huh?"

"Very nice," I said. "Yes."

"Told you so," he said, returning. He had two glasses with what looked like tomato juice in them. "Try this," he said. "I'm getting very good at it."

"Good at it? What is it?" I said, taking the glass from him and smelling the drink.

"They're called Bloody Marys. Ever have one?"

I shook my head.

"Go on, try it. Tell me how it tastes."

I took a sip and immediately choked as the spice brought tears to my eyes. He laughed.

"That good, huh?"

"What's in it?"

"Oh, a little of this, a little of that, and some vodka," he replied.

"Vodka?" I shook my head and started to hand it back to him.

"Oh, go on," he urged. "It won't hurt you. It'll help you relax, chill out," he promised and sat beside me. "What a sound, huh?" he said, nodding at the audio system.

"Have you ever been to a concert?" I asked him.

"Oh sure, lots. My parents have these subscriptions and I go with them from time to time."

"What have you heard?"

"Oh, just about everything. You name it. Drink your drink," he urged. "It grows on you. You'll see."

He practically lifted my glass to my lips for me.

I took another sip. He sat back and closed his eyes.

"What a sound, huh? I could sit here all night and just listen. I hardly watch any television anymore. I'm becoming a real fan of good music, the kind of music you play, I'm sure," he said. "Maybe I should come to your Performance Night, too."

"No," I said quickly. "You can't. We're just permitted two guests each."

"I'll sneak in," he threatened.

"No, don't."

He laughed.

"You know you're about the cutest girl I've ever met. There's something very fresh and honest about you. Where did you say you came from again?"

"I'm from Ohio."

"What do your parents do?"

"They own a corn farm."

How did he forget what I had told him before? Wasn't he listening to me? He certainly made it seem as if he had been hanging on my every word, every syllable!

"Farmer's daughter, of course!" he cried. He tapped his glass to mine. "Here's to the corn on the cob." He started to drink, and then paused when I didn't lift my glass. "Don't you want to drink to that?"

I took another sip.

"You've got some great girlfriends there, Honey. I bet you all have some good times when you party, huh? Especially that Ice. She looks like she could be the life of a party. I know how those quiet ones can be."

"She's not that way and we don't party," I said.

He smiled skeptically.

"We don't," I insisted. "We barely have any time off. This Sunday afternoon is the first since we all started because part of our curriculum is attending shows, concerts, lectures on the weekends," I explained. "I thought you said you knew all about that."

"I did, but I didn't really believe it. That *is* dedication. Which means," he decided, "that you've earned a good time then. Drink up," he urged and tapped my glass again. Hesitantly, I took another sip. "Amazing how it grows on you, huh? I like a drink that comes through the back door, tiptoeing up your spine," he said, trying to make his voice mysterious and running his fingers up my back as if they were the legs of some spider. I jumped, and he laughed. It was a strange laugh. Something about it made me very anxious.

"You're ticklish, huh? That's good. Ticklish girls are

a lot more sensuous. I read that. And," he said winking, "I can tell you it's true."

He was acting now like the Don Juan he claimed he wasn't. What happened to all that innocence, that love pain?

He started to move closer.

"I think I better get going," I said.

"Why? You said you weren't in any rush to get back. Your girlfriends aren't going to be there. They're all having some fun. It's not against the rules for you to have some fun, too, is it?"

"I don't really like this drink," I said, putting the glass on the table. "I'm sorry. It's just not for me, I guess."

"Not for you? What do you drink on the farm, homemade corn whiskey?"

"No. I don't drink whiskey," I said. I didn't like the ridicule in his voice.

"It's just a little vodka, for God's sake. What's the big deal?"

"It's not what I like," I said. "That's the big deal," I added and started to stand.

"Take it easy," he said, pulling me back. "I'm just trying to get to know you better, Honey."

"I don't have to drink vodka to get to know someone," I said.

He stared at me, his eyes suddenly so dark, a stream of pure anger running through them. It put a cold finger on my heart, and I looked longingly now at the door.

"I've got to find my way back," I said softly.

"It's no problem. I'll call you a cab and it will come right to the front of the building. You'll be back in ten minutes, believe me," he said, putting his glass down and moving closer to me.

His arm slipped behind me and his hand popped up like a snake in the grass. His fingers closed tightly on my shoulder and he turned me toward him so he could plant his lips on mine, this time pushing his tongue into my mouth and moving his left hand up the side of my body and over my breast.

I put my hands against his chest and pushed him away.

"Hey!" he cried. "Don't be so unfriendly."

"I don't want to do this."

"Then why did you come up here?"

"To listen to the music," I said. "To see the view you talked about so much."

"Sure."

"Well, that's what you asked me to do, isn't it?"

He tilted his head and smiled.

"What are you, a tease? Is that what they teach you on the farm?"

I started to stand and he reached up, grabbed my arm, and pulled me down roughly.

"Stop it!" I cried, but he was over me, his mouth on my face, down my neck, his fingers fumbling with the zipper on my jeans. I squirmed and pushed and even pounded his shoulder with my fist, but he kept his weight over me. "Tony, stop!" I screamed. "You're hurting me."

His hands went under my blouse and over my bra, the thumbs lifting it roughly away from my breasts so he could strum my nipples. I reached out, seized the glass containing the Bloody Mary, and splashed it into his face. He fell back, cursing, and I jumped up.

"Damn it!" he cried, rubbing at his eyes. "That burns."

"It serves you right," I said. "You tricked me into coming up here. You had no intention of just listening to music."

I hurried to the door. At first, I thought I was locked in until I realized how to open the second lock. He was up and calling to me, but I hurried out and into the hallway, slamming the door behind me.

"Hey, you come back, you tease," he screamed through the closed door and then opened it to follow.

"Stay away from me," I shouted and stopped at the elevator. He was coming down the hallway, still rubbing his eyes.

"Come on back. I was just fooling around. We'll just listen to the music, if you want. Come on."

"No," I said. "Thank you, but I want to go."

The door opened and I stepped in, only he did, too.

"Leave me alone, Tony, or I'll go to the police," I threatened.

"And tell them what? You came up to my apartment to listen to music?" He laughed and moved toward me. "If you just relax, you'll see you can have some fun. Come on," he urged. "I'll forgive you if you'll forgive me."

He put his hands on my shoulders and squeezed his fingers like pincers as he brought his lips toward mine again. Instinctively, I brought my right knee up into his groin sharply, getting him where I knew it would hurt him the most. He cried out and crumpled to his knees just as the elevator door opened.

An elderly lady stood there with a bag of groceries in her hand, gazing in at us with a look of such shock on her face, I thought she might faint or have a heart attack. I stepped past him quickly as he rose by grabbing the railing and pulling himself up the side wall of the elevator.

"What's going on here?" the elderly lady asked me.

"Ask him," I said and hurried out of the lobby. I rushed down the sidewalk, walking as quickly as I could. I looked back once when I crossed a street. Thankfully, he wasn't coming after me. I walked faster, nevertheless, choking back the tears that rushed to my eyes.

People seemed to be looking at me everywhere, I guess because I was practically running and I did still have a frantic expression on my face. *They must think I'm out of my mind,* I thought. I was searching for someone I could ask for directions, but every time I turned toward someone, he or she looked absolutely terrified of me. One woman I called to actually broke into a fast walk to get away, and all I had done was pause to get her to help me.

Finally, I saw a police car and hurried to it. I knocked on the side window and the patrolman rolled it down.

"Yes?"

"I'm lost," I said, and told them where I was trying to go.

"You're not very lost," he said with a soft smile. "Take it easy. All you have to do is go over one block west and then go two more south, okay? Your street will be on the right. You're fine, Miss."

"Thank you," I said and followed his directions. When the Senetsky School came into view, I felt all the tension and panic leave my body. I never thought I would look upon it with such relief. We had all been given keys to the pedestrian gate. I hurried through and up the walkway to the front entrance, not stopping for a breath until I was practically at the door itself. Then I paused, looked back once, and entered.

Fortunately, no one was there to see how I looked. I would hate to have to explain it. My hair looked like a pack of field mice had been chasing each other in it for hours. My lipstick was smeared over my cheek. My blouse was out of my jeans and my face was so flushed, someone would think I had gotten a terrible sunburn. The first thing I did was strip and take a hot shower to calm myself.

When I stepped out and wrapped the towel around myself, I felt a great deal better. *I only hope Cinnamon and Ice don't have similar experiences,* I thought. Rose was going to be so surprised to hear about this, and I hoped her boyfriend Barry would be angry. I was still quite infuriated.

Wiping my hair with another towel, I stepped out of the bathroom. My heart dropped and came up like a yo-yo in my chest. There was no doubt in my mind. Someone had just been in my room. The window was still slightly open and all the clothes I had just worn—my jeans, my blouse, even my panties and bra—were gone.

They were gone!

Pounding like the fist of someone locked in a room, my heart thumped under my breast and took my breath away. Slowly, with my legs almost numb, I went to the window, opened it farther, and leaned out. I looked up, but there was no sign of anyone; neither was there when I looked down. I was about to close the window and retreat when something caught my eye on one of the rungs of the ladder that led upward. I don't know where I found the courage, but I stepped through the window, barefoot and all, the towel still wrapped tightly around my body, and walked up the ladder.

It was my panties.

Whoever it was had dropped them and continued his flight.

I grasped them and lowered myself to my fire escape landing. Fearful I would be seen out here and look quite foolish, I hurried back into my room, where I sat and waited for my heart to calm down and the others to return.

Cinnamon and Ice were back first, Rose about twenty minutes after them. By the time she came up the stairs, I had told Cinnamon and Ice everything. They consoled me, but they were both full of rage and pounced on Rose the moment she stuck her face in the door to see what was happening. It nearly brought her to tears, and she got right on the phone and called Barry. After she described my horrible time with Tony, he asked to speak with me.

"I'm sorry that happened to you, Honey," he said. "I haven't known Tony very long, of course, but I'm surprised he behaved so badly. I'll speak to him."

"I don't want you to have any trouble, Barry. Just forget it," I said.

"I won't have any trouble. The other guys will be just as upset about it. From the little I know about Tony, I see he's quite spoiled. His parents just give him money, let him have whatever he wants. Look how they set him up in that apartment they sublet from a client of his father's," he added.

"A client. I thought it was his uncle's apartment."

Barry was silent a moment.

"Is that what he told you? He's a sick guy. Forget about him. I apologize for bringing him along," Barry said.

I again told him it wasn't his fault and begged him not to get into any problems because of it, and then I handed the phone back to Rose. She said good-bye and, looking so upset herself, hung up.

"That's only half of what's happening," Cinnamon began again.

Rose looked at me.

"What else?"

"Honey had a visitor through the window—and in the daytime, too. Whoever it was is definitely another sicko. He took her clothes."

"What?"

"While I was in the shower. He went up the fire escape, dropping my panties on a rung," I said.

"Did you see him?"

"No."

"But there's no question where he went," Cinnamon said. She looked at Ice. "Tonight, we'll find out what it's all about."

"What do you mean?" Rose asked. "How?"

"We'll pay him a visit, and if it turns out to be Edmond Senetsky..."

"But that's Madame Senetsky's private home."

"I don't care," Cinnamon said. "It's got to stop." She turned to Ice and Rose. "Wait a minute. Didn't you both tell us you were missing clothes?"

"Yes."

"You mean, you think..." Rose choked on the rest of her sentence. "He was actually in my room. In my things, too!"

"Why don't we just tell Madame Senetsky now?" I suggested firmly.

"Let's get it all first, be sure of our facts. It could either be the end of a problem or the end of us here if we don't handle it right," Cinnamon pointed out.

We were all silent.

"Tonight," Cinnamon repeated. "After dinner. We'll change our clothes first. Wear sneakers," she advised. "Going up a fire escape is hard in heels."

Everyone was silent a moment, the same cold fear flowing through our veins. Ice shook her head.

"It was such a nice day, too. Or at least, I thought it was. The park, the restaurant, being on Fifth Avenue and seeing all those expensive stores...for a while I felt like I was in a magical place."

"You were," Cinnamon insisted, "and you'll be there again." She looked at me with determination. "All of us will."

When we went down for dinner, we learned that Madame Senetsky had gone to meet some theater friends for dinner tonight and would not be with us. The dinner itself was finally just a dinner and not so much a learning experience with a guest chef and a lecture about wine and food; nevertheless, at Madame Senetsky's orders, we were treated to chicken Kiev. Ms. Fairchild didn't eat with us, but did give us an introduction to the entree, explaining what it was and where it had originated. She then left the dining room as well.

Howard and Steven were not at the dinner. All Ms. Fairchild told us was that they had other plans, which were approved.

"I'm sure he had nothing special," Cinnamon said, "but he was too embarrassed to face us."

"Who cares?" Ice muttered.

"He's so stuck on himself he thinks everyone is interested in his every breath," Cinnamon said. "You don't know how hard it is to have to work with such a person on the stage. He's always giving me one of his looks that ask, 'Is that the best you can do?' Even Mr. Marlowe is growing impatient with his narcissism."

"His what?" Ice asked, and Cinnamon retold the Greek myth of Narcissus, who fell in love with his own image and died pining away, in love with himself.

"Hell, half the people I know can have that nickname," Ice commented.

"Present company excluded, I hope," Rose said.

We all laughed. The clock was ticking, however, and everyone knew what that meant. After dinner ended, we all cleared the table, helped with the dishes and silverware, and reset the table for the morning. Then, quietly, no one so much as breathing loudly, we paraded up the stairs to our rooms to change. Cinnamon had decided we would go up through my window. They all gathered in my room, but just before we started out, we heard the boys coming up the stairs. Cinnamon indicated we should all be very quiet. We heard them talking and then pausing to listen at my door.

"Maybe they didn't come home yet," Steven said. "They're probably having a great time."

"So?" Howard came back at him. "We had a good time, didn't we?"

"No," Steven replied.

Ice smothered a laugh. We heard them go to their rooms and close their doors.

"Okay," Cinnamon said. She approached my window. "No one speaks. Just take your time going up."

She opened the window and stepped onto the landing. Rose looked at me and I followed, Ice next, Rose last. As quietly as we could, we climbed the metal ladder to the landing above. The light was on in whatever room it was. Cinnamon waited for us all to reach the landing and then she approached the window, which was shrouded by a curtain. She tried the window, and it moved.

"Careful," Ice warned.

Edging it up a little more than an inch at a time, Cinnamon had it open about a foot and then parted the curtain. We gathered around her and the four of us peered into the room. It was a bedroom, not unlike our own. A closet door was open and we could see a row of men's slacks, some sports jackets, and some shirts.

"Look," Cinnamon said, nodding toward the bed.

"Aren't those your clothes, Honey? Your blouse and jeans?"

"Yes," I said.

Suddenly, we heard music. It was the same music I had heard coming from behind the mysterious doors in the costume room. In a whisper, I told the others.

We continued to listen and wait. No one moved. I could hear Rose breathing hard at my left ear. Ice was between Cinnamon and me and Cinnamon leaned into the window. Then she pulled back quickly.

Rose gasped, but Ice held her hand over her mouth.

Edmond Senetsky entered the bedroom and then walked toward the closet. He was wearing a sports jacket, tie, and slacks, but his feet were bare.

"But he doesn't live here, does he?" Rose whispered.

"Shh," Cinnamon said, putting her finger to her lips. We watched him standing at the closet door. He took off his jacket and began to undo his tie with his back to us. Then he reached for a hanger and hung up the jacket. He put the tie on a tie hook and began to unbutton his shirt.

"Now *we're* the Peeping Toms," Ice muttered.

"Just wait," Cinnamon said. "Something's not right."

"Tell me about it," Ice whispered in my right ear.

We continued to watch. When the shirt was completely unbuttoned, he began to peel it off, and that was when we saw what looked like a bandage wrapped around his upper torso. He looked down and began to unwind it.

"What the heck is he doing?" Rose whispered.

No one dared speak or could speak. I think all our hearts were on pause. We barely breathed.

Then he turned—and we saw the bandage free a small, perky bosom. I couldn't move, couldn't swallow. We were clumped together, all of us finding a place to grasp another. Ice had her hand wrapped tightly around my right wrist. Rose was grabbing my blouse and pulling it so hard, I thought it would tear. I had one hand clinging to her blouse and Cinnamon had her left hand pressed against Ice's thigh.

"That's not Edmond Senetsky," Cinnamon whispered.

Whoever it was lowered the slacks. We saw what looked like men's underwear briefs, but when they came down, there was no doubt in any mind this was not a man.

The scene before us was hypnotizing. No one could turn away, nor could anyone move a muscle.

Whoever it was then headed for the bed and picked up my blouse. She put it on and gazed at herself in the mirror.

Cinnamon pulled us all back.

"She can see us in the reflection," she whispered.

"Let's get out of here," Ice said. "Now!"

Without any discussion, Cinnamon backed farther away from the window and nodded toward the ladder. We had to go down in reverse order, Rose first, Cinnamon last. Going down was much harder, not only because we couldn't feel our legs and distrusted the grips our hands had on the metal railings, but because the ladder was at such an incline, it took much more nerve to descend than ascend. I tried keeping my eyes shut tight. We had to be careful we didn't step on each other's hands. I nearly stepped on Ice's. Rose was moving so slowly. At one point she actually froze.

"What's happening?" Cinnamon called down.

"Rose can't move," Ice said.

"Oh, no. Get her to, Ice. Hurry."

Cinnamon and I listened to Ice speaking softly to Rose, trying to calm her, urging her to take one more step and then another. Rose whimpered.

"I'm going to fall," she moaned.

"Not if you hold on tightly and just take your time. Carefully lower your foot to the next rung. Go on. Do it," Ice said a little more firmly.

Finally, Rose began to move again, and then we saw the darkness above us get washed in light, and we all froze once more.

Whoever it was had opened the curtain. Was she coming out?

"Quickly," Cinnamon begged.

Rose found the strength and made it to my landing. We each followed, and all of us hurried through my window and into my room, where we collapsed on the floor. My neck was so damp with nervous sweat, I needed a towel. So did the others.

"Well?" Ice was the first to ask.

"I don't know what to say. Edmond Senetsky is not a man? Was that what we learned?" I asked.

"That can't be so. He's a bit of a dandy, but I never thought he wasn't a man," Cinnamon replied.

"It looked just like him, didn't it?" Rose asked. "Well, didn't it?" she pursued when we were all still silent.

"Yes and no," Cinnamon said. "I don't know. It wasn't a good light. It's all so bizarre. One thing is for sure," she added, looking up at us all, "we don't say anything about this to anyone, not yet at least."

"I wouldn't know how to begin," Rose said. "I feel a little sick to my stomach. How are we going to behave normally tomorrow?"

Cinnamon smiled.

"Just follow Madame Senetsky's advice and focus completely on your work. Remember, a good performer can't see beyond the footlights."

"I don't think I'll have the strength to make one turn, much less dance," Rose complained.

"You will," Cinnamon said. She gazed at Ice and me. "We all will."

"Then what?" Ice asked.

"I don't know. Not yet, anyway."

She laughed.

"How can you laugh about this?" Rose demanded.

"I was just remembering how most of the kids in my school thought I was weird because of the way I dressed and the things that interested me.

"After seeing this, I realize I was as healthy as the whole Brady Bunch put together," she said.

Everyone was quiet, lost in her own thoughts for a few moments.

"I don't know if I'll get any sleep tonight," Rose said softly as she stood up. She looked at her hands. "Ugh." She held them up. They were black from the metal ladder. "I guess I need a shower."

"Me, too," Ice said.

She and Rose went to the door.

"Try to rest, anyway," Cinnamon said. She lingered behind after they had gone to their rooms. "What a day you've had, Honey. I can't believe you won't collapse when your head hits the pillow."

"Me, neither."

She started for the door.

"Cinnamon?"

"Yes?"

"Why do you suppose she's taking our clothes?"

She stood there, thinking for a moment, and then looked at me and said, "She wants to be more like us, I guess."

She shrugged.

"Really?"

"I don't know what else to say, Honey. I suppose we'll find out eventually. Night."

"Night," I replied in a small, broken voice. She walked out and closed the door.

I turned to my window, and then I hurried to it and closed it tightly, closing the curtains as well.

Tonight, I thought, *tonight I'll wrap the darkness around me like an old friend and look for sleep to be the doorway to an escape.*

The morning was suddenly something to fear.

9

Evan Investigates

If we appeared silent and secretive to Howard before, I thought he surely would believe we had committed some heinous crime when he confronted the four of us at breakfast the next day. We were that glum and quiet.

Actually, we didn't have to talk. He did most of it, raving about his day, the people from the theater he had met, going backstage at a hit play, meeting the crew, talking to actors and actresses, and then going to dinner with an agent's assistant who had already shown some interest in him.

After having overheard him and Steven the night before, we felt certain he was lying about it all.

"Why would you meet with another agent? What about Edmond Senetsky?" Cinnamon quickly asked.

"Just because we attend the Senetsky School, we don't have to sign with Edmond Senetsky," he practically whispered. "Sometimes it's better to let a few fight over you. The word gets out and producers take note. That comes in handy at casting time."

"At the moment, Howard," Cinnamon said, "I'm just concerned about getting through our first Performance Night, much less casting for Broadway shows."

"Ridiculous. It's not going to be much of an audience. All of us are having either friends or family. My parents are coming, of course."

"Mine aren't," Steven piped up. He looked at us and added, "They are very busy little beavers, and have to dam up some money in Bermuda."

"Regardless," Howard said, rolling his eyes to indicate his impatience with Steven, "it won't be like playing before thousands, which I did at my school and twice for the community theater."

"All week long, Laura Fairchild has been announcing the names of people attending. They are not just family and friends," I said.

"Besides, Madame Senetsky says an audience of two can make you just as nervous as thousands," Rose added. "She told me that just last week, matter of fact. She also said if you're not nervous, you won't do well, remember?"

"That's just an excuse people who get nervous use. Believe me, it's an old wives' tale," Howard claimed, waving it off.

"What have you decided is an old wives' tale?" Madame Senetsky asked.

She had entered just as Rose had finished, so I was sure she had heard. Howard must have thought so, too. He turned a shade of crimson and then a little blue.

"Nothing very important," he quickly answered.

She stared at him a moment, looked at us, and then took her usual seat at the head of the table. She was not often there at breakfast with us, taking it in her own private quarters instead. The maid came in immediately to pour her a cup of coffee, but she shook her head.

"Nothing for me, thank you," she said and turned back to us. She had a way of capturing us with what people in the theater call the Caesural pause, a dramatic pause that holds your attention. I knew her well enough by now to realize that she was truly doing what she wanted us to do: always perform, take on the demeanor of someone on stage. The effect for me, however, was to feel as if everything she said and did was calculated, contrived.

I wondered if there was ever a time when she was just herself, someone who wasn't conscious of the lighting so she would know how to present her best profile; someone who wasn't waiting for reactions from her listeners and observers; someone who wasn't posturing and looking for constant applause.

What was her real voice like, her real smile, her real laughter, and even her real tears? Had she been an actress so long that it was impossible for her to find herself anymore, to take off the makeup, to remove the costume? Was she like Cinnamon had suggested we were, someone looking always to escape herself, her past, some terrible real pain?

She held her gaze a moment longer on me than she did on the others. It made me wonder if she could see what I was thinking. I looked down quickly and waited, my nerves twanging like the strings of my violin.

"Since we are closing in on our first important date," she began, "I want to be sure we are all going to start this week on the right foot. I would expect that everything you do, everything you say and even think will be of importance," she added, glaring at Howard. He seemed to shrink in his seat.

Steven stirred his coffee and sat with a fat Cheshire cat smile on his face, enjoying Howard's discomfort at being chastised, even slightly.

"I am designing a lighter diet for you all. I want you all to be quick on your feet, energetic, and dedicated. The halls of this house should be filled with music, music, music, and the echo of voices reciting, rehearsing, the consonants and vowels resonating in every corner.

"I have never had an opening Performance Night with a new group of students that did not go very well and leave most of my guests quite impressed, and I do not expect or intend for this one to be any different.

"There will be a small reception in the ballroom afterward. Later this week, I will discuss how I want you all to behave among the agents, actors, and producers who will be there. There is a fine line to walk between modesty and self-confidence. I would like all of you to be attractive and interesting to my guests, but I want you to have an air of innocence and wonder about you."

When she pursed her lips, her eyes lit with a sardonic brightness, rather than a soft smile.

"Most everyone who attends will want to feel like he or she has made a discovery, and not the Senetsky family," she said. She looked like she was holding back a laugh the way someone might swallow back a revolting taste.

"That is just fine. Let them think what they need to think. Egos must be stroked and fulfilled. I don't mind taking a backseat to all of it if you succeed as I know and expect you will," she added.

She sat back. No one uttered a sound. We didn't even breathe loudly.

"I assume you have all heard the name Jack Ferante?"

"Of course," Howard said quickly. "He's the president of the Screen Actors Guild."

"Yes. He is a close friend of mine and he happens to be in New York this weekend. He will attend." She looked from one of our faces to another to see the effect of her announcement. Her blue eyes darkened with her scrutinizing gaze. Except for Howard, none of us looked terribly impressed.

"He has friends in very high places, in the theater, in the opera, in some of the country's finest symphonies," she emphasized, somewhat annoyed at our stoical response.

"Actually," she continued, "he has never been able to attend one of my Performance Nights. He has been on location in a film himself or occupied with SAG business. You should all feel quite honored and quite fortunate.

"I would look with very bitter and disappointed eyes on any action that would detract from our focus this week. I hope that is perfectly clear," she concluded and then rose, paused, and turned to us, her eyes panning each of our faces. "Is it?"

I looked at Cinnamon. It really was almost as if

Madame Senetsky could read our minds, I thought. Cinnamon looked like she agreed with me and nodded slightly, knowing what my look questioned.

"Yes, ma'am," Howard boasted.

"It sure is," Steven said, his smile still sitting on his lips.

"We understand, Madame Senetsky," Cinnamon said, speaking for the four of us.

"Good. To work then," she said, tapped her cane, and left the room.

Howard practically leaped at the rest of us.

"Someone could have warned me she was standing right there," he complained.

"Who could possibly interrupt you when you are giving us one of your lectures, Howard?" Cinnamon asked with feigned innocence.

"You should have expected it anyway," Steven told him. "Living in this place is like living in someone's ear," he said, grimacing.

"What's that mean?" Rose asked.

Little alarms went off in all our hearts.

Steven shrugged.

"You know, with Ms. Fairchild popping out behind us. I check under my bed every night," he said facetiously, but I wondered to myself why it was that the boys never felt as spied upon as we did. Why wasn't this mysterious person at their bedroom windows, too?

I looked at my watch.

"I have to get to my lesson," I said, standing. "I'll talk to you later," I whispered to Cinnamon.

"Knock him dead," Steven called after me.

Knock him dead? Right now, I thought, I was afraid I might not have the strength to hold my violin, much less play it. I was terrified of being too nervous and having Mr. Bergman march me down to the street to play for pedestrians again, so I sucked in my breath, counted to ten, and when I began to perform for him, I concentrated as hard as I could on my work. He listened with those critical eyes so fixed on me, I was sure he was going to rant and rage the moment I lifted the bow. Instead, he nodded softly.

"You're getting there," he said. "You're riding the music well. Now, I want you to think of it as a wild horse you have just trained. It needs direction; it needs authority. Impose yourself upon those notes. Don't play exactly what you see, but how you see it. In short, this is what we mean when we speak of interpretation. I want your personal stamp on this now. I want you to be more than simply a musician playing someone else's creative work. I want you to become part of the process.

"This is a freedom and a task I don't assign to my students until I feel they have the talent and the skill to handle it," he added.

He stopped short of hammering home a compliment and left it hanging in the air for me to pluck and complete instead. I nodded, studied the music for a few moments, and then began again, closing my eyes and thinking of my Uncle Peter, his smile, his words of encouragement. I thought of the farm, Mommy and Daddy and Uncle Simon, and imagined them sitting there listening to me play. I did bring myself and who I was to the melody. I couldn't describe exactly what I had done and I wasn't sure I could ever do it again the same way, but when I was finished, Mr. Bergman was smiling and nodding.

"Yes," he said. "Yes, you will do fine."

With a heart full of hope and excitement, I left my lesson and prepared for the remainder of our day. Unfortunately, Rose wasn't as happy with her work. She said she missed steps, lost rhythm, and just looked clumsy, but Mr. Demetrius assured her she wasn't. Ice said Mr. Littleton gave her unusually enthusiastic compliments, and Cinnamon reported that Howard, squashed a bit by Madame Senetsky at breakfast, was less pretentious on the stage. She admitted she even liked his performance herself and thought it helped her do better. Steven was very happy, too, claiming I had left Mr. Bergman in so good a mood he tolerated his small improvisations.

"No," I told him. "Improvisation, interpretation, that's what he's after now. He wants you to impose yourself on the music, be a part of the creation."

"Listen to her," Steven cried with some surprise. "Our little Honey Child is becoming a sophisticated New York musician."

I blushed with embarrassment.

"That's generally the idea, isn't it?" Cinnamon snapped, stepping up to defend me immediately.

"If you got serious for a minute, you might have the same sort of success," Rose added.

"If you shut off your wise talk, you might," Ice asserted, "but I doubt you can do that."

He looked at the four of us and shook his head, raising his hands as if to surrender.

"Please don't castrate me," he begged. "I'm sorry, girls. I'm sorry," he mocked and walked away.

The four of us looked at each other and laughed. We were truly becoming sisters, looking after each other. We were really becoming a team. Each of us lent something to the others, I thought. Cinnamon was our wit. Ice our muscle. Rose our beautiful face. And me? I was our conscience.

On Thursday Uncle Simon had a bouquet of fresh flowers delivered for each of us with a card wishing us all good luck on our first Performance Night. I had told him how much the girls loved the arrangement he had sent to me. We called him immediately and everyone took a turn thanking him. He was too shy to say much more than, "Don't think anything of it. Living in a city, you need as many flowers as you can get."

Daddy got on and apologized again and again for their not being here my first Performance Night. I tried to make him feel better by telling him it was really just little more than a dress rehearsal.

"The next one will be more important," I said.

Mommy was full of questions about our daily life and how I was adjusting to New York City. I could never lie to Mommy, at least not well enough for her to not see it was a lie. She heard some of my unhappiness in my voice, unhappiness I couldn't yet verbalize or explain.

"Maybe I don't belong in big cities, Mommy."

"Give it time," she advised. "Your wonderful talent will take you to many more cities, Honey, beautiful places. Think of what you would deny those hungry ears if you came home and played only for your Uncle Simon and us."

I laughed and assured her I would be fine, but I missed them all so much that it made me wonder if I ever could become a world-class musician, or actually, if I really wanted the fame and the opportunities as much as the others. At times Rose looked like she had just as many doubts about herself as I did about myself.

Rose's half-brother Evan arrived on Friday. Madame Senetsky granted her permission to meet him at his hotel when he arrived. Since we were performing on Saturday night, we were not given any assignments for Friday night or Saturday, but Ms. Fairchild warned us that time off meant time to relax and prepare ourselves mentally for our big night.

"No wandering about the city," she cautioned. "And no late hours! Pay strict attention to your curfew."

Chandler wasn't arriving until late Friday night and coming to visit late Saturday morning. I had gotten permission for him to join us at lunch. Rose was having Barry as well as Evan. Cinnamon and Ice decided against inviting Larry and Reuben. Neither was special enough to them, certainly not as special as Chandler was to me. I was so excited about seeing him again, I almost forgot about the bizarre scene we had all witnessed through the window the Sunday before, and the taking of my clothing. All of us discussed it Friday afternoon before Rose went to meet her brother. Cinnamon was worried I would say something to Chandler and Rose would tell Barry.

"Until we really know what's going on, it's better we keep it all to ourselves," she strongly suggested.

All agreed.

Shortly after we had our dinner, Rose called Cinnamon from her brother's hotel room. He had arrived and taken the trip well. The hotel had provided him their best room for a disabled person, but she wasn't calling simply to report that.

"I think you should all come here," she told her. "And as quickly as you can."

The three of us started out. Howard and Steven were in the den watching a video of an old American Playhouse production Mr. Marlowe had recommended. Because we didn't want either them or Laura Fairchild to hear or see us leave, we tiptoed to the front door and snuck out, like people escaping. Once down the steps, we all stuck to the shadows and ran to the gate, hurrying to the nearest street corner to see if we could flag a taxicab. We had to make our way to Third Avenue before getting one, but once we did it was only a little more than twenty minutes later that we arrived at Evan's hotel.

When we called from the lobby, Rose came out to meet us and bring us to her brother.

"He's putting on a brave act, but he's exhausted," she explained as we walked down the corridor. "I put him to bed. He's embarrassed, so act like it's nothing unusual."

"Maybe we should have waited until tomorrow then," I said.

"No, he insisted, and after what he told me and what we've experienced, I thought you should come."

Evan looked small and very vulnerable in the king-size bed. Rose introduced us all to him quickly.

"From all she's told me," he said, "I feel like I've known each of you for years."

"Same for us about you, Evan," Cinnamon said.

Knowing how proud Rose was of him brought a glow to his face. He had a soft, round face with long flaxen-blond hair streaming down the sides of his temples and cheeks. Although his eyes confessed his fatigue, they were also bright with excitement at meeting us. I thought he was a good-looking boy, with a slightly cleft chin and beautiful almond-brown eyes.

Rose fixed the pillow behind him so he could sit up, and then he reached over and pulled some notes out of a leather-bound, letter-size folio.

"Rose filled me in on what you guys saw through that window on the third floor of your school building. I don't know if this will help explain it. I don't know if anything could."

We gathered around him, Cinnamon sitting on the bed, Ice at his left shoulder, and me sitting opposite Cinnamon. Rose remained at the foot of the bed, watching. I glanced at her and saw how she was anticipating our reaction. What had Evan found?

"This was one of the hardest, most difficult searches I've undertaken through the Internet," Evan began. "Roadways into places I had to get to were blocked with passwords I didn't have time to break. I had to figure out ways to get around and come in back doors. But," he added with a smile, "it became a real challenge, and I love a challenge."

"Just tell him he can't do something and he deliberately does it," Rose explained.

"Sounds like me," Cinnamon said. "Go on, Evan," she urged, now impatient. "Please."

"Okay. First, a little history about Madame Senetsky. As you know, she has had a great career. By my last count, she had major roles in over two hundred different theater productions and made nearly forty films in Europe. Apparently, she speaks both French and Italian fluently enough to make foreign films. She was never very big in Hollywood, although she has done close to ten films, some independent productions, a few studio films. Usually, a foreign director cast her. The point is, she spent most of her career in Europe, and that was also why it was difficult getting answers.

"Anyway, she married Marshall Senetsky when she was in her early thirties. The Senetsky family emigrated from Poland to France in the early twenties, where they became successful importers of products from North Africa and some things from the Far East. They invested in commercial property and built a sizeable fortune. Marshall Senetsky enjoyed the theater and invested not only in plays but also in theaters themselves. It seems that he built a theater just for his wife.

"For a long time their principal residence was Paris, but they also had a summer home in Switzerland. She didn't become pregnant until she was nearly forty years old."

"Why did she wait so long?" I asked.

"Probably her career came first," Evan said.

"You'd think her husband would have something to say about that," Ice muttered.

"Well, they had a strange relationship. They were apart for long periods of time every year. If you look at her schedule and his, you'd think they were lucky to have been together a week or more sometimes."

"Get to what they have to know, Evan," Rose gently urged. "We don't want to keep you long and we've got to get back to the school before we're missed, too. We weren't supposed to be out late."

"Right. She gave birth both times in Switzerland. There was contradictory information about this, almost as if someone was trying to erase the past, but I finally discovered that she gave birth to a boy first. The boy, as you all know, was named Edmond Corneil Senetsky, Corneil being Madame Senetsky's maiden name. Two years afterward, she gave birth again, this time to a girl. The girl's name was Gerta Louise Senetsky. Louise was Madame Senetsky's mother's name. Gerta was Marshall Senetsky's mother's name."

"We know about her daughter," I said. "She told me herself, remember? She said I reminded her of her daughter, but she had died."

"She told you that?" Evan asked.

"Yes, but she didn't tell me her name or anything else about her. Why are you surprised?"

"There is little history of Gerta. It's like Madame Senetsky would rather forget she ever existed. All the articles I could find that quote her mention only Edmond. They were both brought up in Switzerland, where they attended English schools. Madame Senetsky was traveling often, to make films or to perform in a play. As I said, sometimes she was away from her husband for months and months, but she was also away from her children that long, too."

He paused and looked up at us.

"From what I can tell so far, at the age of fourteen, Gerta disappears, but that's not when she died."

"Disappears?" Ice asked quickly.

"No school records, medical records, nothing. It took a while, but I finally traced her to a clinic in Switzerland."

"What sort of clinic?" Cinnamon questioned, her eyes electric with what I imagined were her memories of her mother's problems.

"A special clinic for disturbed children, mentally disturbed."

"So that's who we saw," Ice muttered. "It had to be. That was surely one disturbed person."

"The resemblance to Edmond would strongly suggest it," Evan said.

"But Madame Senetsky told me she was dead," I reminded them. "Why would she lie about that and why is she being kept hidden?" I asked.

Evan shook his head.

"That's why I said this might not help you understand what's happening in the house. That's all I could find about her so far. It's a very strange story, and after what Rose told me, I thought I should bring it all here to show you."

He handed out some of the articles and pictures he had downloaded from search engines on the Internet. We passed them to each other and read in silence.

"You said she was placed in psychiatric care when she was about fourteen?" Cinnamon asked, looking up from one article in particular.

"It would seem that way from what I could piece together," Evan replied.

Cinnamon thought a moment.

"If I'm correct about the time line, it's not too long after that when Madame Senetsky's husband committed suicide for mysterious reasons. Right?" she asked Evan. "You sent those pages to Rose."

"Yes, that's correct," he said. "They already were living in New York part of the year."

He checked his notes and nodded.

"According to what this says, Marshall Senetsky died a little more than a year after Gerta was committed."

"Wow," I said. "It sounds like there is more drama in Madame Senetsky's real life than there was in any play or movie she acted in."

"Somehow," Cinnamon said, nodding, "I don't think the curtain has come down on it all either."

No one spoke, but it was easy to see drama unfolding in all our faces.

"Let's leave Evan get some rest," Rose said. "He's coming to the house for lunch tomorrow. Madame Senetsky approved of it."

"Good," Cinnamon said. "But let's not talk about any of this in front of anyone else just yet."

"Especially Howard and Steven," Ice pointed out.

"You've taken care of all your travel arrangements, Evan? You can get yourself to the school okay?" Rose confirmed.

He nodded.

"The van will be here about ten. Don't worry about it," he said, obviously proud at how he had managed to handle everything for himself. Independence for someone like him was far more important than it was for any of us, I thought.

"Is there anything else you need before we go?"

"No, I'm fine here. As you see," he said, gesturing toward the bathroom, where we could see railings, "it's all designed for the disabled."

"You're far less disabled than most of the boys I know," Cinnamon told him, which brought a nice smile back to his tired face.

"Thanks," he said.

"There's one other thing you should know, Evan," she continued. "We're practically sisters now. That makes you brother to all of us."

His smile widened.

Each of us kissed him good night.

The beams of happiness in his eyes warmed our hearts. After we left his room, Rose couldn't stop her thank yous.

"Forget it," Cinnamon said. "He's the one who deserves the thanks.

"What is going on in that mansion?" she pondered. "Who was that upstairs? Was it her daughter, and if it was, why did she tell you her daughter was dead?"

"And when will we know?" Ice followed.

We hailed a cab and returned, all of us lost in her own thoughts until we pulled up at the gate and got out.

The house loomed above us, the windows on the third floor dimly lit.

All of it resembling a stage waiting for its next performance.

And with us, strangely enough, participating as an audience trapped in the theater.

Before I went to sleep, I had a call from Chandler to tell me he had arrived and how much he looked forward to seeing me.

"It's been too long," he said. "When you care as much for someone as I care for you, Honey, a week apart is more like a month; a month, more like a year."

"I know, Chandler. I feel the same way," I said.

"I'll be there about eleven," he said.

Knowing he was close by helped me relax and finally get a good night's sleep.

At breakfast, Laura Fairchild told us to report to the parlor as soon as we were finished, where once again Madame Senetsky held court. When I looked at her now, I couldn't help thinking about the revelations Evan had brought to us. How did she keep the turns and twists of her real life from interfering with her performances, her career? A daughter in a mental clinic, a husband who committed suicide? Would I be able to have such control and power over my own emotions?

"When your performances have concluded this evening, you will all report promptly to the ballroom," she began. "The guests will already be there. The reception will begin with champagne and some hors d'oeuvres. I don't want to see any of you gorging yourself on food or gulping champagne. One glass should last each of you the whole evening. Too many young people drink their champagne too quickly and begin to babble ridiculously," she warned. "And I certainly don't want to see anyone with a mouthful of food when he or she is being introduced.

"Gather near me, and I will properly introduce each of you to my guests. No one introduces him or herself, and none of you," she added, eyeing Howard the most, I thought, "assert yourself to anyone.

"Power in the arts comes from being in demand... in every sense... everywhere. When you go to someone instead of him or her coming to you, you weaken your image. Even you, neophytes at the very beginning of your careers, must not give up too much. When you let them know how much you want what they can give, they will have the power over you and not vice versa."

"It sounds more like a war than a career," Ice muttered.

Madame Senetsky smiled coldly, her lips lifting slightly at the corners of her mouth.

"Precisely. Competition is a battle in and of itself. And remember this forever, my precious novices: you will always be in competition, whether you are simply taking a publicity photo, participating in an interview, or at a party or reception such as the one you will be at tonight.

"The people who will be observing you will be comparing you to other potential actors and actresses, dancers and musicians. In their minds you are always competing, so be sure it is in your mind as well. Does everyone understand?"

"Sure," Howard said, looking like a race horse chafing at the bit.

"Good," she said. "Relax for the remainder of the day. Entertain your friends at luncheon and then be sure you all have a good hour or so of rest, quiet, and meditation. Ms. Fairchild will have the program and schedule of performances for you just after lunch."

She paused and looked at us all very hard again.

"I do not wish people in the theater luck. This is not a matter of luck anymore. There might have been some luck involved in getting you here, but once you're on the stage, luck takes a seat at the rear of the theater and your skills, talents, and dedication determine whether you are successful or whether you fail.

"The curtain goes up. It is then entirely in your own hands, each and every one of you. However, I will say, do not disappoint me."

She smiled, almost a genuinely warm smile.

"It's almost as bad as disappointing yourselves," she added and tapped her cane. No one spoke as she walked out.

"If I wasn't nervous before," Cinnamon quipped, "I am now."

It brought some smiles and laughter, even to Howard's normally overconfident face.

An hour later Evan arrived, and Rose showed him about the house. Barry came a little after that, and the three of them visited in the parlor. I was getting nervous about Chandler because it was almost lunch time and he had still not appeared. Finally, twenty minutes before we were all to enjoy the buffet that had been prepared, Chandler arrived, and I introduced him to everyone.

"He is a very handsome boy," Ice whispered in my ear.

We all sat in the parlor and talked. The boys told of their college experiences and we described the work we were doing. Steven and Chandler seemed to get along really well. After lunch, he and Chandler went into the studio and played for each other and we all followed, Cinnamon and Ice taking turns pushing Evan in his wheelchair. When Steven and Chandler began, it was like watching two tap dancers showing each other new steps. Howard didn't like the fact that he was not the center of attention. I could see he quickly became bored and drifted away.

"Steven's amazing," Chandler told me immediately after their impromptu concert ended. "He's going places I haven't even dreamed of yet."

"Everyone's impressed with you, too," I assured him.

Since it was a very nice day, we decided to walk the grounds. On the way out, Barry and Rose caught up with Chandler and me and Barry blurted another apology for the other day. I tried to cut him short, but he kept explaining how he didn't know Tony that well and should never have brought him along. He ended it by saying they were no longer friends and he didn't miss him a bit.

Chandler heard it all, but didn't say anything until we were alone.

"What was that all about?" he asked with a small but disturbed smile.

"We joined Rose when she met Barry on our first free afternoon. We were going to the zoo in Central Park and Barry brought some friends," I explained.

"Uh-huh," Chandler said. "And?"

"I let one of them talk me into listening to his stereo at what was supposed to be his uncle's apartment, and it turned out badly," I said, hoping somehow to leave it at that.

"Badly? How badly?"

"Very badly. He tried to take advantage of me by getting me drunk," I said.

Chandler was very quiet.

"I was just very stupid," I added. "I believed he was really interested in showing me how good the stereo was. I deserve to be called naive, I guess."

"I haven't gone on any dates with anyone else since we left Ohio," he said.

"It really wasn't a date. I was on my way home and I let him talk me into..."

"It's all right, Honey. You don't have to defend yourself. We're not engaged or anything."

"I wish we were," I blurted and he stopped and turned to me.

"Do you? Already? You don't want to experience this city, all the exciting people you will meet, many of them handsome men?"

"No," I said definitively.

He smiled, chuckling to himself.

"I don't!" I insisted.

"Okay, okay. But look how easily you were drawn into something you thought was just going to be an innocent experience. That's all I'm saying. Let's not make promises we can't keep."

"I can keep my promises, Chandler Maxwell. I always have and I always will," I said, steaming.

He laughed.

"I mean it!" I said and stomped away from him. He had to run to catch up.

"Okay, okay. I'm sorry. I'm certainly not upset about it, Honey. I wouldn't want anyone else to make such a promise to me."

I stood there fuming a moment, and then turned my head slightly to look at him.

"And what about you and your promises?" I asked.

He stared at me a moment, dug into his pocket, and then opened his hand to reveal a white gold friendship ring with a small diamond at the center.

"It's close to an engagement ring," he said. "Maybe a step or two away. I wasn't sure if I should give it to you so soon, but..."

"Oh, Chandler, yes," I cried. "Yes."

He took my hand and slipped the ring on my finger.

"It fits perfectly!"

"I found out your ring size from your mother. She was funny, questioning me to see if I was going to offer you an engagement ring. When I told her what it was, she sounded relieved. I don't think it was because she doesn't like me," he added quickly. "Nothing like that. But I know she would feel it's a bit too soon to plan on a marriage, especially when you're planning a wonderful career for yourself and you have all this opportunity," he added, gesturing at the school.

I thought about Madame Senetsky, the things Evan had discovered and told us: her dedicated life, not marrying until she was in her thirties and not having her first child until she was nearly forty. Now who knew what family problems she had?

A part of me wanted to burst out and say, "Oh, Chandler, I don't want anything more than a good husband, a good home, and a family. I don't want to travel from city to city performing, living out of hotels, holding my breath every time a critic appears, worrying about the audiences, competing and competing as Madame Senetsky described."

But I didn't say those things.

Another part of me stood up and cast a shadow over the words.

"You would be dishonest with yourself," it said, "if you denied I was here inside you, too."

"This means a great deal to me, Chandler," I said, running my finger over and over the ring. "Thank you."

He shook his head.

"Thank you, Honey, for wanting it."

He leaned forward to kiss me.

"Hey," we heard Steven call from behind us. He walked our way. "You're not supposed to rile up the performers before the show."

Chandler and I laughed.

But up in a window on the third floor, someone stood watching us.

It looked like the young woman we had seen. A moment later, she was gone.

It put a dark shadow over me.

I embraced myself quickly, seized Chandler's hand, and continued on, with Steven chattering beside us like some bird enjoying an hour out of its cage.

10

Performance Night

Ms. Fairchild gave us the program and schedule of performances for the evening. Steven was to be first, but it didn't seem to bother him at all. Maybe it was better to be as nonchalant and uncaring as he appeared to be, I thought. I was third, after Ice. Rose was scheduled to dance before Howard and Cinnamon were to end the evening with their scenes.

We had another light dinner, as Madame Senetsky had ordered, and then we all went up to dress for our performances. Just before eight, the six of us marched down the stairs and gathered with Ms. Fairchild in the little theater. The first row had been reserved for our teachers.

Evan was already there and set up in an area to the right of the last row when we all arrived. It was the only place where he could fit with his wheelchair because Madame Senetsky wouldn't permit him to sit in an aisle, even down front.

Ms. Fairchild had the audacity to tell Rose that this was a private school and not required to make accommodations for handicapped people. Rose was upset, but Evan assured her, in such a small theater, there was no problem where anyone sat.

Before anyone else arrived, Madame Senetsky ushered us backstage. She was angry about us being out front talking with Evan.

"Never, never mingle with your audience before a performance," she lectured us offstage. "You will destroy that illusion, that magical way in which the people see you as special, as larger than life, sparkling in the spotlights."

"He's only my brother," Rose protested.

"When you're on the stage, you are no longer anyone's sister, anyone's brother, son, or daughter."

"Or mother," Cinnamon muttered loud enough for her to hear. She glared at her a moment and then nodded.

"Precisely, or mother or father. Now let's all attend to our business at hand," she said. "I have to greet our guests."

Ice and Rose went into an antechamber to go through their warm-ups. Steven didn't want to do anything, and I was afraid to touch my violin before my appointed time. Howard wanted Cinnamon to review their lines, but she didn't want to, saying, "If we don't know it by now, Howard, five more minutes isn't going to matter very much."

Still, he went off on his own and carried on as if she was there with him behind the curtains, reciting her lines as well as his own.

"What happened to our confident, stomach-never-full-of-butterflies Howard Rockwell the Third?" Cinnamon quipped.

Everyone who heard her smiled, but we didn't seem to have the strength to overcome our jitters and laugh.

People were arriving! We could hear the low murmur of their voices as they filled the little theater.

Why this should be any more unnerving and frightening to me than the times I played before much larger audiences in Ohio, I didn't know, but it certainly was. I felt tingling and buzzing in places I had never felt them. My throat kept getting so dry, my tongue scratched the roof of my mouth as harshly as it would had a piece of sandpaper been stuck on it.

"Don't drink so much water," Ms. Fairchild snapped at me. "You'll have to pee while you're performing and it will ruin your concentration."

I spit out what was in my mouth. *What a horrible image,* I thought.

Madame Senetsky came backstage to look us all over one more time before the Performance Evening was to begin. She, herself, was going to do the introductory speech, greeting her audience and explaining the program. Before she stepped onto the stage, she looked so hard at each and every one of us, I was sure she would spot a strand of hair out of place. She nodded approvingly at the others, but paused in front of me, her eyes seeming to shrink in her skull. What was wrong? Did I have something on my face, a button undone?

"Before you go into the reception, come back here and wait for me," she ordered.

"Why?"

She didn't reply. She turned, nodded at Laura Fairchild, and then stepped into the wing of the little theater's stage. She paused, sucked in her breath, which lifted her shoulders, and then walked out. There was loud applause.

"Good evening, ladies and gentlemen, and thank you all for attending the first Senetsky School Performing Night," we heard her begin.

I inched closer to Cinnamon.

"Did you hear what she said to me?" I asked.

Cinnamon shook her head and stared at the stage. Suddenly, she looked terrified, her face whiter, her eyes glazed. In fact, they all, including Howard, looked like they were holding their collective breaths.

"I wonder what she wants," I muttered to myself, realizing Cinnamon either couldn't or wouldn't hear me.

"I can assure you, as I have in the past," I heard Madame Senetsky concluding, "that these are very special students. My crème de la crème," she finished.

Howard smiled at us and nodded.

Steven was standing there with his hands in his pockets, his head down.

Each of our teachers was to introduce his student. Mr. Bergman introduced Steven as one of his most promising prodigies. He explained the piece Steven would play and then announced his name. Steven strutted out to a polite round of applause, took his piano seat, and began as if he was in the practice room and there was no one but Mr. Bergman present. I thought he played better than anyone I had ever heard, even professionals, and apparently so did the audience. When he was finished, there was rousing applause. He took his bows the way he had been instructed to do them and then marched off the stage, looking as if he had done this a thousand times, unfazed, nonchalant, even a little bored.

Ice was introduced next. Mr. Littleton accompanied her on the piano. She sang "Green Finch and Linnet Bird" from *Sweeney Todd* and concluded with "Memory" from *Cats.* The applause for her seemed to last nearly twice as long as the applause for Steven had lasted, thundering in the rafters.

They'll hate me, I thought. *I'll make mistake after mistake and look so foolish they'll wonder how I was admitted to this school. How can I compete with that level of talent?*

Mr. Bergman introduced me and my Mozart pieces. I feared my legs wouldn't obey the order I sent down to them when I was called onto the stage. I felt as if I was literally floating from the wings, my feet never touching the floor. When I took my place, I saw Chandler gazing up at me with a soft smile of wonder and excitement in his eyes. I was never so happy to see him as I was at that moment. The sight of a friendly face, the face of someone who reminded me of home, helped put me at ease. I closed my eyes and began.

I never looked at the audience again. I felt myself being lifted by my own music. I thought about what it meant to me, just as Mr. Bergman advised me to do, and when I was finished, I lowered the violin and started off the stage, thinking there was only silence, but that was because of the way the applause cracked in my ears, exploded, deafening me for a moment.

"Wonderful, wonderful," Ms. Fairchild said, applauding from the wings.

"Thanks a lot," Rose moaned. "Now I have to top that, too."

Cameron Demetrius stepped out and spoke about Rose and what she would perform. He concluded by saying she was a breath of fresh air in the world of dance, just when he thought there would never be another, jokingly adding, like himself. That brought a titter of laughter, but not enough to relax Rose.

The stage lights were adjusted for her interpretive dance and, moments later, the music began. She seemed to fly out and sail above the stage floor. Never was she more graceful and beautiful to watch.

"We should have been first," Howard complained when the audience lauded her performance with the same explosive clapping. It sounded more like hundreds of firecrackers.

"How are we supposed to get them up after all this music?" Howard continued. "It would have made more sense to have us in the middle. Who decided on the order of our performances?" he demanded from Ms. Fairchild.

She stared at him a moment and then, with a small, cold smile on her lips, replied, "Why, Madame Senetsky decided. Who else?"

He swallowed back whatever else he had planned to say and turned to Cinnamon.

"Just don't upstage me, Howard," she warned.

In a wonderfully deep and dramatic voice, Mr. Marlowe set up their scene and stepped back into the wings. The stage went dark and then the lights were brought up slowly on Howard and Cinnamon. Despite his protestations, he projected and spoke beautifully. Cinnamon was exciting to watch. The way she moved, held her head, and turned her hands made every part of her body part of her performance. When she and Howard finished, the audience was as appreciative as it had been for any of us, but they rose to a standing ovation when Madame Senetsky took the stage again to conclude the show.

"Thank you, thank you. You're all very generous. We have work to do. We know. But we are proud of our students and what they have accomplished in so short a time. Please join us in the ballroom for a small reception. Thank you for coming."

People began to file out. Ms. Fairchild told us to wait a moment, and then she instructed everyone to follow her.

"Except you," she told me. "Madame Senetsky will be with you in a moment."

Cinnamon finally remembered what I had said earlier and what had been said to me.

"What is it all about?" she asked.

I shook my head.

"I have no idea."

She thought a moment, pressing her lips together.

"Be like a witness in court. Don't say any more than you have to," she advised. "Especially if it has anything to do with you-know-what."

I nodded, my heart now pumping like Daddy's submersible well.

When everyone was gone, the room felt so cold and dark, I wrapped my arms around myself and paced with my head down. Then I paused and I watched the doorway and waited. Where was she? What did she want? Finally, she appeared. It was more like she swelled in the doorway.

"Quickly," she said, gesturing for me to come closer. "I haven't much time."

More curious than afraid, I stepped up to her and she reached down and seized my hand with surprising force, turning up my finger to look closely at the ring Chandler had given me. I cried out as she twisted my wrist and squeezed my fingers.

"What is this?"

"A friendship ring," I said.

"It looks more like an engagement ring," she asserted with dark, suspicious eyes. "Who gave it to you?"

"My boyfriend," I said. "Today. You gave permission for him to be here."

"It looks too much like an engagement ring. I won't have any of my prodigies looking like she is on her way to the altar. I don't waste time on young women who have only dishes, washing machines, and diapers in their eyes. You are not to have a serious relationship yet."

"What?"

"You heard me. No one gets engaged or develops a serious romantic relationship while studying and living here," she ordered. "It takes away from his or her serious concentration and it puts an unnecessary onus on us while we are trying to develop your professional persona. Remove it at once. If you must keep it, keep it where it will not be seen, preferably buried in some drawer.

"I've spoken to you once before about this, and I thought you understood. I want my pupils, especially my young women, to have an air of virginity about them, a purity that makes them wholly desirable. Whether you are a virgin in fact or not," she added with her lips twisted. "Well?"

The tears that were burning my eyes made her look foggy and cloudy.

"Can't I keep it on and tell people I'm not engaged if they ask?"

"I will not debate it. We cannot permit our special guests to wait a moment longer. Are you a part of this school or are you not? Did you waste your parents' time and money or did you not? I'll see to it that you are taken to the airport and put on a plane for home this very night," she threatened.

I sucked back my sobs and slipped off the ring.

"Very good. Come along," she said.

"May I go to the bathroom and wash my face first?" I asked. My eyes felt like shattered marbles.

"No," she said. "It's better that you look a bit frightened. They enjoy it."

She started out, waited for me to follow, and then continued to the ballroom, where everyone was already having champagne and filling the air with laughter and compliments. I heard Edmond Senetsky's voice booming above all others, bragging about how he had found his mother her newest students.

"It's like visiting garden after garden and plucking the most beautiful of flowers. Quite a little bouquet of talent, eh?"

Chandler, who wore a look of worry on his face because I hadn't arrived with my fellow performers, was standing with Barry across the room. He started toward me the moment he saw me enter, but Ms. Fairchild was there first, ordering me to take my place with the others. We were to greet people first, like newly married couples greet their guests, standing in a line. I was handed a glass of champagne and told to take my place between Rose and Howard.

"Where's Evan?" I asked, gazing around and not seeing him.

"I had to send him back to his hotel," Rose said. "He looked tired, and I can't spend that much time with him now. He'll be here tomorrow before he heads back."

I nodded, half listening. My body was still trembling from the demands Madame Senetsky had just made. My hand was shaking so much, in fact, I had to sip some champagne quickly so it wouldn't spill from the glass. I glanced at Ms. Fairchild to see if she was watching and condemning me for drinking too fast. She did have her eyes on me, but she didn't look any different, her eyes still their normal critical selves, searching for a reason to whip one of her precious rules at us.

"Are you all right?" Rose asked.

I started to say no when Chandler approached.

"Hi," he said. "You were terrific." He turned to the others. "All of you were great."

"Excuse me," Ms. Fairchild told him with a plastic smile. She stepped directly between him and me. "Please ask your friends to wait politely at the rear of the room. Introductions to important people are to begin."

She widened that smile and walked away.

Chandler and Rose had overheard.

"How rude," she said. "Like our friends aren't important people. That's why I didn't want Evan hanging around and feeling unwanted and belittled."

"Don't worry. She can't make me feel unwanted," Chandler whispered in my ear. "I'll be eagerly waiting for you in the bleachers."

He looked about and then quickly kissed me on the cheek before hurrying off to join Barry. I caught Madame Senetsky glaring at me with those eyes that could condemn someone to the gallows with a single glance.

"I feel like I'm on display," Rose muttered through a forced smile. "Just like I did when I was in the beauty contest. Why can't we just be ourselves and mingle? This feels so artificial. Who stands in a line like this at a party and lets people gape at them?"

"We do," Howard said proudly. "The crème de la crème."

The train of people began to line up to pass before us, Madame Senetsky introducing each of us, making sure to introduce Jack Ferante first.

"I see some movie-star potential here," he declared, looking at Rose.

Most everyone was enthusiastic about us and our work, raining down his or her appreciation in a shower of compliments. Howard was the best at soaking them up. He seemed to swell with every passing moment, the glow in his face becoming absolutely luminous. Like the rest of us, however, he maintained enough modesty to satisfy Madame Senetsky. I wasn't modest so much as I was too frightened to say anything but a simple "thank you."

After the formal introductions, we were joined by our teachers, who directed us to those more involved in our individual fields. The room was filled with conversations about music, dance, and the theater. Names of famous people were casually thrown about as if they were all close friends with the guests who were present. Some of them probably were. My most interesting conversation was with a viola player who was with the New York Philharmonic. He told me about their rehearsals, how he had been chosen, his own schooling and preparation, and what his life was like living in New York and traveling with the orchestra.

"I have no doubt," he said, "that you will end up with one of our finest symphony orchestras, too. You don't know how lucky you are to have this opportunity. I wish I had been given it when I was your age. For me it was quite a struggle, but for you, with your talent and Madame Senetsky's connections, it should be so much easier. I can think of no one who carries more respect and influence in New York, as well as the world's most important cities, than she does."

I thanked him, and when I turned, I saw Madame

Senetsky had been standing very close, eavesdropping on everything he had said to me and I had said to him. Our eyes met for an instant and I saw the pleasure in her face hearing all the wonderful things about herself. She nodded at me as if to say, "See? Now you know why you had better do exactly as I tell you." Then she turned her attention to Rose.

For a moment, I appeared to be free. There was no one with whom I had to make conversation. It was as if a fresh breeze had come into the room. I could take a deep breath and let myself relax. It was short-lived, however. As soon as I turned toward Chandler, Mr. Bergman was there with a friend of his who taught at Juilliard.

"Madame Senetsky is lucky you didn't audition for me," he said. "You would have had a scholarship and be attending my school.

"But," he added with a small sigh, "I'll have to admit she gets her students placed well and on to very successful careers. She has an amazing track record."

"Which is why I am here in the first place," Mr. Bergman told him.

His friend assured me I would be working for a prestigious orchestra some day soon.

"Just work hard," he said, "and listen keenly to everything Madame Senetsky tells you," he admonished and walked off. *If I hear that from one more person,* I thought, *I'll scream.*

When I gazed about, I saw how all of the others were glowing. Thankfully, it was a very successful evening. Toward the end of the reception, Madame

Senetsky expressed that very sentiment to us. She looked proud and content.

Finally released from my obligatory chatter, I hurried to join Chandler. Barry and Rose fell in with us and the four of us started out of the room, intending to spend some time together in the parlor, but Ms. Fairchild caught up with us in the hallway.

"Remember curfew, girls," she warned. She tapped the face of her watch. "Twenty more minutes and your friends will have to leave the house and you're all to be in bed."

She marched ahead of us to join Madame Senetsky in the entryway saying good night to the guests.

"Twenty minutes! That woman is like a pail of ice water," I moaned.

Her warning did have the effect of cooling down our excitement. From the way we were all seated in the parlor and the looks of disappointment on our faces, anyone would think they had walked in on a funeral.

Steven joined us a moment later, bopping in like his legs consisted of springs.

"What a night, huh?" he cried. I bribed a waiter to give me an extra glass of champagne." He heard no response and looked at each of us. "What happened? Someone's pet rock die?"

"Nothing happened, Steven, except ten minutes ago, Ms. Fairchild made sure to tell us we had less than twenty minutes to spend with each other. Chandler came all the way from Boston!" I cried.

"We don't get to see each other very much even though Barry's here in New York. Our relentless schedule makes it very difficult," Rose added. "You'd think we'd get a little more consideration. I hate these curfews and restrictions. Other people our age don't have them."

"The price of fame!" Steven joked. No one laughed. He gazed at us all for a moment and then, after looking behind him to be sure he wouldn't be overheard, stepped farther into the room and closer to us all. "How about me showing Laurel and Hardy here how to get back into the building after Dracula's daughter bolts the entrance?"

"What?" Chandler asked. "What are you talking about?"

"I'm talking about sneaking you guys back in and upstairs. It's easy. You just go around the side of the building and climb the fire escape to their windows," he said. "They're on the same side and have the same landing."

Rose looked at me and I felt my body freeze.

"How do you know about that?" she asked him.

Steven shrugged.

"I just happened to look out and notice, and then, when I was walking about the grounds, I saw how to do it." He turned to Chandler and Barry. "You'll have to pull yourselves up a bit on the ladder. I don't imagine it will be too clean, so you might spoil your nice clothes, but," he said glancing from Rose to me and then back to Rose, "it might be worth it."

Chandler looked at me to see what I thought of the idea. I couldn't help but be afraid.

"If they get caught," Rose said, "we could be thrown out tomorrow."

"So don't let them get caught. Jeez," Steven said. "Isn't there any adventure in your guys?"

We were all silent.

"Or any male hormones?" he added, followed by his thin, silly laugh as he sauntered out of the parlor.

"What do you think?" Chandler asked Barry.

"I'm game for it if you are. Girls?"

Rose widened her eyes and turned to me. I looked at Chandler, who was staring at my hand, just realizing I wasn't wearing his ring.

"What happened to it?" he asked, nodding at my fingers.

"What?" Rose asked.

I bit down on my lip.

We could hear Ms. Fairchild's voice in the hallway.

"Do it," I blurted rather than answer his question.

"All right," Barry said smiling.

Rose looked terrified and surprised at me. When Ms. Fairchild made her presence nearby obvious, I suggested the boys leave.

"There's only a few minutes left anyway," I said. "Our windows will be open halfway. Steven's right. We're on the same landing, so it's easy."

Chandler smiled.

"I'll be like Romeo, climbing the balcony," he said.

"It's just about as dangerous for everyone," Rose muttered and we stood up to walk with them to the front door. Ms. Fairchild followed us with her gaze and was standing behind us when we all said our good nights.

"You did very well, girls," she told us. "Very well.

Now get what I'm sure is a much-needed night's rest."

She pivoted and marched away, her heels ticking over the tiles until she disappeared around the corner. Rose looked at me. She smiled with excitement. We held hands and hurried up the stairs. At my doorway, we parted.

"Have a much-needed night's rest," she mimicked. I laughed, took a deep breath, and entered my bedroom.

For a moment I stood there staring at the window. Do I dare? Should I just leave it down and forget this idea? Was it worth the risk?

As I approached the window, I felt a tingling start at the base of my stomach. I wanted Chandler. I wanted him to hold me and kiss me and comfort me. I wanted to be loved like I had never been loved. What right had that woman to demand I take off his expression of affection, my beautiful ring? Why should we let her control our very heartbeats, our every quickened breath, our laughter and our tears? No one should have such authority over another.

I slipped the ring back onto my finger and held it up in the moonlight. Its glitter reassured me.

Partly out of defiance and partly out of the longing I had for him, I lifted that window and slowly brought it to a position halfway open. Excitement seemed to explode in my heart, sending a thunderous beat and reverberation through every nerve, dousing me in a warmth that cupped my breasts and made my lips wet with anticipation.

I turned from the window and went into the bathroom, where I stared at myself in the mirror for a few moments. Then, I unbuttoned my blouse and peeled it off. I lowered my skirt and stood there in my bra and panties for a moment. I brushed down my hair and then, after a deep sigh, stepped back into my room.

Chandler was already standing there, silhouetted in the moonlight that poured through my window. He did not speak. I flipped off the bathroom light and crossed to my closet without speaking either. My heart was pounding. I was playing out my own fantasy, imagining he wasn't really there. He was a dream instead. I hung up my blouse and my skirt and then turned back to him. He hadn't moved. His face was still in dark shadows.

I went to my dresser and, with my back to him, I undid my bra and slipped it down my arms. I put it in the drawer and closed my eyes. My body was tingling all over, my nipples so hard, they ached.

"Honey," he whispered. "I do love you so much."

I stood there, waiting. First, I felt his lips on my neck and then he kissed my shoulders and pressed his face against my hair. He wrapped his arms about my waist and held me against him. I let my head fall back and his kisses climbed up my neck again. Then his hands moved over my breasts, cupping them, strumming my nipples, washing wave after wave of excitement up and into my face, which felt so hot, I thought I could cook an egg on my cheek.

Slowly I turned around and we kissed, long and hard, both of us breathing very fast.

"I want you so much, my whole body is in pain," he said. How wonderful that made me feel.

When I was a little girl, my grandad made me believe that desire was the road to hell. He had me terrified of myself, my dreams, my urges and feelings. There was a time when I thought I was the most sinful of people, feeling guilty because I had developed into a woman.

It wasn't until I met Chandler that I began to look at myself differently, and when I learned about Grandad's own sinful acts, I realized why Mommy often chastised him by throwing back at him the Biblical quotes he often whipped at me.

"He without sin cast the first stone," Mommy would tell him, and Grandad would shift his eyes quickly and walk off mumbling to himself.

"Pay him no heed," Mommy would urge me. "He's all twisted up inside."

When all these thoughts battled within my dizzy brain, I heard a voice inside me whispering, telling me that what I felt was not evil, but beautiful. Two people who truly cared for each other, who loved each other dearly, made the most beautiful music in the rhythm of their hearts. The ability to love each other wholly and purely was truly a blessing, not a sin. I longed to bury Grandad's warnings and threats with him, once and for all, now and forever.

And there was only one way to do it.

Chandler and I did not speak. We moved to my bed so quietly, gracefully, it almost seemed not to be happening. He stood beside the bed, gazing down at me. The moonlight played on his eyes, his lips, whitening his face. His slow, deliberate movements combined with that made me feel as if we were both performing an ancient love scene in some Kabuki theater. His clothing fell from him like a curtain. He slipped off my panties. Moments later we were both naked, holding and kissing each other with an increasing desperation.

"We've got to be careful," the sensible side of me managed to say.

"Don't worry. I'm prepared," he whispered.

Grandad had made the act of love into something bestial, ugly, raw, and violent in my mind. He knew nothing of tenderness. He knew nothing about bringing one heart into another, turning two separate people into one. We were both reaching so deeply into each other, we surely touched each other's very souls, I thought. In my musical mind, I felt our lovemaking building to a crescendo. It took my breath away. I clung to him as if I believed I would fall forever and ever if I didn't hold on to him. I was squeezing him so hard, I was sure he was in some pain, but it was an exquisite pain. He did all he could to keep me from stopping, crying, "No, no, not yet," as if his lingering within me would keep us bonded forever.

And then, both spent, we released each other and lay there side by side, catching our breaths, falling back to earth, dropping into our separate bodies.

"I don't see how it's possible to love anyone more than I love you, Honey," he said after a few moments of just listening to each other breathe.

I smiled, turned, and kissed him first on the tip of his nose and then his lips.

"Nor can I, Chandler."

"Why didn't you have the ring on your finger before?" he asked, touching it now and holding my fingers in his hand.

"Madame Senetsky thought it looked too much like an engagement ring."

"So? I don't understand."

"She would prefer her students to look totally dedicated to their professions. She wants us literally to have no other interests or goals in our lives but that."

"How can being in love with someone hurt your effort to become a successful musician?" he asked, grimacing with confusion.

"We'd be distracted. It's what she believes, not what I believe," I added quickly. "But she threatened to send me home if I wore the ring in front of people."

"Oh," he said sadly. "Hey," he said, "don't worry about it. She can't stop the flow of love from me to you."

I smiled.

He started to lift his head to kiss me again when my eyes caught a shadow moving over the wall. I turned to the window and then cried out. We heard her flee up the ladder.

"What...what was that?" he asked.

Now my heart was pounding to a different rhythm, thumping to a different drummer: abject fear.

"Oh, no," I cried.

"Was someone there? Was someone spying on us?" Chandler asked, sitting up quickly. "One of the boys? Steven? What? Tell me, Honey," he pleaded.

Footsteps in the hallway made us both deadly silent

for a moment. We listened and then heard them pass and begin to descend the stairs.

"What's going on?" he whispered.

"Get your clothes on, Chandler," I urged. I went for a nightgown quickly. He started to dress.

"What's happening?"

"I don't know," I said.

"I don't understand. Was there someone out there or not?"

"Yes, there was. There's someone living upstairs, someone none of us have met. We think it might be Madame Senetsky's daughter."

"Well, why is she using the fire escape? Was she spying on you?"

"I don't know. It's all very strange."

"What did you mean by you *think* it's her daughter? Is it or isn't it?"

"We're not sure. She looks like her son, but..."

"So you've seen her?"

"Yes, but..."

"But what?"

"Madame Senetsky told me her daughter died some time ago."

"Huh?" He scratched his head and then shook it. "I don't understand."

"I can't talk about it anymore," I said, hesitating to tell him the rest of it: how she dressed, the missing clothes, Evan's research.

"But..."

Just then, we definitely heard someone on the fire escape and turned to the window.

"Don't move," Chandler said, inching toward it and urging me to lie back.

He lunged at the window, pulling the curtain back farther to see Barry standing there.

"What the hell are you doing?"

"I came to tell you we'd better go. Rose is getting nervous."

"How long were you out here?" Chandler asked him.

"I just stepped up, why?"

Chandler turned back to me.

"I don't understand what you're saying," he continued as if Barry had never interrupted us. "Why haven't any of you met her? Why would she be spying on you? Does this mean she's going to tell Madame Senetsky about us?"

"I don't know, Chandler. Let's leave it be for now. Barry's right. You'd better leave before something else happens, okay?"

"I would feel terrible if I caused you to be thrown out of the school, Honey. Just terrible."

I nodded. I was too frightened to think about it.

"I'll call you in the morning before I leave for the airport," he said.

He kissed me quickly and slipped out the window. I watched him and Barry descend. He looked up and waved and then they both ran to the driveway to disappear in the shadows and sneak out of the compound.

I closed the window and thought. Would whoever that was tell what she had seen? Rose could be in big trouble, too. I put on my robe and quickly went to her room. I knocked softly.

"Who is it?"

"Me," I said, opening the door. Her lights were out.

"Honey? What's wrong?" she asked and turned on the lamp on her side table.

I closed the door softly behind me.

"She was at my window," I said. "While Chandler and I were…"

"While you were making love?"

"Yes. I mean, I don't know how long she was there or what she actually saw, but she surely saw he was there. Once she tells Madame Senetsky…Oh, Rose, how will I ever explain this to my parents?"

I dropped onto her bed and started to weep.

"We'd better tell the other two. Wait here," Rose said. "I'm going to get them."

I sat in the dark, waiting, trembling. Moments later, Rose returned with Ice and Cinnamon right behind her. They closed the door and Rose put on another lamp.

"What exactly happened?" Cinnamon asked in a loud whisper.

I told her and everyone was quiet.

"She might have looked in my window, too," Rose said, "and seen Barry as well."

"This is disgusting, being spied upon like this. We have no lives here," Cinnamon muttered.

"Amen to that," Ice said.

"What should we do?" I asked.

"Nothing. What can we do? We'll have to wait to see what happens tomorrow. I can tell you this," Cinnamon vowed, "if either of you are thrown out of this school because of this, I'm marching out right behind you."

"Me, too," Ice said.

"No. You can't ruin your careers because of me," I moaned.

"Or me," Rose insisted.

"I'll make it on my own. If we have such talent, nothing can stop us. It might take longer, but the price we'll pay for speed isn't worth it," Cinnamon said. "Don't worry about it. We'll all get jobs in the city and rent an apartment together and work at our careers. It might be more fun, anyway."

"My parents wouldn't be happy about it," I said, even though it did sound good to me.

"They'll get happy about it," Cinnamon insisted.

She made me smile.

"I told you—one for all, all for one. Girls?"

"Okay," Ice said. "They go, we all go."

She put out her hand. Cinnamon covered it with hers. Rose gazed at me and then did the same, and then I did. For a moment we held onto each other tightly.

"Let's get some sleep," Cinnamon said and started for the door. She stopped before opening it and turned to the rest of us. "But one more thing...even if nothing comes of this, I want to know what's happening up there. Who is that? Why is she spying on us?

"Let's decide right now to find out."

"How?" Ice asked.

"We'll pay her a visit again. Only this time..."

"What this time?" I asked, holding my breath.

"This time we go into the rooms. We confront her. We ask questions."

No one spoke.

All our hearts beat with the same mad, frightened rhythm.

Cinnamon opened the door.

"I've got to get a boyfriend, too. I need to have someone sneak up here," she joked. "That's a rule I'd enjoy breaking."

Moments later, we were all in our beds, looking into the darkness, wondering what the morning would bring.

11

Oranges and Lemons

Almost telepathically, the four of us emerged from our respective rooms simultaneously to go down to breakfast in the morning. We wore an air of anticipation around and over us like an invisible blanket. Every time someone came into the dining room, our eyes lifted together in expectation. Ms. Fairchild's steely footsteps in the corridor were like tiny knocks on our thumping hearts. Most of the time, she walked by the room without looking in to see what we were doing, but whenever she did, our collective breaths were frozen. All of us waited to hear, "Madame Senetsky wants you to report to her office now!"

But we didn't hear the fatal words.

Without any specific assignments to fulfill, we could have slept later. Steven and Howard certainly did, both appearing when the four of us were nearly finished.

"What's going on here today?" Howard complained. "Usually, it's quieter than a cemetery on a Sunday."

There did seem to be a great deal of activity in the house: doors opening and closing, Madame Senetsky's servants going to and fro, Ms. Fairchild looking in on us and then, without a word, disappearing into the private residence. We were all wondering what it meant.

"So?" Steven asked, flopping into a chair at the table, "how did the rest of the evening go?"

No one spoke. Surprised at the question, Howard looked at us and at Steven.

"What rest of what evening?" he asked.

"Didn't you hear any scurrying about the building last night? For a while there, I thought we were going to have an earthquake in New York."

"No," Howard said. "What are you talking about now, Steven?"

"Nothing," he said, smiling lustfully at Rose and me. "Or was it something?"

Cinnamon was about to tell him off when Ms. Fairchild appeared in the doorway again.

"The boy in the wheelchair is here," she announced with a grimace twisting her lips.

"He's not the boy in the wheelchair. His name is Evan and he's my brother," Rose retorted.

"Nevertheless, he's here and someone should assist him into the building. Everyone is too busy this morning to cater to anyone's guests."

We started out with Rose.

"If you need any help, call," Howard shouted after us.

"If I needed any help, he'd be the last one I'd call," Cinnamon muttered.

The van was parked in front and the lift was lowering Evan in his chair. Rose went down to him immediately. The driver came around to assist. It was a cloudy day, with threats of rain coming from the north. I felt a real chill in the air.

"Hi. You guys were all great last night," Evan said as we approached.

We all thanked him. He stared at us a moment and then looked to Rose.

"What?" she asked, sensing he had something more important to tell us.

"I've got about an hour," Evan said, "before I have to leave for the airport. Is there some place we can go to talk in private?"

"Privately? Why?" Cinnamon asked quickly.

"I did some more work last night. Couldn't sleep and went on-line with my notebook computer."

No one spoke. Cinnamon looked back at the house.

"What's wrong?" Evan asked.

"If we go inside, Howard and Steven will be all over us," she replied. "And we can't get him upstairs into any of our rooms."

"It looks like it's going to rain any minute," Ice said. "We can't stay out here."

"Look," I cried, and everyone followed my gaze to the third-floor front windows. A curtain quickly closed.

"Was it her?" Ice asked.

"I think so," I said.

"It can't be her," Evan said. "Or at least who you all think it is."

"Why not?" Cinnamon asked.

Evan looked back at the van. His driver was sitting with the seat back, his eyes closed.

"Just take me for a walk. The rain's a little way off," he said. "It won't take me long anyway."

Rose got behind the wheelchair and we all started down a path toward the north side. Groundspeople were working. Their mowers and trimmers hummed.

"What else have you learned?" Cinnamon practically demanded as soon as we were far enough from the house.

We stopped at one of the benches. Ice and I sat. Rose and Cinnamon stood, with Evan at the center.

"I went back to try to find out when Gerta left the clinic and came to live in New York with Madame Senetsky. When Honey said that Madame Senetsky told her that her daughter had died, I began to check the European newspapers."

"And?" Cinnamon asked.

Evan looked up at her.

"A search for the name revealed an item on the obituary pages. It's true. Gerta Senetsky died."

"How?" Ice asked.

"They didn't say specifically in the obituary, but from what I could read in small news clippings, it looks to me like either a suicide or an accident."

"If Gerta Senetsky is really dead, who is that up there?" Rose asked, gazing back at the building.

"I don't know what to tell you. I haven't found any other relatives I could suggest," Evan said.

"When did she die?" I asked.

"A little less than a year after she entered the clinic," Evan replied.

All of us stared at him.

"Maybe that's a student who broke some rules and was locked up in the tower of Senetsky," Cinnamon grumbled, gazing back at the building.

"How weird," Rose said and lowered herself slowly beside Ice and myself.

"Maybe it's her ghost," Cinnamon suggested, half-kiddingly.

"Please, not your spirits again," Rose moaned.

We all stared at Evan for a long moment, and then Cinnamon's eyes widened.

"From what you told us previously, Madame Senetsky's husband did commit suicide about that time, too, right?"

"Yes, very soon afterward, but it's all been kept so vague. There are so few details."

"This is getting too complicated. What do we do?" I asked.

"If we keep trying to find out, this whole thing could explode in our faces," Rose suggested in a loud whisper.

"Or Madame Senetsky's," Cinnamon countered. She stared at the house again and then turned back to us, her face etched with determination. "Tonight, girls, we go up there and confront our Peeping Missy, whatever her name is."

"I don't know," Ice said, shaking her head. "Poking around like that."

"We're not the ones who have been poking around,

Ice. We have to find out what's going on. Rose is right. It's so weird, and who wants to be gaped at and spied upon and robbed of clothes and..."

"Cinnamon's right," Rose concluded. "I don't care what the consequences are. Let's get to the bottom of it."

"I wish I could go up there with you," Evan said. "I've got a few more ideas I want to pursue. If you find out anything concrete, call me tonight. Call me any time, Rose."

She nodded.

"It's starting," I said when the first raindrop hit my cheek.

"Come on in and have something hot to drink before you go, Evan," Rose said.

We helped him into the house and to the dining room, where Steven and Howard were still having their breakfast. For the time being, we put aside our mystery and instead talked about the Performance Night, the people we had each met, and some of the things we were told. I saw how much Evan enjoyed our company, and I felt sorry for him having to return to a big home where his only companion was his computer and what its electronic tentacles could latch onto for him.

We're all isolated in different ways, I thought. Even people who were in a city as big as this one, with so great a population, found themselves trapped in their own pockets of loneliness. Some brought their own isolation upon themselves with their conceited manner, living as if they were looking down at the rest of the world from an ivory tower. Despite her grand lifestyle and her many, many important acquaintances, Madame Senetsky struck me as someone who was not really happy. She was too concerned with being Madame Senetsky. I had yet to hear an authentic, free, and wonderful peal of laughter coming from her, see an honest smile or a look of pure wonder in her eyes.

Mommy and Daddy lived on a farm in a very unsophisticated world by Madame Senetsky's standards. They worked very hard, but the work seemed naturally part of who and what they were. That was certainly true for Uncle Simon. The word *work* had an entirely different meaning for him when it came to his flowers. There was none of this contrivance, this myriad of defenses to construct around yourself so your reputation and your power over other people was constantly protected. Back home, they just nourished their work, not their image. It seemed that here our images were almost as important, if not more important than our talents, and protecting and building that image was a continuous, never-ending responsibility. Disaster for Madame Senetsky was probably being caught with her hair down.

There were tears in Rose's eyes when she said good-bye to Evan. I had tears in my eyes, too, after Chandler called to say good-bye for a while.

"Did you get into any trouble? Don't lie to me, Honey," he followed quickly, before I could contrive a false answer if there was need for one.

"No, Chandler. No one has said a word about any of it this morning, and we've seen Ms. Fairchild a few times already."

"Good," he said with relief in his voice. "Anyway, I'm going to work out another trip back here very soon. I've got some exams, and after that, I'll return."

"I'll be waiting for you, Chandler."

"Don't fall in love with any handsome actors, singers, or producers until I do return," he warned with a small laugh. His sincere fear was palpable.

"I'm already in love, Chandler. I don't have room in my heart for another. This one takes up too much room," I told him.

"And I'll keep the ring under my pillow so I can dream about you every night."

I could almost hear his smile.

We said our good-byes and then I cradled the phone and wiped the errant tears from my cheeks. I was in my room, sitting on my bed, reliving our wonderful lovemaking. My eyes shifted to my closet, and for a moment or two, I stared at my clothing without understanding why something was nudging at me. Then I rose and went to the rack.

Moments later, I was downstairs again. Cinnamon, Rose, and Ice were watching television. Howard and Steven had gone to a movie.

I paused in the doorway, my hand at the base of my throat.

"What is it?" Cinnamon asked quickly.

"My clothes," I said in a breathy voice, "the ones that had been taken?"

"Yes."

"They're all back in my closet!"

"Really?" Cinnamon turned to Rose.

"I'll go up and check mine," she said, rising. We all followed her and, sure enough, her missing clothing was back as well.

"Do you think any of this had to do with all the commotion this morning?" I asked.

"Maybe," Cinnamon said, nodding.

"Why didn't anyone ask us about the clothing, why we didn't report it missing?" Rose wondered aloud.

"Maybe they hoped you didn't notice," Ice suggested.

"She's right, I bet," Cinnamon said. "It doesn't matter though. After dinner, tonight, we're going up that fire escape again, and this time, we're going into the room," she added, nailing down her determination with a look in her eyes that clearly said, "Don't disagree."

It was still frightening, but with the way Cinnamon looked at us, we were all trying to decide what was more frightening: confronting the mystery or defying our very determined sister.

Conducting our investigation without attracting Howard or Steven's attention was the first task. They returned from their movie and hovered about us, suggesting different ways to spend the evening together. Cinnamon and Rose claimed they had letters to write.

"I'm long overdue," Cinnamon said.

"You just saw your brother," Howard told Rose. "Why don't you join us in a game of Scrabble?"

"I have my mother to write, you know," she said with feigned indignation. "She doesn't live as close by as your parents do."

"What about you two?" he asked Ice and me, ignoring her.

"Scrabble?" Ice said. "I think I'd rather twiddle my thumbs. It's more exciting."

"I'm just tired," I said. "I guess the emotional pressure was more than I realized."

"Jeez," Howard complained. "If this is the level of energy you people bring to the theater, I pity the audiences."

Steven sat there with a silly smile on his face, listening and observing. The way his eyes fixed on me made me nervous.

"I wouldn't worry about their level of energy, Howard," Steven said.

"Right."

"I don't know why you're complaining about us not joining you this evening, Howard," Cinnamon said as she rose. "You've told us so many times what good company you are. You shouldn't be upset about spending time with yourself."

Steven laughed hard and slapped his knee.

"Go on, ridicule me all you like. Some day you'll wish you had spent more time with me, Cinnamon Carlson," Howard cried after her.

We followed her out, leaving him and Steven. When we were upstairs, Cinnamon turned and whispered, "Ten minutes, Honey's room. Put on sneakers and wear black."

"You're sure about this?" Ice asked one more time.

"Absolutely," Cinnamon replied.

We broke up and went to change clothes. A little less than ten minutes later, they were all in my room, everyone whispering. Cinnamon went to the window, paused, and then opened it as quietly as she could.

It was a very cool night. It had rained on and off all day and the sky was still overcast. It wasn't until we were all out on the landing and Cinnamon started up the ladder that we realized the metal was wet and slippery. Ice's foot slid off a rung and she nearly fell onto Rose. She uttered a small scream, and we all froze.

"You all right?" Cinnamon called in a loud whisper.

"Yes."

"Everyone take your time," Cinnamon ordered.

Once again, we started up. We moved like a dark snake, slowly climbing toward the landing above us, where the glow of the light from within spread a pool of pale white illumination over the iron, turning it into the color of faded bones. The cool air dropped a chill down my back. My teeth clicked and I shuddered. *Don't look down,* I kept telling myself.

When we were all finally on the landing, we crouched and hovered close to each other, gazing into the bedroom. There was no one there, even though the lights were on, but like before, we could hear music—the very same tune, in fact.

"What is that?" Rose asked.

"I've heard the tune before, but I can't place it," Ice said. "Anybody?"

We all shook our heads.

"It sounds like a children's song or something," Rose suggested.

"Okay," Cinnamon said. "This is it. If we don't do it now, we won't."

She opened the window and then started in. Rose put her hand on her shoulder, and she paused.

"There's no going back once we're in there, Cinnamon."

"Exactly," Cinnamon replied and entered the room.

Ice followed, and then Rose and I. The bed was a four-poster canopy. Against the pink and white pillows were two large teddy bears. They seemed to be watching us. We stood there for a moment, listening. The music continued, and then someone began to sing along.

We heard a very childlike voice.

" 'Oranges and lemons, say the bells of St. Clement's. You owe me five farthings, say the bells of St. Martin's.' "

Cinnamon shook her head and scrunched her nose. Ice shrugged, and the four of us moved very slowly and quietly to the doorway of the bedroom.

The singing continued.

" 'When will you pay me? say the bells of Old Bailey. When I grow rich, say the bells of Shoreditch.' "

We all peered through the door into a living room. At first we saw no one. The room had a sectional with its back toward us, two large cushion chairs facing it and a pretty burgundy and black oval rug. There was a standing lamp with a pale yellow shade on the right of the sectional, which provided the only light in the room at the moment.

The walls were quite different from the walls in the rest of the house. These walls were paneled in a dark maple wood. There was a fireplace to the right, but in it was a potted plant. Above the mantle was a rich oil painting of a much younger Madame Senetsky standing on a balcony, in what looked to me to be a scene from *Romeo and Juliet.* She had her eyes turned upward and her hands outstretched, palms upward, as if she had just asked, " 'Wherefore art thou Romeo?' "

The window in this room had a heavy, dark brown velvet curtain with gold tassels drawn closed over it. On the opposite side of the room was a pedestal holding a small bronze statue of a cherub. Scattered over the floor beneath it were what looked like cutout dolls, found in children's games.

There was a door on the side that made me think this was the door I had seen when I had gone to the rear of the costume room and Ms. Fairchild had come in on me.

The music continued, and we quickly realized it was coming from the front of the sectional. The voice continued, ending with, " 'Here comes a candle to light you to bed. Here comes a chopper to chop off your head.' "

The woman we had seen before rose. Her hair was in pigtails and she wore a light pink wool nightgown with a fringed collar and short sleeves. As she rose, she emphatically said, " 'Chop, chop, chop. The last man's dead!' "

She clapped her hands and then turned and saw us all standing there. Her look of shock and surprise was almost instantly replaced by a broad smile. Now that we were standing only a few feet from her and looking directly at her, the resemblances we had found between her and Edmond Senetsky were not as pronounced. There were still, I thought, some similarities in their eyes and noses.

The recording of the song ended, but she was playing it on an old phonograph she had on the floor. The phonograph needle was caught and grinding.

"Oh, it's stuck!" she cried, and knelt down to fix it. We walked farther into the room and saw she had a small pile of old records there as well.

She stood up again. Her nightgown was hemmed just below her knees and she wore what looked like a man's pair of old, soft, leather slippers.

"Have you come to play oranges and lemons?" she asked, her face lighting up with expectation.

"No," Cinnamon said. "We've come to find out exactly what's going on."

Her smile went out like a blown bulb. She looked like she might burst into tears.

"We've come to find out who you are and why you've been spying on us through the windows," Cinnamon continued.

There was something in the woman's face that made me feel bad about Cinnamon's aggressive tone.

"I don't think she understands," I whispered.

Cinnamon's eyes narrowed.

"Is this where you live?" Rose asked the woman.

Despite her childlike manner, the way she wore her hair, the little teddy bear figures on her nightgown and the teddy bears on her bed, I thought she was well into her twenties, if not her thirties.

"Yes, I do. I do live here. Yes," she said. She nodded and looked very thoughtful for a moment. "Once I lived there," she continued, "but now I live here."

"Where was there?" Ice asked.

She laughed.

"There was not here, silly. Silly girl. Silly. Who wants to play first?"

"What is this?" Cinnamon muttered to us. I shook my head. I couldn't help but be both frightened and fascinated.

"What's your name?" Rose asked. She smiled at her. "My name is Rose. This is Cinnamon, and Ice, and this is Honey."

"Rose? Name?" She laughed. "Yes," she said with that thoughtful look again. Then she turned, gazed at Madame Senetsky's portrait and, raising her hand slowly, her fingers twitching as if she was imitating the first flight of a baby bird, cried, " 'What's in a name? A rose by any other name would smell as sweet.' "

She looked at us and laughed.

"Come on. Who's first? Who will play with me first? Who will be the lemon and who will be the orange? I'll be the orange," she said quickly. "You," she said, pointing at me. "You can be the lemon. Come on. Give me your hands. Come on," she urged, holding out her hands.

I looked at Cinnamon, who just shook her head, and then I put my hands out.

She seized them and raised them so we formed an arch.

"Not so close," she said to me. "Step back. Make room for them. Go on, you foolish, silly girls. Go on." She looked at Cinnamon, Rose, and Ice. "The rest of you go under as we sing along."

Then she began to sing.

" 'Oranges and lemons, say the bells of St. Clements.' "

She paused and looked angrily at Ice, Cinnamon, and Rose.

"Are you going to go under or not? How are we to play if you don't go under?"

"What the hell is she talking about?" Cinnamon groaned.

"Let's just do it," Ice said, and went under the arch.

She smiled.

" 'You owe me five farthings, say the bells of St. Martin's.' "

With her head, she urged Cinnamon and Rose.

" 'When will you pay me? say the bells of Old Bailey. When I grow rich, say the bells of Shoreditch.' "

She paused.

"Keep going under, silly girls. Come on." She wagged our arms.

Ice did it again.

" 'When will that be? say the bells of Stepney.' "

Cinnamon and Rose went under again as she sang on.

" 'I'm sure I don't know, says the great bell at Bow.' "

Just as Ice entered, she brought down our arms around her, trapping her between them.

" 'Here comes a candle to light you to bed. Here comes a chopper to chop off your head.' Well?" she asked Ice.

"What?"

"Decide. Are you a lemon or are you an orange? Come on, silly."

"I'm an orange."

"Good, get behind me. Quickly," she said, raising our arms so Ice could pass and go around behind her. "Next."

Rose went under, and again she brought our arms down, trapping her and singing the ending of the song. " 'Here comes a chopper to chop off your head.' Well? What are you?"

"A lemon," Rose said.

"Get behind her," she said, nodding at me. "Next."

Cinnamon shook her head and entered and the arms came down. Now the girl sang, " 'Chop, chop, chop. The last man's dead!' Well?"

"Lemon," Cinnamon said. "I feel like one."

"Get behind her," she ordered, which she did. "Grab waists. Come on. Grab waists. Now, everyone pull. It's a tug of war. Who's stronger, the orange or the lemon? Pull," she cried.

She was pulling so hard, my arms felt like they would come out of their sockets. Cinnamon released Ice and Ice released me and I went falling forward onto her. She fell back against Rose, and the three of us toppled onto the sectional.

She laughed and laughed and clapped her hands.

"That was wonderful. What a wonderful game."

She sat up and gazed at us and we realized she had been wearing a wig, which had fallen off. Her hair was cut very short—chopped, was more like it.

"Who wants to do it again?"

"No," Cinnamon said. "We're not here for that. We want to know your name. Tell us your name. Why are you living up here? Why do you look in our windows? Why did you take clothing and then put it back?"

She shook her head.

"I didn't put it back," she said.

"Well, why did you take it?"

"I liked it. Don't scowl at me like that. Go sit in the corner."

She embraced herself, pursed her lips, and sat sternly. Then she saw her wig, looked at us, and quickly put it back on her head, adjusting it as comfortably as she could.

"I can choose any one I want," she said. "And I can wear anything I want, even the queen's crown. I just go in there and pick and pick when the door is unlocked."

"You obviously aren't supposed to go into our rooms and pick and pick," Cinnamon muttered.

"Are you related to Madame Senetsky?" Rose asked softly. She didn't respond. She just stared. "I don't care if you took my clothes. It's all right," Rose added. The woman's eyes shifted to her, to search for truth in Rose's face. Contented, she relaxed.

"I don't have any new clothes anymore. Just the costumes. She doesn't take me shopping."

"Who doesn't?" Ice asked.

"Mommy, Mommy, Mommy. Can we go shopping tomorrow? Can we walk in the big stores? Can we see the animals in the park? Tomorrow, tomorrow, always tomorrow. When will tomorrow come?" She looked up at Madame Senetsky's portrait again.

" 'Tomorrow and tomorrow and tomorrow creeps in this petty pace from day to day.' "

We all looked at each other.

"Will you come back tomorrow? Will you take me shopping?" she asked us.

Rose smiled at her and nodded.

"Sure we can. If your mother says it's all right. Is your mother Madame Senetsky?"

"Yes, yes, yes."

"Your name is Gerta, isn't it?" Cinnamon said.

"Of course," she replied.

"Why did she tell me she was dead? And how could Evan have located her obituary?" I whispered. Rose nodded.

"Gerta Berta. I'm Daddy's little Greta Berta. Let's go shopping, and we'll have ice cream on a stick."

"How long have you been living here, Gerta?" Cinnamon asked.

She scowled back at her.

"You're a lemon," she said, pointing her finger at her. "And you let go. You're not supposed to let go."

"I know. I got tired. You were too strong."

"Oranges are stronger. Today, oranges are stronger. Maybe not tomorrow. Who's coming back to play tomorrow?"

"We're all coming back, Gerta. We want to learn who you are and how you got here and why you don't come downstairs," Rose said smiling.

"I'm not allowed downstairs. If I go downstairs, I'll be put somewhere ugly again. A place where they touch you all over," she said, running her hands over her breasts and down to her thighs, "and make you cry out and then keep doing it until you promise to laugh and never tell.

"Swear," she said, "swear never to tell. Swear."

She paused and fell into what looked like a deep melancholy.

"So much for worrying that we would be turned in," Cinnamon said.

"This is very sad," I said. "She's, like, trapped up here."

She opened her eyes and looked at me.

" 'Yankie pokie, Yankie fun, how do you like your tatties done?'

" 'First in brandy, then in rum, that's how I like my tatties done.' "

She clapped her hands and laughed.

We heard some footsteps on a stairway and a door slam.

"We'd better get out of here," Cinnamon said.

"We have to go," I told Gerta. "Maybe we'll come back to see you."

"Come back, come back, oh, come back," she sang.

We walked into the bedroom and to the window. She followed and watched us go out and onto the landing.

"Be careful," Cinnamon whispered to me as I started down the ladder.

They all began to follow.

"Good night," we heard from the window. " 'Good night, sweet prince.' "

"She's very confused. She's liable to follow us," Rose cautioned.

"Go back inside," Cinnamon called up to her. "Go on. Close the window."

We waited to see what she would do.

"Lemon," she cried, and slammed the window shut.

I was down the ladder in seconds and moments later in my room, the others right behind.

"I have a little experience around mental patients," Cinnamon said when we settled down. "That's a case and a half up there."

"What's wrong with her? She looks like someone about thirty, doesn't she?" Rose asked.

"Yes, but she's a child, mentally."

"And yet, she comes out with the most amazing things," I said. "Those were lines from Shakespearean plays she quoted, weren't they?"

"Yes," Cinnamon said.

"It's like something's trapped her in her mind as well as up in that apartment," Ice mused.

"What should we do?" Rose asked.

"Forget about her," Ice said quickly. She looked at Cinnamon. "Right?"

"I can't help feeling sorry for her," I said.

Cinnamon's eyes widened when she looked at me. She nodded.

"When my mother was trapped in her mental dungeon, locked up by all her unhappiness, I felt so helpless, so ineffective. I had to humor her when all I wanted to do was shout, 'Mommy, you lost the baby. There is no baby. You've got to stop this ridiculous pretending and come back to us.' I knew, however, she wouldn't have heard me. She would have just smiled at me as if I was the one who was disturbed."

"Why doesn't Madame Senetsky try to get her help

instead of keeping her locked in up there?" Rose wondered, gazing toward the ceiling. "And why tell Honey that her daughter died long ago?"

"Apparently, she's not only telling Honey. Don't forget about the obituary," Ice reminded her.

"But why?"

"My guess," Cinnamon said with a deep sigh, "is that she is embarrassed by her. Madame Senetsky can't have a daughter like that. Not our Madame Senetsky, the Queen of Theatrical Perfection. She'd die if there was a picture of Gerta and the story in a newspaper. I remember how embarrassed my grandmother was when my mother went loony. And that was just my grandmother worrying about people who knew us and would gossip! And we weren't celebrities, remember."

"It's not fair," I said. "She's a very lonely person. Did you see how happy she was when we appeared—and how trusting, just like a child would be."

Everyone was quiet.

"We could just march downstairs and tell Ms. Fairchild we want to meet with Madame Senetsky and demand she let her out," Rose suggested.

Ice smirked.

"Oh, she would just say 'Sure thing, girls. I'm so happy you pointed out my mistake.' "

"Ice is right," Cinnamon said. "Forget that."

"Then what, forget about *her?"*

No one spoke for a moment.

"I've got to call Evan and let him know what we've discovered. Maybe there was a mistake in his information or he got something confused," Rose said.

"I doubt it," Cinnamon said. "When Madame Senetsky wants to forget something, she definitely has a funeral and buries it. Who knows what else she's buried?"

"Maybe we could go back up there and try to help her," I suggested.

"Back up there? You're kidding, right?" Ice said. "How can we help her?"

"I don't know. Maybe if we spend some time with her, she'll..."

"Snap out of it? It doesn't work that way," Cinnamon said. "It takes intense therapy and medication sometimes. But..."

"But what?" Ice asked.

"But I guess we can visit her again, learn more about her, maybe help her a little."

"You're the crazy one now," Ice insisted.

"Maybe. Rose, what do you think?"

She thought, smiled, and shrugged.

"I'm for it, if y'all are."

"Honey, you sure?"

"Yes. I don't care who gets mad at us."

Cinnamon looked at Ice.

"If you're all going to be thrown out of here, I guess I'd better join you. I won't be happy staying with Howard and Steven."

"What about them?"

"Don't dare let them know a thing," Cinnamon said. "Steven would not take it seriously and get us in trouble faster, and Howard..."

"What?" I asked.

"Would probably turn us in."

Everyone nodded in silent agreement.

"Besides," Cinnamon said with a smile, "the next time I'm going to be an orange."

All of us laughed, even Ice.

"Let's just let a few days pass to be sure neither Ms. Fairchild or Madame Senetsky has found out about our little expeditions into their private world and that we've discovered their big secret," Cinnamon suggested.

Everyone nodded.

"It's like waiting for a second shoe to drop," Ice said. "My daddy always says that. Especially after he and my mother had an argument and she went off to sulk or drink. I walked around holding my breath most of the time. My teachers thought I was some kind of mute."

"Until you opened your mouth and sang, I bet," Rose said.

"Singing is freedom to me," Ice replied.

Cinnamon smiled.

"I like that. I guess, in a real sense, that's what drives all of us. Ironic, in a way, that we've all come here to achieve that freedom, and we find someone practically imprisoned."

"What a strange old house this is," I said. "There really is more theater going on in here than there is on Broadway!"

It sounded silly, but it also sounded like an understatement.

Everyone laughed, but it was laughter mixed with nervousness and uncertainty.

They left my room as quietly as they could, slinking back to their own rooms.

I got ready for bed, but before I crawled under my blanket, I gazed out the window and up the ladder. Above us, the light was still on.

I thought I could hear "Oranges and lemons, say the bells of St. Clements."

Then the light went out.

And darkness fell faster than it had the night before.

12

Keeping Secrets

Carrying the secret of Gerta was like wearing a mask all day, except for when we were practicing and performing for our teachers. We tried not to speak about it at all while we were downstairs. Whispering would only draw more attention. However, our more frequent goings and comings from each other's rooms started to attract Steven and Howard's interest, especially Howard's. Sometimes we had to include them in our girl talk to keep them from developing any suspicions. Steven would grow bored quickly and leave, but Howard, who prided himself on having an opinion about everything, remained to argue, most often with Cinnamon.

Almost a week after our first visit upstairs, we decided to go up again. Rose had called Evan and told him of our discovery. He reinvestigated and reported back to her, assuring her his information was correct. The newspaper had reported that Gerta Senetsky died and was buried in a cemetery in Switzerland. A few days later, he called to say he had even learned the name of the cemetery.

When we climbed up the ladder the second time, we hovered on the landing and waited to be sure Gerta was alone. We knew that Madame Senetsky had left the house to attend a preview of a Broadway play, but we weren't sure where Ms. Fairchild was. For a good ten minutes, we gazed into the bedroom, waiting for signs of Gerta. She did not appear.

"Maybe they took her away," Rose suggested.

"Looks like someone is still using this bedroom though," I said.

Finally Cinnamon decided to open the window and climb in. She thought it might be better if only she went. The rest of us waited and watched. She stood in the doorway, looking into the living room, and then she returned and beckoned us to follow. Once inside, we found Gerta sitting on the living room sofa, one of the teddy bears from her bed in her lap. She was in an eighteenth century dress and a wig of golden hair with two rather large curls, which lay in front of her shoulders. The dress had a hoop so wide, she looked quite silly. I saw she had even put a fake beauty mark on the crest of her right cheek.

She didn't appear to notice we had entered, but continued instead to stare with glazed eyes at the floor.

"Hi, Gerta," Rose said. "How are you?"

She didn't respond; she didn't move her eyes. I noticed she was stroking the teddy bear mechanically with her right hand.

"We came to play Oranges and Lemons again," Cinnamon said.

Still Gerta did not respond, did not move, turn her head, or do anything to indicate she had heard either Rose or Cinnamon.

"Why are you dressed like this today? Are you in a play?"

"She's in a daze," Ice said.

"It looks more like a coma," Cinnamon told us.

She crossed the room and went to the door, trying the knob.

"It's locked," she whispered. She tried the door that went to the costume room. The first one opened, but not the second. "Locked as well. They really have her imprisoned in here."

"I'm surprised they didn't lock the window, too," Rose said. "Nail it shut so she couldn't get onto the fire escape once they found our clothes in her closet." She turned and looked at Gerta. "This is not right," she said, shaking her head. "It's downright cruel. Look at her. She needs professional help, not incarceration."

"That's some costume," I told her. "I bet it took you a long time to get it on, didn't it, Gerta?"

Her eyelids fluttered.

"Gerta," Rose said, sitting beside her, "aren't you feeling well tonight? Do you need something? We're here to help you. We'd like to help you, right, girls?"

"Yes," I said quickly.

Ice, who was looking at the pile of records, suddenly turned toward her, holding one of the records in her hands, and began in to sing a soft voice:

“ ‘Put on the skillet, slip on the lid, Mama’s gonna make a little short’nin’ bread. That ain’t all she’s gonna do, Mama’s gonna make a little coffee too.’ ”

Ice laughed.

“My mama used to sing me this one. ‘Short’nin’, short’nin’, short’nin bread.’ ”

Gerta raised her eyes and slowly began to smile. Ice looked at us and went into the chorus.

“ ‘Mama’s little baby loves short’nin’, short’nin, Mama’s little baby loves…’ ”

Gerta cried, “ ‘Short’nin bread.’ ”

Together they sang, “ ‘Mama’s little baby loves short’nin, short’nin….’ ”

And then we all joined in to finish with, “ ‘Mama’s little baby loves short’nin bread.’ ”

Gerta laughed.

“I never had short’nin bread,” she said.

“Well, we oughta go out and get some for her,” Rose declared.

“I was supposed to go out today,” Gerta said, “but it got canceled, so I decided to put on a different dress and hair.”

“Where were you supposed to go, Gerta?” Cinnamon asked her.

“To buy new clothes.”

Cinnamon looked thoughtful for a moment and then walked quickly back to the bedroom.

“Let’s sing again,” Gerta said. “Put on the record.”

“Okay,” Ice said.

“Everyone, come in here!” Cinnamon called to us.

“One moment, Gerta,” Ice said.

We joined Cinnamon, who was standing at the closet, the doors wide open.

"Look at this. All that's here are men's clothes: jackets, slacks, even men's shoes." She opened the dresser drawers, glancing in each one. "Except for some undergarments and a few nightgowns, she has nothing feminine."

"So with the exception of the costumes, which I'm sure she can't wear long, if anyone sees her dressed, he or she would think he had seen a man," Rose said.

"Exactly," Ice said. "And that may be why she stole your clothes, Rose, and yours, Honey," Cinnamon concluded.

"She wants to be who she is, but they're not letting her," I said.

"Maybe," Cinnamon said, her eyes taking on that look of deep thought again. "And maybe there's some more deeply psychological reason. I've been through the effects of depression, remember. There are all sorts of reasons for something like this."

Everyone nodded.

"When are we going to get short'nin bread?" Gerta asked. She had come to the bedroom doorway.

"In a few days," Cinnamon told her. "She probably won't remember anyway," she whispered. "But for now, let's all just sit and talk, okay?"

"And sing?"

"And sing," Cinnamon agreed. "Honey," she told me as she started back to the living room, "you stay in here and search some more. See if you can find anything that would help explain any of this."

I nodded and waited until they were all in the living room again. Then I began with the dresser drawers. There was nothing but the articles of clothing. The closet presented no hints either. I was about to give up when I thought about my own private places back home, and got on my knees to look under her bed. There I found a shoe box and brought it out.

They were singing again in the living room, this time along with the recording. I opened the box. Inside was a pink ribbon, a pretty woman's watch, and a very faded picture of a boy who looked about ten standing beside a little girl. Behind the little girl was a tall man in a suit and tie, his hands on her shoulders. I looked closely at the watch. It was pretty, but apparently not working. When I turned it over, I read the inscription: *To Gerta Berta. Love, Daddy.*

Cinnamon came to the doorway.

"Well?"

I stood up and showed her the box. She came over and looked at the watch and the picture.

"This could be her and that could be Edmond. I bet that's their father," she said. "Look how stiffly Edmond is standing next to her, not holding her hand or anything. Is this it?"

"So far," I replied.

She took the picture back and showed it to Gerta.

"Who is this?" Cinnamon asked, pointing to the little boy she thought was Edmond.

Gerta took the picture into her hands and looked.

"It's me," she said.

"No, isn't this you?" Cinnamon asked, touching the picture.

Gerta shook her head.

"That's Gerta Berta," she said.

"What?" I asked.

Suddenly Ice and Rose were beside us.

"Someone's at the costume room door," Ice whispered. "We heard the lock being opened."

We pulled back just as Laura Fairchild stepped into the living room.

"What are you doing, Gerta?" she demanded harshly.

"Singing."

"It's time I put the costume back and you went to sleep. Your mother wants you to go to sleep early tonight."

"I don't want to go to sleep. I want to sing."

"Do what you're told," Laura said firmly. "You want to go buy new clothes, don't you?"

"Yes."

"Then do what you're told or you won't go. It's enough singing and you've worn the costume long enough. I promised your mother I'd see that you went to bed. Go on, take it off," she ordered. "And I'll put it back where it belongs. C'mon."

"I was having fun," Gerta whined. "I don't want to go to bed. I'm not tired."

"Gerta, do you want me to have to cut off your hair again and shave your head?"

"I'll just wear a wig," she replied.

"No, you won't. You won't if we say no. And that goes for the costumes, too. If you don't go to bed right now, I'll come back when you're fast asleep and shave your head bald this time," Laura Fairchild threatened. "Clean up your records, take off the costume so I can put it back, and then you go to bed. Now! Go on. Take it off quickly, or I won't get you any other things to wear when you want," she threatened.

Cinnamon nodded toward the window and we all made our way out as quietly as we could. Slowly, she lowered the window, but, about halfway down it seemed to stick. She cursed under her breath. Ice pushed on the other side and together they got it to move again.

"Move," Cinnamon urged, and we all started down the fire escape ladder.

Suddenly, the window was thrown open again. Everyone froze.

We looked up and saw Laura Fairchild. She was looking out, but she apparently did not see us. After a moment she lowered the window, and we heard the definite sound of it being locked in place.

"Does she know we were in there?" I whispered.

"Just keep moving," Cinnamon said, and we did. No one breathed until we were back in my room.

"That was close," Cinnamon said.

"Are you sure she didn't see us?" Rose asked.

"No, but I can't imagine her seeing us and not screaming at us."

"That's for sure," Ice agreed.

"She locked the window. I heard her," I said. "She wants to stop anyone coming in through it."

"Maybe she was just being cautious and making sure Gerta doesn't go out."

"If it stays locked, how are we going to get back in there?" I asked.

"I don't know," Cinnamon said. "Maybe we should think twice about going back anyway."

Everyone was quiet.

"Cinnamon's right," Ice said, nodding. "That was almost it for us. We can't do anything for her anyway. It's not our problem. We're not here for that."

"But they're being pretty nasty to her. She was so hopeful, so happy when we promised to take her shopping and get her the short'nin' bread," Rose said with a smile. "That was nice when you began to sing for her, Ice."

Ice nodded.

I put on the light by my bed.

"Look at us!" Cinnamon cried.

Everyone was streaked with soot from the fire escape ladder.

"Let's clean up," she said.

They all started out.

Just as they stepped into the hallway, Howard came up the stairs.

"Hey, how's the Ladies' Sewing Circle doing?" he asked, laughing.

"Fine," Cinnamon said.

I stood in the doorway. He turned to me, his smile suddenly disappearing.

"What happened to you?" he asked.

"Why?"

"What's that on your face?"

"Nothing. We were fooling around with makeup," Cinnamon said quickly.

"Makeup? That doesn't look like theatrical makeup to me."

"You don't know everything about the theater yet, Howard Rockwell," Cinnamon told him. "Good night, girls," she said with emphasis.

They all headed for their rooms. I closed my door, but Howard stood there gaping at me until I did. Then I went to the bathroom and looked at myself in the mirror. There was a thick line of soot down my cheek where I had pressed my face against the ladder, waiting for Laura Fairchild to retreat and close the window.

Howard is too smart, I thought. We'd have to come up with something.

Cinnamon returned just after I had washed my face and hands.

She knocked softly and then slipped into the room, closing the door quietly behind her.

"You all right?"

"Yes, but I think Howard's onto us," I said.

"I know. I'm going to confide in him," she said.

"Is that smart?" I asked.

She smiled.

"No. What I'm going to tell him is you were out secretly to meet your boyfriend."

"But he knows Chandler returned to Boston."

"Who says it has to be Chandler?"

"What?"

"Just play along with it. He'll buy into it and we won't have him spying on us or asking us a whole lot of tricky questions."

"I can't do that."

"Sure you can. Think of it as a play, a role you've taken," she advised.

"I'm not an actress, Cinnamon. You're the actress. You should be the one pretending to have a boyfriend you secretly meet, not me."

She smiled.

"You had the smudge on your face, not me. Besides, have you forgotten Madame Senetsky's words? We are *always* performing. We are always on one stage or another. Don't worry about the cover story. I was always good at this," she said proudly. "I raised fabrication to an art form. Believe me, when I'm finished with him, Howard will believe it."

"That's what I'm afraid of," I said.

As quickly as she slipped in, she slipped out. My heart began to beat drums of warning. Lies weren't the same as assuming an artistic persona, I thought. Cinnamon was playing with fire and she was doing it with *my* love life. I'd be the one who got burnt, not her.

Suddenly Mommy's concerns about my being safe here were not as foolish as Daddy had thought when we all first arrived. It was a fortress, yes. It had security, but all that was to keep danger out.

What about the dangers that were already living in this grand house?

And what about those living in us?

"He bought it all," Cinnamon told me the following day. "Especially when I begged him not to tell Steven, who might just slip up and get you in trouble."

However, instead of getting him to lose interest in

me and stop him from asking questions, it seemed to have had the completely opposite effect. Suddenly, in his eyes, I became the most interesting of the four. I began to wonder just what sort of things Cinnamon had told him about me. What were the details she left out?

Late the next afternoon, after all our sessions had ended, I heard a knock on my door. I had just sat down to write Uncle Simon a letter.

"Yes?" I called, and Howard appeared.

"Hi," he said. "What are you doing?"

"Just writing my uncle a letter. Why?"

"Why don't you just phone him?"

"He likes having the letters, Howard. Why is that a problem for you?"

"It's not. I just wondered. I can actually understand why he'd want the letters. It establishes more of a bond. You make a phone call, you talk, you hang up, and there's just silence."

"Exactly."

"Doesn't he have E-mail?"

"No. This uncle hasn't spent ten minutes with a computer. He has absolutely no interest in that sort of thing."

"What sort of thing?"

"Anything technological," I replied. "He's more into natural things."

What did he want? Why was he standing there, smiling at me? He had been giving me looks all day, looks that made me more and more nervous.

"That's kind of why I came around," he said with a slight shrug. "You see how beautiful it is today? Here we are, all caged in most of the day, rehearsing, practicing. We're ignoring nature. It's still quite nice. Warmer than usual for this time of the year here."

"Yes, it does look like a beautiful day."

"So why spend the last part of it inside? Feel like going for a walk?"

"A walk? You want me to go for a walk with you?"

"Just around the block. There's a dead-end street that looks out over the East River. I'd like to show it to you. I found it quite by accident one day. It's in a very ritzy neighborhood."

I continued to stare at him.

"You want me to take a walk to see the river?"

"We hardly ever talk. I don't mean when we're all together. We've been here weeks and weeks and all I really know about you is your name, you're from Ohio, and you play the violin as beautifully as Itzhak Perlman."

"Hardly," I said.

"Not hardly. Soon," he corrected.

I laughed. His arrogance annoyed me as much as it annoyed the others, but he wasn't acting that way right now.

"I'm just talking about a walk," he said. "It's not holy matrimony. We won't have to go down the fire escape for some clandestine rendezvous," he added with a smile.

Perhaps I had better go with him, I thought. Why make him any more suspicious?

"Okay. I'll finish this later."

"Sure. It won't go out until tomorrow anyway. That's nice, your writing to an uncle. You must be very close," he added while I put on my jacket.

"We are. We've always been. Where's Steven?" I asked when we started down the stairs.

"Playing with one of his computer games or something. He's a genius on the piano, but I really can't have an intelligent conversation with him. And I'm not trying to sound superior," he quickly added.

"Somehow, Howard, you don't have to try," I said, and he laughed, but differently from his usual condescending or satirical laugh. This laugh seemed so much more sincere.

He opened the door for me and I nodded my thank-you and stepped out. He was right, of course; it was one of those days when the clouds just seemed daubed against the blue, little puffs of them here and there, the breeze gentle, everything still looking remarkably fresh. Most of the trees had lost their leaves, but the grass remained an almost kelly green.

"When New York has this kind of weather, it's unbeatable," Howard said. We walked slowly down the drive. "I like taking these walks in the city."

"I didn't know you went out on your own much, Howard."

"Oh, no? Well, when you girls are all locked up in one of your rooms or another and Steven has his nose in a computer game, I just wander away. I like to feel the energy here. The city almost has a palpable heartbeat. Excitement, lights, people, traffic. It's just...great," he declared.

I smiled at his exuberance.

"Not for you though, huh?" he asked.

"Well, yes and no. It is exciting, but I can't deny that I miss the quiet nights, the sight of an owl, or the fresh breezes combing through the corn stalks, the sight of the geese in formation going south or north, the deep aroma of freshly turned earth. Let's just say there is music in both places, but entirely different from each other and equally moving," I concluded.

He walked without speaking. We were almost to the gate.

"Of all the girls here, you're the most interesting to me, Honey," he said.

"Me? Why? Cinnamon is the actress and filled with great stories about spirits and stuff. Ice comes from a much harder place, with stories that will make your hair stand up, yet she has so much softness inside her. And Rose, Rose is very beautiful to watch. Her walk is a dance."

He laughed.

"You're the best public relations agent they'll ever have, only you left out yourself. You're the first farmer's daughter I have ever met," he added.

"So?"

"Didn't you ever hear any of those jokes about the farmer's daughter?"

"No," I replied with some suspicion. Tony had said something resembling this, I recalled. "What sort of jokes?"

"There's all these jokes about traveling salesmen who break down in a storm and go to the farmhouse where they take him in for the night and the farmer's daughter sleeps with him."

"They don't tell those jokes where I live," I said.

"I bet not. Well, it doesn't matter. You obviously don't fit any stereotype."

We stepped out of the compound and onto the sidewalk.

"We go left," he said, nodding. "Getting back to you. You come from what anyone here might call the hinterland, yet you have a certain sophistication that is especially apparent in your music. Yes, Ice is going to sing her way out of poverty. Cinnamon acts almost as a means of self-defense. I agree that Rose is pure grace and beauty. She couldn't help but be what she is, just as you said. But you, you play classical music on a violin and were brought up with the sound of cows mooing and farm equipment grinding. Who'd expect you to take up a violin and play like you do?"

I nodded, stared at the sidewalk as we strolled, and smiled softly to myself.

"I don't play it. It plays me," I whispered.

"Huh?"

"I had an uncle who was killed in a plane accident. He was the one who put the violin in my hand. Literally. He bought it for me and paid for my lessons."

"Amazing," Howard said. "I have to tell you, Honey. You are the most sincere one."

"No, I'm not."

"I think you are. Down this street," he directed. The apartment houses did look full of rich people. They had private gates and security guards and little gardens. "There," Howard pointed. There was a fence at the end of the street. Across the way, over the highway, was the East River, just as he had promised. "Well?"

"Very unexpected. You're right. How did you find this again?"

He smiled.

"A friend of my father's lives in that building," he said, nodding at the apartment house on our left. "He has a private elevator that opens only on his apartment."

"Why did you tell me you discovered it by accident?"

"I thought it would sound more romantic."

"It did," I said, "but I didn't need the embellishment. The truth isn't necessarily dull."

He laughed and squatted by the fence.

"Relax," he said, patting the space beside him. "Have a seat."

I looked at the ground with some trepidation.

"A farmer's daughter shouldn't be afraid of sitting on the grass," he added.

I did.

"So," he said, "Speaking of the truth—now that we're alone, why don't you tell me what's really going on with you girls?"

"He asked you that?" Rose cried when I had returned and gotten them all together.

"Yes."

"He really is quite an actor, our Howard Rockwell," Cinnamon said, her face full of fury. "I thought he bought my story hook, line, and sinker. He put on this big performance about how shocked and surprised he was that Honey would cheat on Chandler. He even said he thought you were the purest of heart. I feel like punching him in his perfect, handsome face."

"That's what he told me, too," I said. "When he

asked me, I looked sharply at him and told him I didn't know what he meant."

"What did he do?" Ice asked.

"Laughed and said he would never believe I snuck out at night to meet some boy secretly and risk not only my position in the school but my relationship with Chandler. 'You're a one-boy girl, Honey,' he told me.

"Of course, he's right, and I couldn't deny it. He saw it clearly in my face.

" 'So what's going on?' he repeated and I got up quickly and ran from him, ran all the way back here."

"That should throw off all suspicion," Cinnamon muttered. "Smart."

"She didn't know what else to do," Rose said, coming to my defense. "I would have done the same thing, Honey."

"I would have kicked him," Ice claimed, but then looked at me and shrugged. "I don't know what I would have done. The thing is, what do we do now?" she asked, turning to Cinnamon.

"We could tell him you're pregnant," she replied.

"What? Why don't we tell him *you're* pregnant?" Ice countered.

"I'm only kidding. No matter who we claimed was pregnant, it would hold him off only a few months before he realized it wasn't so."

"Let's not tell him anything," Rose concluded. "Why should we have to, just because he's suspicious?"

"That will work all right if we don't go back up there," I said.

"I thought we decided we wouldn't," Ice insisted.

"We didn't say that exactly," Rose reminded her.

"Well, are we?"

No one answered for a moment.

"I can't believe she threatened to shave her head," I said.

"Again. You heard her. She's done that before," Rose said. "Gerta has no one to defend her. It's so sad."

"Her mother should be defending her," Cinnamon snapped.

"But she isn't, is she?" Rose countered. "Mothers don't always stand up for their daughters."

"I have trouble falling asleep now that I know she's up there, locked in like that," I said.

"She's probably singing 'Short'nin Bread,' " Rose mused with a smile.

Ice shook her head.

"Damn," she said.

Everyone eyed everyone else. It was easy to see how we all felt about it.

"Ms. Fairchild locked the window. The only way to get back up there is to go through the doors off-limits to us," Cinnamon warned. "We'd have to wait until Madame Senetsky left the house."

"I heard she's going to a dinner at Gracie Mansion, the mayor's home, on Thursday," Rose said. "Mr. Littleton told Mr. Demetrius."

"This is going to end up bad," Ice said. "I can feel it in my bones."

No one disagreed.

But we did all sleep better that night.

Over the next few days, we all concentrated on our work. Howard learned he might get an opportunity to fill a two-line role in a film being shot nearby. Edmond Senetsky knew the producer and had given him Howard's head shots. Fortunately for us, that was all Howard wanted to discuss. At every dinner, he lectured about the differences between stage acting and film acting.

"The reason all those actors in the early movies look so silly to us is they were still performing the way they did on stage. It was their only training. So they made all these grand gestures and exaggerated facial expressions, not realizing the power of the camera," he explained.

Cinnamon caught on early, realizing that as long as he was obsessed with himself, he was disinterested in us. She encouraged his talks and encouraged us to ask him questions, act impressed and interested. Only Steven, sitting back with that satirical smirk on his face, understood what we were doing.

As luck would have it, Howard had to go see the movie producer Thursday night. There was a reading Edmond asked him to attend. With Madame Senetsky going to an event and Howard out of our hair, we all felt a bit more confident about violating the boundaries of the house and paying Gerta another visit.

Ice remained downstairs while Cinnamon, Rose, and I pretended to be tired and went up to bed. Steven lingered a while and then grew bored and went to his room and his games. A little less than a half hour later, Ice told us Ms. Fairchild had retired for the evening, warning her to be sure everything was turned off and things left neatly before she went up to sleep.

Still quite nervous and frightened, we all descended the stairway, pausing occasionally to listen. All I heard was the pounding of my own heart, the blood thumping through my veins and echoing in my ears. A grandfather clock bonged the hour. Floorboards creaked, but other than that, the house was very quiet.

At the doorway to Madame Senetsky's private rooms, we paused one final time. All of us knew that once we entered, there was no turning back. Secrets would spill over. There would be serious consequences. Our careers would be seriously set back. What drove each of us to go forward with these realizations bubbling under our skin was not very different, I thought. We each saw something of ourselves in Gerta, in her plight and in her loneliness.

During one of her frequent lectures, Madame Senetsky had emphasized how a good performer always brings something of himself or herself, some personal, even traumatic experience to his or her performance.

"It is the way we see ourselves in others, especially in roles we are asked to perform, that will determine how well we will exhibit our talents," she explained. "Whether it be music or dance or acting, the commonality we all share is the well from which you will draw your aesthetic sense and strength.

"Be perceptive, use your compassion and your sensibilities to draw from those around you.

"That is what I have always tried to do."

Because all of us had become so close, we shared our most painful memories as well as our happiest. Cinnamon's sense of isolation from her peers was something all of us had felt at one time or another. Ice's estrangement from her mother, her pain and difficulty in expressing herself struck a sympathetic note, especially with Rose, whose mother had literally deserted her for a long time. And my oppressive grandad, my loss of Uncle Peter, made me timid and afraid of stepping out into the world.

Who could possibly be more different from her peers than Gerta? How difficult it was for her to really communicate with anyone. Look how estranged she was from her own mother. How terrified she was of the world outside? In one way or another, we were all Gerta.

The door creaked on its hinges as if it wanted to warn Ms. Fairchild that it was being violated. No matter how slowly Cinnamon pulled it open, it groaned. We held our breaths and listened for any sound of her footsteps. Cinnamon opened it a little farther, and we were all able to slip in, closing it as softly as we could behind us.

We all looked at one another.

No one had to say it.

Now, it was too late to turn back.

13

Gerta's Story

When we closed the door behind us and turned, we all stopped and stared in awe. The long, dark hallway was dimly lit by black candles in ivory holders mounted on the walls. Light dripped down in a waxy pool over the tiled floor. The candles flickered as though they'd been left by someone hurrying past, fleeing from discovery, diving into the darkness like a toad seeking the cover of murky water. All was still, but from somewhere above us, we could hear muffled voices. They sounded like words trapped in the building's ancient pipes, words spoken ages ago by others as young as we were and just as afraid. Of course, we assumed it was Gerta playing her records.

"Why is the hallway like this?" Rose was the first to ask. "I feel like I'm descending into a cavern or something."

"How strange," I said.

"Obviously, Gerta is not the only one living in her own private world," Cinnamon muttered.

"I don't think we should go any farther," Ice said. The chill in her voice made my own teeth start to chatter.

"What's there to be afraid of?" Cinnamon pondered, sounding more like she wanted us to agree than give her an answer. "So she goes for a dramatic decor. Big deal. Right?" she asked Rose.

"I don't know," Rose said, obviously having trouble swallowing.

"Oh, just come on," Cinnamon directed and started forward. When no one moved, she stopped and looked back at us. "Well, are you coming or not?"

We practically inched our way down the corridor. Along the way we passed a niche that contained a statue of a woman holding up a baby and gazing toward the heavens as if she was offering the child as some sort of sacrifice. The child's eyes were closed and looked already dead and gone.

"Not exactly a very joyful work of art," Ice muttered.

Cinnamon grunted her agreement and we continued, pausing to look at a window drape that was hanging from one corner. There was a large rip in it as well. On the tile below it was what looked like large drops of blood. The blood trailed to the doorway of the room on the left. It nailed our feet to the floor.

"What happened here?" Rose wondered aloud.

"Whatever it was, it happened a while ago. Why keep it like this?" I asked.

"Let's get out of here," Rose whispered. "We're going to get into so much trouble."

"We've come this far," Cinnamon said. "It's too late to turn back."

Now that we were much deeper into the house, we realized the sound we heard in the walls was not voices from any recording of a song. It sounded more like someone chanting and moaning. Drawn by a morbid curiosity that seemed overpowering enough to move our numb bodies, we stepped up to the doorway and gazed into the room.

No one could speak; no one could utter a sound.

The room was in chaos. A chair was turned over and the small settee was toppled on its back. A lamp was sprawled over it and still lit. A bottle of wine lay broken on the right. Then our eyes fell to a large knife, the blade stained with what surely was blood. When we all moved a few inches to the right, Rose grabbed my arm so fast and so hard, I was positive she had driven her nails through the skin. Her cry was like a dagger itself, piercing my breast.

"What's that?" Ice cried, pointing.

It was an arm and a hand just visible behind the overturned settee.

I felt my own blood drain from my face.

No one spoke or moved until Cinnamon stepped forward and walked around the settee. She stood there gaping, and then she shook her head and smiled.

"What's so funny?" I asked.

"Come here and look for yourselves," she said.

We all did.

There on the floor was a wax figure of a woman in a black dress, a slash across her right wrist. It was very lifelike—or I should say, deathlike, because the eyes were glassy, like the eyes of a corpse, but the skin looked so real. There was even a wedding ring on her finger and a working, expensive looking watch on her wrist.

"What's going on here?" Rose asked.

Cinnamon started to shake her head and then stopped, her eyes widening.

"Of course," she said, laughing. "This is like a museum."

"What? How?" Ice demanded. "It looks like a madhouse to me."

"That's because you guys haven't been forced to watch Madame Senetsky's greatest performances as part of your curriculum here. Howard and I have, and this corridor, all the trappings, even the statue...it's all from a German film she did called *Mein Medea—My Medea.* It's something of a twist on the famous Greek story, a modern-day version. Madame Senetsky played this wife, betrayed by her husband. Just like Medea, she gets back at him by killing their child and then she takes her own life in a very dramatic finale. It's a dark and depressing movie, but according to Mr. Marlowe, it's considered a classic, and Madame Senetsky's performance described as pure brilliance."

"What's that have to do with all this?" Rose asked.

"She's built the set that was used in the movie for the final scene, and that's why I say it's like a museum or a homage to the performance. If you look closely at this waxwork," Cinnamon added, moving around to gaze down at the face more closely, "you'd see it's a very accurate depiction of a young Madame Senetsky."

We all studied the face and nodded in agreement.

"Didn't she make any good, happier films?" Ice asked.

"Yes, of course, but this is considered one of her masterpieces."

She continued to gaze down at the waxwork.

" 'What greater punishment can you inflict on a man who betrays you than to take his child?' That's a line from the film," she said. "Of course, she couldn't live with herself afterward and so…this tragic and gruesome ending."

We continued to stare at the wax version of our mentor. There was great detail, right down to the small birthmark on the edge of her chin.

"I just thought of something strange," Rose said.

"Stranger than this?" I asked.

"Well, Evan told us that there was the possibility of Gerta committing suicide, right? There was some talk of that in the stories he found in the old papers, remember?"

"But Gerta didn't die. She's upstairs!" I cried.

"Yes, but that was what Evan said he read. And then Madame Senetsky's husband committed suicide soon afterward. That was definite, wasn't it, Cinnamon?"

She thought, her eyes narrowing.

"Yes, I see what you're saying." She looked at the wax figure.

"But the wife committed suicide in this movie, not the husband," Ice pointed out.

"Minor point," Cinnamon said with a smile.

"Madame Senetsky dies on the stage and in movies in many productions, but not in real life.

"In real life, she lives on to perform again and again."

Suddenly, a shadow seemed to slide across the wall. We were all still, listening.

"I don't like this," Rose said, embracing herself. "There are too many dark places here. Let's go back. Let's stop trying to learn about her past and Gerta's before..."

"Before what?" I asked.

"Before we find out too much," Cinnamon answered for her. "Right, Rose?"

"Yes," Rose said, nodding. She was reliving her own family tragedy, her father's suicide. I could see it playing behind her eyes. Reviving something like that surely turned her spine to cold stone.

The sounds from above changed. Now, we heard music.

"Isn't that 'Short'nin Bread'?" I asked Ice. She smiled and nodded.

"We've got to keep going. We're in this far. How can we turn back now?" Cinnamon pondered.

Rose wasn't happy about it, but we continued into the private residence.

Once past the corridor of candles, as it became known in my mind, we found more normal accommodations: a small kitchen with a round wooden table and four chairs, another living room with plush furnishings, but also pieces that looked like they would be more at home on a stage, like a royal-purple velvet lounging chaise embellished with gold cording, albeit looking never used. There were two large oil paintings, one of which Cinnamon identified as a portrait of the famous actress Sarah Bernhardt and the other as a portrait of the French playwright Molière. There were Tiffany lamps, crystals glittering like pieces of ice in the lamp light, a small secretary in the far right corner, and a hutch filled with expensive-looking memorabilia.

One door down we discovered what had to be Madame Senetsky's bedroom. It was a very large room with a bed Cinnamon described first as a small stage. It was round, with a crest of big fluffy pillows against the grand, curved headboard built out of what looked like rich mahogany, and in which was carved the words, "To hold as t'were the mirror up to nature."

"What does that mean?" Ice asked.

"It's from *Hamlet,* part of what Hamlet says is the purpose of theater," Cinnamon explained while she gaped at the oversized furniture, with mirrors everywhere, even in the ceiling. There was a large magnifying mirror at the vanity table, which ran the length of the room and was covered with a variety of makeup, brushes, and pencils. There were jars after jars of skin creams, many of whose labels boastfully announced the end of wrinkles. In an open closet to our left we saw shelves of wigs, some of which we recognized as ones Madame Senetsky had worn at dinners and on other occasions. The clothing closet on the right looked as long and wide as each of our bedrooms.

The walls of the room were papered in pink with figures of mythological creatures like satyrs, sileni, gorgons, and centaurs. Statues of what looked like Greek gods and goddesses stood on pedestals in every available corner.

Most interesting, perhaps, was the tile floor. Each tile was about a foot in diameter and depicted a scene from a famous play. It looked like the entire history of the theater was painted on the floor.

"Someone could go mad in here, never being able to not look at herself and see every blemish or hair out of place," Rose commented, turning from one mirror to the next.

"Doesn't that look like a spotlight?" Ice asked, pointing to a can light in the ceiling directed at the bed.

"Bizarre," Cinnamon said. "I bet she performs her death bed scene from *Othello* often."

We walked on until we came upon a stairway that spiraled up. It wasn't as grand as the one that greeted us on entry to the house, but, like that one, it had a rich-looking mahogany balustrade and carpeted steps.

We contemplated it, and then Cinnamon nodded.

"This has to be the way to Gerta's apartment. Let's go up," she said, and we started up the steps. At the top we found a door with a key in the lock.

"This is it," Cinnamon declared. She turned the key and we entered what we knew to be her living room. The needle was stuck on the record again. For a moment we all stood in the opened doorway, gaping. Then Ice moved to the phonograph and stopped it from grinding.

"Gerta?" Cinnamon called.

There was no response. Cinnamon nodded at the bedroom and we walked slowly across the room to the doorway. She was there, sitting in a chair, her arms and hands resting on the chair's arms. Now she was fully dressed in her manly clothes, a dark brown suit and brown tie, wearing a wig that resembled Edmond's hair with a deep part down the right side, and looking more like Edmond than herself. She sat calmly, staring at us, her legs crossed.

"Whom do you wish to see?" she asked in a deeper and more adult-sounding voice.

It took us all by surprise, and for a long moment, no one, not even Cinnamon, could respond. The only lamp that was lit in the room threw a pale glow over Gerta, deepening the shadows around her eyes, making them look more like small pools of ink in her pale face.

"We've come to see Gerta," Cinnamon said.

"Gerta? I'm afraid you're too late," she replied. "Gerta is gone."

"Gone?" Rose asked. "Where did she go?"

"She's out, shopping for new clothes," she replied.

"Shopping for new clothes? What is she saying? I don't understand her," Rose complained, with her lips pulled back and her eyes set to shed tears of frustration and fear.

"Let's get out of here," Ice said in a throaty whisper, her gaze cold and full of warnings.

"Take it easy," Cinnamon said. "Relax, everyone."

"I'm with Ice," I said. "Let's go, Cinnamon."

"Wait." She turned back to her. "How can Gerta be out? Doesn't she have to stay in here?" Cinnamon asked, moving closer to her.

"Not if she doesn't want to, not anymore. She found

a way to go wherever and whenever she pleases," she replied with a bright smile.

"What way? How can she do that?" Cinnamon asked more firmly.

"Cinnamon," Rose urged, grasping her arm. "Don't."

"How can Gerta leave?" Cinnamon continued, ignoring Rose's plea.

Gerta turned away. I thought she wasn't going to respond and that would be that, but she snapped her head back so fast and hard, I thought she could have cracked her neck. Her face was now dressed in a rage, her lips pulled up and back so her clenched teeth were showing.

"Don't you blame her. Don't you dare blame her, too," she warned, spitting her words through those teeth.

"We don't blame her. Right, girls? No one here blames her a bit. We just want to know about her. We're her friends. That's why we came back to see her."

Gerta considered us, studying everyone's face very carefully, I thought. Then she leaned forward slowly.

"She was very unhappy where she was. She wanted to go home, even if it meant being Gerta Berta," she said with obvious bitterness in her voice. "But they wouldn't let her go, no matter how she cried and begged. There were bars on her windows and her door was always kept locked until they came to take her out for walks or to go eat or to go to the rec room or to see the doctor."

She sat back.

"No one can blame her," she emphasized again. "How else could she have gotten out?"

"Right," Cinnamon said. "We understand and we don't blame her a bit. How did she do it?"

Gerta smiled.

"She figured it out. She wasn't stupid."

"No, she wasn't. How did she do it?" Cinnamon insisted on hearing.

"First, she had to get out of her body. They were keeping her body locked up. Sometimes, she could do it easily. When her body was asleep, she could very quietly slip away, but she couldn't be away long enough. Her body always realized she was gone and woke and pulled her back inside.

"Once, she was just outside the window. She was on her way home and then, her body trembled and shuddered until it woke and *poof,*" she said, clapping her hands so quickly, sharply, and unexpectedly, we all jumped. "She was brought back again, back into her body."

"So what did she do?" Cinnamon pursued.

I wished she hadn't. I had enough already to provide me a few weeks of nightmares, and from the looks on Ice's and Rose's faces, I saw they had enough, too.

"There was only one way. She had to put her body to sleep for good so it couldn't pull her back. Under her bed hung a broken bedspring. She crawled there and bent it back and forth, back and forth until it snapped off. It was sharp enough to run it over her wrist until it unzipped her skin and let the blood drip out. Her body was screaming and begging and promising never to call her back again, but she didn't believe it. Bodies lie, you know. They tell us things that aren't true all the time.

"They tell us we're hungry and we're not really hungry. As soon as we begin to eat, we throw up.

"They tell us we're not tired, but when we try to do something, we can barely move.

"They tell us it's morning when it's still night. They tell us we're warm when we're really cold. They lie, lie, lie to keep us quiet.

"So, she said no, she wouldn't zip up her skin. She sat there watching it stop and go until it finally just flowed and then she closed her eyes and waited. She knew that as soon as her body was permanently asleep, she could be off. She could be gone.

"And so she was, because when they found her body in the morning, she was already gone and they couldn't get her back."

"Look at her wrist," Rose said with a small gasp. "Is that scar what I think?"

"Yes, wait," Cinnamon said. She turned back to Gerta. "And when she was free, she came here?" Cinnamon continued.

"Yes, of course. She came home. But he was gone, too. His body was in the ground and he wasn't here to call her his Gerta Berta. She was happy and sad, happy and sad. I told her I would help her. I would always help her. Sometimes, she needed to be back in a body, you know."

"I think I'm getting sick," Rose said. "I don't know about y'all, but I think I want to just leave."

"Hold on. You don't know what this means yet," Cinnamon insisted. She turned back to Gerta. "So, you let her go into you?"

"Of course. She's my little sister. It wasn't her fault. What he did to her wasn't her fault."

"What did he do to her?"

Gerta's eyes grew small, suspicious. I felt my chest tighten. My heart was beating fast, but low, thumping like someone's fingers on a tabletop.

"She didn't tell you?" she asked Cinnamon.

"No. She couldn't do it. She said we should come to ask you."

"Poor Gerta."

"Right," Cinnamon said. "What happened to her? What did he do?"

"He made her his Gerta Berta. When she had nightmares and she went to him, he showed her how to forget them, but that wasn't nice. Her body lied again. Her body thought it was nice."

"Didn't she tell her mother?" Cinnamon asked.

"Oh, yes. Of course, my mother told her everything must be kept secret. Only whisper to yourself and never tell. Never tell."

She looked about the room.

"These walls are full of whispers, you know. They are like sponges, and if you press your ear against one hard enough, you can squeeze out some whispers."

"This is disgusting," Ice practically spit.

Rose turned away and hurried to the doorway of the living room, clutching her stomach.

Cinnamon stared after her a moment and then looked at us.

"You've got to transfer your fears, put your emotions into something constructive," she recited as if we were all training for a dramatic presentation. "None of us want to hear such things, but they happen."

"Let's get out of here," Rose urged from the doorway.

"She's right, Cinnamon," I said. "What can we do for her?"

"We've got to do something," Cinnamon said with fury in her eyes.

She was remembering what had happened to her mother, I thought.

"Not tonight," Ice said. "Let's go. I've heard enough anyway."

Cinnamon looked at me and I nodded.

"They're right. We should go."

"Okay. We'll come back to see Gerta," she told her. "Will you tell her that? Tell her we like her and we want to help her go shopping."

"That's very nice," she said. "She'll be happy to hear that."

She turned toward the wall on the right and just stared.

"Cinnamon," Ice urged, tugging at her arm.

Cinnamon backed up and we all started for the door. Just as we walked out, however, we heard a door slam below.

"Oh, no. Madame Senetsky's back, or it's Laura Fairchild," I said.

We froze and listened to the footsteps below. They were getting louder and approaching.

"Back out the window," Cinnamon said, retreating.

"But the door will be unlocked. She'll know someone came in here," I said.

"Or she'll think she just forgot to lock it," Cinnamon said. "C'mon. We don't have time to argue about it."

We closed the door softly and hurried back into the bedroom. Gerta was still sitting the same way, staring at the wall. She didn't seem to hear us. We went to the window. It, too, had been locked, so we had to open that and go out, closing the window behind us and hurrying off the landing and down the stairs to my room.

"Ms. Fairchild is going to figure it out," Ice warned as we all descended. "The door was unlocked and the window was unlocked."

"Gerta could have done the window. Just keep cool and reveal nothing," Cinnamon fired back.

We stepped on the landing and I opened my window so we could all crawl in. Just as we did, the lights went on.

Rose cried out. I gasped, and Cinnamon and Ice turned with surprise.

Standing there with a big, fat smile on his face was Howard Rockwell.

"What are you doing in my room?" I cried.

He wasn't fazed at all. He stood there, cocky as ever with that arrogant smile, his arms folded over his chest, and leaned against the closed door.

"When I came home and found none of you about, I began to check your rooms. This was the last and just as I stepped in to look, I heard the racket on the fire escape and waited. So, what are you, a bunch of burglars?"

No one spoke.

"You had no right coming into my room without my permission," I fired back at him.

"Really? And I suppose you girls have a right to climb the fire escape to the rooms above?" he asked, his eyes lifting toward the ceiling.

"This is trespassing," I charged.

He shrugged.

"And what you're doing isn't? We were all told what was and wasn't off-limits here."

He shrugged.

"I suppose you could always tell on me. Ms. Fairchild and Madame Senetsky would call me on the carpet and I would have to describe this scene, I guess. Whatever you want. Maybe we should march down to Ms. Fairchild's quarters right now. What do you think?"

He started for the door, put his hand on the knob, and turned.

"Well?"

"You're a real bastard, Howard," Cinnamon said.

"Is there any other kind?" he countered. "So, what will it be, girls?" he asked after we all looked at each other. "Am I going to be brought in on this or do I have to conduct a more elaborate investigation? Is Steven in on it?" he added quickly.

"No, Steven is not poking his nose into our business, thank you," Rose said.

"That's his choice. I have more of an inquisitive mind. It's part of what makes me a good actor."

"No, what makes you a good actor is your ability to be two-faced," Ice said.

We all laughed. Howard's smile wilted.

"What's going on here?" he demanded. "And don't give me any junk about Honey's love affairs."

The three of us looked at Cinnamon. She considered and then nodded.

"Okay, Howard. We'll tell you all of it, but if you

say anything to anyone else, you'll make big trouble for yourself as well as us, believe me," she warned.

He suddenly looked more worried than arrogant.

"So, if you still insist on knowing..." she continued.

"I insist," he said.

"All right," she said, and she began to tell him everything.

"I want to see her," he decided when Cinnamon concluded.

Rose, Ice, and I sat on my bed and let Cinnamon relate the story. Howard sat in the chair and listened, looking from her to us every once in a while to be sure what she was describing was not something she was making up on the spot. Our glares, half angry, half interested in his reaction, affected him.

"You can't see her, Howard. As far as we know, they don't take her out of the house. They don't bring her downstairs, unless it's done very late when we're all asleep or something," Cinnamon explained.

"I'll just go up when you go up again," he decided.

"Who said we're going up there ever again?" Ice asked him.

He smiled, looked from her to the rest of us, and nodded.

"You will. I can see it in your faces. Well," he said, rising and pondering, "I have to admit this is very interesting, more interesting than I had imagined."

"If you do anything, say anything, we'll all get thrown out of here, Howard, including you, now that you know it all!" Cinnamon emphasized.

He shook his head.

"I doubt it."

"Why?" I asked.

"From what you've told me, the last thing in the world our Madame Senetsky would want is this story leaked to the rag papers. No, if anything, should we be found out, I think we can expect the best possible treatment. Maybe we will make sure we're found out, in fact. Our careers may move faster than we all think," he concluded.

"You're sick, Howard. You're that ambitious that you would try to blackmail Madame Senetsky and use poor Gerta," Rose flared at him.

"All's fair in love and war, they say, and you've heard Madame Senetsky's speech about being in continuous battle, continuous competition. There are many, many talented people out there, girls. There are probably a dozen girls on this block and the next who sing as beautifully as you do, Ice. Go down to Broadway and look at the line of dancers competing for a Broadway opportunity, Rose. And the number of openings for positions in orchestras isn't exactly overwhelming, Honey. As for us, Cinnamon, you know what the competition will be like."

"Is this the great Howard Rockwell the Seventh or Eighth admitting he is not God's gift to the theater and therefore guaranteed to win the Tony Award?" Cinnamon quipped.

"All I'm saying is, when it comes down to it, whatever you can use to your advantage, you use. It's the same in every business, every field of work."

"It isn't for my father," I said. "We don't blackmail people to get them to buy our corn."

"You would if it came down to whether you would sell it or not," he insisted with confidence.

He turned to Cinnamon and glared at her with a face that could stop a charging tiger.

"You're going back up there very soon, and I'm going with you," he said. "I want to see all this for myself. Then I'll decide what we should do, if anything."

"It might be impossible to get back up there, Howard," Cinnamon said, her voice revealing a certain degree of retreat. "If the window is locked and if we can't get up through Madame Senetsky's..."

"We'll find a way," he said confidently. He looked at the rest of us. "No one say anything to Steven. He's unpredictable," he said.

He turned to the door and opened it. Then he turned back to us.

"Isn't it nice how well we're all getting along? Trust, girls. It's all a matter of trust."

He laughed and walked out, closing the door softly behind him.

"How can someone so good-looking be so cold-hearted?" Rose wondered.

"Didn't you ever look at a cobra? They're beautiful, but deadly," Cinnamon replied.

She started for the door. Ice and Rose followed.

"It's almost as if life is a series of stages, one curtain lifting to reveal another and then another and another," Cinnamon said. "Until you reach the final curtain, take your bows, and leave the stage."

"Hoping you'll hear applause," Rose added.

"Instead of boos and catcalls," Ice followed.

"Good night, sweet ladies, good night," Cinnamon said. We all hugged and they left.

I stood there alone, the whole evening ringing in my ears.

Later, after I had gone to bed and my head rested on my pillow, I turned toward my window and gazed out at the night. It seemed to me that a dark shadow flew by and up.

Gerta, I thought, *returning to her body.*

Surprisingly, the idea didn't chill me. It brought me comfort to know that even someone as desperately alone as Gerta could find a way home.

She wasn't there yet.

Not yet.

Maybe we could help her, which in a strange and wondrous way would help us as well.

14

Betrayal

The following day it was impossible for us to concentrate on anything. I should say, with the exception of Howard, and of course Steven, who had no reason not to do his usual good work. All of us girls looked like we had slept on a bale of hay, whereas Howard looked as rested and chipper as ever. He seemed to take pleasure in our discomfort, too. I could see he liked having the upper hand, especially over Cinnamon, who didn't come back at him with her usual biting quips whenever he criticized one of us or ridiculed something we had said.

The only time we were all alert was when Ms. Fairchild appeared. She surely had discovered the unlocked door and the unlocked window in Gerta's apartment. Would she dare to interrogate all or one of us about it, since none of us had brought up any questions about Gerta or made any remarks? Or would she assume that Gerta had opened the window and she had left the door unlocked herself?

Her eyes, like some searchlight, moved slowly over our faces, lingering, it seemed to me, the longest on mine. I was usually uncomfortable with the way she looked at me as it was, much less now, knowing I was trying to appear innocent. Ice and Cinnamon especially, but Rose as well, were better at putting on their masks of deception. They had lived with and among people whom it was necessary to fool.

Rose often talked about Evan's aunt, how cold and cruel she was to him. He had shown her methods he often employed to confuse and deceive her, the best one being his manipulations of his own trust funds. Because of the way Ice's mother was, she often had to keep things hidden from her so she wouldn't take out her anger on Ice's father. Ice had even kept her pursuit of singing something of a secret from her. In many ways, she told us, her mother was competing with her, fighting age desperately and "practically blaming me for her gray hairs and wrinkles."

Cinnamon readily admitted many times that she had made lying and deceiving a science in her home and in her world. She described her grandmother as a tyrant in the house who had to be deliberately misinformed in order to keep the peace between her and Cinnamon's mother.

"Madame Senetsky is right," she once said with a bit of sadness in her voice, "we are always performing."

Well, if that was true, I knew I wasn't good at it. Trust was more than a word in my home. It was closely tied to love. And when Grandad was alive, any deception, no matter how small, was considered a crack in the moral fiber that made our fortress against evil and Satan that much weaker. I didn't think my nose would grow, but when I was younger, he had me convinced a lie breaks out like a pimple and is easily discovered, so I was not very good at being deceptive and conniving.

When Ms. Fairchild finally left, I felt positive she had read everything in my face. I told Cinnamon so.

"Even if she did, she won't dare accuse you or anyone else. Howard's right about that. Just go on about your business and pretend none of this happened," she advised.

Despite their experience, it was advice neither she nor my new sisters could follow easily themselves. All that day and the next we anticipated something, some sign in Madame Senetky's lectures, some evidence in Ms. Fairchild's orders. At dinner we felt our hearts leap with every long pause in the conversation. All eyes turned toward Madame Senetsky. If she suspected anything, she was surely the world's best actress.

Nevertheless, every footstep outside our doors, every knock or mention of our names brought a cold wave of fear. It was coming. I felt it in my bones the way Grandad used to feel a coming storm. The end here was coming.

But it didn't. Nothing happened out of the ordinary until Thursday at lunch, when we were all summoned to the parlor for a rather severe bawling-out by Madame Senetsky.

Naturally we anticipated the executioner's ax. We sat quietly, waiting. The grandfather clock bonged and she entered briskly, taking the chair she usually took, her hand on her cane. She looked like the queen of dramatics she was purported to be. Our eyes went from her to each other to the floor. The silence was deafening. Finally, she spoke, her words falling like heavy hail, each syllable crisp, sharp, and meant to sting like darts.

"I have spoken with all of your instructors and, to a man, they have the same complaint: you're all badly distracted. You've all let up on your efforts. You all are revealing yourselves as less dedicated and determined, and this with a second Performance Night just around the corner. I won't stand for it.

"I have a suspicion," she said, eying me, "that some of you are thinking about other, far less important things—childish romances, whatever—and that is taking a dramatic toll on your achievement here. I can't remember the last time I had to give a group of Senetsky candidates a pep talk to motivate them. I pride myself on choosing candidates who are so self-motivated, they are frustrated by their own rate of development. They are usually after me to rush their careers along, as if I could wave a magic wand over them and, *poof,* make them all into movie stars, stage stars, musical stars, as if I created the constellations in the entertainment sky.

"Well, I do, but not without total commitment."

She paused and slowly panned us all, her gaze no less stinging than her words.

"Sadly, that is not the case with you girls. I haven't had this said so much about our two young men," she added, with a brief nod at Steven and Howard.

Howard smiled. Steven looked unimpressed, even a bit impatient and anxious to get back to his games.

"Therefore," she announced, rising like a never-ending giant in our midst, her words exploding like cannon fire, "I am prohibiting you girls from leaving this property or having any guests for the next three weekends, which will bring us to the second Performance Night. Is that perfectly clear?"

"But..." I started to say. Chandler had worked out another trip in two weeks. We had wonderful plans to tour the city and spend private time together. I felt I needed him more than ever. How could I tell him it was impossible?

She raised her eyebrows and stiffened her neck, pounding the cane once.

"Yes?"

I looked down without speaking. Mentioning his name would surely be the kiss of death.

"Nothing," I muttered.

"Good. Then it's settled. I expect to hear about a vast improvement beginning tomorrow. I suggest you all give what I have said a great deal of consideration. Go upstairs to your rooms and contemplate yourselves in your mirrors and ask yourselves once and for all, what do I want to do with my life? Who do I want to be?"

She turned and walked out. I looked at the others, my eyes tearing. They knew why I was so upset.

"What am I going to tell Chandler?" I moaned.

"Same thing I'm going to tell Barry," Rose said. "The bridge over the moat has been pulled up."

Steven laughed.

"Girls," he said, holding out his arms, "you always have me any time you want me."

The looks on our faces when we all glared back at him raised his eyebrows.

"Well, you heard our leader. I'm off to do a little extra," he said quickly and practically leaped off his chair and ran out the door.

"Talk about your disturbed people," Howard muttered. Then he turned on us, his face stern. "What's wrong with you? How many times do you have to be told that when you are performing, when you are on a stage, even in practice, you leave your real lives in the wings? If you're not able to do that, you won't make it. When they say the show must go on, they mean it," he declared. "This dressing down was certainly not necessary, especially for me. Unfortunately, I'm grouped in with the rest of you, and to tell you the truth, I'm totally embarrassed. Despite what she said, all of it will affect my career, too."

"What we certainly don't need at this moment is a lecture from Howard Rockwell," Cinnamon snapped back.

"No?" He stared for a moment and then sat back. "Maybe you're right. You won't benefit by it. I can see that." He rose and walked to the door before turning to add, "Tonight, girls."

"What?" I cried.

"We're going up tonight."

"And exactly how are we supposed to do that, Howard?" Cinnamon demanded. "We've told you about the window being locked."

He smiled that now-familiar beam of arrogance that tightened all our stomachs.

"I remembered something you told me. Honey found that door in the costume room, remember? I went up on my own late last night and tried it. Well, guess what, my little geniuses? The key is right there in the door. We can get in that way."

He stopped grinning.

"We're going in, say about nine. Ms. Fairchild retires to do whatever it is she does with her narrow, limited little life, and Madame Senetsky, I've learned, has been invited to a cocktail party at the Guggenheim Museum. The coast, as they say in melodrama, is clear."

"Are you crazy?" Cinnamon asked him. "After what just happened, you want to risk her rage, too?"

"Precisely because of that," he replied coolly. "Wouldn't it have been nice to say something like, 'We've had a hard time sleeping with all that singing coming from above.' "

"But we don't hear that," I said. "At least, I don't."

He smiled.

"Little Miss Honesty," he quipped. "Somehow, I doubt that would occur to her and be any sort of argument. Right, Cinnamon?"

She glared at him without speaking.

"Right?" he insisted.

"I don't know," she muttered.

"Well, I do. Nine o'clock. Everyone quietly, without attracting Steven's attention if possible, meets at the foot of the stairway. See you later, girls."

He flashed a smile and was gone.

"He's crazy," Rose muttered.

"As a fox," Cinnamon said. "We'll have to be there. If he went up without us, it could be worse. He might frighten Gerta, too."

None of us could stop thinking about it the remainder of the day. One look at any of our faces could tell that, yet somehow we managed to do better in our classes and hold back our raging nerves and tension at dinner. At one point I thought Steven had caught on to something. Everything he suggested that he and Howard do, Howard rejected.

"What are you going to do, Howard?" he slammed back at him, "sit in your room and contemplate your navel all night?"

"I'm doing some reading, some very intense concentration, if you have to know. I'm not as fortunate as you are, Steven. My talent has to be nurtured, developed."

"Give me a break."

He looked at us.

"Anyone here up for a game of Killer Spunk on my computer? I just got it day before yesterday. The graphics are incredible. You're a killer, Cinnamon. What do you say? Up for the challenge?"

"When I was a child, I thought as a child, I understood as a child, Steven. Now that I am a woman, I have put away childish things."

Howard roared.

"What the hell is that supposed to mean?" Steven cried, his face twisted in a grimace of frustration.

"It's from the Bible, a paraphrase," Howard explained. "It means it's time to grow up, Steven. Very good, Cinnamon."

She nodded, but with a look that said, "I don't need your compliments."

"You're all a bunch of deadheads," Steven declared, disgusted, and stood and left the dining room.

"Hey, you didn't stay to do your share of cleanup," Howard called after him.

"Let him go, Howard. It's better," Cinnamon advised, her eyes taking on that narrow glint that said, "Don't disagree or else."

Howard nodded.

"Right," he said. "Okay, let's get to it."

"You're making a mistake," Rose told him.

"*We're* making a mistake," he corrected, with his smile as punctuation.

Quietly, we went about our duties and then all walked upstairs. It was practically a funeral procession. We met in my room before we met with Howard at nine.

"We'll get in and out of there as quickly as we can," Cinnamon began. "Don't do too much talking and certainly don't start her on her music," she told Ice. "Maybe he'll get bored with it and that will be that."

"I feel like we're betraying her in some way," Rose muttered, "exposing her to him, I mean."

Ice nodded.

"It might be worse for her if we don't," Cinnamon suggested.

As the clock's hands drew closer and closer toward nine, I felt my stomach burning inside as if the ends of my nerve wires were sparking. The others looked just as tense. Nothing anyone said or did could take away the anxiety. Almost as soon as the big hand kissed the twelve, there was a gentle rap on my door. We looked at each other, and then Cinnamon opened the door. Howard was there, in a black turtleneck and black pants.

"What do you think this is, a spy mission?" she teased.

"In a way, I suppose it is. Always dress for the part you're about to play in life," he said.

"Give us a break, will you, Howard? Let up on the theatrics for just a few hours. Girls."

We followed her out and slipped down the corridor as quietly as possible past Steven's closed door, to the stairway leading up to the costume room. No one spoke. Howard led the way. At night the small corridor looked even more gloomy and desolate, the small light barely casting a shadow on the wall. Howard opened the costume room door as quietly as he could. It squeaked nevertheless, and although it was not a very loud sound, to us it seemed like a fire alarm.

When the door was completely open, we waited a moment to see if anyone—Ms. Fairchild, especially—had heard anything. There were no sounds coming from below. The house held its breath as tightly as we held ours. Howard smiled, nodded, and continued into the room.

We filed past the costumes and reached the door. Howard lifted the dresses away from it and turned the key in the lock to open the first door. He looked at Cinnamon, who shook her head as one final appeal to him to retreat. Smirking, Howard opened the second door, which took us into the living room of Gerta's apartment. Howard closed the door behind us and we all stood for a moment. Gerta wasn't in the living room.

"That's her bedroom?" he asked, nodding at the door.

"Yes," Cinnamon said. "She might be asleep."

He moved slowly, quietly to the door, looked in, and then turned to us and shook his head.

"What?" Cinnamon asked in a loud whisper.

"She's not there," he said, and we all moved up beside him and looked at the empty bed.

We all wondered the same thing. Was she gone? Had they decided to take her away?

"Try the door to the hall," Cinnamon told Ice. "Maybe it was left unlocked and she went down to her mother's residence."

Ice tried the door and found it locked.

"The window," Cinnamon thought aloud and went to it herself, but found that locked as well. She turned and shrugged. "She's gone."

Howard looked from her to the rest of us, skepticism writing lines along his forehead and pulling his lips in at the corners of his mouth.

"This was all a lot of bull, wasn't it?" he charged. "You thought you'd have some fun with me, is that it?"

"Don't be completely stupid, Howard," Cinnamon told him.

"You've got something else going on and you tried to pull this on me. I want you to know I never really fell for it," he said, folding his arms across his chest. "That's why I insisted on coming up here. If you really thought I had swallowed this fantastic story about a disturbed daughter practically kept a prisoner just so

Madame Senetsky wouldn't be embarrassed, well, you've all got another think…"

Gerta was so quiet, stepping out from behind the closet door, we almost didn't see her. She wore a wig of long black hair that trailed over her shoulders. She was dressed in an ankle-length nightgown. She didn't seem to see us, but instead looked past us. Then she smiled.

" 'My mother had a maid called Barbary; She was in love, and he she loved proved mad, and did forsake her. She had a song of "Willow," an old thing 'twas, but it express'd her fortune, and she died singing it.' "

"What is she saying?" Ice asked with a grimace.

Howard shook his head in awe.

"Those are Desdemona's lines in *Othello* before she is murdered by him. Cinnamon, what is this? Have you been working with her, teaching it to her?"

"Of course not," Cinnamon replied.

"But…" He looked at us. "It's part of what Cinnamon and I are preparing for our next Performance Night."

I turned quickly to Cinnamon. Had Gerta somehow been listening in on their rehearsals? For a moment her eyes twinkled with the same suspicion. Then she shook it out of her thoughts.

"Just coincidence," she muttered for my benefit.

Gerta stepped forward.

" 'The song tonight will not go from my mind; I have much to do but to go hang my head all at one side and sing it like poor Barbary,' " she continued.

She paused and lowered her head.

"That's very good," Howard told her. He looked

skeptically at Cinnamon. "Too good to be any sort of coincidence."

"I told you, Howard, I've had nothing to do with it. She just knows lines from plays."

Gerta lifted her head, her face back to the face we had seen before, that childlike smile of trust on her lips.

"Hello," Howard said to her.

She ignored him and turned to us.

"Are you all here for the show?" she asked excitedly.

"What show is that, Gerta?" I asked.

"My mother's new show. We're supposed to be very quiet, you know. Not a peep. Sit and pay attention and smile at people who smile at you, but not a peep," she warned. "This way, please," she said and walked into the living room.

Howard turned to us, astounded.

"Is she for real?"

"Well, have you had enough, Howard?" Cinnamon asked him. "You see for yourself we were not lying to you. Are you satisfied? Do you want to apologize?"

"Yes, yes," he said, waving his hand at her. "I'm sorry, I'm sorry. You're all as honest as the day is long." He looked after Gerta. "She's like an idiot savant, rattling off those lines. You said you have heard her recite others?"

"So what?" Ice asked him.

"So what? That's not exactly a television commercial jingle, you know, and she performed it rather well, I thought. Maybe even better than you do," he told Cinnamon.

"That doesn't bother me, Howard. This is just all very sad to us. Can we go now?"

"Let me just see what else she knows," he said, and followed her into the living room.

"He's a piece of work, our Howard Rockwell," Cinnamon muttered. We all trailed after him.

Gerta was on the sofa. She picked up some needlework she had been doing and continued as if none of us were there. Howard watched her, fascinated, for a moment.

"Gerta?"

She didn't look up at him.

" 'I do believe 'twas he,' " he said.

Gerta looked up at him.

" 'How now, my lord? I have been talking with a suitor here, a man that languishes in your displeasure.' "

"Holy cow," Howard said, turning back to us. "She knows the whole thing. Desdemona's part." He stared at her a moment. "I wonder... 'How now?' " he cried in a loud, angry voice, " 'What do you here alone?' "

Gerta's face changed, her body stiffened.

" 'Do not you chide; I have a thing for you.' "

Howard's eyes looked like they would pop out of his head.

"That's Emila's line. She knows the whole play by heart!"

"Howard," I said. "Maybe that's enough, okay?"

"No, wait a minute. Let's try... *Macbeth*." He turned back to Gerta and in a loud whisper said, " 'If we should fail?' "

She gazed at him, her face now turning angry.

" 'We fail? But screw your courage to the sticking place, and we'll not fail.' "

She leaned forward to whisper.

" 'When Duncan is asleep, whereto the rather shall his day's hard journey soundly invite him, his two chamberlains will I with wine and wassail so convince, that memory, the warder of the brain, shall be a fume and the receipt of reason a limbeck only. When in swinish sleep their drenched natures lies as in a death, what cannot you and I perform upon the unguarded Duncan? What not put upon his spungy officers who shall bear the guilt of our great quell?…' "

"That's it!" Howard cried. "Lady Macbeth's planning of the murder of the king. She knows it all by heart."

Gerta returned to her needlework.

"Can we go now, Howard? Are you satisfied?"

"No. How did she get like this? How come I never read or heard anything about her? What's her name, Gerta, Berta? What?"

Gerta's head snapped up.

"No Gerta Berta. No!" she cried, her face in a grimace.

"Huh?" said Howard, stepping back quickly and turning to Cinnamon.

"Now you've done it. You've riled her up."

"What did I do?"

"It's all right, Gerta," I told her and put my hand on her shoulder. "You're Gerta. You're all right now. You're safe. Don't worry."

She stared up at me. Her eyes calmed and she returned to her needlework.

"What is going on?" Howard muttered. "Why did that disturb her?"

"Let's get out of here before we're discovered," Rose pleaded.

We started toward the door to the costume room. Howard lingered, watching Gerta work until Cinnamon grabbed his arm and turned him.

"All right," he said, "I'll leave. But I want to know what this is all about."

"She was abused by her father, who called her Gerta Berta, if you have to know."

"Abused?" He looked back at her, his eyes growing smaller. "You mean, sexually?"

"That's what we think, yes. Can we get out of here, please?"

Reluctantly, he joined us at the door. We gazed back at Gerta and then we closed the first door, stepped into the costume room and closed and relocked the second. As quietly as we could, we trailed back through the room, closed the door behind us, shuddering at the squeaks, and then hurried down the stairway.

"Let's all go to sleep now," Cinnamon ordered

Howard stood there, thinking. I didn't like the way he was behaving and neither did the others.

"Howard?"

"What? Oh, yeah. Thanks. Good night," he said and went to his room. We watched him until he closed his door.

"He was fascinated and amazed. I think it was pathetic and sad," Rose said.

"Me, too," Ice agreed.

"He would have stayed up there for hours feeding her lines just for his own amusement," I said.

Cinnamon nodded.

"The only living thing more self-centered than our Howard Rockwell is an amoeba," she declared.

It brought some smiles, but we were all emotionally exhausted.

I was sure we all went to sleep that night with Gerta's dramatic recitations echoing in our thoughts and spinning webs of nightmares off the spindle of our dreams.

Over the next few days, we actually thought Howard was going to let it all go. He had seen Gerta and the strange arrangements she had. He was satisfied that he was now sharing our great secret. Cinnamon said he was very energized in drama class. As we had learned, they were preparing cuts from Shakespeare's *Othello,* Tennessee Williams' *The Glass Menagerie,* and Strindberg's *Miss Julie,* under the heading Woman and Romantic Disappointments. In vocal class Howard's voice actually carried above Ice's at times, and he was even more enthusiastic about our dance lessons.

The second Performance Night loomed in the very immediate future now. This one seemed to be more important. We were told that, because of the success of the first, more important managers, producers, and even performers were requesting seats. Howard lectured to us about it, saying some of it might just be good hype generated by Edmond Senetsky.

"It takes a great deal of experience to be able to distinguish between what is just good public relations and what is reality," he declared.

"But naturally *you* have an instinct for telling the

difference, right, Howard?" Cinnamon asked him and he readily agreed.

All we could do was shake our heads and smile. He was so arrogant about it that he missed her sarcasm or refused to see it. If self-confidence was like money in the bank, Howard would have enough to loan out sufficient amounts to all of us, I thought. I'd certainly line up to make such a request, although I was enjoying Mr. Bergman's enthusiasm for my work more and more these days. I was going to play a more difficult piece for the second Performance Night, and so was Steven.

As the evening drew closer, our excitement built, especially for me because my parents were going to try to be here. Ice's father said he would come, too, but she had not yet heard from her mother. Cinnamon's father was feeling better, so he and her mother said they would attend. Only Rose remained in doubt about her mother and then, one afternoon, she received a post card with a picture of the Eiffel Tower on the front of it. All it said was:

Dear Rose,

I got married in Las Vegas today.
Wish me luck.

Mom

We all gathered in her room to console her. She wagged her head to shake off her tears and then declared with conviction, "I don't care. You are my only family now, and the theater is my only home."

No one spoke, but I felt that, despite our work and our talents, that would not be a good substitute for my family and home. Grease paint, costumes, props, and scenery were all part of the illusion. You could pretend to love someone on stage, embrace a family, have wonderful, close friends, but it wouldn't work when the curtain came down.

Later that evening, I decided that before I went to bed, I would visit Rose once again to see if I could cheer her. Just as I stepped out into the hallway, I heard a loud creak and looked at the stairway that led up to the costume room. Howard Rockwell stopped midway. He looked very guilty, shifting his eyes to avoid my shocked gaze.

"Where were you?" I asked.

"Costume room," he said quickly. Much too quickly, I thought.

"Why?"

"I wanted to check on my costume for Performance Night. Who do you think you are, cross-examining me like this, anyway?" he added and hurried down and to his room. I waited until his door was closed and then I hurried across the hall to Cinnamon's room instead of Rose's. I knocked and went in. She was in bed, reading her script.

"What's wrong?" she asked, sitting up after taking one look at my face.

"I just found Howard coming down the stairs. I think he might have gone into Gerta's apartment."

"What? Why do you think that?"

"Just the way he looked... very guilty."

She threw off her covers.

"I'm not positive," I added, seeing how enraged she

was becoming. "He did claim he was checking his costume for the second Performance Night."

"Is that what he told you? It's a downright lie. He knows his costume was sent out to be cleaned and pressed."

She shoved her feet into her slippers and practically lunged for her robe on the way out of the room. The look on her face frightened me. She seemed capable of bludgeoning him to death. I hoped I wasn't making a mountain out of a molehill.

"C'mon," she said.

"Where?"

"We'll go up to see Gerta and learn if he was there without us or not."

"Should we get Ice and Rose?"

"No," she said firmly. "It'll be quicker and less chance of being discovered."

We moved quietly to the stairs, but they creaked just as they had under Howard's feet. No one came out of his or her room, and moments later, we were in the costume room. We could see where the dresses were moved to permit someone to open the door. Cinnamon looked at me knowingly, turned the key, and continued. My heart was beating like a hailstorm against a window.

The lights were out in the living room, but there was some dim illumination coming from Gerta's bedroom. We walked quietly to the door and looked in to see her lying in bed, wearing the wig that had the long, gold pigtails.

She turned to us.

"Hi, Gerta, how are you?" Cinnamon asked her.

Gerta's face began to crumble.

"I was bad again," she said. "I was Gerta Berta."

Cinnamon hurried to her bedside. I followed.

"What do you mean, Gerta?"

"Daddy was here," she said. "I was bad."

"Daddy wasn't here," Cinnamon insisted, but she shook her head.

"Yes, he was. He said he wanted to stop the nightmares. He was right here," she added, patting the large fluffy pillow beside her.

Cinnamon looked at me. I shook my head.

"What is she saying?"

"Howard," Cinnamon replied.

"What do you mean?"

Cinnamon's eyes grew dark.

"He came up here and did some role-playing with her. He must have been coming up here. Who knows how many times?"

I shook my head.

"What..."

"Can't you see? She's naked under the blanket," Cinnamon pointed out. Her face was so full of rage, I thought her eyes might explode. The muscles in her cheeks and jaw were taut enough to outline the bone.

The realization struck me like a punch in my stomach.

"That's horrible," I said.

She nodded.

"Horrible's too soft a word for it."

"Please tell me a story," Gerta said. "Tell me something nice. Tell me a happy story."

Cinnamon looked at her and then muttered to me. "I'm flat out of happy endings."

"Let me," I said, moving past her to take Gerta's hand and sit on the bed.

"Let me tell you the story of the little princess who got lost," I began.

Cinnamon smiled, but her thoughts clearly went back to Howard Rockwell. She stepped aside to wait for me to finish, fuming so intensely, I could almost feel the heat of her anger across the room.

Gerta's eyes closed finally and I stood up. Cinnamon and I moved silently out of the apartment and through the costume room, locking the door behind us, and then went down the stairs, neither of us saying a word. Disgust and horror made us mute.

"What are we going to do?" I asked her when we reached the bottom of the stairs.

She glared at Howard's closed door.

"Bring down the curtain," she vowed.

"How?"

"Get some sleep. We're all going to need it," she replied and went to her room.

Get some sleep? I thought.

She might as well have asked me to build a house or fly to the moon.

15

The Play's the Thing

If someone had asked me, after the first few weeks at the Senetsky School of Performing Arts, who among the four of you girls do you believe could most easily toss it all away, I think I would have chosen myself. I played the violin with love, but I was always torn between home and the places I knew my musical career would take me. I wasn't sure if I wanted to make all those sacrifices. I wasn't sure if I really was as ambitious as the others. Personal glory didn't seem as important to me. Going home would not be a defeat and a punishment.

Ice wanted to succeed for her father even more than she wanted it for herself. During the times she and I were alone, she often spoke of him with deep affection, and made it clear to me that she believed she was his hope, the only thing that brought sunshine to his days and filled his heart with dreams anymore. She told me about his own longing to be a successful musician and how he had been forced to give up his pursuit. Like so many people, she said, he had to surrender his ambitions in order to provide for his family and himself. He moved through life now as if he were a shadow of a person, doing most things simply to survive, but the one thing that he didn't do out of any necessity was to get behind her development as a singer.

"I'm his future, his justification for all his terrible sacrifices," she said. "I will succeed."

She said it with such vehemence and intensity, she made my heart skip beats. I thought the look on her face was wonderful, and I thought it was all there in her voice, in the way she made the audience freeze in awe of her talent.

Rose had come here at what she hoped was to be the end of a trail of betrayals. She had loved her own father very much and she talked often about the way he had made her feel special, but she also admitted she had sensed something very insubstantial about him, something so carefree and irresponsible that he was more like a little boy. His adulterous affair had left her and her mother destitute as well as in shock and disbelief. Her mother, however, looked at it as a betrayal only of her, as if Rose wouldn't suffer anywhere near as much.

When Evan's aunt, Charlotte Alden Curtis, the sister of her father's lover, came to them for help with Evan, making them feel they had to bear the responsibility of what her father had done, she readily accepted the consequences. Slowly, Charlotte corrupted Rose's mother, deliberately setting her up with a womanizer just to enjoy some sick revenge. Ironically, however, all this brought Rose closer to her handicapped brother, and together they found a way for her to develop her dancing talent and defeat Charlotte's revenge. A child of betrayals, Rose could never betray Evan's efforts, for he saw his own validation in her successes.

Cinnamon was most puzzling from the beginning. There was always a sharpness, an underlying bitterness behind every look and word. She seemed to be able to touch a deeper, darker world and draw upon it to strengthen herself. Ghosts, spirits, shadows fertilized and enriched her view of life, rather than frightened her. Despite her distaste for Howard Rockwell, she enjoyed being on stage, even if it had to be with him. Watching her perform, I felt she didn't memorize lines and pretend to be someone, but instead permitted and enjoyed having that new persona possess her, just the way she claimed the spirits that lived in her home had possessed her. The theater was really her world, far more than Howard Rockwell would ever appreciate or ever know.

Nevertheless, what Cinnamon proposed, even though she knew what impact that proposal could have on her own future, truly surprised me. It wasn't until lunch hour that she and I were able to relate to Ice and Rose what we had discovered the night before. They were both as sickened and disgusted about it as we were.

"The fact is," Cinnamon pointed out, "I don't know who we should blame more for all this, our sick Howard Rockwell or Madame Senetsky, whose need to protect her image and reputation far outweighs her own daughter's needs."

"It amazes me how indifferent and aloof some parents can be toward their own children," Rose said, her own life clearly an example. "When that umbilical cord is cut, it's cut. It's almost as if they feel they've done their duty in just giving birth, fulfilled some responsibility to the species or something, and then go on to travel the Selfish Highway, terrified that we'll somehow cause them to lose one moment's pleasure."

"Whatever," Cinnamon said, impatient to tell us what she wanted us to do. "I have a plan, and I'll need everyone's cooperation."

When she described it to us, we were all speechless. We tried to talk her out of it, but she was adamant.

"You'll take the most blame," I pointed out to her.

She shrugged it off.

"I admire Madame Senetsky for her accomplishments, of course, but I ask myself, would I like to be her?" She smiled and shook her head. "I have no problem with that answer, and I'd bet everything I have and will have that none of you do either. However, if anyone here would rather not be a part of this, I certainly understand."

"I'll help," I said without hesitation.

"Of course I'll help," Rose said.

"Me, too," Ice added.

"Look at it this way," Cinnamon said. "We'll be like producers and directors."

"What will we call this major production of ours?" Rose asked.

Cinnamon thought a moment.

"How about 'Falling Curtain'?"

No one laughed. If anything, it made us all pause and give it some deep thought.

Falling curtain.

It was too true, too descriptive, and too much of a prophecy to belittle or ignore.

As if Fate knew what was best for us and had decided to take a hand in what was to follow, unexpected events dictated we would be alone when we most needed support. Mommy called me the next day, very upset. Daddy's new combine had broken down, and he was tied up with that and some other problems on the farm.

"We just can't get away, sweetheart. I know how much you wanted us to be there."

I was about to say, "No, you don't, Mommy," but instead I assured her I would be fine. *Maybe I am a good actress after all,* I thought. *Maybe it rubs off.*

Cinnamon learned the next day that her mother had come down with a severe chest cold and was unable to travel even ten miles. That evening, Ice's father called to tell her about the death of his uncle and how his need to attend the funeral in South Carolina would prevent him from coming to New York as well. Rose's mother had already written off any attempt to attend our next Performance Night.

We had only ourselves.

We hoped it was enough.

"Now we'll take on one of our most difficult acting jobs," Cinnamon instructed. "Grin and bear it, ladies. We'll all treat Howard Rockwell the same as usual. Pretend we know nothing about what he has done."

"I'll be biting my lip so hard, I'll get blisters," Rose complained.

"It'll be hardest for you on that stage, Cinnamon, rehearsing with him," I pointed out.

"I like a challenge," she replied, and Ice laughed.

"I have other words for him beside 'challenge' that I'm sure are much more descriptive, and you know me, girls, I'm not one to rely on words," she said.

We laughed.

It amazed and even excited me how close the impending danger and risk made us all. *Would I ever again have friends as wonderful as these?* I wondered. If nothing else ever came of my experience here, this alone was worth it.

We did what Cinnamon ordered, however. We put on the act. Rose even added a nice touch by asking Howard questions at dinner, as if he was truly our resident expert about theater, agents, producers, and audiences. He gave long-winded answers rife with references to this performer and that, quoting directors and producers. All of us listened, our eyes barely shifting toward each other for fear we might laugh aloud or in some way give away our own performances. It was so easy to humor someone who had an ego as swollen as Howard's ego was.

It was far more difficult to keep our intentions hidden from Madame Senetsky. Fortunately, she was busier than usual preparing for this particular Performance Night. Ms. Fairchild made it a point to impress upon us how hard Madame Senetsky was working to bring in the most influential and well-known people. The names were leaked out in dribs and drabs: told to our teachers in front of us, casually mentioned at lunch and dinner, thrown in with orders to staff and to Mrs. Churchwell while we were present.

It was almost as if Madame Senetsky had decided to psych us out, to bring us to the cliff of nervousness and taunt us with being pushed over the edge just to see how well we would perform and stand up to it all. She was turning up the pressure like some sadist working a torture chamber to discover what we were really made of. Could we survive in this competitive world? Better to find out now, she surely thought, and not waste anyone else's time.

Building up the night this way made us even more anxious about Cinnamon's plan.

"Maybe we should wait," Rose suggested. "Maybe when there aren't so many important people here."

"No," Cinnamon insisted. "The more significant the audience, the better it will be. I want to repeat what I told you all at the start. If anyone feels more comfortable not being a part of this, no hard feelings. I can't blame anyone. All of you have worked hard to get to this point. It's understandable you wouldn't want to throw it away."

"So have *you* worked hard," Ice said sharply.

"I've got to do this," Cinnamon replied.

"So do we," I said. I looked at Rose. She nodded.

"I just wondered," she said with a shrug.

"No," Cinnamon corrected, "just a case of basic stage fright."

"And remember," we all chanted imitating Madame Senetsky, "even the most seasoned actors and musicians experience stage fright, butterflies, shattered nerves before stepping on stage."

Our laughter at ourselves brought us our only small moments of relief. The rest of the time, tension was our shadow, following us everywhere, even into our dreams.

On the morning of Performance Night, we were brought together for our instructions concerning the usual reception that would take place immediately at the end of the show. We were reminded about our behavior and what Madame Senetsky's expectations would be.

We were then permitted to relax and prepare ourselves mentally and emotionally for the evening's activities. Steven went off to his computer games. Howard decided to review his lines and practically demanded Cinnamon join him, but she turned him down again, claiming a bad headache this time. Rose occupied herself with warm-ups in the dance studio. Ice went for a walk and then retreated to her room, and I took my violin and sat alone, playing some of the music I remembered Uncle Simon loved to hear. We were all like firecrackers, afraid to get too close to each other because we might set each other off and blow ourselves to bits.

When I went upstairs to get ready for the show, I met Steven in the hallway.

"What is it with everyone today?" he asked. "No one wants to talk. I nearly got my head chopped off when I poked it in to watch Rose go through her exercises, and Cinnamon just glared at me as if I was a child pornographer or something. I feel like I'm in the movie *High Noon* and it's ten to twelve. The clock is a monster!" he cried, throwing his arms up.

I had to laugh.

"That's it," he said quickly, encouraged by my mirth. "If you're too serious, you'll make mistakes."

"You know something, Steven," I said. "When I first met you, I thought you had to be a mistake, but now I'm convinced that, of all of us, you have the best chance of success in this business."

"Huh?" he said.

"See you downstairs," I said, and left him scratching his head.

I tried to get some rest. Mommy called again to wish me luck and Uncle Simon got on to apologize for not sending flowers in time. I kept thinking about what we were about to do and how it would affect all of us. I hoped my family wouldn't be disappointed in me if it went badly, but I was in firm agreement with Cinnamon. It was something we had to do. No opportunity, no chance for success was worth having to live with not doing something to correct what we were all convinced was a terrible wrong.

Incredibly, I fell asleep, and woke in time to dress and prepare for my performance. Ms. Fairchild had already informed us that Madame Senetsky wished us to follow the same order of appearance, which worked fine for Cinnamon. In fact, it was what she had hoped would happen. What she forgot to consider was how we would all perform, knowing what we knew was about to occur. It was like stepping on a hot stove, not a stage.

Edmond Senetsky came backstage twenty minutes before it was to begin. Except for his attending some dinners and occasionally stopping by to watch and listen to us work in class, we hadn't had much opportunity to speak with him or he with us. He looked very dapper and energized in his bright red ascot and black tuxedo.

"I have someone here to consider each and every one of you tonight," he began. "I don't want that to make any of you unduly nervous, but as my mother often says, you are always being judged out there anyway. You shouldn't have any more or any less concern than you normally would. That's the character of a true professional, and it's my firm belief that every one of you has what it takes to be one. So, good luck. Break a leg and help me make my ten percent."

Steven was the only one who really laughed. Howard looked too serious and took every word literally. We simply stared at Edmond, all of us wondering the same thing. How much did he know? How much did he care? What would he be saying before this evening ended?

He left to take his seat. While Madame Senetsky greeted our audience, Steven stepped into the wings, waiting to be introduced. He had his head down and kept opening and closing his hands. Then he looked up at me, smiled, and said, "I feel like I'm a surgeon about to operate on someone's brain."

"As long as it isn't mine," I told him.

He laughed, looked at me seriously for a moment and said, "You're great, Honey. I really will miss you when this is over."

Of course, he had no idea what that might mean at the time, but it was eerie.

As soon as Madame Senetsky left the stage, Mr. Bergman began to introduce Steven. I stepped back into the shadows, my heart so caked in fear, I could barely feel its beat. Moments later he was at his piano. Steven's beautiful music followed, and that was soothing. Every once in a while, Rose, Ice, or Cinnamon would look my way and we would lock our eyes like the conspirators Howard so often accused us of being. He paced about like some zoo beast in its cage. Occasionally we heard him mumbling lines to himself, saw him pause, take a dramatic stance, and then nod and continue.

When Steven finished and the applause came, it was just as loud and enthusiastic as it had been for his first recital. I turned to look at Ice. She was to be the first of us four, and I knew it would be extra difficult for her tonight. As she walked by me to take her position in the wings, we grasped hands and held each other's for a moment.

"Don't worry," she whispered. "I'm fine. I'm all music," she added with a smile. I nodded, wished her luck, and watched her go on stage.

Cinnamon lingered in the rear doorway. I was next to perform and then came Rose. She wouldn't leave to do what she had to do until Rose was introduced. We knew how long we each took out there, so we had our timing down fine. I only hoped I could do as well as Ice was doing, I thought as she began to sing.

It was all going along as it should. The audience's reaction to Ice was more overwhelming than it had been the first time. Her voice seemed richer, stronger, resonating with a timbre that touched hearts. I felt it in my bones. She was going to be a star. When she came off-stage, she hugged me.

"It's a piece of cake," she said. "Just as soon as you step into the spotlight, it all happens. You'll see. It's magic out there."

Mr. Bergman was introducing me. I glanced back at Cinnamon, who still looked very confident. She nodded at me. Rose in her dance tights came up beside her. She was so radiant, so beautiful, I thought. I knew in my heart I couldn't let them down. It all had to work. We had to be better than anyone imagined.

I pulled myself up when my name was given and then I walked out on the stage. In a real sense, I wished my parents were out there tonight and not just out there in my heart and mind, I thought. When it was over, they would surely be even more proud of me. I had to remind myself they were here, Uncle Peter was here, Uncle Simon, all of them. Wherever I go, they go, for they are always in me, a part of me, a part of who and what I am.

I raised the bow and the music came, as it always did. I played as if I was trying to keep Death himself at bay. I would charm the devil. It was almost as if the violin was truly connected to my very soul. I didn't think about it. I was like a tightrope walker who never looked down, but just kept his eyes forward, his concentration fixed on the goal, the finale, but I did sense how well I was playing. I could feel every note.

When it ended, I had a wonderful sense of completion, a sweet exhaustion, and I bathed in the applause. *I'm meant for this,* I thought. *Oh, yes I am. There's no doubt. No matter what, Honey Forman,* I told myself, *you'll be back out here. One way or another, you'll be back.*

Rose looked flushed in the wings. Her face seemed on fire when she pressed her cheek to mine and whispered how wonderful I had been. We were taking the audience higher and higher, which was just what Cinnamon wanted. The explosive resolution would be that much more dramatic. It was as if we were all relay runners, passing the baton. Rose took it from me and glided out on that stage to dance as she had never danced before, her every turn, spin, and leap slicing the air with grace and beauty.

I looked back. Cinnamon was gone. We had all completed the preparations earlier; now we had to follow our plan. Ice was distracting Steven. I looked for Howard, who was backstage going through his voice exercises. I drew closer to be sure he didn't go looking for Cinnamon. He looked up at me.

"How much longer?"

"Four minutes, maybe," I said.

"Where's Cinnamon?"

"In the wings, taking her position on the other side of the stage from you," I replied.

"You don't do that," he said, smirking with disgust. "You don't stand there like someone looking for a handout from the audience. You make them wait. You fill yourself with the power," he bragged. "She'll miss a beat," he predicted. "You'll see, I'll end up having to carry her through each piece we perform."

"With your broad shoulders of talent, Howard, that should be no problem," I said.

He looked at me with a little smile of confusion and then shrugged it off and returned to his exercises. Finally, he decided to take his position stage left. Cinnamon was to be in position stage right, both of them waiting for Mr. Marlowe to come on stage after Rose's exit.

I sucked in my breath.

The time had come. She was whisked in like a shadow, unnoticed in the pool of darkness behind stage.

Mr. Marlowe set the scene.

"Our first cut," he began, "is from Shakespeare's immortal *Othello.* Othello has come to Desdemona's bedroom to kill her because he is convinced she has betrayed him with Cassio."

The lights went out.

A bed was rolled on the stage in the darkness for Desdemona.

The lights came on.

Howard stepped onto the stage and, looking at the audience, began.

" 'It is the cause, it is the cause, my soul,' " he recited. " 'Let me not name it to you, you chaste stars. It is the cause. Yet I'll not shed her blood, nor scar that whiter skin of hers than snow, and smooth as monumental alabaster. Yet she must die, else she'll betray more men.'

" 'Put out the light,' " he continued moving toward the bed and Desdemona, " 'and then put out the light...' "

On through the speech he went, never more dramatic, never more convincing until he reached his final lines...

" 'This sorrow's heavenly, It strikes where it does love.' "

Desdemona turned in the bed and Howard cried, " 'She wakes.' "

He turned and froze, like Lot's wife in the Bible. I thought he'd never move again.

Gerta, in the correct costume and wig, cried back, " 'Who's there, Othello?' "

Howard's mouth opened and closed, but nothing emerged. Panicked, he turned toward the audience and then back toward Gerta, who went on with, " 'Will you come to bed, my lord?' "

"Madame Senetsky!" Howard screamed.

"Bring down the curtain," we heard her shout back.

And it fell like lead.

16

The Final Scene

Ironically, none of us truly appreciated the strength and the poise of Madame Senetsky as much as we did after the bedlam and confusion had begun. Without hesitation, she had Laura Fairchild sweep Gerta away, leading her back through the private residence and up to her apartment with a minimum of witnesses. We were told to report immediately to her office, and then she took the stage and addressed her guests calmly.

"My performers are, after all," she began, "still amateurs. There's been an unfortunate mix-up. Please, follow my son Edmond and the faculty to the ballroom, where we will begin our reception. I'll join you all as soon as I can. Thank you."

We heard the loud murmuring as the audience filed out. Behind the curtain, Howard was still sitting on Desdemona's bed, his head in his hands, no doubt moaning over the sabotaging of his great performance.

Steven, the most confused, chanted, "What's going on? What's happening? Who was that? Huh? What's going on?"

None of us spoke. We marched quietly to the office. Steven lingered to see what Howard was going to do and then finally caught up with us in the hallway just outside the office.

"Hey," he cried. "What the hell is happening? Won't anyone tell me anything? Cinnamon, why weren't you out there to do the scene with Howard? Who was that?"

Cinnamon turned to him, her face cold and stern.

"Howard has been working with someone else in secret," she said.

"Huh?"

He looked at the rest of us, who stared with one solid wall of silent wrath. It was enough to make him step back and calm down. We entered the office and sat on the nail-head red leather settee that was angled toward the large, dark oak desk. It was neatly organized with a gold framed picture of Madame Senetsky receiving a Tony award for her role of Katherine in *The Taming of the Shrew.*

Steven waited in the hallway and then entered with Howard, whose face was still the color of a ripe apple. He stood there, looking at us.

"Did someone here actually think that was a funny thing to do?" he asked in a very controlled voice of rage.

"No," Cinnamon said. "Actually, we were expecting you to continue with your role-playing and start to call her Gerta Berta."

Howard's crimson quickly paled to the color of cherry blossoms.

"What?" he managed to ask in a throaty voice.

"Can someone please tell me what this is all about?" Steven cried, his arms up.

"It's about Madame Senetsky's daughter and how she was first abused by her father and then by a so-called budding thespian, who took disgusting advantage of her," Cinnamon told him, throwing a look full of darts at Howard.

"Now, just a minute," Howard began.

"The night Honey saw you coming down the stairs, she and I went up to see Gerta, Howard. We saw what you had done. She told us."

"That's just her crazy imagination. You don't expect anyone is going to take her word against mine. Why..."

"Never mind your bickering," we heard, and saw Madame Senetsky in the doorway. "Both of you, sit," she ordered Howard and Steven. They moved instantly to the two chairs across from us. She closed the office door.

"I don't know how much of that you heard, Madame Senetsky," Howard began, "but I can assure you—"

She raised her hand like a traffic cop, and Howard pressed his lips together so hard, someone would think they were glued shut. The door opened and Edmond stepped in. He closed it softly behind himself and stood there, leaning against it.

"You should be with our guests, Edmond," Madame Senetsky said.

"No, Mother, I believe I should be here," he replied. He was so firm in his reply, she did not disagree. Instead, she turned to us.

"How long have you known about Gerta?" she

asked. From the way her eyes fixed on me, it looked as if she was directing herself solely to me.

"Some time now, Madame Senetsky. Weeks," I replied. I glanced at Edmond, who didn't look as angry at us as he did troubled and sad. "It began when we realized someone was on our fire escape landing in the evening, looking into our rooms. Rose's and mine, especially. We didn't know who it could be," I said.

"It wasn't me," Steven said quickly, somehow thinking that was the most important issue.

Howard smirked and looked away.

"You thought it might have been me?" Edmond said, reaching his own conclusion from the way my eyes shifted to him and then quickly away. "Because of how she was dressed," he added, "correct?"

"Edmond," Madame Senetsky chided.

"Correct?" he pursued, raising his voice like a prosecutor.

"Yes," Cinnamon said. "Especially after we found what we believed was your ascot."

He nodded and looked at Madame Senetsky.

"Apparently, taking advantage of her identity problem and having her play me worked, Mother, but not the way you expected it to work."

"Edmond, return to our guests," she ordered gently.

"It's too late, Mother. Let's just finish all this."

Madame Senetsky raised her eyes toward the ceiling and then looked back at us.

"Go on," she said. "What happened next?" Once again, she centered her gaze on me.

"We watched for whoever it was one night and saw

a figure go up the fire escape to the landing above. Shortly after that, I was missing some clothing."

"Yes, the clothing. Why didn't you report it?"

"I... we..." I turned to Cinnamon.

"We weren't ready to make any accusations yet. Rose and Ice were missing some things as well. For a while, they doubted they had brought them," she explained.

"Go on."

"One night we went up the ladder and we saw... saw Gerta dressed in man's clothing, but we also saw she wasn't a man. It frightened us, and we retreated. We didn't know what to think and we didn't want to make a scene. We were afraid," I added. "Afraid of you."

"Not that afraid apparently," she muttered. "So?"

"Rose's brother is an expert on the computer and he found out some things about your family."

"That article about my husband," Madame Senetsky recalled. She turned to Cinnamon. "The one you claimed you found in your closet. That was something this brother dug up?"

"Yes," Cinnamon said.

She nodded.

"I didn't mean to leave it behind," Rose cried. "I—"

"That's not important now. What else did your brother dig up, as you say?" she asked Rose.

"He found out you had a daughter named Gerta in a clinic in Switzerland and he found out she had died. Which," she added looking to me, "you had told Honey."

Madame Senetsky gazed at me. Suddenly, the sternness and the anger drained from her face. She sat back, looking more like an exhausted elderly woman. It was an instant metamorphosis, as if she had removed a mask.

"It was bound to happen someday, Mother. I told you this years ago," Edmond said.

She nodded.

"I've never had nor expected to have a group of determined little detectives living in my midst," she said.

"We didn't mean to pry," Cinnamon said. "We were naturally very curious and we went back and met Gerta. We felt very sorry for her, and for a while we thought we might give her some companionship."

"How did that include putting her on stage to be seen by all these people?" she demanded, the fury rushing back into her face.

"That came about for another reason," Cinnamon said, looking to Howard.

His face exploded in a panic.

"Whatever they say isn't true," he cried. "It was them. They were toying with her, making her play silly games, humoring her in those costumes, reciting lines to get her to repeat speeches from plays. I saw it myself, firsthand."

"So you were up there, too, then?" she asked him. "That's not a lie then, is it?"

"What? Well, I saw that they were up to something, and I made them take me up there one night to see for myself."

"Why didn't you come to me to tell me about it if you say they were toying with her?" Madame Senetsky asked almost calmly.

"Well, I was...I was going to, but...we had this Performance Night..."

"He went up there without us afterward," Cinnamon said boldly. "More than once. And we are sure he took advantage of her. We went up after him and found her crying, claiming she had been bad again."

"That's a lie. This whole thing about Gerta Berta is just..."

Madame Senetsky's eyes blazed. She leaned forward, looking at us first.

"She told you all of that?"

"Yes, Madame," I said.

She turned to Cinnamon.

"Are you saying he pretended to be my husband?"

Cinnamon could only nod.

We all looked down, but I could see Howard's eyes shifting from side to side like a trapped rodent.

"Steven apparently knows nothing about all this." Madame Senetsky concluded, looking at him. He had never looked more stunned and confused.

"No, ma'am," he said.

She nodded.

"I would like to speak privately with the young ladies, first. Edmond, would you please take Howard to the parlor, and then take Steven and please look in on the reception and tell everyone I'll be there as soon as possible. Please," she begged him.

"All right, Mother, but I'll be right back."

"I understand," she said.

Edmond looked down at Howard.

"Come with me immediately," he ordered. Steven

was already up and to the door. He couldn't get away fast enough. Howard glanced back at us.

"They're just going to tell you a bunch of lies about me," he threw back and walked out.

Edmond closed the door.

The silence was heavy. Everyone looked like she was holding her breath.

"It seems so very, very long ago," she began, "when I was as young as you all are now. I was one of those people who are described as having the theater in her blood, I suppose. I was putting on shows for my own parents when I was barely old enough to speak," she said, smiling at the memories.

"For me, there was never anything more exciting than an audience. I suppose it is no exaggeration to say I was and still remain obsessed."

Again she looked mostly at me.

"Marriage, a family, a loving husband, were never as important. I have often lectured you about dedication and I have even been hard on you to keep you determined. Maybe that's wrong. Maybe that's a certain sort of madness. I don't know. I just do what I think I must do to turn my rough-cut precious stones into jewels. I've had many successes.

"If you have all the research you claim you have, you know that I didn't get married until I was in my thirties, and reluctantly. My husband wanted a trophy more than a wife, and I wanted to rid myself of the nagging obligation to marry and have a family. I didn't want anything to hinder my career, even if it meant doing something I had half a heart for. My husband was sympathetic, cooperative, I should say, in the beginning. He tolerated my loving the theater far more than I would ever love him. But in time, he drifted into his world and left me to mine.

"We had Edmond because he demanded he have an heir and that was part of our bargain, and then, I had an affair with a leading man in a production I was in, and I became pregnant with Gerta. My husband found out and insisted I give birth to her despite this. He was more concerned about his reputation, and wanted the world to believe the child was his.

"I was a fool to believe he would not harbor any resentment about it, but his resentment, I thought, was tempered when we found out that Gerta had certain disabilities, and yet a remarkable ability to memorize facts, information she couldn't use. The plays you heard her quote, the parts, most of them I played and I think she was motivated to learn them because of that, but she has other facts stored in her mind that astound me.

"She was always a very sensitive child. She seemed unable to go beyond a certain age, although I have always hated the term retarded. I refuse to accept such a word for her. I have had some specialists tell me she is akin to an idiot savant. At times, as I suspect you have come to realize, she is truly amazing.

"Like any child, she longed to be loved and cherished and I'm afraid Marshall, my husband, took advantage of that. It had a devastating effect on Gerta and she, as you know, had to be institutionalized. I kept it all as quiet as I could. It reached a terrible climax when she attempted to commit suicide. Marshall was living in New York and I was in a production of Molière's *The Misanthrope* in Paris. I had to rush back to Switzerland.

"There were a number of rag newspaper reporters hot on the story. Someone I trusted very much came up with the idea to pretend Gerta was indeed gone. Our hope was she would never be pursued or abused again."

She paused to take a breath. None of us dared.

"Perhaps it was my anger, my utter disgust, but I let Marshall believe the story about Gerta's death was true. I even had a quick funeral before he could return, and there is actually a grave with a tombstone that bears her name. One of my greatest performances occurred at that gravesite," she added, with a look on her face that suggested to me she was proud of it. "Especially when I stood there with Marshall. I enjoyed his suffering."

She was silent a moment, and then, after a deep breath, continued.

"Marshall, as you already know from that article, took his own life soon afterward. I have my moments of regret, but they are short-lived. Some people can't live with the evil in themselves and what they do is what they need to do. So it was with my husband.

"I brought Gerta back, hoping to give her some comfort. The rest you now know."

"But it seems very cruel to keep her locked up like that," I said.

"And Ms. Fairchild is not exactly a warm companion for her," Cinnamon added bitterly.

"She does what she thinks I want her to do."

"Chop off her hair and threaten to do it again and again!" Ice snapped.

Madame Senetsky widened her eyes.

"Gerta did that to herself."

"No, she didn't, Madame. We were upstairs in Gerta's bedroom when Ms. Fairchild threatened her."

She stared at us and then nodded softly, following that with a deep sigh.

"Laura can be overly exuberant when she is asked to carry out an order, I suppose."

"Like a Nazi," Rose muttered.

Edmond stepped back into the office.

"It's all right out there," he said softly. He looked at us and then his mother. "Well?"

"I've told them everything and they have told me some things as well. You've been right about all this, Edmond. Changes will be made immediately."

He smiled.

"That's good, Mother."

Madame Senetsky rose.

"We have to attend to our guests," she said.

"The show must go on," Cinnamon muttered loud enough for all to hear.

"Yes," Madame Senetsky said in the tone of one who had to admit the inevitable. "It must if *we* are to go on. Edmond?"

"Actually," he said, "despite the disaster of the final act, there are people chafing at the bit to meet you all. I have a record company producer who is very interested in you, Ice. Rose, there's a casting director out there who's looking for dancers for a Broadway show. It will be just as part of the chorus, but it's a very nice opportunity. Jack Ferante was apparently more impressed with Cinnamon than he was with Howard, and he passed her name on to Mark Coleman, Mother."

"I didn't see Mark there tonight."

"He was there and was disappointed not to see you, but he came up to me immediately when I brought Steven to the reception and asked to have Cinnamon come to an audition for his new film, *The Runaways.* It could be a star-maker."

"That's very interesting, Edmond, but I don't want to rush these people."

"Mother," he warned. "Are we going to get into the same old argument?"

He turned to us and smiled.

"Mother and I disagree about when and where talented people should be exposed to the public at large. She forgets how she was pushed out on stage at the age of fourteen."

"That's different."

"Why? Because it was you?"

She stiffened.

"We'll talk about it later, when it is appropriate to talk about it," she said firmly.

He smiled.

"I have some interesting prospects for you as well, Honey, but I do believe the more you work with Mr. Bergman, the better you're going to be. Before this year ends, you'll have a position in a significant orchestra, I'm sure."

"What about Steven?" I asked.

Edmond looked at Madame Senetsky.

"There's a manager who is very interested in taking him on," he replied.

"Not that Hungarian horse thief, Magdar," she said.

"He gets it done, Mother."

"He ruins them," she countered.

"We'll talk," Edmond said softly.

"That, my son, we will do," she assured him with her characteristic regal control.

She started out and then turned to us.

"Well? Why are you all still sitting there? You have responsibilities. I've spent hours and hours, days and days preparing you for meeting people in events such as these. I don't expect anyone will let me down. Ice, fix your hair. Cinnamon, straighten out that ridiculous skirt. Rose, didn't I tell you to use less lipstick? Wipe it off and put it on lightly, lightly. Honey..."

"Yes, Madame Senetsky."

"Come along, I have someone I want to introduce you to myself. Quickly," she ordered, and I jumped up, looked at the others and then followed her and Edmond. Just outside the door, I paused and turned back to face my three sisters.

No one spoke.

No one had to.

We all simply hugged each other.

And then we went to the reception.

Epilogue

Howard was gone before morning. I thought to myself that it was the surprises that made our lives interesting and even exciting. To live in a predictable world was to live in a world without high drama, a world without Madame Senetskys. Wasn't it really only when my music reached another level, an unexpected original turn that Mr. Bergman, and the audiences to follow, would smile or feel genuinely touched?

Of the six of us, Howard Rockwell began with the most assurance he would succeed. He was so convinced of it, he convinced us as well, and for a while, I think that gave me a distaste for success. If this was the sort of person who found accomplishment in the arts, then maybe the arts were really not for me after all.

Madame Senetsky said very little about him specifically. At dinner the following evening, she spoke about compassion and how important an ingredient that was in creating a successful actor, a successful performer in any field of artistic endeavor.

"The truly great actors of my time were those men and women who could empathize and sympathize with the tragic characters they played. If they thought themselves better or above sincere human emotions, they would never have touched so many. One can master the technique, but he or she has to have soul."

Howard would probably find his way into something, I thought, but he would never be satisfied; he would never be happy, and if you can't be satisfied with yourself, be happy with yourself, you could never satisfy others, you could never make others happy.

I didn't have to travel all this way and live in a big, sophisticated city to know that. My family had taught me that long ago.

Uncle Peter had taught me that.

I had gone flying with him a few times before his tragic death. Mommy wasn't happy about it, but I had such confidence in him, I wasn't afraid. And when we were up there above the clouds, where there was only pure blue sky around us, I did feel some of the beauty he felt.

"We're on God's front porch," he would tell me.

"It's wonderful," I said. "I should take flying lessons, too, I suppose."

He smiled at me and shook his head.

"No, Honey. You'll get here your own way, through your music. You'll fly with your violin. You'll be on the wings of angels."

I didn't know what to make of those words. I was too young then.

Years and years later, after I left Madame Senetsky's School, I was on a stage in front of thousands of people. I was doing a solo. The music did make me soar. I thought about Uncle Peter.

And when I closed my eyes, I knew.

I was on God's front porch.